Raves for
The Gates of Sleep

"Putting a fresh face to a well-loved fairytale is not an easy task, but it is one that seems effortless to the prolific Lackey. In a brilliant twist, the author sets the classic story of Sleeping Beauty in Edwardian England, imbuing her characters with the power of elemental magic, including the cursed child herself, Marina Roeswood. Beautiful phrasing and a thorough grounding in the dress, mannerisms and history of the period help move the story along gracefully. Marina's character, along with those of her guardians, her friends and Arachne, are fully fleshed out and credible. This is a wonderful example of a new look at an old theme."

              —Publishers Weekly

"Everything's here—christening gifts, thorn hedge, sleeping servants—but with an innovative charm of Ms. Lackey's own. Using elemental magic instead of fairies updates this classic with verve. Her robust characters echo the English countryside setting, further distancing this tale from its French origins."   *—Romantic Times*

"The period touches are charming . . . the elemental magic is unusual enough to be interesting. A lovely variation on a familiar fairy tale."   *—Locus*

"With colorful characters, Lackey makes her variation of the Sleeping Beauty story great fun to read."   *—Booklist*

*Forthcoming in hardcover from DAW Books

THE GATES OF SLEEP

MERCEDES LACKEY

DAW BOOKS, INC.
<u>DONALD A. WOLLHEIM, FOUNDER</u>
375 Hudson Street, New York, NY 10014
ELIZABETH R. WOLLHEIM
SHEILA E. GILBERT
PUBLISHERS
www.dawbooks.com

First Paperback Printing, March 2003
1 2 3 4 5 6 7 8 9

DAW TRADEMARK REGISTERED
U.S. PAT. OFF. AND FOREIGN COUNTRIES
—MARCA REGISTRADA.
HECHO EN U.S.A.
PRINTED IN THE U.S.A.

Dedicated to the Port Authority Police and their Port Authority
co-workers who perished, saving others,
September 11, 2001

Joseph Amatuccio; Officer Christopher C. Amoroso; Jean A. Andrucki; Richard A. Aronow; Ezra Aviles; Arlene T. Babakitis; James W. Barbella; Officer Maurice V. Barry; Margaret L. Benson; Daniel Bergstein; Edward Calderon; Officer Liam Callahan; Lieutenant Robert D. Cirri; Carlos Dacosta; Dwight D. Darcy; Niurka Davila; Officer Clinton Davis; Frank A. De Martini; William F. Fallon; Stephen J. Fiorelli; Officer Donald A. Foreman; Officer Gregg J. Froehner; Barry H. Glick; Officer Thomas E. Gorman; Joseph F. Grillo; Ken G. Grouzalis; Patrick A. Hoey; Officer Uhuru G. Houston; Officer George G. Howard; Officer Stephen Huczko; Inspector Anthony P. Infante Jr; Prem N. Jerath; Mary S. Jones; Officer Paul W. Jurgens; Deborah H. Kaplan; Douglas G. Karpiloff; Sergeant Robert M. Kaulfers; Frank Lalama; Officer Paul Laszczynski; Officer David P. Lemagne; Officer John J. Lennon; Officer John D. Levi; Executive Director Neil D. Levin; Margaret S. Lewis; Officer James F. Lynch; Robert H. Lynch; Myrna Maldonado; Captain Kathy Mazza; Officer Donald J. McIntyre; Officer Walter A. McNeil; Director/Supt. of Police Fred V. Morrone; Officer Joseph M. Navas; Pete Negron; Officer James Nelson; Officer Alfonse J. Niedermeyer; David Ortiz; Officer James W. Parham; Nancy E. Perez; Officer Dominick A. Pezzulo; Eugene J. Raggio; Officer Bruce A. Reynolds; Francis S. Riccardelli; Officer Antonio J. Rodrigues; Officer Richard Rodriguez; Chief James A. Romito; Kalyan K. Sarkar; Anthony Savas; Officer John P. Skala; Edward T. Strauss; Officer Walwyn W. Stuart; Officer Kenneth F. Tietjen; Lisa L. Trerotola; Officer Nathaniel Webb; Officer Michael T. Wholey.

PROLOGUE

ALANNA Roeswood entered the parlor with her baby Marina in her arms, and reflected contentedly that she loved this room better than any other chamber in Oakhurst Manor. Afternoon sunlight streamed in through the bay windows, and a sultry breeze carried with it the scent of roses from the garden. The parlor glowed with warm colors; reds and rich browns, the gold of ripening wheat. There were six visitors, standing or sitting, talking quietly to one another, dressed for an afternoon tea; three in the flamboyant, medievally inspired garb that marked them as artists. These three were talking to her husband Hugh; they looked as if they properly belonged in a fantastic painting, not Alanna's cozy parlor. The remaining three were outwardly ordinary; one lady was in an up-to-the-mode tea gown that proclaimed wealth and rank, one man (very much a countrified gentleman) wore a suit with a faintly old-fashioned air about it, and the last was a young woman with ancient eyes whose flowing emerald gown, trimmed in heavy Venice lace like the foam on a

wave, was of no discernible mode. They smiled at Alanna as
she passed them, and nodded greetings.

Alanna placed her infant carefully in a hand-carved cradle, and seated herself in a chair beside it. One by one, the
artists came to greet her, bent over the cradle, whispered
something to the sleepy infant, touched her with a gentle finger, and withdrew to resume their conversations.

The artists could have been from the same family. In fact,
they were from two. Sebastian Tarrant, he of the leonine red-
brown locks and generous mustache, was the husband of
dark-haired sweet-faced Margherita; the clean-shaven,
craggy fellow who looked to be her brother by his coloring
was exactly that. All three were Hugh Roeswood's childhood playmates, and Alanna's as well. The rest were also
bound to their hosts by ties of long standing. It was, to all
outward appearances, just a gathering of a few very special
friends, a private celebration of that happiest of events, a
birth and christening.

Alanna Roeswood wore a loose artistic tea gown of a delicate mauve, very like the one that enveloped Margherita in
amber folds. It should have been, since Margherita's own
hands had made both. She sat near the hearth, a Madonna-
like smile on her lips, brooding over the sensuously curved
lines of newborn Marina's hand-carved walnut cradle. The
cradle was a gift from one of her godparents, and there
wasn't another like it in all of the world; it was, in fact, a
masterpiece of decorative art. The frothy lace of Marina's
christening gown overflowed the side, a spill of winter white
against the rich, satiny brown of the lovingly carved wood.
Glancing over at Sebastian, the eldest of the artists, Alanna
suppressed a larger smile; by the way he kept glancing at the
baby, his fingers were itching to sketch the scene. She wondered just what medieval tale he was fitting the tableau into
in his mind's eye. The birth of Rhiannon of the Birds, per-

haps. Sebastian Tarrant had been mining the Welsh and Irish mythos for subjects for some time now, with the usual artistic disregard for whether the actual people who had inspired the characters of those pre-Christian tales would have even remotely resembled his paintings. The romance and tragedy suited the sensibilities of those who had made the work of Dante Rossetti and the rest of the Pre-Raphaelites popular. Sebastian was not precisely one of that brotherhood, in no small part because he rarely came to London and rarely exhibited his work. Alanna wasn't entirely clear just *how* he managed to sell his work; it might have been through a gallery, or more likely, by word of mouth. Certainly once anyone actually *saw* one of his paintings, it generally sold itself. Take the rich colors of a Rossetti, add the sinuosity of line of a Burne-Jones, and lay as a foundation beneath it all the lively spirit of a Millais, and you had Sebastian. Adaptor of many styles, imitator of none; that was Sebastian.

His brother-in-law, mild-eyed Thomas Buford, was the carver of Marina's cradle and a maker of every sort of furniture, following the Aesthetic edict that things of utility should also be beautiful. He had a modest clientele of his own, as did his sister, Margherita (Sebastian's wife) who was as skilled with needle and tapestry-shuttle as her husband was with brush and pen. The three of them lived and worked together in an apparent harmony quite surprising to those who would have expected the usual tempestuous goings-on of the more famous (or infamous) Pre-Raphaelites of London. They lived in an enormous old vine-covered farmhouse — which Sebastian claimed had once been a medieval manor house that was home to one of King Arthur's knights — just over the border in Cornwall.

This trio had been Alanna's (and her husband Hugh's) friends for most of their lives, from their first meeting as children in Hugh's nursery, sharing his lessons with his tutors.

The remaining three, however disparate their ages and social statures — well, it had only been natural for them all to become friends as adolescents and young adults first out in adult society.

And *that* was because they were all part of something much larger than an artistic circle or social circle.

They were all Elemental Masters; magicians by any other name. Each of them commanded, to a greater or lesser extent, the magic of a specific element: Earth, Air, Fire, or Water, and they practiced their Magics together and separately for the benefit and protection of their land and the people around them. There was a greater Circle of Masters based in London, but Hugh and Alanna had never taken part in any of its works. They met mostly with the double-handful of Masters who confined their workings to goals of smaller scope, here in the heart of Devon.

Marina stirred in her nest of soft lace, but did not wake; Alanna gazed down at her with an upswelling of passionate adoration. She was a lovely baby, and that was not just the opinion of her doting parents.

Hugh and Alanna were Earth Masters; their affinity with that Element was the reason why they seldom left their own land and property. Like most Earth Masters, they felt most comfortable when they were closest to a home deep in the countryside, far from the brick-and-stone of the great cities. Margherita was also an Earth Master; her brother Thomas shared her affinity, and this was why they had shared Hugh's tutors.

For the magic, in most cases, passed easily from parent to child in Hugh's family, and there was a long tradition in the Roeswood history of beginning training in the exercise of power along with more common lessons. So tutors, and sometimes even a child's first nurse, were also Mages.

Hugh's sister Arachne, already an adult, was long gone from the household, never seen, seldom heard from, by the time he was ready for formal schooling. Magic had skipped her, or so it appeared, and Hugh had once ventured the opinion that this seemed to have made her bitter and distant. She had married a tradesman, a manufacturer of pottery, and for some reason never imparted to Hugh, this had caused a rift in the already-strained relationship with her parents.

Be that as it may, Hugh's parents did not want him to spend a lonely childhood being schooled in isolation from other children his age—and lo! there were the Tarrants, the Bufords, and Alanna's family, all friends of the Roeswoods, all Elemental Mages of their own circle, all living within a day's ride of Oakhurst, and all with children near the same age. The addition of their friends' children to the Roeswood household seemed only natural, especially since it was not wise to send a child with Elemental power to a normal public school—doubly so as a boarder. Such children saw things—the Elemental creatures of their affinities—and often forgot to keep a curb on their tongues. And such children attracted those Elemental creatures, which were, if not watched by an adult mage, inclined to play mischief in the material world. "Poltergeists" was the popular name for these creatures, and sometimes even the poor children who had attracted them in the first place had no idea what was going on about them. Worst of all, the child with Elemental power *could* attract something other than benign or mischievous Elemental creatures. Terrible things had happened in the past, and the least of them was when the child in question had been attacked. Worse, far worse had come when the child had been lured, seduced, and turned to evil himself. . . .

So five children of rather disparate backgrounds came to live at Oakhurst Manor, to be schooled together. And they matched well together—four of the five had the same affinity. Only Sebastian differed, but Fire was by no means incompatible with Earth.

Later, Sebastian's father, educated at Oxford, had become Hugh's official tutor—and the teacher of the other four, unofficially. It was an arrangement that suited all of them except Sebastian; perhaps that was why *he* had been so eager to throw himself into art!

Hugh and Alanna had fallen in love as children and their love had only grown over the years. There had never been any doubt whom he would marry, and since both sets of parents were more than satisfied with the arrangement, everyone was happy. Hugh's parents had not lived to see them married, but they had not been young when he was born, so it had come as no great surprise that he came into his inheritance before he left Oxford. The loss of Alanna's mother and father in a typhoid epidemic after their marriage had been more of a shock. If Alanna had not had Hugh then—she did not think she could have borne the loss.

At least he and Alanna had the satisfaction of knowing that their parents blessed their union with all their hearts.

Sebastian had taken longer to recognize Margherita as his soul mate. Fate had other ideas, Thomas claimed later; Sebastian could be as obnoxious to his schoolmate as any other grubby boy, but overnight, it seemed, Margherita turned from a scrawny, gangly brat to a slender nymph, and the teasing and mock-tormenting had turned to something else entirely.

Such was the magic of the heart.

Insofar as that magic that Alanna and Hugh both carried in their veins, there was no doubt that their firstborn daughter had inherited it. One day little Marina would wield the forces of Elemental Magic as well, but *her* affinity, beautifully portrayed in the curves and waves of her cradle, the tiny mermaids sporting amid the carved foam, was for Water. Not the usual affinity in the Roeswood family, but not unknown, either.

Though they had not been part of that intimate circle of schoolfellows, the others here to bestow magical blessings on the infant were also Elemental Mages, and *were* part of their Working Circle. Two wielded Air magic, and one other, like Marina, that of Water. That third had left an infant of her own behind, in the care of a nurse; Elizabeth Hastings was Alanna's first friend outside of her schoolmates, and one of the wisest people Alanna knew. She would have to be; she had kept her utterly ordinary husband completely in the dark about her magical powers, and it was unlikely that he would ever have the least inkling of the fact that his lovely, fragile-looking wife could probably command the ocean to wipe a good-sized fishing village from the face of the earth if she was minded to.

Not that gentle Elizabeth would ever so much as consider doing such a thing.

This, the afternoon of the ceremony at the village church, was a very different sort of christening for Marina. Each of these friends was also a godparent; each had carefully considered the sort of arcane gift he or she would bestow on the tiny child. In the ancient days, these would have been gifts of defense and offense: protections for a helpless infant against potential enemies of her parents. In these softer times, they would be gifts of grace and beauty, meant to enrich her life rather than defend it.

There was no set ceremony for this party; a godparent simply moved to Alanna's side, whispered his or her gift to the sleeping baby, and lightly touched her silken hair with a gentle finger. Already four of the six had bestowed their blessings—from Margherita, skillful hands and deft fingers. From Sebastian, blithe spirits and a cheerful heart. Thomas' choice was the gift of music; whether Marina was a performer herself, or only one who loved music, would depend on her own talents, but no matter what, she would have the ear and mind to extract the most enjoyment from it. A fourth friend, a contemporary of their parents, Lady Helene Overton (whose power was Air), she of the handsome tea gown and silver-white hair, had added physical grace to that. Now the local farmer in his outmoded suit—a yeoman farmer, whose family had held their lands in their own right for centuries (and another Air Master)—glided over to Alanna's side. Like most of his Affinity, in England at least, he was lean, his eyes blue, his hair pale. The more powerful a Master was, the more like his Elementals he became, and Roderick Bacon was *very* powerful. He smiled at Alanna, and bent over the cradle.

"Alliance," he whispered, and touched his forefinger to the baby's soft, dark hair.

Alanna blinked with surprise. This was a gift more akin to those given in the ancient days! Roderick had just granted Marina the ability to speak with and beg aid from, if not command, the Elemental creatures of the Air! He had allied *his* power with hers, which had to be done with the consent of his Elementals. She stared at Roderick, dumbfounded.

He shrugged, and smiled sheepishly. "Belike she'll only care to have the friendship of the birds," he replied to her questioning look. "But 'tis my line's traditional Gift, and I'm a man for tradition."

Alanna returned his smile, and nodded her thanks. Who was she to flout tradition? Roderick's Mage-Line went back further than their status as landholders; they had *become* landholders because of Magical aid to their liege lord in the time of King Stephen and Queen Maud.

She was grateful for the kinds of Gifts that had been given; her friends were practical as well as thoughtful. They had not bestowed great beauty on the child, for instance; great beauty could be as much of a curse as a blessing. They hadn't given her specific talents, just the deftness and skill that would enable her to make the best use of whatever talents she had been born with. Even Roderick's Gift was mutable; it would serve as Marina decided it would serve. While she was a child, the Elementals of the Air would watch over her, as those of her own Element would guard her—no wind would harm her, for instance, nor was it possible for her to drown. Once she became an adult and knew what the Gift meant, she could make use of it—or not—as she chose.

Only Elizabeth was left to bestow her gift. Alanna smiled up into her friend's eyes—but as she took her first step toward the baby, the windows rattled, a chill wind bellied the curtains, and the room darkened, as if a terrible storm cloud had boiled up in an instant.

The guests started back from the windows; Margherita clung to Sebastian. A wave of inexplicable and paralyzing fear rose up and overwhelmed Alanna, pinning her in her chair like a frightened rabbit.

A woman swept in through the parlor door.

She was dressed in the height of fashion, in a gown of black satin trimmed with silk fringe in the deepest maroon. Her skin was pale as porcelain, her hair as black as the fabric of her gown. She raked the room and its occupants with an imperious gaze, as Hugh gasped.

"Arachne!" he exclaimed, and hurried forward. "Why, sister! We didn't expect you!"

The woman's red lips curved in a chill parody of a smile.

"Of course you didn't," she purred, her eyes glinting dangerously. "You didn't invite me, brother. I can only wonder why."

Hugh paled, but stood his ground. "I had no reason to think you would want to attend the christening, Arachne. You never invited me to Reginald's christening—"

Arachne advanced into the room, and Hugh perforce gave way before her. Alanna sat frozen in her chair, sensing the woman's menace, still overwhelmed with fear, but unable to understand why she was so afraid. Hugh had told her next to nothing about this older sister of his—only that she was the only child of his father's first marriage, and that she had quarreled with her father over his marriage to Hugh's mother, and made a runaway marriage with her wealthy tradesman.

"You should have invited me, little brother," Arachne continued with a throaty laugh, as she continued to glide forward, and Hugh backed up a step at a time. "Why not? Didn't you think I'd appreciate the sight of the heir's heiress?" Another pace. A toothy smile. "I can't imagine why you would think that. Here I am, the child's only aunt. Why shouldn't I wish to see her?"

"Because you've never shown any interest in our family before, Arachne." Hugh was as white as marble, and it seemed to Alanna that he was being *forced* back as Arachne advanced. "You didn't come to father's funeral—"

"I sent a wreath. Surely that was enough, considering that father detested my husband and made no secret of it."

"—and you didn't even send a wreath to mother's—"

"She could have opposed him, and chose not to." A shrug, and an insincere smile. "You didn't trouble to let me know of your wedding to this charming child, so I could hardly have attended *that*. I only found out about it from the society pages in the *Times*. That was hardly kind." A theatrical sigh. "But how could I have expected anything else? After Father and Mother determined to estrange me from our family circle, I wasn't surprised that you would follow suit."

Alanna strained, with eyes and Sight, to make sense of the woman who called herself Hugh's sister. There was a darkness about her, like a storm cloud: a sense of lightnings and an ominous power. Was it magic? If so, was it her own? It was possible for a mage to bestow specific magic upon someone who wasn't able to command any of the powers. But it was also possible for one of the many sorts of Elementals to attach itself to a non-mage as well.

As thunder growled and distant lightning licked the clouds outside, Alanna looked up and met Arachne's eyes— and found herself unable to move. The rest of their guests stood like pillars, staring, as if they, too, were struck with paralysis.

Hugh clearly tried to interpose himself between Arachne and the cradle, but he moved sluggishly, as if pushing his way through thick muck, and his sister darted around him. She bent over the cradle. Alanna tried to reach out and snatch her baby away, but she could no more have moved than have flown.

"Well, well," Arachne said, a hint of mockery in her voice. "A pleasant child. But *so* fragile. Nothing like *my* boy. . . ."

As Alanna watched in horror, Arachne reached out with a single, extended finger, supple and white and tipped with a long fingernail painted with bloodred enamel. She reached for Marina's forehead, as all of the godparents had. The darkness shivered, gathered itself around her, and crept down the extended arm. "You really should enjoy this pretty child—while you have her. You never know about children." Her eyes glinted in the gloom, a hint of red flickering in the back of them. The ominous finger neared Marina's forehead. "They can survive so *many* hazards, growing up. Then one day—say, on the eighteenth birthday—"

The finger touched.

"Death," Arachne whispered.

Like an animate oil slick, the shadow gathered itself, flowed down Arachne's arm, and enveloped Marina in a shadow-shroud.

Lightning struck the lawn outside the window, and thunder crashed like a thousand cannon. Alanna screamed; the baby woke, and wailed.

With a peal of laughter, Arachne whirled away from the cradle. In a few strides she was out the door and gone, escaped before any could detain her.

Now the paralysis holding all of them broke.

Alanna snatched her child out of the cradle and held the howling infant to her chest, sobbing. As lightning crashed and thunder rolled, as the baby keened, all of her godparents descended on them both.

"I don't know how she did this," Elizabeth said at last, frowning. "I've never seen magic like this. It doesn't correspond to any Element—if I were superstitious—"

Alanna pressed her lips tightly together, and fought down another sob. "If you were superstitious—what?" she demanded.

Elizabeth sighed. "I'd say it was a curse. Meant to take effect between now and Marina's eighteenth birthday. But I can't tell *how*."

"Neither can I," Roderick said grimly. "Though it's a damned good job I gave her the Gift I did. She got *some* protection, anyway. This—well, call it a curse, my old granddad would have—with the help of the Sylphs, this curse is drained, countered for now—else it might have killed her in her cradle. But how someone with no magic of her own managed to do this—" He shrugged.

"The curse is countered—" Alanna didn't like the way he had phrased that. "It's not *gone*?"

Roderick looked helpless, and not comfortable with feeling that way. "Well—no."

Elizabeth stepped forward before the hysterical cry of anguish building in her heart burst out of Alanna's throat. "Then it's a good thing that *I* have not yet given my Gift."

She took the baby from Alanna's arms; Alanna resisted for a moment, before reluctantly letting the baby go. She watched, tears welling in her eyes, hand pressed to her mouth, as Elizabeth studied the red, pinched, tear-streaked face of her baby.

"This—abomination—is too deeply rooted. I cannot rid her of it," Elizabeth said, and Alanna moaned, and started to turn away into her husband's shoulder.

"Wait!" Elizabeth said, forestalling her. "I said I couldn't rid her of it. I didn't say I couldn't change it. Water—water can go *everywhere*. No magic wrought can keep me out."

Shaking with hope and fear, Alanna turned back. She watched, Hugh's arms around her, as Elizabeth gathered her power around her like the skirts of her flowing gown. The green, living energy spun around her, sparkling with life; she murmured something under her breath.

Then, exactly like water pouring into a cavity, the power spun down into the baby's tiny body. Marina seemed too small to contain all of it, and yet it flowed into her until it had utterly vanished without a trace.

The darkness that had overshadowed her face slowly lifted. The baby's eyes opened; she heaved a sigh, and for the first time since Arachne had touched her, she smiled,

tentatively. Alanna burst into tears and gathered her baby to
her breast. Hugh's arms surrounded her with comfort and
warmth.

Elizabeth spoke firmly, pitching her voice to carry over
Alanna's weeping.

"I did not—I *could* not—remove this curse. What I
have done is to change it. As it stood, it had no limit; it
could have been invoked at any time. Now, if it does not fall
upon her by her eighteenth birthday, it will rebound upon
the caster."

Alanna gulped down her sobs and looked up quickly at
her friend. Elizabeth's mouth was pursed in a sour smile.
"Injudicious of Arachne to mention a date; curses are tricky
things, and if you don't hedge them in carefully, they find
ways of breaking out—or leaving holes. And injudicious of
her to come in person; now, if it is awakened at all, she will
have to awaken it in person, and I have buried it deeply.
It will not be easy, and will require a great deal of close
contact."

"But—" Alanna felt her throat closing again, and Elizabeth held up her hand.

"I have not finished. I further modified this curse; should
Arachne manage to awaken it, Marina will *not* die." Elizabeth sighed, wearily. "But there, my knowledge fails me. I
told you that curses are difficult; this one took the power and
twisted it away from me. I can only tell you that the curse
will not kill outright. I cannot tell you what it *will* do. . . ."

Alanna watched a hundred dire thoughts pass behind
Elizabeth's eyes. There were so many things that were
worse than death—and many that were only a little better.
What if the curse struck Mari blind, or deaf, or mindless?
What if it made a cripple of her?

Then Elizabeth gathered herself and nodded briskly.

"Never mind. We must see that it does not come to that. Alanna, we must hide her."

"Hide her?" Hugh said, from behind her. "By my faith, Elizabeth, that is no bad notion! Like—like the infant Arthur, we can send her away where Arachne can't find her!"

"Take her?" Alanna clutched the infant closer, her voice rising. "You'd take her away from me?"

"Alanna, we can't hide her if *you* go with her," Hugh pointed out, his own arms tightening around her. "But where? That's the question."

Hot tears spilled from Alanna's eyes, as the others discussed her baby's fate, heedless of her breaking heart. They were taking her away, her Marina, her little Mari—

She heard them in a haze of grief, as if from a great distance, as her friends, her husband, decided among them to send Marina away, away, off with Sebastian and Thomas and Margherita, practically into the wilds of Cornwall. It was Hugh's allusion to Arthur that had decided them. Arachne knew nothing of them; if she had known of Hugh's childhood schoolmates, she hadn't recognized the playfellows that had been in the artists of now.

Elizabeth tried to comfort her. "It's only until she's of age, darling," her friend said, patting her shoulders as the tears flowed and she shook with sobs. "When she's eighteen, she'll come back to you!"

Eighteen years. An eternity. An age, in which she would never see Marina's first step, hear her first word, see her grow. . . .

Alanna wept. Wept as they bundled Marina up in a baby-basket and carried her away, leaving behind the little dresses that Alanna had embroidered during the months of her confinement, the toys, even the cradle. She wept as her friends smuggled the child into their cart, as if she was nothing more than a few apples or a bottle of cider.

She wept as they drove away, her husband's arms around her, her best friend standing at her side. She wept and would not be consoled; for she had lost her heart, and something told her she would never see her child again.

1

BIRDS twittered in the rose bushes outside the old-fashioned diamond-paned windows. The windows, swung open on their ancient iron hinges, let in sunshine, a floating dandelion seed and a breath of mown grass, even if Marina wasn't in position to see the view into the farmyard. The sunshine gilded an oblong on the worn wooden floor. Behind her, somewhere out in the yard, chickens clucked and muttered, and two of Aunt Margherita's cats had a half-minute spat. Marina's arm was starting to go numb.

The unenlightened might think that posing as an artist's model was easy, because "all" one had to do was sit, stand, or recline in one position. *The unenlightened ought to try it some time,* she thought. It took the same sort of simultaneous concentration and relaxation that magic did—concentration, to make sure that there wasn't a bit of movement, and relaxation, to ensure that muscles didn't lock up. If the pose was a standing one, then it wasn't long before feet and legs were aching; if sitting or reclining, it was a certainty that *some* part of the body would fall asleep, with the resulting pins-and-needles agony when the model was allowed to move.

Then there was the boredom—well, perhaps *boredom* wasn't quite the right word. The model had to have something to occupy her mind while her body was frozen in one position; it was rare that Marina ever got to take a pose that allowed her to either read or nap. She generally used the time to go over the basic exercises of magic that Uncle Thomas taught her, or to go over some more mundane lesson or other.

Oh, modeling was work, all right. She understood that artists who didn't have complacent relatives paid well for models to pose, and in her opinion, every penny was earned.

She'd been here all morning posing, because Uncle had got a mania about the early light; enough was enough. She was hungry, it was time for luncheon, and it wasn't fair to make her work from dawn to dark. How could anyone waste such a beautiful autumn day inside the stone walls of this farmhouse? "Uncle Sebastian," she called. "The model's arm is falling off."

A whiff of oil paints came to her as Sebastian looked up from his canvas. "It isn't, I assure you," he retorted.

She didn't pout; it wasn't in her nature to pout. But she did protest. "Well, it *feels* as though it's falling off!"

Sebastian heaved a theatrical sigh. "The modern generation has no stamina," he complained, disordering his graying chestnut locks with the same hand that held his brush, and leaving streaks of gold all through it. "Why, when your aunt was your age, she could hold a pose for six and seven hours at a time, and never a complaint out of her."

Taking that as permission to break her pose, Marina leaned the oriflamme, the battle banner of medieval France, against the wall, and put her sword down on the floor.

"When my aunt was my age, you posed her as a reclining odalisque, or fainting on the couch, or leaning languidly in a window," she retorted. "You never once posed her as Joan of Arc. Or Britannia, in a heavy helmet and breastplate. Or Morgan Le Fay, with a snake and a dagger."

"Trivial details," Sebastian said with a dismissive gesture. "Inconsequential."

"Not to my arm." Marina shook both of her arms vigorously, grateful that Sebastian had not inflicted the heavy breastplate and helmet on her. Of course, that would have made the current painting look rather more like that one of Britannia that he had recently finished than Sebastian would have preferred.

And since the Britannia painting was owned by a business rival of the gentleman who had commissioned this one, it wouldn't do to make one a copy of the other.

This one, which was to be significantly larger than "Britannia Awakes" as well as significantly different, was going to be very profitable for Uncle Sebastian. And since the rival who had commissioned "Saint Jeanne" was a profound Francophobe. . . .

Men, Marina had long since concluded, could be remarkably silly. On the other hand, when the *first* man caught wind of this there might be another commission for a new painting, perhaps a companion to "Britannia Awakes," which would be very nice for the household indeed. And then—another commission from the second gentleman? This could be amusing as well as profitable!

The second gentleman, however, had made some interesting assumptions, perhaps based upon the considerable amount of arm and shoulder, ankle and calf that Britannia had displayed. He had made it quite clear to Uncle Sebastian that he wanted the same model for *his* painting, but he had also thrown out plenty of hints that he wanted the model as well, perhaps presuming that his rival had also included that as part of the commission.

Marina wasn't supposed to know that. Uncle Sebastian hadn't known she was anywhere near the house when the client came to call. In fact, she'd been gathering eggs and had heard voices in Uncle Sebastian's studio, and the Sylphs had told her that one was a stranger. It had been quite funny—she was listening from outside the window—until Uncle Sebastian, with a cold remark that the gentleman couldn't possibly be referring to his dear *niece,* had interrupted the train of increasingly less subtle hints about Sebastian's "lovely model." Fortunately, Sebastian hadn't lost his temper. Uncle Sebastian in a temper was apt to damage things.

Marina reached for the ribbon holding her hair in a tail behind her back and pulled it loose, shaking out her heavy sable mane. Saint Joan was not noted for her luxuriant locks, so Uncle had scraped all of her hair back tightly so that he could see the shape of her skull. Tightly enough that the roots of her hair hurt, in fact, though she wasn't apt to complain. When he got to the hair for the painting, he'd construct a boyish bob over the skull shape. In that respect, the pose for Britannia had been a little more comfortable; at least she hadn't had to pull her hair back so tightly that her scalp ached. "When are you going to get a commission that *doesn't* involve me holding something out at the end of my arm?" she asked.

Her uncle busied himself with cleaning his palette, scraping it bare, wiping it with linseed oil. Clearly, *he* had been quite ready to stop as well, but he would never admit that. "Would you rather another painting of dancing Muses?" he asked.

Recalling the painting that her uncle had done for an exhibition last spring that involved nine contorted poses for her, and had driven them both to quarrels and tantrums, she shook her head. "Not unless someone offers you ten thousand pounds for it—in advance." She turned pleading eyes on him. "But don't you think that just *once* you might manage a painting of—oh—Juliet in the tomb of the Capulets? Surely that's fashionably morbid enough for you!"

He snatched up a cushion and flung it at her; she caught it deftly, laughing at him.

"Minx!" he said, mockingly. "Lazy, too! Very well, failing any other commissions, the next painting will be Shakespearian, and I'll have you as Kate the Shrew!"

"So long as it's Kate the Shrew sitting down and reading, I've no objection," she retorted, dropped the cushion on the window seat, and skipped out the door. This was an old-fashioned place where, at least on the ground floor, one room led into the next; she passed through her aunt's workroom, then the room that held Margherita's tapestry loom, then the library, then the dining room, before reaching the stairs.

Her own room was at the top of the farmhouse, above the kitchen and under the attics, with a splendid view of the apple orchard beyond the farmyard wall. There was a handsome little rooster atop the wall—an English bantam; Aunt Margherita was very fond of bantams and thought highly of their intelligence. They didn't actually have a farm as such, for the land belonging to the house was farmed by a neighbor. When they'd taken the place, Uncle had pointed out that as artists they made very poor farmers; it would be better for them to do what they were good at and let the owner rent the land to someone else. But they did have the pond, the barn, a little pasturage, the orchard and some farm animals— bantam chickens, some geese and ducks, a couple of sheep to keep the grass around the farmhouse tidy. They had two ponies and two carts, because Uncle Sebastian was always taking one off on a painting expedition just when Aunt Margherita wanted it for shopping, or Uncle Thomas for *his* business. They also had an old, old horse, a once-famous jumper who probably didn't have many more years in him, that they kept in gentle retirement for the local master of the hunt. Marina rode him now and again, but never at more than an amble. He would look at fences with a peculiar and penetrating gaze, as if meditating on the follies of his youth—then snort, and amble further along in search of a gate that Marina could open for him.

There were wild swans on the pond as well, who would claim their share of bread and grain with the usual imperiousness of such creatures. And Uncle Thomas raised doves; he had done so since he was a boy. They weren't the brightest of birds, but they were beautiful creatures, sweet and gentle fantails that came to anyone's hands, tame and placid, for feeding. The same couldn't be said of the swans, which regarded Aunt Margherita as a king would regard the lowliest serf, and the grain and bread she scattered for them as no less than their just tribute. Only for Marina did they unbend, their natures partaking of equal parts of air and water and so amenable to *her* touch, if not to that of an Earth Master.

She changed out of her fustian tunic with the painted fleur-de-lys and knitted coif, the heavy knitted jumper whose drape was meant to suggest chain mail for Uncle Sebastian's benefit. Off came the knitted hose and the suede boots. She pulled on a petticoat and a loose gown of Aunt Margherita's design and make, shoved her feet into her old slippers, and ran back down the tiny staircase, which ended at the entryway dividing the kitchen from the dining room and parlor. The door into the yard stood invitingly open, a single hen peering inside with interest, and she gave the sun-drenched expanse outside a long look of regret before joining her aunt in the kitchen.

Floored with slate, with white plastered walls and black beams, the kitchen was the most modern room of the house. The huge fireplace remained largely unused, except on winter nights when the family gathered here instead of in the parlor. Iron pot-hooks and a Tudor spit were entirely ornamental now, but Aunt Margherita would not have them taken out; she said they were part of the soul of the house.

The huge, modern iron range that Margherita had insisted on having—much admired by all the local farmers' wives—didn't even use the old chimney. It stood in splendid isolation on the external wall opposite the hearth, which made the kitchen wonderfully warm on those cold days when there was a fire in both. Beneath the window that overlooked the yard was Margherita's other improvement, a fine sink with its own well and pump, so that no one had to go out into the yard to bring in water. For the rest, a huge table dominated the room, with a couple of tall stools and two long benches beneath it. Three comfortable chairs stood beside the cold hearth, a dresser that was surely Georgian displayed copper pots and china, and various cupboards and other kitchen furniture were ranged along the walls.

Margherita was working culinary magic at that huge, scarred table. Quite literally.

The gentle ambers and golds of Earth Magic energies glowed everywhere that Marina looked—on the bread dough in a bowl in a warm corner was a cantrip to ensure its proper rising, another was on the pot of soup at the back of the cast-iron range to keep it from burning. A pest-banishing spell turned flying insects away from the open windows and doors, and prevented crawling ones from setting foot on wall, floor, or ceiling. Another kept the mice and rats at bay, and was not visible except where it ran across the threshold.

Tiny cantrips kept the milk and cream, in covered pitchers standing in basins of cold water, from souring; more kept the cheese in the pantry from molding, weevils out of the flour, the eggs sound and sweet. They weren't strong magics, and if (for instance) Margherita were to be so careless as to leave the milk for too *very* long beyond a day or so, it would sour anyway. Common sense was a major component of Margherita's magic.

On the back of the range stood the basin of what would be clotted cream by teatime, simmering beside the soup pot. Clotted cream required careful tending, and the only magic involved was something to remind her aunt to keep a careful eye on the basin.

Occasionally there was another Element at work in the kitchen; when a very steady temperature was required— such as beneath that basin of cream—Uncle Sebastian persuaded a Salamander to take charge of the fires in the stove. Uncle Sebastian was passionately fond of his food, and to his mind it was a small enough contribution on his part for so great a gain. The meals that their cook and general housekeeper Sarah made were good; solid cottager fare. But the contributions that Margherita concocted transformed cooking to another art form. Earth Masters were like that, according to what Uncle Thomas said; they often practiced as much magic in the kitchen as out of it.

Of all of the wonderful food that his spouse produced, Uncle Sebastian most adored the uniquely Devon cream tea—scones, clotted cream, and jam. Margherita made her very own clotted cream, which not all Devon or Cornish ladies did—a great many relied on the dairies to make it for them. The shallow pan of heavy cream simmering in its water-bath would certainly make Uncle Sebastian happy when he saw it.

"Shall I make the scones, Aunt?" Marina asked after a stir of the soup pot and a peek at the cream. Her aunt smiled seraphically over her shoulder. She was a beautiful woman, the brown of her hair still as rich as it had been when she was Marina's age, her figure only a little plumper (if her husband's paintings from that time were any guide), her large brown eyes serene. The only reason her husband wasn't using *her* as his model instead of Marina was that she had her own artistic work, and wasn't minded to give it over just to pose for her spouse, however beloved he was. Posing was Marina's contribution to the family welfare, since she was nowhere near the kind of artist that her aunt and uncles were.

"That would be a great help, dearest," Margherita replied, continuing to slice bread for luncheon. "Would you prefer cress or cucumber?"

"Cress, please. And deviled ham, if there is any."

"Why a Water-child should have such an appetite for a Fire food, I cannot fathom," Margherita replied, with a laugh. "I have deviled ham, of course; Sebastian would drive me out of the house if I didn't."

Margherita did not do all of the cooking, not even with Marina's help; she did luncheon most days, and tea, and often made special supper dishes with her own hands, but for the plain cooking and other kitchen work there was old Sarah, competent and practical. Sarah wasn't the only servant; for the housecleaning and maid-of-all-work they had young Jenny, and for the twice-yearly spring and fall housecleaning, more help from Jenny's sisters. A man, unsurprisingly named John, came over from the neighboring farm twice a week (except during harvest) to do the yard-work and anything the uncles couldn't do. There wasn't much of that; Thomas was handy with just about any tool, and Sebastian, when he wasn't in the throes of a creative frenzy, was willing to pitch in on just about any task.

Marina stirred up the scone dough, rolled it out, cut the rounds with a biscuit cutter and arrayed them in a baking pan and slipped them into the oven. By the time they were ready, Margherita had finished making sandwiches with brown and white bread, and had stacked them on a plate.

Sarah and Jenny appeared exactly when they were wanted to help set up the table in the dining room for luncheon: more of Margherita's Earth magic at work to call them silently from their other tasks? Not likely. It was probably just that old Sarah had been with the family since the beginning, and young Jenny had been with them nearly as long—she was only "young" relative to Sarah.

After being cooped up all morning in the studio, Marina was in no mood to remain indoors. Rather than sit down at the table with her uncles and aunt, she wrapped some of the sandwiches in a napkin, took a bottle of homemade ginger beer from the pantry, put both in a basket with one of her lesson books, and ran out—at last!—into the sunshine.

She swung the basket as she ran, taking in great breaths of the autumn air, fragrant with curing hay. Deep in the heart of the orchard was her favorite place; where the stream that cut through the heart of the trees dropped abruptly by four feet, forming a lovely little waterfall that was a favorite of the lesser Water Elementals of the area. The bank beside it, carpeted with fern and sweet grass, with mosses growing in the shadows, was where Marina liked to sit and read, or watch the Water Elementals play about in the falling water, and those of Air sporting in the branches.

They looked like—whatever they chose to look like. The ones here in her tiny stream were of a size to fit the stream, although their size had nothing to do with their powers. They could have been illustrations in some expensive children's book, tiny elfin women and men, with fish-tails or fins, except that there was a knowing look in their eyes, and their unadorned bodies were frankly sensual.

Of course, they weren't the only Water Elementals she

knew. She'd seen River-horses down at the village, where her little stream joined a much greater one, and water nymphs of more human size, but the amount of cold iron in and around the water tended to keep them at bay. She'd been seeing and talking with them for as long as she could remember.

She often wondered what the Greater Elementals were like; she'd never been near a body of water larger than the river that supplied the village mill with its power. She often pitied poor Sarah and Jenny, who literally couldn't see the creatures that had been visible to *her* for all of her life— how terrible, not to be able to see all the strange creatures that populated the Unseen World!

Her minor Elementals—Undines, who were about the size of a half-grown child, though with the undraped bodies of fully mature women—greeted her arrival with languid waves of a hand or pretended indifference; she didn't mind. They were rather like cats, to tell the truth. If you acted as if you were interested in them, they would ignore you, but if you in your turn ignored them you were bound to get their attention.

And there were things that they could not resist.

In the bottom of her basket was a thin volume of poetry, part of the reading that Uncle Sebastian had set for her lessons—not Christina Rossetti, as might have been assumed, but the sonnets of John Donne. She put her back against the bank in the sun, and with her book in one hand and a sandwich in the other, she immersed herself in verse, reading it aloud to the fascinated Undines who propped their heads on the edge of the stream to listen.

When the Undines tired of listening to poetry and swam off on their own business, Marina filled her basket with ripe apples—the last of the season, left to ripen slowly on the trees after the main harvest. But it wasn't teatime by any stretch of the imagination, and she really wasn't ready to go back to the house.

She left the basket with her book atop it next to the stream, and strolled about the orchard, tending to a magical chore of her own. This was something she had been doing since she was old enough to understand that it needed doing: making sure each and every tree was getting exactly the amount of water it needed. She did this once a month or so during the growing season; it was the part of Earth Magic to see to the health of the trees, which her aunt did with gusto, but Margherita could do nothing to supply the trees with water.

She had done a great deal of work over the years here with her own Elemental Power. The stream flowed pure and sweet without any need for her help now, though that had not always been the case; when she had first come into her powers a number of hidden or half-hidden pieces of trash had left the waters less than pristine. The worst had been old lead pipes that Uncle Thomas thought might date all the way back to Roman times, lying beneath a covering of rank weed, slowly leaching their poison into the water. Uncle Thomas had gotten Hired John to haul them away to an antiquities dealer; that would make certain they weren't dumped elsewhere. She wished him well as he carted them off, hoping he got a decent price for them; all she cared about was that they were gone.

Still, there was always the possibility that something could get into the stream even now. She followed the stream down to the pond and back, just to be sure that it ran clean and unobstructed, except by things like rocks, which were perfectly natural; then, her brief surge of restlessness assuaged, she sat back down next to her basket. She leaned

up against the mossy trunk of a tree and took the latest letter from her parents out of the leaves of her book and un-
folded it.

She read it through for the second time—but did so more
out of a sense of duty than of affection; in all her life she had
never actually seen her parents. The uncles and her aunt
were the people who had loved, corrected, and raised her.
They had never let her call them anything other than
"Uncle" or "Aunt," but in her mind those titles had come to
mean far more than "Mama" and "Papa."

Mama and Papa weren't people of flesh and blood.
Mama and Papa had never soothed her after a nightmare, fed
her when she was ill, taught her and healed her and—yes—
loved her. Or at least, if Mama and Papa loved her, it wasn't
with an embrace, a kiss, a strong arm to lean on, a soft
shoulder to cry on—it was only words on a piece of paper.

And yet—there were those words, passionate words.
And there was guilt on her part. They *were* her mother and
father; that could not be denied. For some reason, she could
not be with them, although they assured her fervently in
every letter that they longed for her presence. She *tried* to
love them—certainly they had always lavished her with
presents, and later when she was old enough to read, with
enough letters to fill a trunk—but even though she was in-
timately familiar with Uncle Sebastian's art, it was impossible to make the wistful couple in the double portrait in her
room come alive.

Perhaps it was because their lives were also so different
from her own. From spring to fall, it was nothing but news
of Oakhurst and the Oakhurst farms, the minutiae of country squires obsessed with the details of their realm. From fall
to spring, they were gone, off on their annual pilgrimage to
Italy for the winter, where they basked in a prolonged summer. Marina envied them that, particularly when winter

winds howled around the eaves and it seemed that spring would never come. But she just couldn't *picture* what it was like for them—it had no more reality to her than the stories in the fairy tale books that her aunt and uncles had read to her as a child.

Neither, for that matter, did their home, supposedly hers, seem any more alive than those sepia-toned sketches Uncle Sebastian had made of Oakhurst. No matter how much she wished differently, she couldn't *feel* the place. *Here* was her home, in this old fieldstone farmhouse, surrounded not only by her aunt and uncles but by other artists who came and went.

There were plenty of those; Sebastian's hospitality was legendary, and between them, Thomas and Margherita kept normally volatile artistic temperaments from boiling over. From here, guests could venture into Cornwall and Arthurian country for their inspiration, or they could seek the rustic that was so often an inspiration for the artist Millais, another leader in the Pre-Raphaelite movement. Their village of a few hundred probably hadn't changed significantly in the last two hundred years; for artists from London, the place came as a revelation and an endless source for pastoral landscapes and bucolic portraits.

Marina sighed, and smoothed the pages of the letter with her hand. She suspected that she was as much an abstraction to her poor mother as her mother was to her. Certainly the letters were not written to anyone that she recognized as herself. She was neither an artist nor a squire's daughter, and the person her mother seemed to identify as *her* was a combination of both—making the rounds of the ailing cottagers with soup and calves-foot jelly in the morning, supervising the work of an army of servants in the afternoon, and going out with paintbox to capture the sunset in the evening. The Marina in those letters would never pose for her uncle (showing her legs in those baggy hose!), get herself floured to the elbow making scones, or be lying on the grass in the orchard, bare-legged and bare-footed. And she was, above all else, nothing like an artist.

If anything, she was a musician, mastering mostly on her own the lute, the flute, and the harp. But despite all of the references to music in *her* letters, her mother didn't seem to grasp that. Presents of expensive paints and brushes that arrived every other month went straight to her Uncle Sebastian; he in his turn used the money saved by not having to buy his own to purchase music for her.

Oh, how she loved music! It served as a second bridge between herself and the Elemental creatures, not only of Water, but of Air, the Sylphs and Zephyrs that Uncle Sebastian said were her allies, though why she should need *allies* baffled her. She brought an instrument out here to play as often as she brought a book to read. *I'm good,* she thought idly, staring at words written in a careful copperplate hand that had nothing to do with the real *her. If I had to — I could probably make my own living from music.*

As it was, she used it in other ways; bringing as much pleasure to others as she could.

Just as she used her magic.

If she didn't make the rounds of the sick and aged of the village like a Lady Bountiful, she brought them little gifts of another sort. The village well would never run dry or foul again. Her flute and harp were welcome additions to every celebration, from services in the village church every Sunday, to the gatherings on holidays at the village green. They probably would never know why the river never overtopped its banks even in the worst flood-times, and never would guess. Anyone who fell into the river, no matter how raging the storm, or how poor a swimmer he was, found himself carried miraculously to the bank — and if he then betook himself to the church to thank the Lord, that was all right with Marina. Knowing that she had these powers would not have served them—or her. *They* would be frightened, and she would find herself looked at, not as a kind of rustic unicorn, rare and ornamental, but as something dark, unfathomable, and potentially dangerous.

Her uncles and aunt had never actually said anything about keeping her magics a tacit secret, but their example had spoken louder than any advice they could have given her. Margherita and Thomas' influence quietly ensured bountiful harvests, fertile fields, and healthy children without any overt displays—Sebastian's magic was less useful to the villagers in that regard, but no one ever suffered from hearth-fires that burned poorly, wood that produced more smoke than heat, or indeed anything having to do with fire that went awry. It was all very quiet, very *domestic* magic; useful, though homely.

And working it paid very subtle dividends. Although the villagers really didn't know the authors of their prosperity, some instinct informed them at a level too deep for thought. So, though they often looked a bit askance at the bohemian visitors that were often in residence at Blackbird Cottage, they welcomed the four residents with good-natured amusement, a touch of patronization, and probably said among themselves, "Oh, to be sure they're lunatics, but they're *our* lunatics."

They did grant full acknowledgement of the mastery of the talents they could understand. They thought Aunt Margherita's weaving and embroidery absolutely enchanting, and regarded her lace with awe. If they didn't understand why anyone would pay what they did for Uncle Sebastian's "daubs," they recognized the skill and admired his repainted sign for the village pub, which was, almost inevitably, called "The Red Lion." And then there was Uncle Thomas. There wasn't a man for miles around who didn't know about Thomas' cabinet-making skills, and admire them.

Marina's room was a veritable showplace of those skills. In fact, it was a showplace of all three of her guardians' skills. Uncle Thomas had built and carved all of the furniture, from the little footstool to the enormous canopy bed. Aunt Margherita was responsible for the embroidered hangings of the bed, the curtains at the windows, the cushions in the window seat, all of them covered with fantastic vines and garlands and flowers. Uncle Sebastian had plastered the walls with his own hands, and decorated them with wonderful frescos.

He had nobly refrained from painting his beloved medieval tales—instead, he'd given her woods filled with gentle mythological creatures and Elementals. Undines frolicked in a waterfall, a Salamander coiled lazily in a campfire for a pair of young Fauns with mischievous eyes, a Unicorn rested its horn in the lap of a maiden that bore more than a passing resemblance to Marina herself. The room had grown as she had; from a cradle and a panel of vines to the wonder that it was now. The number of hours that had gone into its creation was mind-boggling, and even now that she was grown, she could come into the room to find that Uncle Sebastian had touched up fading colors, or Aunt Margherita had added a cushion. It was the visible and constant reminder of how much they cared for her.

No one could possibly love her as much as her aunt and uncles did, and never mind that the titles of Aunt and Uncle were mere courtesy. She had never questioned that; had never needed to. There was only one question that had never been properly answered, so far as she was concerned.

If my parents love me so much, why did they send me away—and why have they never tried to be with me again?

That there was a secret about all this she had known from

the time she had begun to question the way things were. She
had never directly questioned her parents, however—something about the tone of her mother's letters suggested that
her mother's psyche was a fragile one, and a confrontation
would lead to irreparable harm. The last thing she wanted to
do was to upset a woman as sweet-natured and gentle as
those letters revealed her to be!

*And somehow, I think that she is so very fragile emotion-
ally* because *of the reason she had to send me away.*

She sighed. If that was indeed the case, it was no use asking one of her beloved guardians. They wouldn't even have
to lie to her—Uncle Sebastian would give her a *look* that
suggested that if she was clever, she would find out for herself. And as for the other two, well, the look of reproach that
Aunt Margherita could (and would) bend upon her would
make her feel about as low as a worm. And Uncle Thomas
would become suddenly as deaf as one of his carved bed-
posts. It really wasn't fair; the chief characteristic of a Water
Master was supposed to be *fluidity.* She *should* have been
able to insinuate her will past any of their defenses!

"And perhaps one day you will be able to—when *you are
a Master,"* giggled a voice that bubbled with the chuckling
of sweet water over stones.

She turned to glare at the Undine who tossed her river-
weed-twined hair and with an insolent flip of her tail, stared
right back at her.

"You shouldn't be reading other people's thoughts," Marina told her. "It isn't polite."

"You shouldn't be shouting them to the world at large,"
the Undine retorted. *"A tadpole has more shields than you."*

Marina started, guiltily, when she realized that the Undine was right. Never mind that there wasn't real *need* for
shields; she knew very well that she was supposed to be
keeping them up at all times. They had to be automatic—

otherwise, when she really *did* need them, she might not be able to raise them in time. There were unfriendly Elementals—some downright hostile to humans. And there were unfriendly Masters as well.

"I beg your pardon," she said with immediate contrition to the Undine, who laughed, flipped her tail again, and dove under the surface to vanish into the waters.

She spent several moments putting up those shields properly, and another vowing not to let them drop again. What had she been thinking? If Uncle Sebastian had caught her without her shields, he'd have verbally flayed her alive!

Well, he hadn't. And what he didn't know, wouldn't hurt him.

And besides, it was time for tea.

Checking again to make sure those shields were intact, she picked up her basket, rose to her feet, and ran back up the path to the farmhouse, leaving behind insolent Undines and uncomfortable questions.

For now, at any rate.

2

SEBASTIAN had paint in his hair, as usual; Margherita forbore to point it out to him. He'd see it himself the next time he glanced in a mirror, and her comments about his appearance only made him testy and led to growling complaints that she was fussing at him. Besides, he looked rather—endearing—with paint in his hair. It was one more reminder of the impetuous artist who had proposed to her with a brush behind one ear and paint all over his hands.

At least these days he generally got the paint off his hands before he ate!

Instead, she passed the plate of deviled ham sandwiches to him, and said, "Well, they're off to Italy. They caught the boat across the Channel yesterday, if the letter was accurate."

No need to say *who*. Alanna and Hugh Roeswood, unable to bear their empty house in the winter, had fled to Italy as soon as their harvest was over that first disastrous year, and had repeated the trip every year after. It was a habit now,

Margherita suspected; Earth Masters tended to get into comfortable ruts. The Roeswoods always took the same Tuscan villa, and Alanna was able to pass the time in a garden that was living through the winter instead of stark and dormant. As an Earth Master herself, Margherita suspected that it helped her cope with her grief. By now, the earth there knew them as well as the earth of Oakhurst did.

Sebastian helped himself to sandwiches, and nodded. He seldom read Alanna's letters; Margherita suspected they were too emotional for him. Like all Fire Masters, his emotions were volatile and easily aroused. And Alanna's letters could arouse emotion in a stone.

As Margherita had suspected he would, he shifted the subject to one more comfortable. "I'll be glad when winter truly comes for us. With all the harvesters moving in and out, it fair drives me mad trying to keep track of the strangers in the village."

Strangers—the unspoken danger was always there, that Marina's *real* aunt had finally found out where she was, that one of those strangers was her spy.

Never mind that Marina was known as "Marina Tarrant" and everyone thought she was Sebastian's niece. Never mind that they managed to preserve that false identity to literally everyone in the world except her real parents and that handful of guests at the ill-fated gathering after the christening. Such a transparent ruse would never fool Arachne, if the woman had any idea where to look for the child. The single thing keeping Marina safe was that Thomas, Sebastian, and Margherita were the Roeswoods' social inferiors, and it would probably never enter Arachne's head to look for her brother's child in the custody of middle-class bohemians. She had, in fact, looked right past them when she had made her dramatic entrance; perhaps she had thought they had been invited only because they were part of something like the great Magic Circle in London. Perhaps she had even thought they were mere entertainers, musicians for the gathering. It had been clear then that to her, they might as well not exist.

And why should they come to her notice then? Their parents had been the equivalent of Roeswood servants; Sebastian was hardly known outside of the small circle of patrons who prized his talent. As for Thomas, he was a mere cabinetmaker; he worked with his hands, and was not even the social equivalent of a farmer who owned his own land. That was their safety then, and now. But they had always known they could not rely on it.

The danger was unspoken because they never, ever said Arachne's name aloud and tried not even to think it. Arachne's curse lay dormant, but who knew what would happen if her name was spoken aloud in Marina's presence? Names had power, and even if that sleeping curse did not awaken, saying Arachne's name still might draw her attention to this obscure little corner of Devon. Whether Arachne's magic was her own or borrowed, it still followed no rules of Elemental power that Margherita recognized, and there was no telling what she could and could not do.

That was why they had kept the reason for Marina's exile a secret from her all these years, and up until she was old enough to keep her own counsel, had even kept her real name from her. If she knew about the curse, about her real aunt—she might try to break the curse herself, she might try to find Arachne and persuade her to take it off, she might even dare, in adolescent hubris, to challenge her aunt.

She might not do any of those things; she *might* be sensible about it, but Margherita had judged it unwise to take the chance. Marina was sweet-natured, but there was a stubborn streak to her, and not even a promise would keep her from doing something she really wanted to. Marina had a very agile mind, and a positively lawyerlike ability to find a way, however tangled and convoluted the path might be, of getting around any promises she'd made if she truly wanted something. That was a Water characteristic—the ability to go wherever the will drove. Perhaps they had done her no favors by keeping her in ignorance, but at least they had done her no harm.

Other than the harm of separating mother from child.

It hadn't been Marina that had suffered, though; Margherita would pledge her soul on that. The happy, carefree child had grown into a remarkable young woman, and if she had not had all the advantages her parents' relative wealth could have bought her, she had obtained other advantages that money probably could not have purchased. Freedom, for one thing; she'd learned her letters and reckoning from Margherita, and all the other graces that young ladies were supposed to require, and a great deal more. From Thomas, who had a scholarly turn, she'd learned Latin and Greek as well as the French she got from Margherita—and from Sebastian, Italian. She learned German on her own. When she was little, they'd given her formal lessons, but when she turned fourteen, they let her choose her own subjects for the most part, though she'd still had plenty of studying to do. This year was the first time they'd let her follow her own inclinations; there was no telling what she'd choose to do when she passed that fateful eighteenth birthday and her parents collected her. Thomas hoped that she would go to Oxford, to the women's college there, even though women were not actually given degrees.

Meanwhile, she had the run of the library, and devoured books in all five languages besides her native English. Winter-long, there wasn't a great deal to do besides work and read, for the long winter rains kept all of them indoors. Margherita reflected that she would have to keep an eye on Sebastian and his demands for Mari's time as his model; it had already occurred to him that by next summer he would lose her, and he was painting at a furious rate. Mari was being very good-natured about all the posing, but Margherita knew from her own experience that it was hard work, and that Sebastian was singularly indifferent to the needs of his models when a painting-frenzy was on him.

Thomas reached for the teapot and let out his breath in a sigh. "Eight months," he said, and there was no indication in his voice that the sigh was one of relief. Margherita nodded.

They had always known that this last year, Marina's seventeenth, would be the hardest. Even if Arachne was not aware that her curse now had a limitation on it, she would still be trying to bring it to fruition in order to achieve that self-imposed deadline. The older Marina got, the stronger she would be in her powers, and the better able to defend herself. Nor could Arachne count on Marina remaining alone; although the help that her friends could give her was, by the very nature of the magic that they wielded, somewhat limited, that did *not* apply to true lovers, especially if they happened to be of complementary Elements. In a case like that, the powers joined, magnifying each other, and it would be very difficult for a single Power to overwhelm them. The older Marina was, the more likely it became that she would fall in love, and Magic being what it was, it was a foregone conclusion that it would be with another Elemental magician.

Arachne would want to prevent *that* at all costs, for her curse would rebound on its caster if it was broken, and heaven only knew what would happen then.

So this seventeenth year of Marina's life would be the most dangerous for her, and her guardians were doing everything in their power to keep her out of the public eye.

Not her *image*—that was harmless enough. She didn't look strikingly like either of her parents; the resemblance had to be hunted for. She had Hugh's dark hair, a sable near to black, but it was wavy rather than straight as his was, or as curly as her mother's. In fact, virtually everything about her was a melding of the two; her face between round and oblong, her mouth neither the tiny rosebud of her mother's, nor as wide as her father's. She was tall, much taller than her mother. And her eyes—well, they were nothing like either parent's. Hugh's were gray, Alanna's a cornflower blue. Marina's were enormous and blue-violet, a color so striking that everyone who saw her for the first time was arrested by the intensity of it. There had been no hint of that color when she'd been a baby, and as far as anyone knew, there had never been eyes of that color in either family.

So Sebastian had been using her as a model all this past year, both because she was a wonderful subject and to keep her busy and out of the village as much as possible. And if because of that his pictures took on a certain sameness, well, that particular trait hadn't hurt Rossetti's popularity, nor any of the other Pre-Raphaelites who had favorite models.

In fact, the only negative aspect to using Marina as a model had so far been as amusing as it was negative—that certain would-be patrons had assumed that the model's virtue was negotiable. After the first shock—the Blackbird Cottage household was known in the artistic community more as a model for semi-stodgy propriety than otherwise—Sebastian had rather enjoyed disabusing those "gentlemen" of that notion. If going cold and saying in a deathly voice, "Are you referring to *my niece?*" was not a sufficient hint, then turning on a feigned version of a Fire Master's wrath certainly was. No one ever faced a Fire Master in his full powers without quailing, whether or not they had magic themselves, and even theatrical anger was nearly as intimidating as the real thing.

And Sebastian being Sebastian, he usually got, not only

an apology, but an increase in his commission out of the encounter. He'd only lost one patron out of all of the years that he'd been using Marina, and it was one he'd had very little taste for in the first place. "I told him to go elsewhere for his damned 'Leda,' if he wanted the model as well as the painting," was what he'd growled to Margherita when he'd returned from his interview in London. "I wanted to knock him down—"

"But you didn't, of course," she'd said, knowing from his attitude that, of course, he hadn't.

"No. Damn his eyes. He's too influential; I'm no fool, my love, I kept my insults behind my teeth and managed a cunning imitation of sanctimonious prig without a sensual bone in my body. But I wanted to send his damned teeth down his throat for what he hinted at." Sebastian's aura had pulsed a sullen red.

"Serve the blackguard right," Margherita returned. Sebastian had smiled at last, and kissed her, and she had known that, as always, his temper had burned itself out quickly.

But common perceptions were a boon to Marina's safety; Arachne would never dream that Marina Roeswood would be *posing for paintings* like a common—well—*artist's model*. The term was only a more polite version of something else.

For that matter, if Alanna had any notion that Sebastian's lovely model was her own daughter, she would probably faint. It was just as well that the question had never come up. The prim miniatures that Sebastian sent every Christmas showed a proper young lady with her hair up, a high-collared blouse, and a cameo at her throat, not the languid odalisques or daring dancers Sebastian had been painting in that style the French were calling Art Nouveau.

"Once harvest's over and winter's begun," Sebastian said

through a mouthful of deviled ham, "it will be easier to keep the little baggage indoors."

"Unless she decides it's time you made good on your promise to take her to London," Thomas pointed out.

"So what if she does?" Sebastian countered. "London's as good or better a place to hide her than here! *How* many Elemental magicians are there in London? Trying to find her would be like trying to find one particular pigeon in Trafalgar Square! If she wants a trip to the galleries and the British Museum, I'll take her. I'm more concerned that she doesn't get the notion in her head to go to Scotland and meet up with the Selkies."

Thomas winced. "Don't even think about that, or she might pick the idea up," he cautioned, and sucked on his lower lip. "We've got a problem, though. *We* can't teach her any more. She needs a real Water Master now, and I think she's beginning to realize that. She's restless; she's bored with the exercises I've set her. She might not give a hang about the Roeswood name, fortune, or estate, but she's going to become increasingly unhappy when she realizes she needs more teaching in her Power and we can't give it to her."

Sebastian and Margherita exchanged a long look of consternation; they hadn't thought of *that.* Of all the precautions they had taken, all the things they had thought they would have to provide for, Marina's tutoring in magic had not been factored into the equation.

"Is she going to be *that* powerful?" Sebastian asked, dumbfounded.

"What if I told you that every time she goes out to the orchard she's *reading poetry to Undines*?" Thomas asked.

That took even Margherita by surprise. Sebastian blanched. Small wonder. When Elementals simply appeared to socialize with an Elemental mage, it meant that the magi-

cian in question either *was* very, very powerful, powerful
enough that the Elementals wanted to forge friendships with
her, or that she *would be* that powerful, making it all the
more important to the Elementals that they forge those
friendships *before* she realized her power. One didn't coerce
or compel one's friends . . . it just wasn't done.

"Oh, there is more to it than that," Thomas went on. "I've
caught Sylphs in her audiences as well. I can only thank God
that she hasn't noticed very often, or she'd start to wonder
just what she could do with them if she asked."

So the Air Elementals were aware of her potential power
too. The Alliance granted her by Roderick did go both
ways. . . .

Thomas was right; they couldn't leave her at loose ends.
If she began trying things on her own, they might as well
take her to London and put her on top of Nelson's column
with a banner unrolling at her feet, spelling out her name for
all—for Arachne—to see.

"What about asking Elizabeth Hastings for a visit—or
more than one?" Margherita asked slowly.

Sebastian opened his mouth as if to object—then shut it.
Thomas blinked.

"Would she come?" her brother asked, probably guess-
ing, and accurately, that she had been feeling Elizabeth out
on that very subject in her latest letters. "She's not an artist,
after all. And we are not precisely 'polite' society."

"We're not social pariahs either, brother mine," she
pointed out. "Silly goose! She wouldn't harm her reputation
by visiting us, even if anyone actually knew that was what
she was doing here. A mature lady just might take up the invitation of a perfectly respectable couple and the wife's
brother, all well-known for their scholarly pursuits—"

Thomas primmed up his face, and Sebastian drew himself up stiffly, interrupting her train of thought with their posing.

"Stop that, you two!" she said, torn between exasperation and laughter. She slapped Sebastian's shoulder lightly, and made a face at Thomas. "Like it or not, we *are* respectable, and only old roués like some of *your* clients, Sebastian, think any different!"

"Dull as dishwater, we are," Thomas agreed dolefully, as Sebastian leered at her. "We don't even amuse the village anymore. We give them nothing to gossip about."

"Oh, but if they only knew. . . ." Sebastian laughed. "Now, acushla, don't be annoyed with us. There's little enough in this situation to laugh about, don't grudge us a joke or two."

He reached out to embrace her, and she sighed and returned it. She never could resist him when he set out to charm her.

"Now, what about Elizabeth? Obviously you two women have been plotting something out behind our backs," Sebastian continued.

"Well, to be honest, it never occurred to me that we'd *need* to have her here, I just thought it would be good for Mari to be around another Water-mage, and even better to have someone around who was—well—more like Hugh and Alanna. Someone who could get her used to the kinds of manners and social skills she'll have to have when she goes to them." Margherita sighed. "I don't want her to feel like an exile. And she likes Elizabeth. I thought if Elizabeth could come for a few weeks at a time, it would help the transition."

"So, that makes perfect sense; all the better, that you've clearly got something in motion already," Thomas said, with his usual practicality. "So, what was your plan? How did she figure to get away from all of *her* social obligations? I should think given the season that it would be nearly impossible."

"Not this year!" Margherita said in triumph. "You *know* she hates both the shooting season and the hunting season—"

" 'The unspeakable in pursuit of the inedible,' " her brother muttered, quoting Wilde.

"—and now that her daughter's married and both her sons are at school, she's got no real reason to stay and play hostess if she truly doesn't want to," Margherita continued. "Her husband, she tells me, has always wanted to try a season in Scotland instead of here. He's had tentative invitations he never pursued because *she* didn't care to go."

She stopped there; both her brother and her husband were canny enough to fill in the blank spaces without any help from her. The Hastingses had been the host to more than enough pheasant-shoots and fox-hunts over the years that they must have an amazing backlog of invitations that Stephen Hastings—always a keen hunter—could pursue with a good conscience without worrying that Elizabeth was going to make no secret of being bored.

"So he'll get to be that most desirable of social prizes, the 'safe single man,' " Margherita observed with irony. "He can escort the older widows to dinner without feeling put-upon, and he won't target or be a target for unsuitable romance. He won't cause a quarrel with anyone's fiancé, and he can be relied upon, if there's a country dance, to make sure all the wallflowers get a waltz."

"That alone will probably ensure he gets his choice of shoots," Sebastian said, his face twitching as he tried not to laugh.

Elizabeth had said as much herself, pointing out the rest of her husband's good points as a sporting guest. He was a good and considerate gun too; not a neck-or-nothing rider, but that wasn't necessary in a middle-aged man to preserve his standing in the Hunt Club. All things considered, in order to give him a free conscience in accepting one or more of those long-standing invitations, all that Elizabeth would have to do would be to find some excuse that could reasonably take her off to this part of the country for some extended period of time.

"Let's put our heads together on this one," Sebastian said immediately. "What on God's green earth could Lady Elizabeth Hastings want in *this* part of the world?"

Thomas blinked again—and said, "Folk tales and songs."

Margherita clapped her hands like a girl, and Sebastian's smile lit up the entire room. "Brilliant, Thomas!" he shouted. "By gad, I *knew* I'd made a good choice of brother-in-law! Absolutely brilliant!"

The collection of folk ballads and oral tales was always an appropriate and genteel pursuit for a lady with a scholarly bent; this close to Cornwall there were bound to be variations on the Arthurian mythos that no one had written down yet. During the seasons of planting, tending, and harvesting, no farmer or farm-worker would have time to recite the stories his granny had told him—but during the winter, if Elizabeth wanted to lend verisimilitude to her story, all she would have to do would be to have Thomas run her down to the pub in the pony-cart now and again to collect a nice little volume of tales and songs.

"We've already had her out here during the summer and spring over the years, so she's seen the May Day celebrations and the fairs," Margherita said, planning aloud, "She can look through her sketches and notes and 'discover' what a wealth of untapped ballads we have here and make visits the rest of the winter. One long one up until the Christmas season, say, and another between the end of January and spring."

"That's a rather long time. You're sure her husband won't mind?" Sebastian asked, suddenly doubtful, remembering the other half of the Hastings equation.

Margherita smiled. "I didn't *think* you two ever listened when I read her letters aloud. Let me just say that they are on cordial terms, the best of terms, really, but Elizabeth has gotten confirmation about some of her suspicions about her husband's frequent visits to London."

Thomas shook his head; Sebastian snorted. "Actress?" he asked bluntly.

"Dancer," she replied serenely. "Well, if Elizabeth chooses to look the other way, it is none of *my* business, and if Stephen has another interest, *he* won't be unhappy if Elizabeth doesn't go in to London with him this winter."

"Stephen got his local Parliament seat last year, didn't he?" Sebastian asked, showing that he had paid a little more attention to Elizabeth's letters than Margherita had thought.

"He did, and Elizabeth loathes London." The plan unrolled itself in Margherita's mind like a neatly gridded tapestry. "Stephen can pretend to live at his club and visit his dancer while Parliament is in session, and *she* can stay with us." Her lips twitched in a bit of a smile. "Perhaps if he gets a surfeit of the girl he'll tire of her."

"He probably will," Sebastian predicted loftily. "It's nothing more than an attempt to prove he isn't middle-aged, I suspect. If he doesn't tire of her, *she'll* tire of *him*. There'll be a dance-instructor or a French singing-master hanging about before the New Year, mark my words. And at some point, Stephen will show up at her establishment unexpectedly, and discover that there's something other than lessons going on."

Margherita hid a smile. Sebastian had met Stephen several times, and on each occasion she was reminded of a pair of dogs circling one another in mutual animosity, prevented from actually starting a fight by the presence of their masters. Sebastian was the utter opposite of Stephen Hastings, describing him as a "hearty gamesman" and intimating that the only reason he'd actually gotten his Cambridge degree was that his instructors wanted to see the last of him. There might have been some truth in that. He *certainly* hadn't taken a First, and seemed to be absurdly proud of the fact.

It wasn't her business why Elizabeth had married him, when all was said and done. Perhaps, besides a certain amount of affection, it had been because he was so *very* incurious, so utterly without imagination, that she could carry on her Magical Workings without rousing any interest in him. That arrangement wouldn't have suited Margherita— but it was infinitely better than having to sneak about in deathly fear of being caught. And if one couldn't find some-one to love—society being what it was, a woman of Elizabeth's position had little choice except to marry—the best compromise was to find someone it was possible to be friends with.

"I'll write her," Margherita said. "Unless you want to use a dove to send her a message?" She cast a glance of inquiry at Thomas. He shook his head.

"It's not that urgent, not while Marina has other things to occupy her. There's plenty to do around here until the end of harvest," he said.

"I'll *find* things for her to do," Margherita and Sebastian said together, then looked at each other and laughed.

"It's settled, then," Margherita said for both of them, and felt a certain relief. That would be one more person here to watch over Marina as well. One more pair of eyes—one more set of powers.

Most importantly, someone to help the child master the powers that would protect her better than any of them could.

"And just what is it that you are thinking about that makes you frown so?" asked the Undine. Her pointed chin rested on her hands, her elbows propped on the bank of the brook. The faintly greenish cast to her skin was something that Marina was so used to seeing that she seldom noticed it unless, like now, she stopped to study an Undine's expression.

The Undines didn't trouble themselves with individual names; at least, they never gave *her* their names. Though that might simply have been excessive caution on their part. Names had power, after all.

"Was I frowning?" Marina asked. She rubbed her forehead; on the whole, she really didn't want to discuss her internal conflicts with an Undine that wouldn't understand anyway. Undines didn't have parents, at least, not so far as Marina knew, just sisters. Marina had never seen anything but female Undines. "Just concentrating, I suppose."

"Well, at least you aren't shouting your thoughts anymore," the Undine replied, with a toss of her green-blond hair. *"You ought to stop thinking and come have a swim. It won't be long before it's too cold—for you, anyway. Enjoy yourself while you still can."*

"You're right," she agreed, only too pleased to leave the problem of her parents to sort itself out another day. The Undine laughed liquidly, and plunged under the surface of the brook to become—literally—one with the water. For all intents and purposes, the Undine vanished in a froth of foam and a wave.

Marina followed the brook upstream, above the little falls, to a pond the family waterfowl seldom visited. It stood in the midst of a water meadow, and the verge was dense with protective reeds. An intensely green scent hung over the pond; not the scent of rotting vegetation, nor the stale smell of scum, just the perfume of a healthy watering hole densely packed with growing things. In fact, the water was pure and clear, thanks to a fine population of little fish and frogs. Herons came here to hunt, and the smaller, shy birds of the reed beds, but never any people—if the folk of the neighboring farm knew about this place, they didn't think it held fish large enough to bother with, and her own family left her alone here. This was Marina's summertime retreat by common consent, and had been since she was old enough to come up here alone. It wasn't as if she could get into any trouble in the water, after all—even in the roughest horse-play, the Undines would never permit her to come to harm in her proper element. She had been able to swim, and be safe in the water, since before she could walk.

She slipped out of her dress and petticoat and underthings and left them folded on a rock concealed among the reeds, where they would remain safe and dry without advertising the fact that there was someone swimming here to anyone who might be passing. This time of year there were always strangers, itinerant harvesters, and gypsies passing through the village. The villagers themselves might not come here, but the strangers, looking for a place to camp, might happen upon it by accident. Not the gypsies, though; the Undines managed to warn them off.

There hadn't been anyone around the pond today, or the Undine wouldn't have invited her to swim. They might not understand much about a mortal's life, but they did understand that strange men lurking about could be a danger to Marina.

She took a moment to tie her hair loosely at the nape of her neck, then slipped into the sun-warmed water wearing nothing more than her own skin.

Immediately she was surrounded by Undines wearing nothing more than theirs, and an exuberant game of tag began. She was at a partial disadvantage, not being able to breathe underwater, but she managed to compensate with her longer reach. There was a great deal of splashing and giggling as they chased one another. The warm water caressed Marina's skin like the brush of warmed silk; as the Undines slid past her, a tingle of energy passed between them, a little like the tingle in the air before lightning strikes. The pond was surprisingly deep for its small size, and as she dove under to elude a pursuer or to chase her own quarry, she reveled in the shock of encountering a cooler layer of water beneath the sun-warmed surface. Other, lesser Elementals gathered to watch, chattering excitedly among the reeds, applauding when someone made a particularly clever move. A family of otters appeared out of nowhere and joined in the fun, and the game changed from one of tag to one of "catch the otter" by common consent.

The otters took to this new game with all the enthusiasm that they brought to any endeavor, and soon the pond was alive with splashing and shrill laughter. Undines chased otters in every direction; slippery otters slid right through Marina's fingers, though truth to tell, she didn't try very hard to hold them. It was more fun watching them twist and turn in the water to avoid capture than it was to try and wrestle a squirming body that just might deliver an accidental nasty kick—with claws!—if you weren't careful.

Only when Marina was completely out of breath did she retreat to her rocks and watch the Undines continue the game on their own. The smallest of the otters evidently ran out of energy at the same time, and joined her. After she combed out her hair with her fingers and coaxed most of the water out of it, she stroked the otter's smooth, dense fur and scratched its head as it sighed with content and erected its stiff whiskers in an otter-smile. It rolled over on its back, begging for her to scratch its tummy. She chuckled, and obliged.

But the sun was westering; it was past teatime, and neither the Undines nor the otters seemed prepared to give up their game any time soon. They might be perfectly free to play until dark and afterwards, but she did have things to do. Reluctantly, she donned her clothing again—reluctantly, because after the freedom of being in the water, it seemed heavy and confining—pulled her skirts up above her knees, and waded back to dry land.

She stopped in the orchard long enough to retrieve her basket of apples and her book. With the basket swinging from one hand, she took her time strolling back to the farmhouse.

In the late afternoon sunlight, the gray granite glowed with mellow warmth. When winter came, the stone would look cold and forbidding, but now, with all the doors and windows open, flowers in the window boxes, and roses twining up trellises along the sides, it was a welcoming sight.

Tea was over, but as she'd expected, Aunt Margherita had left her scones, watercress sandwiches, and a little pot of clotted cream in the kitchen under a cheesecloth. There was no tea, but there was hot water on the stove, and she quickly made her own late repast. She arranged the apples she'd brought in a pottery bowl on the kitchen table, and retreated to her room to fetch her work. After her swim, she was feeling languid, and her window seat, surrounded by ivy with a fine view of the hills and the sunset, seemed very inviting. Uncle Sebastian would be fiddling with his *Saint Joan,* working on the background, probably; Uncle Thomas was carving an occasional table, a swoopy thing all organic curves. And Aunt Margherita was probably either at her embroidery or her tapestry loom.

Her uncles expected a great deal of her in her studies; they saw no reason why she couldn't have as fine an education as any young man who could afford the sort of tutor that Sebastian's father had been. Granted, neither Sebastian nor Thomas had attended university, but if they'd had the means or had truly wanted to they *could* have. So, for that matter, could Aunt Margherita. Perhaps women could not aspire to a university degree, but they were determined that should she choose to attend the single women's college at Oxford regardless of that edict, she would be as well or better prepared than any young man who presented himself to any of the colleges there. She was not particularly enamored of the idea of closing herself up in some stifling building (however hallowed) for several years with a gaggle of young women she didn't even know, but she did enjoy the lessons. At the moment she was engaged in puzzling her way through Chaucer in the original Middle English, the *Canterbury Tales* having caught Uncle Sebastian's fancy. She had a shrewd notion that she knew what the subjects of his next set of paintings was likely to be.

Well, at least it will be winter by the time he gets to them. If she was going to have to wear the heavy medieval robes that Uncle Sebastian had squirreled away, at least it would be while it was cold enough that the weight of the woolens and velvets would be welcome rather than stifling.

At the moment, it was the Wife of Bath's Tale that was the subject of her study, and she had the feeling that she would get a better explanation of some of it from Aunt Margherita than from the uncle that had assigned it to her. Uncle Sebastian was not *quite* as broad-minded as he thought he was.

Or perhaps he just wasn't as broad-minded with regard to

his "niece" as he would have been around a young woman who wasn't under his guardianship. With Marina, he tended to break out in odd spots of ultra-middle-class stuffiness from time to time.

She curled herself up in the window seat, a cushion at her back, with her Chaucer in one hand, a copybook on her knee, and a pencil at the ready. If one absolutely *had* to study on such a lovely late afternoon, this was certainly the only way to do so.

3

SEBASTIAN had gone down to pick up the post in the village; no one else wanted to venture out into the October rain and leave the warmth of the cottage. Marina was supposed to be reading Shakespeare—her uncle was making good his threat to paint her as Kate the Shrew and wanted her to become familiar with the part—but she sat at the window of the parlor and stared out at the rain instead. Winter had definitely arrived, with Halloween a good three weeks away. A steady, chilling rain dripped down through leafless branches onto grass gone sere and brown-edged. Even the evergreens and the few plants that kept their leaves throughout the winter looked dark and dismal. The air outside smelled of wet leaves; inside the foyer where the coats hung, the odor of wet wool hung in a miasma of perpetual damp. Only in the foyer, however. Scented candles burned throughout the house, adding the perfume of honey and cinnamon to counteract the faint chemical smell of the oil lamps, and someone was always baking something in the kitchen that formed a pleasant counter to the wet wool.

And yet, for Marina at least, the weather wasn't entirely depressing. Water, life-giving, life-bearing water was all around her. If the air smelled only dank to the others, for her there was an undercurrent of *potential*. She sensed the currents of faint power that followed each drop of rain, she tasted it, like green tea in the back of her throat, and stirred restlessly, feeling as if there ought to be something she should do with that power.

She heard the door open and shut in the entranceway, and Uncle Sebastian shake out his raincape before hanging it up. He went straight to the kitchen, though, so there must not have been any mail for her.

She didn't expect any; her mother didn't write as often in winter. It was probably a great deal more difficult to get letters out from Italy than it was to send them from Oakhurst in England.

Italy. She wondered what it would be like to spend a winter somewhere that wasn't cold, wet, and gray. Was Tuscany by the sea?

I'd love to visit the sea.

"I don't suppose you remember Elizabeth Hastings, do you?" asked Margherita from the door behind her. She turned; her aunt had a letter in her hand, her dark hair bound up on the top of her head in a loose knot, a smudge of flour on her nose.

"Vaguely. She's that Water magician with the title, isn't she?" Marina closed the volume in her lap with another stirring of interest. "The one with the terribly-terribly correct husband?"

Margherita laughed, her eyes merry. "The *only* one with a 'terribly-terribly correct husband' that has ever visited us, yes. She's coming to spend several weeks with us — to teach *you.*"

Now she had Marina's complete interest. "Me? What — oh! Water magic?" Interest turned to excitement, and a thrill of anticipation.

Margherita laughed. "She certainly isn't going to teach you etiquette! You're more than ready for a teacher of your own Element, and it's time you got one."

The exercises that Uncle Thomas had been setting her had been nothing but repetitions of the same old things for some time now. Marina hadn't wanted to say anything, but she had been feeling frustrated, bored, and stale. Frustrated, because she had the feeling that there was so much that was just beyond her grasp — bored and stale because she was so *tired* of repeating the same old things. "But — what about Mrs. Hasting's family?" she asked, not entirely willing to believe that someone with a "terribly-terribly correct husband" would be able to get away for more than a day or two at most, and certainly not *alone.*

"Elizabeth's sons are at Oxford, her daughter is married, and her husband wants to take up some invitations for the hunting and fishing seasons in Scotland this year," Margherita said, with a smile at Marina's growing excitement. "And when the hunting season is over, he intends to go straight on to London for his Parliament duties. Elizabeth hates hunting and detests London; she'll be staying with us up until Christmas."

"That's *wonderful!*" Marina could not contain herself any more; she leapt to her feet, catching the book of Shakespeare at the last moment before it tumbled to the floor out of her lap. "When is she coming?"

"By the train on Wednesday, and I'll need your help in getting the guest room ready for her —"

But Marina was running as soon as she realized the guest

would arrive the next day. She was already halfway up the stairs, her aunt's laughter following her, by the time Margherita had reached the words "guest room."

Once, all the rooms in this old farm house had led one into the other, like the ones on the first floor. But at some point, perhaps around the time that Jane Austen was writing *Emma*, the walls had been knocked down in the second story and replaced with an arrangement of a hall with smaller bedrooms along it. And about when Victoria first took the throne, one of the smallest bedrooms had been made into a bathroom. True, hot water still had to be carted laboriously up the stairs for a bath, but at least they weren't bathing in hip baths in front of the fire, and there was a water-closet. So their guest wouldn't be totally horrified by the amenities, or lack of them.

It would be horrible if she left after a week because she couldn't have a decent wash-up.

She opened the linen-closet at the end of the hall and took a deep breath of the lavender-scented air before taking out sheets for the bed in the warmest of the guest rooms. This was the one directly across from her own, and like hers, right over the kitchen. The view wasn't as fine, but in winter there wasn't a great deal of view anyway, and the cozy warmth coming up from the kitchen, faintly scented with whatever Margherita was baking, made up for the lack of view. Where her room was a Pre-Raphaelite fantasy, this room was altogether conventional, with rose-vine wallpaper, chintz curtains and cushions, and a brass-framed bed. The rest of the furniture, however, was made by Thomas, and looked just a little odd within the confines of such a conventional room. Woolen blankets woven by Margherita in times when she hadn't any grand commissions to fulfill were in an asymmetrical chest at the foot of the bed, and the visitor would probably need them.

She left the folded sheets on the bed and flung the single window open just long enough to air the room out. It didn't take long, since Margherita never really let the guest rooms get stale and stuffy. It also didn't take long for the room to get nasty and cold, so she closed it again pretty quickly.

Fire. I need a fire. There was no point in trying to kindle one herself the way that Uncle Sebastian did. She was eager, almost embarrassingly eager, for their visitor to feel welcome. When Elizabeth Hastings arrived, it should be to find a room warmed and waiting, as if this house was her home.

Marina solved the problem of the fire with a shovelful of coals from her own little fire, laid onto the waiting kindling in the fireplace of the guest room. She might not be able to kindle a fire, but she was rather proud of her ability to lay one. Once the fire was going and the chill was off the air, she made the bed up with the lavender-scented sheets and warm blankets, dusted everything thoroughly, and set out towels and everything else a guest might want. She made sure that the lamp on the bedside table was full of oil and the wick trimmed, and that there was a box of lucifer matches there as well.

She looked around the room, and sighed. No flowers. It was just too late for them—and too late to gather a few branches with fiery autumn leaves on them. The bouquet of dried strawflowers and fragrant herbs on the mantel would just have to do.

She heard footsteps in the hall outside, and wasn't surprised when her Aunt pushed the door open. "You haven't left me anything to do," Margherita observed, with an approving glance around the room.

"Well, really, there wasn't that much work needed to be done; that tramping poet was only here last week." The "tramping poet" was a rarity, a complete stranger to the household, who'd arrived on foot, in boots and rucksack, letter of recommendation in hand from one of their painterly friends. He'd taken it in his head to "do the Wordsworth"— that is, to walk about the countryside for a while in search of inspiration, and finding that the Lake District was overrun with sightseers and hearty fresh-air types, he'd elected to try Devon and Cornwall instead. He was on the last leg of his journey and had been remarkably cheerful about being soaked with cold rain. A good guest as well, he'd made himself useful chopping wood and in various other small ways, had not overstayed his welcome, and even proved to be very amusing in conversation.

"You can't possibly be a successful poet," Sebastian had accused him. "You're altogether too good-natured, and nothing near morose enough."

"Sadly," he'd admitted (not sadly at all), "I'm not. I do have a facile touch for rhyme, but I can't seem to generate the proper level of anguish. I've come to that conclusion myself, actually. I intend to go back to London and fling myself at one of those jolly new advertising firms. I'll pummel 'em with couplets until they take me in and pay me." He'd struck an heroic attitude. "Hark! the Herald Angels sing, 'Pierson's Pills are just the thing!' If your tummy's fluttery, hie thee to Bert's Buttery! Nerves all gone and limp as wax? Seek the aid of brave Nutrax!"

Laughing, Margherita and Marina had thrown cushions at him to make him stop. "Well!" he'd said, when he'd sat back down and they'd collected the cushions again, "If I'm doomed to be a jangling little couplet-rhymer, I'd rather be honest and sell butter with my work than pretend I'm a genius crushed by the failure of the world to understand me."

"I hope he comes back some time," Marina said, referring to that previous guest.

"If he does, he'll be welcome," Margherita said firmly. "But *not* while Elizabeth is here. It would be very awkward, having a stranger about while she was trying to teach you Water Magic. Altogether too likely that he'd see something he shouldn't."

Marina nodded. It wasn't often that someone who wasn't naturally a mage actually saw any of the things that mages took for granted—that was part of the Gift of the Sight, after all, and if you didn't have that Gift, well, you couldn't See what mages Saw. But sometimes accidents happened, and someone with only a touch of the Sight got a glimpse of something he shouldn't. And if magic made some change in the physical world, well, that could be witnessed as well, whether or not the witness had the Sight.

"Now that the room's been put to rights, come down with me and we'll bake some apple pies," Margherita continued, linking her arm with Marina's. "There's nothing better to put a fine scent on the house than apple pies."

"I couldn't agree more," Marina laughed. "And besides, if you give me something to do, I won't be fretting my head off."

"Tch. You're getting far too clever for *me*. It's a good thing Elizabeth is coming; at least there will be someone here now whose habits you don't know inside and out."

That's a lovely thought. One of the worst things about winter coming on was that she was bound to be mostly confined to Blackbird Cottage with people she knew all too well—loved, surely, but still, she could practically predict their every thought and action. But this winter would be different.

Oh, I hope it's very, very *different!*

As usual, it was raining. Uncle Sebastian had intended to go to the railway station in the pony cart, but Aunt Margherita had stamped her foot and decreed that under no circumstances was he going to subject poor Elizabeth to an open cart in the pouring rain. So he had arranged to borrow the parson's creaky old-fashioned carriage, which meant that there was enough room for Marina to go along.

Marina peered anxiously out the little window next to the door; the old glass made the view a bit wavery, and the rain didn't help. Finally Sebastian arrived with the carriage, an old black contraption with a high, arched roof like a mail coach, that looked as if it had carried parsons' families since the time of the third George. The parson's horse, the unlikely offspring of one of the gentry's hunters and a farmer's mare, a beast of indeterminate color rendered even more indeterminate by his wet hide, looked completely indifferent to the downpour. The same could not be said of Sebastian perched up on the block where he huddled in the non-existent coachman's stead, wrapped up in a huge mackintosh with a shapeless broad-brimmed hat pulled down over his eyes.

He shouldn't complain; he'd have been just as wet on the pony cart.

Marina, her rain cape pulled around her and her aunt's umbrella over her head, made a dash across the farmyard for the carriage and clambered inside. The parson's predecessor had long ago replaced the horsehair-covered seats with more practical but far less comfortable wooden ones, and as the coach rolled away, she had to hang on with both hands to guard herself from sliding across the polished slats during the bumps and jounces. When the coach was loaded with the parson's numerous family, the fact that they were all wedged together against the sides of the vehicle meant no one got thrown against the sides, but with just Marina in here, she could be thrown to the floor if she didn't hang on for dear life. The coach creaked and complained, rocking from side to side, the rain drummed on the roof, and water dripped inside the six small windows, for the curtains had long since been removed in the interest of economy as well.

Poor Elizabeth! She'll be bounced to bits before we get home!

The station wasn't far, but long before they arrived, Marina had decided that their guest would have been far more comfortable in the pony cart, rain or no rain.

But then I wouldn't have been able to come meet her.

She'd thought that she'd be on fire with impatience, that the trip would be interminable. It wasn't, but only because she was so busy holding on, and trying to keep from being bounced around like an India rubber ball from one side of the coach to the other. It came as a welcome surprise to get a glimpse, through the curtain of rain, of the railway station ahead of them, and realize that they were almost there. She didn't even wait for the coach to stop moving once they reached the station; she flew out quite as if she'd been launched from the door, dashing across the rain-slicked pavement of the platform, leaving her uncle to tie up the horse and follow her.

She reached the other side of the station and peered down the track, and saw the welcome plume of smoke from the engine in the distance, rising above the trees. As Sebastian joined her on the platform, the train itself came into view, its warning whistle carrying through the rain. Marina remembered not to bounce with impatience—she *wasn't* a child anymore—but she clutched the handle of the umbrella tightly with both hands, and her uncle smiled sideways at her.

It seemed that she was not the only one impatient for the train to pull into the station. There was one particular head that kept peeking out of one compartment window—and the very instant that the train halted, that compartment door *flew* open, and a trim figure in emerald wool shot out of it, heedless of the rain.

"Sebastian!" Elizabeth Hastings gave Uncle Sebastian quite as hearty an embrace as if he had been her brother, and Marina hastened to get the umbrella over her before the ostrich plumes on her neat little hat got soaked. "Good gad, this appalling weather! Margherita warned me, and I didn't believe her! Hello Marina!" She detached herself from Sebastian and gave Marina just as enthusiastic a hug, with a kiss on her cheek for good measure.

"You didn't believe her about what?" Marina asked.

"Oh, the rain, of course. She swore that in winter, this part of Devon got more rain than the whole of England put together, and I swear to you that it was bright and sunny a few miles back!" She took the umbrella from Marina, as a porter hauled her baggage out of the baggage car onto the platform behind them. "Not a cloud, not a *sign* of a cloud, until we topped a hill, and then—like a wall, it was, and just a wall of clouds, and most of them *pouring* rain!"

"That's what you get for not believing Margherita when she tells you something," Sebastian said, with laughter in his eyes. "You should know the Earth Masters by now! They don't feel it necessary to exercise their imagination unless it's in the service of art. When they tell you something, it's unembroidered fact!"

"Oh, you tiresome thing, I *told* you that it was my own fault!" She shook her head, and little drops of rain flew from the ornaments on her bonnet as she laughed. "Come along with you, let's get my things into whatever contraption you've commandeered to get me, and get ourselves home, before we all drown!"

"You're a Water Master," Sebastian teased, a grin creasing his face. "You can't drown. Now *me*, if I don't find my-

self drowning in this antagonistic Element, I'm probably
going to perish of melancholy."

But as the train pulled away from the station with a whistle and a great rush of steam and creaking of metal, he
rounded up the stationmaster's boys and got Elizabeth's
baggage fastened up behind and atop the coach. There was
quite a bit of it; three trunks and some assorted boxes. But
she was staying for weeks, after all, and given the weather,
couldn't count on regular washdays.

*Oh, I wonder what she's brought to wear. She's a lady,
and in society—what kind of gowns did she bring?* Marina
was torn between hoping that Elizabeth had brought all
manner of fine things, and *fear* that she had, and that her
wardrobe would be utterly unsuitable for Blackbird Cottage
and a Devon winter.

The rain did not abate in the least, and Sebastian looked
up at the sky before he climbed aboard the coachman's box,
his hat brim sending a stream down the back of his mackintosh. "I don't suppose you're prepared to do anything about
this, are you?" he asked Elizabeth.

Elizabeth paused with one foot on the step. "In the first
place, I'm a Water Master, not an Air Master; storms are *not*
my venue, and I would need an Alliance with Air at the very
least to clear this muck away permanently—or at least, for
more than a day. In the second place, all I can do by myself—without interfering in a way that would shout to
everyone with a Gift that a Magus Major was here—is
to create just enough of a pause in the rain to give you time
to get the horse turned toward Blackbird Cottage. Now if
that's what you want—or if you really think it's prudent to
let every Power in the county know that I've arrived—"

Sebastian heaved a theatrical sigh. "No, thank you, Elizabeth," he said, and reached up, grabbing the rail at the side
of the box, and climbing up onto his perch. Elizabeth closed

the umbrella and handed it to Marina, then climbed inside. Marina followed her and laid the umbrella at her feet. It would end up there anyway.

"Good gad, he borrowed the parson's rig, didn't he?" Elizabeth exclaimed, as she settled herself on the hard wooden bench across from Marina. "I'd almost rather he'd brought the pony cart!"

The coach swayed into motion, and they both grabbed for handholds.

"Your lovely hat would have gotten ruined," Marina protested weakly.

"Yes, and all the rest of my turnout as well," Elizabeth agreed ruefully. "I fear I've cut rather too dashing a figure for this weather of yours. Well, no fear, my dear, I haven't come laden like a professional beauty; this is about as fine a set of feathers as I've got with me. And there's a certain relief in being among the savage Bohemians; *you* don't feel required to attend church every Sunday, so if the weather's foul, neither shall I! And at long last, I'll be able to get through a day without changing my dress four or five times!"

Marina laughed. She had forgotten how outspoken Elizabeth was, and—to be honest—how very pretty. She could easily be a professional beauty, one of those gently-born, well-connected or marginally talented ladies whose extraordinary good looks bought them entree into the highest circles. The PBs (as they were called) had their portraits painted, sketched, and photographed, figured in nearly every issue of the London papers, and were invited to all important social functions merely as ornaments to it. And even to Marina's critical eyes, educated by all of her exposure to art and artists as well as the press, Elizabeth Hastings, had she chosen to exert herself, could have had a place in that exalted circle. She must be nearing forty, and yet she didn't look it. Her soft cheeks had the glow that Marina saw on her own in the mirror of a morning; her green-green eyes had just the merest hint of a crow's-foot at the corners. That firm, rounded chin hadn't the least sign of a developing jowl; the dark blonde hair was, perhaps, touched a trifle with silver, but the silver tended to blend in so well that it really didn't show. And in any case, as Marina well knew, there were rinses to change the silver back to gold.

"Remarkably well-preserved for such a tottering relic, aren't I?" Elizabeth asked, the humor in her voice actually managing to get past the gasps caused by the jouncing of the coach.

Was I thinking loudly again? A rush of blood went to Marina's cheeks. "Oh—*bother!*" she exclaimed, as she felt tears of chagrin burn her eyes for a moment. "Lady Hastings, I apologize for—for being so—"

But Elizabeth freed a hand long enough to pat her knee comfortingly. "Please, dear, *you* are a Water child, and a powerful one—anyone of the same Element would have picked up the train of your thoughts no matter how much energy you put into those basic shields Thomas taught you."

Marina shook her head. "But I wasn't really trying hard enough—"

"Perhaps, but he *hasn't* taught you how to make those shields effortless and unconscious; well, I can't fault him for that. It isn't as if Earth Masters are often called on to work combative magics."

"What has that to do with my being rude?" Marina asked, the flush fading from her cheeks.

"That is what you will learn for yourself. And it's *Elizabeth,* my dear. Or Aunt Elizabeth, if you prefer. I *am* one of your godparents, after all." Elizabeth smiled into Marina's astonished eyes. "You didn't know? I should have thought someone would have told you."

"No, Aunt Elizabeth," Marina said, faintly. "But—"

Elizabeth chose to change the subject, bending forward to peer out one of the dripping windows. "I will be very glad when we're all safely in Margherita's kitchen, dry, and with a hot cup of tea in front of us." The coach hit a deep rut, and they both flew into the air and landed hard on their seats. "Good heavens! When was this coach last sprung? For Victoria's coronation?"

"Probably," Marina said, torn between laughing and wanting to swear at her bruises. "The parson hasn't much to spare, what with having all those children; his hired man fixes *and* drives this rig along with all his other duties—"

"Well, I hope that the parsonage ladies are considerably more—" the coach gave another lurch "—more *upholstered* than we are."

Marina's laugh was bitten off by another bump, but it was very clear to her that she and "Aunt" Elizabeth were going to get on well together. Heretofore, Elizabeth Hastings had been something of an unknown quantity; like the artists that arrived and left at unpredictable intervals, she was the friend of Marina's guardians, and hadn't spent much time in Marina's company.

Oh, Marina had certainly had *some* interaction with Elizabeth in the past, but there had been that distance of "adult" and "child" between them.

Between that last visit and this, that relationship had changed. For the first time Elizabeth Hastings was treating her as an adult in her own right, and Marina was discovering that she *liked* the older woman. Certainly Elizabeth was making it very easy to become a friend; inviting friendship, welcoming trust and offering it.

Without knowing she'd been worried about that, Marina felt a knot of tension dissolve inside her. So, as well as they could amid the bouncing of the coach, they began to learn about each other. Before very long, it almost seemed as if she had known Elizabeth Hastings all her life.

Sebastian brought the coach as close to the door as he could, and a herd of flapping creatures enveloped in mackintoshes and rain capes converged on it as soon as it stopped moving—Uncle Thomas, Sarah, and Jenny, with Aunt Margherita bringing up the rear. Elizabeth was ushered straight into the kitchen by Margherita; Marina stayed outside with her uncles and the servants just long enough to be loaded with a couple of bandboxes before being shooed inside herself.

She shed her rain cape and hung it, dripping, on its peg, then brought her burden into the kitchen. Elizabeth had already divested herself of hat, coat, and jacket, and Marina found herself eyeing the fashionable emerald trumpet skirt with its trimming of black soutache braid and the cream silk shirtwaist with its softening fall of Venice lace with a pang of envy. Not that she didn't love the gowns that her Aunt Margherita made for her, but . . . but they weren't *fashionable.* They were lovely, *very* medieval, and certainly comfortable, but they weren't anything like fashionable. Plenty of magazines found their way here, and Marina had been known to peruse the drawings in them from time to time, gazing with wonder at the cartwheel hats, the bustle skirts, the PBs in their shoulder-baring gowns and upswept hair. The village was hardly the cynosure of fashion; most of the people who came to stay at the cottage were of the same ilk as her guardians. Only Elizabeth Hastings came in the feathers and furbelows of couture, and Marina's heart looked long and enviously at its representative. *She* wanted an emerald suit, an ostrich-plumed hat.

But you'd have to wear corsets! a little voice reminded her. *Look at her waist—think about how tight you'd have to lace them!*

But oh—replied another side of her—it would be worth it to look like that, to wear clothing like that.

She shook herself out of her reverie and joined them over their hot tea.

"—and no, I am *not* going to prance around your farmyard in a ridiculous rig like this!" Elizabeth was saying as Marina took a seat at the table. "Honestly, if you must know, the reason I tricked myself out like a PB on a stroll through Hyde Park was so I would be treated with disgusting servility by the railroad staff. A woman traveling alone needs all the advantage that perceived rank and wealth gives her. I wanted porters to present themselves to me without having to look for them. I wanted instant service in the dining car and no mashers trying to seat themselves at my table. I *didn't* want to find myself sharing my compartment with some spoiled little monkey and his or her nursemaid; in fact, I didn't want to share it at all, and I couldn't get a private compartment on that train. The best way to ensure privacy is to dress as if you're too important to bother. It's what I do when I go to suffrage meetings. *No one* raises his hand or voice against me when I'm dressed like this. I may get surly looks, but they're *deferential* surly looks, even from the police."

Margherita shook her head. "I can't picture you as a suffragist, somehow."

"I only go often enough to make it clear where my sympathies are. And I supply money, of course," Elizabeth replied matter-of-factly. "But frankly, the Magic takes up so much of my time I can't give the Cause the physical support I'd like to." She shook her head. "Enough of that; if you really want to know about it, I'll talk about it some evening with you. Now, I want you to know clearly that—*exactly* as last time I visited—I'm not expecting any more service than any of your other guests. I can take care of myself quite nicely, thank you, I don't need to be waited on hand and foot by a maid, and *not* dressing for dinner is going to be something of a relief."

Aunt Margherita broke into a gentle smile that warmed her eyes. "You know, I think that I had known that, but it's good to hear it from your own lips. We've never had you for longer than a long weekend, you know, and a weekend guest is very different from a long-term guest."

"True enough." Elizabeth drank the last of her tea, stood up, and picked up her hat and jacket. "Now, since the bumping and swearing in the staircase has stopped, I think we can assume that the men have finished hauling my traps up the stairs, and I can change into something more appropriate." She dimpled at Marina. "Then *you* will stop treating me as if I didn't want to be bothered."

All three of them laughed. "I'll show you your room," Marina offered, and took the lead up the stairs, the bandboxes in hand.

"Oh lovely—you gave me the other kitchen-room!" Elizabeth exclaimed as soon as she recognized what part of the house she was in. She breathed in the scent of baking bread from below appreciatively. "These are the best rooms Blackbird Cottage has in the winter."

"I think so too," Marina said, as Elizabeth hung her jacket up in the wardrobe and bent to open one of the three trunks. Then, suddenly shy, she retreated back down to the kitchen to help her aunt.

Elizabeth came down to join them in a much shorter time than Marina would have thought, and the plain woolen skirt and shirtwaist she wore were nothing that would be out of place in the village on a weekday. Marina couldn't help a little pang of disappointment, but she tried not to show it.

Then came a supper that was astonishingly different because of a new face and some new topics of conversation around the table. This time, though, Marina was included in the conversation as a full equal. There was no discussion; it just happened, as naturally as breathing.

And one of the new topics was magic. . . .

"The Naiads and I had to drive a River-horse up the Mersey, away from people," Elizabeth said over the apple pie, as light from the candles on the table made a halo of her hair. "We don't know where it came from, but it seems to have been retreating from the poisoning of its stream. You haven't seen anything of water-poisoning around here, have you, Marina?"

She shook her head. "No. After I cleaned out all of the mess that had been left from before we took the land, I haven't had any trouble."

"It's probably just some disgusting factory then," Elizabeth said with a frown. "Honestly! You would think that when fish and animals begin to die, the owners would figure out for themselves that the poison they've dumped in the water is *going* to spread!" Her eyes flashed with anger. "How can they *do* this?"

"But it never spreads to where they live," Sebastian pointed out dryly, though anger smoldered in the back of his eyes as well. "That's the thing. If it was their children that suffered, coughing out their lives in black air, dying from poisoned water, it would be different. It's *only* the children of the poor, of their workers. And there are always more children of the poor to take their places."

"It's doing things to the magic." Elizabeth's frown deepened. "Twisting it. Making it darker. I don't know—if I were able to find a Left Hand Path occultist behind some of this, I wouldn't be in the least surprised. But I haven't, and neither has anyone else."

"Then it has to be just a coincidence," Thomas said

firmly. "Don't look for enemies where there are none. We have enemies enough as it is."

Elizabeth let out a long breath. "Yes, and I should be concentrating on—and training our newest Mage to deal with—those existent enemies, shouldn't I? Well said, Thomas."

Enemies? We—I—have enemies?

"The least of the many things you need to teach her, and I am profoundly grateful that you are here, my dear," Thomas replied with a smile. "I hope I have given her a thorough grounding, but your teaching will be to mine as university education is to public school."

It is? The thought of enemies evaporated from her mind.

"Which leads to the question—when do you want to start?" Margherita asked.

"Tomorrow," Elizabeth replied, to Marina's unbounded joy, though for some reason, there seemed to be a shadow over the smile she bestowed on her new protégée. "Definitely tomorrow. No point in wasting time; we have a lot to share, and the sooner we start, the better."

4

BREAKFAST was a cheerful affair, despite the gray clouds outside. The rain had stopped at least, and one of Margherita's favorite roosters crowed lustily atop the stone wall around the farmyard. Sarah did the breakfast cooking. She excelled at solid farm food, and her breakfasts were a staple at Blackbird Cottage. Everyone ate breakfast together in the kitchen, including little Jenny the maidservant, with Sarah joining them when she was sure no one else would want anything more.

This morning there was a new face at the table when Marina came down: Elizabeth, with her hair braided and the braid coiled atop her head, a shawl about her shoulders, cheerfully consuming bacon and eggs and chatting with old Sarah.

The cook was one of those substantial country women, once dark-haired, but now gone gray in their service. She was seldom without a shawl of her own knitting about her shoulders; plain in dress, plain-spoken, she had mothered

Marina as much as Margherita, and usually was the one to
mete out punishments that the soft-hearted Margherita could
not bear to administer.

What she thought of the strange guests that often stayed
here, she seldom said. Certainly she was plied for information about her employers whenever she went down to the
village, but if she ever gossiped, no harm had come of it.
And she was the perfect servant for this odd household; she
was the one who found the new maidservants (usually from
among her vast network of relatives) when their girls were
ready for more exacting duties (and higher pay) in larger
households. The hired man John was one of her many
nephews. Sarah was the unmoving domestic center of the
household, the person who made it possible for all three
artists to get on with their work without interruption. She
trained the succession of maids—Jenny was the eighth—
and made them understand that the free-and-easy ways of
this household were not what they could expect in the next.
Thus far, the girls had all chosen to move on when places in
wealthier households opened, but it looked as if Jenny might
stay. She was timid by nature; they all treated her with consideration for her shyness, and Sarah had confided to Marina
one day that the idea of going into a Great House was too
frightening for Jenny to contemplate. Sarah had seemed
pleased by that; Marina thought that their cook was getting
tired of the continual succession of girls, and would welcome an end to it.

"Oh, bless you, mum," Sarah said, in answer to some
question of Elizabeth's that Marina hadn't heard. "E'en
when this table's crowded 'round with daft painterly chaps,
I'd druther be workin' for Master Sebastian."

"And why would that be, Sarah?" Thomas asked, grin-
ning over a slice of buttered toast. "Could it be that our com-

pany is so fascinating that you would be bored working for anyone else?"

"Lor' help you, 'cause none of *you* lot ever wants break-fuss afore eight." Sarah laughed. "Farmer, now, they're up before dawn, and wants their breakfuss afore that! As for a Great House, well e'en if I could get a place there, it'd be cooking for the help, an they be at work near as early as a farmer. Here, I get to lie abed like one of th' gentry!"

"You *are* one of the gentry, Sarah," said Margherita from the doorway, her abundant dark brown hair tumbling down around her shoulders, shining in the light from the oil lamp suspended above the kitchen table. "You're a Countess of Cooks, a Duchess of Domestic Order."

Sarah giggled, and so did little Jenny. "Go on with you!" Sarah replied, blushing with pleasure. "Anyroad, as for going on to a Great House, like I says, my cooking's too plain for the likes o' they. And I'm not minded to fiddle with none of your French messes. Missus Margherita can do all that if she wants, but plain cooking was good enough for my old mother, and it's good enough for me."

Margherita took her place at the broad, heavy old table and Sarah brought over the skillet to serve her fresh sausages and eggs.

Marina poured more tea for herself and her aunt. She wanted to ask their guest what they were going to start with, but she was constrained by the presence of the two servants.

"I think I'll borrow one of your workrooms for my visit, Margherita," Elizabeth said casually. "The little one just off the library. I'd like to organize the notes I brought with me, then get started on my project."

"Project, ma'am?" said Sarah, who was always interested in at least knowing what the guests at Blackbird Cottage were about. Perhaps in any other household, she'd have been rebuked or even sacked for her curiosity, but curiosity wasn't considered a vice here, not even in servants.

And Elizabeth already knew that from her previous visits, so she answered Sarah just as she would have another guest, or a visitor from the village. "I'm trying to do something scholarly, collecting old songs, Sarah," she said. "Very old songs—the ones that people might have heard from their grandparents."

"What, them old ballads? Robin Hood an' Green Knights an' witches an' ghosts an' all?" Sarah answered, looking both surprised and a little pleased. "Is this something for them university chaps?"

"Why, exactly! How did you know?" Elizabeth might very well really have been here to collect folk ballads from the way she responded. Marina wasn't surprised that Sarah knew that scholars were collecting folk songs for their studies; with all of the talk around this table, Sarah picked up a great deal of what was going on in the world outside their little village.

"Well, stands to reason, don't it? Clever lady like you? Went to university yourself, didn't you?" Sarah chuckled, and tenderly forked slices of thick bacon onto Marina's plate, then onto little Jenny's. After all these years, she knew exactly what each of them liked best, and how much they were likely to want. "I could ask around, down in village for you," she offered deferentially. "Some folks might know a song or two, and a pint would loosen tongues, even for a strange lady."

"If you would be so kind, I would greatly appreciate your help, Sarah," Elizabeth replied with all sincerity, though her eyes were twinkling. Marina knew why; her feigned errand had gotten an unexpected touch of veracity.

"Pleased to, ma'am," Sarah replied, and turned back to her cooking with a flush of pleasure.

But Marina knew that the "little workroom" was the one room in the house used for serious and involved Magical work. Margherita had put compulsions upon the door that worked better than any orders forbidding Jenny or Sarah—or anyone else who was not a magician—from entering. That was a special ability of the Earth-Master, to create compulsions that worked even on those without a hint of magic in their souls. Oh, others could do it, but the trick came most easily to Earth Masters.

Each compulsion was gently tailored to the individual. For Jenny, the moment she touched the door, she would be under the impression that she had just cleaned the room and was leaving. Sarah, on the other hand, would suddenly think that there must be something on the stove or in the oven that needed tending. Visitors would believe that the door was locked, even though it wasn't, and would promptly forget about the room the moment they turned away.

"That will be fine, Elizabeth. Would you like Marina to help you?" Margherita replied casually.

"I certainly would! You know me—completely hopeless when it comes to organization!" Elizabeth laughed, and the conversation went on to other things, leaving Marina tingling with excitement and anticipation.

Elizabeth lingered over her tea until Marina finished her breakfast, then nodded at her as she rose. Marina jumped to her feet, and followed the older woman out of the kitchen and down to the workroom. As an Elemental Master herself, Elizabeth was not affected by the compulsions on the door, and opened it without a pause, beckoning to Marina to follow.

According to Uncle Thomas, many Elemental Masters preferred to have a religious cast to their magical workrooms; they often had an altar and religious icons such as crucifixes, statues of ancient gods or goddesses, censers for incense, and other religious paraphernalia. But since this room was shared by three—counting Marina, *four*—magicians, all of whom had their own very definite ideas about their magic, the compromise had been reached of leaving it bare. Uncle Thomas had installed cupboards with shutters to close them on all of the walls, and whatever each person felt was absolutely necessary to his or her working lived in the cupboards until needed. There were two benches pushed up against one wall, and a small table (which could presumably serve as an altar) against another. Although the room did not have a fireplace of its own, the back wall of the library fireplace radiated quite enough warmth for the small space.

And it had only one small window, ivy-covered and high. Marina would have had to stand on tiptoe to see through it. So it would be fairly difficult for anyone to spy on whatever was going on in here.

The floor was of slate, like the rest of the ground floor of the farmhouse; the panels of the shutters were of wood with grain that suggested far-off landscapes and distant hills. Between the panels, Uncle Thomas had carved the graceful trunks of trees that never grew in any living forest. The two benches were also Uncle Thomas' work, as was the table.

"Close the door, dear," Elizabeth said, and pulled one of the benches out further into the room while Marina did as she asked. "Now, come sit down, please."

Obediently, Marina did so.

"One of the great advantages of using a permanent workroom is that the basic shields are already in place, and one needn't bother with putting them up," Elizabeth said with satisfaction. "I know that you've been taught perfectly well in all the basics, so I shan't bother going over them again. Nor am I going to put you through a *viva voce* exam on the subject."

Oh! Well that's a relief! Marina had been expecting

something of the sort, and was very pleased to discover she was going to escape it.

"No," Elizabeth continued, "What you need first from me is the understanding of how you access the energy of your own element."

"Shouldn't we be outside for that?" Marina asked curiously. "Near the stream or something?"

But Elizabeth shook her head. "Nothing of the sort. Water is all around you; in the ground beneath your feet, in the air—good heavens, *especially* in the air around here!" She laughed, and Marina giggled nervously. "You would be hard pressed to isolate yourself from a single element; even in the heart of the driest desert on earth there is water somewhere, if only in your own body. Each element has a sphere in which it can *dominate,* but none can be eliminated. Now, I assume you know how to recognize the energy of Water?"

Marina nodded.

"Good. Then call upon your inner eye, and watch what I do."

Marina clasped her hands in her lap and let fall the guard she usually kept on that sense that Thomas called Sight, but which was so much more than merely *seeing* beyond the material world. And the moment she did so, she was aware that the room was alive with energies.

The golds and browns of Earth Magic and the reds of Fire invested the shields around them, forming an ever-changing tapestry of moving color, scent, taste, and sensation. Earth magic had a special scent to Marina, of soil freshly-turned by the plow; its taste, rich and smooth, vanilla-flavored cream. And it seemed to wrap her in warm fur. Whereas Fire tasted of cinnamon, smelled of smoke, and felt like the sun on her skin just before she was about to be sunburned.

Water, though, smelled exactly like the air the moment before it was about to rain, mingled with new-mown hay; it tasted of all the waters of the world, faintly sweet and cool, and it felt exactly like chilled silk sliding across her bare arms. In color it was every shade of green there had ever been, from the tender, yellow-green of unfolding leaves, to the deep black-green of ancient pines in a thunderstorm. This was what she saw now, investing the very air of the room, condensing out of it like fog, or like her breath on a frosty morning, or a cloud blooming overhead in the sky. Tender threads, tiny tendrils of it, coalescing out of no-where, each one a different shade of green; they sprang up and flowed toward Elizabeth, joining thread to thread to make cords, streams, all of them flowing to her and into her, and she began to glow with the growing power she had gathered into herself.

"Oh, my!" Marina breathed. But she wasn't going to just sit there and admire—Elizabeth had said to watch what the older woman was doing, and she set herself to finding out just *how* Elizabeth was doing this.

It took some time of studying and puzzling before she figured it out.

The clue was in what Elizabeth had said earlier, that the energy was everywhere. It *was,* and it could be coaxed into a more coherent form by application of the energies of her own mind, the ones that Uncle Thomas had already taught her how to use.

"You see?" Elizabeth said softly, and she nodded. "Good." Abruptly the older woman stopped gathering in the energies and looked at her pupil expectantly. "Now you try it."

Knowing how it was done and doing it herself were two different things . . . akin to the difference between knowing how to ride a horse and actually staying on its back. But this was what she'd wanted, wasn't it?

Be careful what you ask for, she reminded herself ruefully, and set to work.

And *work* it certainly was. Elizabeth made it look so effortless, but compared with dipping energy out of the aura of a free-flowing stream, a spring, or a deep well, it was anything but effortless.

Exhausting was more like it. It took a peculiar combination of relaxation and concentration that was infernally hard to master, and by the time she had managed to coax the first tentative tendrils of power out of the aether, she was limp with fatigue.

"That will do for now," Elizabeth said, and she let the burgeoning streamlets go with no little relief. "Luncheon, I think; then a little rest for both of us, perhaps an hour or so, and we'll start again."

So soon? she thought with concealed dismay. Uncle Thomas had never made her work for this long! But it couldn't be helped; if that was what Elizabeth wanted, then there was probably a reason for it.

"I want you to have a firm grasp on this technique today," Elizabeth said, as she got up and offered Marina her hand to aid her to her feet. Marina took the offered help; her knees felt so shaky she wasn't certain she could have stood up without it. "If we left things at the point where they are now, by tomorrow it would all have to be done over again. We have to make a pathway in your mind and spirit that rest or sleep can't erase. *Then* you can take a longer respite."

Marina sighed, and followed her out; her stomach gave a discreet growl, reminding her not only that she had used a great deal of *physical* energy, but that she would feel better about resuming once she wasn't so ravenous.

Aunt Margherita seemed to have anticipated how hungry she would be, for the main course of luncheon was a hearty stew that must have been cooking since breakfast or before.

With fresh bread slathered with butter and Margherita's damson preserves, and cup after cup of strong tea, Marina felt better by the moment. Sarah, Margherita and Elizabeth chattered away like a trio of old gossips on wash-day, while Marina ate until she couldn't eat any more, feeling completely *hollow* after all her exertion.

Finally, when she'd finished the last bit of the treacle tart Sarah had given her for dessert, Elizabeth turned away from her conversation with the others. "Have you any lessons or other work you need to do this afternoon?" she asked, but somehow managed not to make it sound as if she was asking a child the question.

"Work, actually. German," she replied, with a lifting of her spirits. "*Die Leiden des Junges Werther*, I'm translating it for Uncle Sebastian; he thinks he might want to paint something from it."

"Oh good heavens, *Sturm und Drang*, is it?" she laughed. "Obsessed poets and suicide! Oh well, I suppose Sebastian knows what is likely to sell!"

"Sebastian knows very well, thank you," her uncle called from the doorway. "Beautiful young dead men sell very well to wealthy ladies with less-than-ideal marriages of convenience. It gives them something to sigh and weep over, and since the young men are safely dead, their husbands can't feel jealous over even a painted rival."

Marina didn't miss the cynical lift of his brow, and suspected he had a particular client in mind.

Evidently, Elizabeth Hastings hadn't missed that cue either. "Well," she said dryly, "If the real world does not move them, they might as well be parted from some of that wealth in exchange for a fantasy, so that others can make better use of their money than they can."

"My thoughts exactly," Sebastian said, and with the chameleon-like change of mood that Marina knew so well, beamed upon Sarah as he accepted a bowl of stew from her hands. "Sarah, you are just as divine as Miss Bernhardt! In a different sphere, of course—"

"Tch! The things you say! I doubt Divine Sarah'd thank ye for that!" their own Sarah replied with a twinkle, and turned back to her stove.

"I'll come fetch you from your room in an hour or so," Elizabeth said to Marina, who took that as her cue to escape for some badly needed rest.

Translating *Werther* was not what she would have called "work," even though Uncle Sebastian said it was. She had taught herself German from books; she couldn't speak it, but she read it fluently enough. German seemed useful, given all of the medieval poems and epics that the Germans had produced that could give Uncle Sebastian subjects for his paintings, and so she had undertaken it when she was twelve.

Mind, she thought, as she wrote yet another paragraph of Werther's internal agony, *I can't do much with figures. And as for science—all I know is what the old alchemists did!* She supposed her education had been rather one-sided.

She was amused, rather than enthralled, by Goethe's hero. She couldn't imagine ever being so utterly besotted with *anyone* as to lose her wits over him, much less kill herself because she could not have him. Poor silly Werther.

But he'd make a fine subject for a painting, her uncle was right about that. Pining over his love, writing one of his poems of wretchedness and longing, or lying dead with the vial of poison in his hand.

I suppose I'll have to pose for him, *too.* It wouldn't be the first time that she'd stood in for a young, callow man. Uncle Sebastian simple gave her a little stronger chin and thinner lips, flattened her curves, and took care to give her a sufficiently loose costume and there she was. More than one lady had fallen in love with the masculine version of herself; Uncle Sebastian never enlightened them as to her sex.

A tapping at her door told her that another sort of lesson—and work—awaited her.

"Come in!" she cried, and put the book aside. "I'll just be a moment."

Elizabeth pushed the door ajar, and gazed with delight on the room. "I swear, I wish I could get your guardians to create something like this for *me*," she said with a chuckle.

"It would take them eighteen years, I'm afraid," she replied, tidying her desk and making sure that the ink bottle was securely corked.

Elizabeth sighed. "I know. And it would cost me a *hideous* amount of money, too—I certainly couldn't ask them to work for less than their normal commissions."

"You'd be surprised how many would," Marina said sourly, thinking of all the people who, over the years, had attempted to trade on past acquaintance to get a bargain.

"No magician would," Elizabeth said firmly. "No magician *could*. Well, enough of that; back to work for us."

Back down to the little workroom they went, and Marina saw when Elizabeth opened the door that she had brought in a lamp and had moved the table to the center of the room. And in the center of the table was a clear glass bowl full of water.

"What's that for?" Marina asked, as Elizabeth closed the door behind them.

"Later," her tutor told her. "When I'm sure you've mastered the first lesson."

Marina raised an eyebrow, but didn't argue; Elizabeth was the Master here, and had presumably taught more pupils in the art of the Element of Water than she. She took a seat on one of the benches, and took up where they had left off.

It was easier this time; at Elizabeth's signal, she released the power, then gathered it in again. A dozen times, perhaps more, she raised the power and let it flow out again, until the gathering of it was as natural as breathing and almost as easy.

Only then did Elizabeth stop her, this time before she released it.

"Good. Now, hold the power, and watch me again." Elizabeth cupped her hands around the bowl, and gazed into the water.

Then Marina sensed something curious—she felt a tugging within her, as if she heard a far distant call or summons.

Strange—

Was the summons coming from—Elizabeth?

Yes! It was! Marina concentrated on it, and on her mentor. Slowly she deciphered the silent message written in power, sent out into the world. Not a summons, but an invitation.

But how on earth did Elizabeth expect it to be answered? There were no streams here for the Undines to follow, no way for them to get into this sealed room.

How—

Something stirred in the bowl, like a trail of bubbles in the clear water, a momentary fog passing over the surface. The water in the bowl rippled, as if Elizabeth blew on it, or moved the bowl, but she did neither.

And then—there, perfect in miniature, were an Undine and a Naiad, looking up at Elizabeth in expectation.

And Elizabeth looked up at her pupil, a roguish smile on her lips.

"But—but—" Marina could only stare. How could the Elementals have gotten there—and how, why were they so *small?*

"They're creatures of spirit and magic, not flesh, no matter how they look to us, Marina," the older woman said softly, as the two Elementals gazed around themselves with curiosity. "They don't follow the rules of the flesh-and-blood world. Like the energies of Water, they can go where they will, so long as there is a place of their Element waiting for them."

Now Marina thought about all the times she'd been with the Undines and Naiads, the other elemental creatures of spring and stream—how they would appear and disappear, seeming to dissolve into the water only to appear elsewhere. Why hadn't that occurred to her before?

"And you just call them?" she asked.

"It isn't *quite* that easy, but I'll show you how to form several sorts of summons. They all require Water energies, of course." She bent over the bowl. "Thank you, my friends. Would you care to go, or stay?"

"Shall we go, and see if our Fleshly Sister can properly call us too?" asked a tinkling voice that was as much in Marina's head as in her ears. The Undine cast an amused glance at Marina, then turned her attention back to Elizabeth.

"I think that would be very gracious of you, if you would be so kind," Elizabeth replied gravely.

"Then we shall." The two tiny figures seemed to spin in the water for a moment; it sparkled in the light from the lamp, then there was only a trail of bubbles, then they were gone.

Elizabeth looked up into Marina's eyes. "Now then—your turn."

Marina was glad that she had eaten a full lunch, because somehow teatime slipped right past them. It wasn't until after dark that Elizabeth was ready to let her go, and she still hadn't mastered that most basic of summonings, the simple invitation. As Elizabeth had warned, it was harder than it looked.

Marina felt as limp as wilted lettuce when Elizabeth decreed an end to the work for the day, and as her mentor opened the door and the aroma of tonight's meal hit her nose, her stomach gave a most unmannerly growl.

Elizabeth laughed at that, and picked up the bowl of water. "Blow out the lamp, dear, and let's get you something to eat before you faint. That sort of behavior might be *de rigueur* for debutantes, but I think your uncles would have more than a few harsh words with me if they thought I was overworking you."

"You're not!" Marina protested. "I could have asked you to stop any time, couldn't I?"

"Yes, you could. I trusted that you had gone far enough in magic to be able to judge for yourself when you needed to stop." Elizabeth waited while Marina closed the door behind herself, and the two of them went out into the library.

Candles and lanterns had already been lit, and warm pools of light shone around them. A savory aroma drifted in from the kitchen, and Marina's stomach complained— silently, this time.

"Have you any notion where I could pour out this bowl of consecrated water?" Elizabeth asked. "It doesn't do to just pour it down a drain, it really ought to go somewhere it can do some good."

"Aunt Margherita has a little conservatory off her loom room," Marina replied, after a moment of thought. "She grows herbs and things in there—"

"Just the thing; that's probably her personal workroom. Go join everyone and tell them I'll be there in a moment." Elizabeth took the left-hand door that went further into the house. After a moment of hesitation, Marina took the right.

Supper was just being served in the dining room; a shaded oil lamp above the table shone down on the pristine linen tablecloth, and wisps of steam arose from the dishes waiting in the center. Thomas and Margherita were there and already eating, but Uncle Sebastian wasn't, yet. Marina sat down and helped herself from a random bowl in front of her; it proved to contain mashed squash, of which she was inordinately fond. "Elizabeth had a bowl of water—" she began.

"Ah. She'll be watering my herbs with it, then," her aunt said immediately. "Just the thing."

"That's what she said—" Sebastian came in at just that moment, trailed by Elizabeth, who still had the now empty bowl.

"I found this prowling in your workroom, dearest, what would you like me to do with it?" Sebastian said, pulling a laughing Elizabeth forward by the wrist.

"Invite it to supper, of course, you great beast. I trust everything went well for the first lesson?" Margherita replied, with a playful slap at her husband's hand.

"Zee student, she progresses with alacrity!" Elizabeth said, in a theatrical, faux-French accent, which garnered a laugh. She took her place between Margherita and Marina, and spread her napkin in her lap.

"I'm glad to hear it. I assume that means we can socialize this evening?" Thomas wanted to know.

"Certainly. All work and no play—speaking of which, Sebastian, are you going to need the student for work tomorrow?"

Sebastian chewed meditatively on a forkful of rabbit for a moment, thinking. "I *could* use her. I need more work on the hands at the moment; hard to get them right without her. And I'd like to do some sketches for the next projects. *Werther* and the Wife of Bath."

"Then I absolve you of lessons in the morning, but in the afternoon, we'll take up where we left off," Elizabeth decreed, and reached for the platter nearest her plate. "Now, what have we here. Stewed rabbit! Nothing illegal, I hope?"

"Sarah's hutches, and she brought them up this morning. Really, Elizabeth, I hope you don't subscribe to the notion that *everyone* living in the country poaches!" Thomas looked indignant, and Marina had to smother a laugh, because she knew very well that Sarah didn't have rabbit hutches, and that her dear uncle had been talking to Hobson, who did poach, just that morning, for she'd seen him out of her bedroom window.

"Now, don't you try to pull the wool over my eyes, sirrah!" Elizabeth retorted. "I know the taste of wild bunny from hutched, and this little coney never saw the inside of a wire enclosure in his life!"

"I am appalled—" Thomas began.

"And I did not fall off the turnip-cart yesterday!" Elizabeth shot back.

The two of them wrangled amicably over dinner, until Margherita managed to interject an inquiry about what Elizabeth's husband was up to. That led to a discussion of politics, which held absolutely no interest for Marina. In fact, as the conversation carried on past dessert and into the parlor, Marina found it hard to keep her eyes open.

She finally gave up, excused herself, and left politics and a pleasant fire for the peace and quiet of her equally pleasant room. Jenny had left a warm brick in the bed and banked the fire; Marina slipped into a flannel nightgown, brushed and braided her hair, and with the sound of rain on her window, got into bed. She thought she'd stay awake long enough to read, but after rereading the same page twice, she realized there wasn't a chance she'd get through a chapter. And the moment she blew out her candle, that was all she knew until morning.

5

RAINING again, rain drumming on the window of the workroom, making the air alive with the energy of the storm. Marina had always been fond of rain, but now it meant so much more than a cozy day indoors, watching the fat drops splash into puddles. Now it meant a ready source of power, power she was only just beginning to learn how to use.

"Watch carefully," Elizabeth said—as she had so many times during the lessons. But then she added, "Of all the things that you can do with the magical energy you gather, this may be the most important. Everything depends on it."

Marina was hardly going to be *less* attentive, but those words put just a fraction of a tingle of warning down her spine.

Because Elizabeth was right, of course. This *was* the most important thing she could learn to do—because now that she could gather in Water energies almost without thinking, and summon Elementals to the most unlikely places, she was going to learn the shields peculiar to a Water Master.

The basic shields, those walls of pure thought that she placed around her mind and soul, were not enough, she had already learned that much this summer. They couldn't even contain her thoughts away from anyone else of the same affinity—or her Elementals—when she was thinking hard, or her emotions were involved. How could she expect them to defend her if something really did decide to test them?

So she watched Elizabeth with every particle of concentration she had, her brow furrowed with intent, her hands clasped tightly in her lap. The workroom seemed very quiet, the sound of the rain on the window unnaturally loud.

She had watched Thomas build the shields of an Earth Master and had dutifully tried to copy them, but with no success. He had built up layer upon layer of heavy, ponderous shields, patiently, like building a series of brick walls; somehow she could not manage to construct even a single layer, and had felt defeated and frustrated.

And now, watching Elizabeth, she knew why she had failed—

Elizabeth had taught her how to bring in power from the very air, then had shown her how to touch, then handle, the stronger currents that tended to follow the courses of the waters of the physical world. For instance, there was a water source, an artesian well that was in turn fed from a deep spring, from which the farmhouse pumps got their water. It actually was right underneath Blackbird Cottage; it was also a wellspring of the energies they both used, and Elizabeth tapped into it now.

Marina watched the power fountain up in answer to Elizabeth's call and waited, her breath catching in her throat, to see how Elizabeth could possibly turn the fluid and mutable energies of Water into the solid and immutable shields that

Uncle Thomas had shown her. What did she do? Freeze them, somehow? But how could you do *that?*

Green and sparkling, leaping and swirling, the energies flowed up and around Elizabeth until they met, above, below, surrounding her in a sphere of perpetually moving force. Marina felt them brushing against the edge of her senses, tasted sweet spring water on the tip of her tongue, and breathed in the scent of more than the rain outside. From within the swirling sphere, Elizabeth summoned yet another upwelling of power, and built a second dancing sphere within the first. And a third within the second.

Layer upon ever-changing layer, she built, and Marina waited for the energies to solidify into *walls.*

Until suddenly it dawned on her that they weren't going to solidify; that these were what the shields of a Water Master looked like. Not walls, but something the exact opposite of walls; something that did not absorb attacks, but deflected them, spinning them away—or yielded only to return, renewed.

Perhaps eventually a shield would be ablated away, but that was why all shields were built in layers. Destroy one, and you were only confronted by another, still strong, still intact.

But no wonder I couldn't make the power do what I wanted it to do! Marina thought with elation. *It couldn't! You can't make water into bricks, you can only make it do what is in its nature to do!*

She clasped her hands unconsciously under her chin, and her beaming smile must have told Elizabeth that she had seen and understood, because Elizabeth returned that smile, and with a gentle gesture of dismissal, allowed the energies to swirl back whence they had come. In mere moments, she stood unprotected again, her hands spread.

"You see?" she asked. "I use a much simpler version

most of the time, and obviously I don't need to bother with shields at all when I'm within the protections of my house or this one."

"Oh yes, I do see!" Marina cried. "Please, may I try now?"

"You may, but remember—just as with all else I have taught you, it will be much more difficult than it looked the first time—and indeed, for many of the subsequent trials," Elizabeth cautioned. "Take your time, and don't be discouraged."

"I won't," Marina promised, and took a deep breath, calmed her elation, and reached for the deep-flowing energies as Elizabeth had taught her.

"You look exhausted, Mari," her Uncle Sebastian observed, clearly startled, as she paused with one hand on the doorframe of his studio to steady herself.

She smiled; it was a tired smile, but a real one, and he looked a little more reassured. "I *am,* Uncle—but I'm not at all unhappy about being exhausted."

"Elizabeth put you through a steeplechase, did she?" Her uncle grinned. "She told me she was going to give you shield-techniques today. And your progress?"

Marina didn't answer immediately. Instead, she took her place on the rumpled, unmade pallet on the posing-stand that stood in for the bed in young Werther's garret room. With great care, she arranged herself half on, half off the bed, taking great care to put her head and outflung arms within the chalk marks on the floor. Even when her uncle set her the reclining pose she had not-so-jokingly requested, he couldn't make it a simple one!

Sebastian came over to her and tweaked and arranged the folds of her jacket and shirt to his liking, then checked the disordered bedclothes and put the empty "poison" bottle beside her outflung right hand.

"I haven't made much yet," she admitted, as Sebastian picked up palette and brush and went to work. "But then, I don't at first. I think that was why Elizabeth started me on other things first, instead of going from energies straight to shielding—so I'd know how difficult the specific Elemental magics are, and wouldn't be disappointed when I didn't master shields immediately."

"I think you're probably right." Sebastian sounded as if he wasn't listening to her, but she knew from past experience that he heard every word and was paying close attention. It wasn't his *mind* that was painting so feverishly, or so he often told her. His eye and his hand were practically connected when he worked, and the less interference from the thinking part of him that there was, the better and truer the painting.

She hardly noticed the ubiquitous scent of linseed oil and paint in here anymore—except, as now, when a particularly strong waft of it drifted over to her and she had to fight to keep from wrinkling her nose in distaste.

"At any rate," she sighed, "I haven't managed much, yet. But I will. It's awfully tiring, though—I have to use everything I have to control the energies I'm calling up. Should I have my eyes open, or closed?"

"It will be less tiring with practice," Sebastian promised. "Open eyes, please. You're not supposed to be quite dead yet."

"Am I going to get better?" she teased, staring up at the beams and boards of the ceiling. It felt very good to be lying down, even if it was in this odd position. Uncle Sebastian had found a small, flattish cushion that didn't show under her hair for her to rest her head on, and for once, this was a position where nothing had gone numb—or at least, it hadn't the last time she'd taken this pose.

"No, as you know very well, minx, since you translated Werther's story for me. But I want the lady who buys this painting to fantasize that *she* might save him," Sebastian replied, and that was the last she got out of him, as the rain finally cleared off and the clouds thinned. In fact, he didn't say a word until the light of the setting sun pierced the many leaded panes of the studio window, and he sighed and stuck his brush behind his ear.

"All right, my wench—that's enough for today. You can get up now."

She did so—slowly. Nothing was numb, but after three hours of posing, broken only briefly by two breaks to get up and walk around, she was stiff. At least the posing-platform was wood rather than the flagstones of the floor, and Werther's clothing, a shabby boy's suit, was comfortably warm.

"Don't be discouraged in these shielding lessons of yours, even though it's likely to take longer than you think, poppet," Sebastian said, taking up the conversation where it had left off—a disconcerting habit of his, but one that Marina was used to. "Where's my brush?"

"In your hair," she answered promptly. "How long do *you* think it's going to take?"

"Ah—" he reached up and retrieved the brush, and began to clean it carefully. "I suspect you won't have mastered shields before Elizabeth has to go home for the Christmas holidays with her family."

She couldn't help it; her dismay must have shown on her face, as he shrugged sympathetically and pulled the brush from behind his ear. "It took *me* at least that long," he admitted. "And I was reckoned to be quick at learning magic."

"Oh." She couldn't help but feel a pang of disappointment, but she decided she might as well put a brave face on it. "I had no idea," she admitted, squaring her shoulders and trying to look as if she was prepared for that much work.

"Proper shielding is hard, poppet." He grimaced, and ran his fingers through his hair, leaving a set of ocher streaks to go with the vermilion ones already there. "Really, it uses everything you've ever learned about magic. Once you learn personal shields, then you have to learn how to expand them to fit your work space or your home, how to make them permanent, and how to disguise them inside the common shields you already know. *Then* you have to learn how to make them seem to disappear altogether, so that you look perfectly ordinary to anyone who might look at you with the Sight."

She'd had no idea, and for a moment, the mere thought of all the work that still lay ahead of her made her heart quail with dismay.

Her uncle seemed to sense that, and put a supporting arm around her shoulders. "You can do it, Mari. If *I* could, you certainly can."

She leaned her head against him for a moment of comfort, then managed a laugh. "Oh, Uncle Sebastian, you just said you were *quick* at learning magic!"

"I was. I was also lazy." He gave her a quick squeeze and let her go. "Why don't you hop upstairs and change for supper? You're probably hungry as well as tired, and you'll feel better once you've eaten."

"You're probably right," she agreed, and dropped a kiss on his cheek. "I love you, Uncle Sebastian."

"I love you too, poppet," he said, as she left him among his paints and canvases. "Never forget that."

As if I ever would!

The rains of October had given way to the cold of November, and then to the deeps of December. It didn't rain nearly as often, but the skies still remained gray and overcast most of the time. Every morning the ground was coated with a thick cover of hoarfrost, and the windows bore delicate, fernlike traceries of frost on the inside.

Marina had finally progressed to the point where she could bring up and maintain a single shield, and was just able to bring up a second one inside the first, though she could not yet manage to juggle the complicated structures for very long.

It was far easier to build the common shields and disguise her special shield within them—and for some reason she had mastered the ability to camouflage the common shields as the random and chaotic patterns of a perfectly normal person almost immediately. Why that should be, she couldn't begin to imagine, but it seemed to make her guardians happy.

In spite of the fact that she no longer had formal schooling, she was working harder, and she had less leisure, than ever before. During the best hours of daylight, she posed for Sebastian; the morning and late afternoon and sometimes even the evening belonged to Elizabeth Hastings. There were no rest days for her, and she found herself almost looking forward to the second week of December, when Elizabeth would leave them for Christmas, and not return until after Boxing Day. *Almost,* but she enjoyed Elizabeth's company so much. . . .

But the work was so hard. It wasn't just physical work, either, it involved everything: mind, body, spirit—

And now she wasn't just sitting there when she posed for Uncle Sebastian, she was practicing those shields; not the full and strong ones that she practiced in the work-room, but wispy little things that were easier to bring up.

Yet Elizabeth was working just as hard, and for no personal gain that Marina could see. When Marina was posing, Elizabeth would either be down at the village making good her pretense of collecting folk ballads, or in the workroom doing—

—well, Marina wasn't quite sure what she was doing. It obviously had *something* to do with magic, but she couldn't tell what it could be.

She was tempted, more than once, to cry halt to all of this. She was so tired that she fell asleep without being able to read in bed as she liked to do for an hour or so at bedtime, and she hadn't a single moment to herself when all was said and done. But there was some palpable tension in her guardians that made her hesitate whenever she considered asking for a respite. They weren't saying anything, but for some reason, she sensed that they were extremely anxious about her progress, and she couldn't bear to increase their anxiety with any delay.

It was, after all, a small enough price to pay for *their* peace of mind. After all the years that they had given to her, it was something of a blessing that she could finally give something back to them.

The faun tapped his hoof on the floor, and shook his shaggy head. *"I am sorry, Lady. It is a Gordian Knot, and there is no sword or Alexander to cut it."* His slanted eyes— normally full of mischief in a faun—held regret, and his mobile, hairy ears drooped a little. Margherita had an extraordinarily good relationship with the fauns; normally around a woman they were ill-mannered and lewd, but they called her Lady, and seemed to consider her as a sort of mother-figure.

Margherita sighed, and dismissed the little goat-footed faun with her thanks. He bowed to her, sinking down on his heels, then continued sinking, sinking, into the stone floor of the workroom, until he was gone. She looked to Elizabeth, who shrugged, and spread her hands wide.

"I had no better luck than you," her friend said, grimacing. "The curse is still there, and I can neither remove it nor change it further. What about Sebastian?"

"In this case, a Fire Master is no use to us." Margherita rested both her elbows on the workroom table and propped her chin on her hands. "It's the inimical Element, remember? His Elementals refuse to touch her for fear of angering their opposite numbers in Water. If he pushes his own powers much further trying to get rid of that horrible curse, he could hurt her."

Elizabeth massaged her own temples, unwonted lines of weariness creasing her forehead. Margherita had the distinct feeling that she herself looked no better. "I wish we had an Air power here. I *wish* Roderick were still alive. Or that I could get any interest out of Alderscroft." The expression on her face suggested that she would like very much to give the latter gentleman a piece of her mind.

"We're small potatoes to the like of Lord Alderscroft," Margherita said with some bitterness. "*He* only bothers with things that threaten the whole of Britain, not merely the life of one girl."

Elizabeth's jaw tightened. "Pray do not remind me," she said shortly. "I plan to have a word or two in person with Lord Alderscroft over the holidays. Not that I think it will change his mind, but at least it will relieve my feelings on the subject. Still—" Her expression lightened a little. "—the curse hasn't re-awakened, either. The—relative—still hasn't made any moves, magically *or* otherwise. And even if she actually traced where Marina is and sent someone to find her instead of coming in person, at this time of year, any stranger to the village would be as obvious as a pig in a parlor."

Margherita nodded. "That's true enough," she agreed, once again taking comfort in their surroundings; not a great city like Bath or Plymouth, where strangers were coming and going as often as one's long-time neighbors, but a tiny place where nothing was secret.

Strangers did come to the village, but unless they were taking the rare permanent position as a servant that *wasn't* immediately filled by a local, they rarely stayed. Temporary harvest help arrived and left again; travelers in the summer and spring, sometimes; people on walking tours, for instance. Peddlers came through, of course, and the booth-owners and amusement-operators for the fairs. But that was only in the warm seasons—not in winter. *Never* in winter, and rarely, once the cold set in, during the fall.

The moment a stranger entered their village at this time of year, people would take note and the gossip would begin. If the stranger stayed, well—he'd have to find a room somewhere. The pub wasn't an inn; he'd have to find someone willing to let a room to him—not likely, that. In summer, the gypsies and tramping sorts could camp on the common, but he could hardly do that now.

To have any plausible reason to stay, he'd have to find a job somewhere nearby. According to Sarah, there were *no* positions available in the village or the surrounding farms, or even the two great houses. Of course, if Arachne sent a spy, she might arrange an "accident" to create a position for her hireling, but that itself would cause talk.

People talked a great deal about anything or anyone new in a village this small. And old Sarah, bless her, heard everything, and would faithfully repeat everything she heard to the people she considered as friends as well as employers.

"There are many advantages to being in a small village,"

Elizabeth observed, with a faint smile. "Even though we have the *dis*advantage of being gentry, and people don't talk as freely to us as they would to someone like you."

"Oh, the villagers don't talk to us directly," Margherita admitted. "We're newcomers—why, we haven't a single ancestor buried in the churchyard! But Sarah tells us everything, and everyone talks to her."

"Watchdogs without ever knowing it—and something you-know-who would never think of. Although I must admit that *I* never thought of it either, when we decided you should take Marina with you." Elizabeth tactfully did not mention the third reason—that she had already known that Margherita couldn't conceive, following a terrible bout with measles a year or two before Marina was born.

Taking care of Marina had filled a void that Margherita had not even known was within her until the baby had been in her arms.

"Well, Sebastian should be finished for the day by now," she said, shaking off her somber mood. "And both of them are probably starving."

"Marina will be, anyway. I worked her particularly hard today," Elizabeth said, with a look that Margherita recognized very well. The pride of a teacher in a student who excelled past expectation. Margherita knew it well, because her face wore that look often enough. "She's doing very well; she's quick, and willing, and intelligent. I wish every student of mine had that particular combination of traits."

They cleaned up the workroom after themselves; Margherita found it easier to summon Elementals when she had the help of incense, salt, and other paraphernalia. All this had to be packed back up and put away in one of the cupboards. Only then did they dismiss the shields that hid their work from the outside world and leave the workroom.

Those shields were so very necessary. Elizabeth had not

exaggerated when she had warned Sebastian that any great exercise of her powers would shout to the world that a Magus Major had come to stay in this tiny little backwater village. Thomas—well, he was indeed an Earth Master, but his magic came out in the skill of his hands and his marvelous craftsmanship. It seemed that wood and stone and clay obeyed his will and formed themselves before he ever set tool to them. His power was so contained within himself that it never showed; he had never really needed to shield himself.

Sebastian seldom *used* his power as a Fire Master; it was ill-suited to his life as a painter. In fact, in all the time that Marina had been with them, he hadn't (at least to Margherita's knowledge) worked a greater magic more than a half a dozen times. When he *had* summoned Elementals or used great amounts of power, it had been in attempts to rid Marina of the curse that burdened her.

As for Margherita—though she had used magic more often and more openly than either of the men, it hadn't even been in exercise of the healing magics that came so naturally to Earth Masters. No, hers had been kitchen witchery, the magic of hearth and home, more often than not. And again, when she had invoked greater power, it had generally been for Marina's sake.

There had been magic openly at work in this little corner of Devon, but it had all been minor. Elizabeth had been very wise to be cautious. There was no point in hiding Marina all this time, only to give her presence away in the last year of her danger.

They left the workroom arm-in-arm, and encountered Marina fresh from a hot bath, cheeks glowing, hair damp, enveloped in one of the warm, weighty winter gowns that Margherita had made for her, a caftan of soft olive wool that Margherita had shamelessly copied from a Worth original, with a sleeveless overgown of the same fabric, lined in cream-colored linen, and embroidered with twining forest-green kelp and blue-green fish with fantastically trailing fins.

"Oh, I do like this frock, Mari!" Elizabeth exclaimed involuntarily. "Imagine it in emerald satin! Your embroidery design, of course, Margherita?"

"Yes, but Marina did at least half of the embroidery," Margherita hastened to point out. "Probably more. She's as good with a needle as I am."

"I enjoyed it," Marina said, blushing a little. "But Elizabeth, I thought the suit you arrived in was just stunning."

"Hmm. It *is* one of my favorites, though I can't say that I'm altogether fond of those trumpet-skirts," Elizabeth replied. "Your gown is a great deal more sensible. And comfortable. But there it is; fashion never *does* have a great deal to do with sense or comfort, now, does it?"

"And I suppose I'd look a complete guy, trotting around the orchard in a trumpet-skirt with a mermaid-tail train," Marina admitted ruefully.

"Believe me, my dear, you would; fashion is not made for orchards. And you'd probably break your neck into the bargain." They were the first to reach the dinner table after all, and took their places at it, clustering at one end so that they could continue the conversation.

"But a suit like yours is perfectly comfortable in town, isn't it?" Marina asked, with a wistful expression. "I mean, if I went into London—"

Elizabeth got a mischievous look on her face. "Young lady, if you go into London, I am going to see to it that your wardrobe contains *nothing* but Bloomer fashions! I want every young man who sees you think that you are a hardened Suffragist with no time for mere males!"

The look of dismay on Marina's face made both of the older women laugh.

"But Elizabeth, if you dressed me in those, mightn't they think I'm—fast?" Marina said, in tones of desperation. "After all, aren't some Suffragists proponents of Free Love?"

"Not in those clothes, they won't," Elizabeth responded, still laughing. "Uncorseted, buttoned up to the neck, with more fabric in a single leg of those contraptions than in two trumpet-skirts?"

"I hate to say this, but those Bloomer fashions *are* hideous," Margherita admitted, as Thomas and Sebastian entered, listened to the topic of conversation for a moment, and exchanged a thoroughly masculine *look* of bafflement. "I *know* that they are sensible and practical, but do they have to be so ugly?"

Elizabeth shook her head ruefully. "Frankly, no, I don't think so. Well, look at those lovely gowns you make for yourself and Mari! Really, I'm envious of your skill, and if I could find a seamstress to copy them, I would. Those are practical *and* handsome."

Mari looked a little surprised. "Are they really?" she asked. "They aren't fashionable—"

"They aren't the fashions you see in the society sketches, true," Margherita agreed, and sighed, exchanging a look with Elizabeth. "I don't *like* most of the fashions that PBs wear. I couldn't breathe, much less work.in them, and they're so tightly fitted I can't imagine how a lady gets through an hour without splitting a seam."

"Oh, society!" Elizabeth laughed, after a moment. "PBs and debutantes don't live in the real world, much less *our* world! Can you imagine for a single moment the Jersey Lily summoning Elementals to her? Or one of those belles at Margherita's loom?"

The mere thought was so absurd, of course, that Marina laughed; Margherita smiled, and Sebastian and Thomas looked ridiculously relieved. "Speaking of summoning Elementals—" began Thomas.

"Not over supper!" all three of them exclaimed, and laughed, and turned the conversation to something more entertaining for all five of them.

Marina woke with a start, her heart racing. What had startled her awake?

She listened, heard nothing, and pulled back the covers. Feeling both foolish and groggy, she went to her window to look outside. The clouds were returning, scudding across the face of the full moon, passing shadows across the ground. As the shadows passed, the pale, watery light slicked the bare branches of the tree beside her window with a glaze of pearl.

There was nothing moving out there.

It must have been a cat. Or an owl. But why would a cat or an owl have awakened her? It hadn't been a sound that made her heart pound—it was a feeling. Marina was troubled, uneasy, and she didn't know why. She couldn't sleep, yet her mind wouldn't clear, either; she felt as if there was something out there in the darkness looking for her. This was nothing as concrete as a premonition; just a sense that there was something very wrong, something hostile, aimed at her, but nothing more concrete than that.

There was no logical reason for the feeling. It had been a lovely evening, Uncle Thomas had consented to read aloud to them, something he very rarely did, although he had a wonderful reading voice. Then she herself had brought her musical instruments down and played, while the other four danced in the parlor, with Sarah and Jenny as a cheerful audience. She had come up to bed in a pleasant and mellow mood, thinking only of what she planned to try tomorrow with Elizabeth in the workroom.

But the sudden fear that had awakened her, the unease that kept her awake, wasn't going away.

She listened carefully to the sounds of the house. There was nothing from next door, where Elizabeth was. And nothing from the bedrooms down the hall, either. Whatever was disturbing her, it was nothing that any of the others sensed.

Perhaps their *shields are a little* too *good.* . . .

After all, shields obscured as well as protected.

Now that was an uncomfortable thought.

And yet, there still was nothing concrete out there, nothing she could put a finger on. She thought about getting a glass of water and summoning an Undine, but—

But if there is something looking for me, that's the surest way to tell it where I am.

But the unease only grew, and she began to wonder if there was any possibility she could get downstairs into the workroom—which would at least have the primary shields on it—when something else occurred to her.

She didn't *have* to summon anything, at least, not of *her* Element. She had Allies; she had always known about the interest of the Sylphs and other Air Elementals, but Elizabeth had taught her that they had a special connection to her, how to ask them for small favors. And a call to one of them would not betray her presence.

The thought was parent to the deed; she opened the window, and whistled a few bars of "Elf Call" softly out into the night. It didn't have to be that tune, according to Elizabeth; it could be anything. Whistling was the way that the Finns, who seemed to have Air Mastery in the national blood, had traditionally called their Elemental creatures, so it worked particularly well for one who was only an Ally. It was nothing that an Air Elemental could take offense at. After all, any within hearing distance could always choose to ignore a mere whistle, even one with Power behind it.

There was a movement out of the corner of her eye, a momentary distortion, like a heat shimmer, in the air when she turned to look in that direction.

Then, as she concentrated on the Sight, the heat shimmer became a Sylph.

It did look rather like one of the ethereal creatures in a children's book—a gossamer-pale dress over a thin wraith of a body, and the transparent insect wings, too small to hold her up in the air, even at a hover; pointed face, silver hair surmounted by a wreath of ivy, eyes far too big for the thin little visage.

She looked, in fact, like one of the child-women ballet dancers often sketched in the newspapers. Except that no ballet dancer ever hovered in midair, and no matter how thin a ballet dancer was, you couldn't see the tree behind her *through* her body.

"*Little sister,*" said the Sylph, "*I know why you call.*"

Marina had often heard the expression, "It made the hair on the back of my neck stand up." Now she understood it.

"*There is danger, little sister,*" the Sylph said urgently. "*Great danger. She is moving, and her eye turns toward you. It is this that you sense.*"

"She? Who is *she*?" Marina asked, urgently.

"*Beware! Be wary!*" was all the Sylph would say.

Then she was gone, leaving Marina not at all comforted, and with more questions and next to no answers.

6

A LUSTILY crowing rooster woke Marina with a start, and she opened her eyes to brilliant sun shining past the curtains at her window. She sat straight up in bed, blinking.

The last she remembered was lying in bed, trying to decipher what the Sylph had said. It had seemed so urgent at the time, but now, with a rooster bellowing to the dawn, the urgency faded. She threw off the blankets, slipped out of bed, ran to the window and pulled the curtain aside.

The window was closed and latched, and although she did recall closing and latching it when she went to bed, she didn't remember doing so after summoning the Sylph. She thought she'd left it open; she'd been in such a state of confusion and anxiety that she'd gone straight to her bed from the window.

Had she summoned a Sylph? Or had it all been a particularly vivid dream? Other than the window being shut, and that was problematical, there was nothing to prove her fears of last night had been real or imagined.

Except that last night there were clouds crossing the moon and a steady wind—and today there's barely a breath of breeze and not a cloud in the sky. Could the weather have changed that drastically in a few hours? She didn't think so, particularly not here, where winter was basically rain interrupted by clouds.

She opened the window, and closed it again quickly—it was also *cold* out there! It couldn't be much above freezing, and she didn't recall it being that cold last night. Surely it would have been colder last night than it was now!

That seemed to settle it—she must have dreamed the whole thing.

There was an easy way to check on it, though. Despite her misgivings of last night—which now seemed very misplaced—her guardian's shields surely were *not* strong enough to keep them from sensing trouble.

She turned away from the window, and hurried over to the fire to build it up again, then quickly chose underthings and a gown and dressed for the day. Perhaps her thick woolen stockings were unfashionable, but at the moment, she would choose warm feet over fashion! Then she made for the kitchen, pausing only long enough in the little bathroom to wash her hands and face in the warm water that Jenny had brought up and left there, clean her teeth, and give her hair a quick brushing. *I almost wish snoods were fashionable again, as they were ages ago,* she thought, pulling the brush through the thick locks, with impatient tugs. *Then I could bundle my hair up into the net and be done with it for the day. Sometimes I think I ought to just cut it all off.*

But if she did that, Uncle Sebastian would never forgive her.

Or he'd make me wear horrid, itchy wigs. He already did that now and again, and the things made her skin crawl. Bad enough to be wearing someone else's hair, but she could never quite rid herself of the thought that insects would find the wigs a very cozy home. It was horrible, sitting there posing, sure that any moment something would creep out of the wig and onto her face!

She ran down the stairs to the kitchen, wanting to be there when everyone else came down. If anyone else had awakened with a fright or even an uneasy stirring in the night, they'd be sure to talk about it. In a household full of magicians, night-frights were no laughing matter.

The problem was, of course, that she didn't have enough experience to tell a simple nightmare from a real warning. And with all the praises being heaped on her for her current progress with Elizabeth, she was rather loath to appear to be frightened by a silly dream.

And it wasn't as if there had actually *been* anything menacing her, either! Just a vague feeling that there was something out there, some sinister hunter, and she was its prey. Now how could she ever explain an hysterical reaction to something as minor as *that?*

"Good morning, Sarah!" she called as she flew in at the kitchen door, relieved to see that she was the first down. She wouldn't have missed anything, then.

"Morning to you, miss," the cook replied, after a surprised glance. "Early, ain't you?"

"Cocky-locky was crowing right outside my window," Marina replied, taking the seat nearest the stove, the perquisite of the first down. Even in high summer, that was the favored seat, for whoever sat there got the first of everything from Sarah's skillets. "I know he's Aunt's favorite rooster, but there are limits!"

"I'll tell Jenny not to let them out until you've all come down of a morning," Sarah replied with a chuckle. "She won't mind, and it don't take but a minute to take down the door. She can do't when she's done with fetchin' water upstairs."

She handed Marina a blue-rimmed pottery bowl full of hot oat porridge, which Marina regarded with resignation, then garnished with sugar and cream and dug into so as to get rid of it as soon as possible. Sarah had fed her a bowl of oat porridge every cold morning of her life, standing over her and not serving her anything else until she finished it, and there was no point in arguing with her that she never made the uncles eat oat porridge first. She would only respond that Aunt Margherita ate it, and what was good enough for her lovely aunt was good enough for her. Never mind that Aunt Margherita actually *liked* oat porridge.

For that matter, so did the uncles. They just never were made to finish a huge bowlful before getting served Sarah's delectable eggs fried in the bacon fat, her fried kidneys, sliced potatoes, her home-cured bacon, country ham, and home-made sausages. Not to mention her lovely thick toast, cut from yesterday's loaf, which somehow was always golden, warm enough to melt the butter, and never burned—

—though Marina had long suspected the touch of one of Uncle Sebastian's Salamanders for that particular boon.

Or scones, left over from tea or made fresh that morning, with jam and butter or clotted cream. Or cake, or pie. That oat porridge left very little internal room for all the good things that bedecked the breakfast table.

No, the uncles got a much smaller bowl, and unless Sarah was running behind, they got it along with the rest of their breakfast. Sarah never scolded *them* if they left some of it in the bottom of the bowl.

Such were the trials of having the same person serve as cook and nursery-maid, she supposed, trying not to think about the porridge she was eating. It wasn't so much the flavor, which reminded her strongly of the taste of iron but could be disguised with cream and sugar. It was the texture.

By the time she had only half finished her bowl, she heard a clatter of footsteps on the stair, and the rest of the household came down in a clump, trailed by Jenny carrying the last of the hot water cans. Properly dressed for the day, too—a cold morning didn't encourage lounging about in one's dressing gown!

"Well, finally, a sunny morning!" Elizabeth was saying as they came into the kitchen. "Good morning, Sarah."

"Morning, ma'am. 'Twon't last," Sarah predicted.

"Oh, try not to burst my illusions too quickly, will you?" Elizabeth laughed. "After all, I'll be leaving in a week or so, can't I at least hope that I won't have to depart in a downpour?"

Sarah turned from the stove, spatula in hand. "Oh, ma'am, are you going that soon?" she asked, looking stricken. "But you haven't heard half the things the village folk have dug up—and—you haven't even had a *taste* of one of my mince pies—and—"

"Sarah, I'm only going away over the holidays! I'll be back just after Twelfth Night!" Elizabeth exclaimed, though she looked pleased at Sarah's reaction. "I had no idea that I was anything but an additional burden to your duties."

"Burden? Oh, ma'am, what's one more at table? 'Tis been like having another in the family here." Sarah tenderly forked bacon and sausage onto Elizabeth's plate, giving her so much that Elizabeth transferred half of it to Marina when Sarah's back was turned. Marina ate it quickly before Sarah could notice that *she* hadn't finished her porridge.

"Well, Sarah's right about that," Sebastian said, with a wink for his wife. "Though I must say it's ruined every one of the arguments we've had since she's been here."

"Oh? In what way has my presence interfered, pray?"

Elizabeth responded, with a toss of her head. "Other than that the sheer weight of my intellect overpowers you light-minded painterly types?"

"Well, when it comes to a division between the sexes, it used to come out a draw, and Margherita and Marina had to compromise," Sebastian pointed out, sounding for all the world as if it was the two females of the household who were unreasonable when it came to sitting down for negotiations. "Now there's the three of you, and you run right over the top of us poor befuddled males."

"If you'd learn to listen to reason, you wouldn't be befuddled *or* find yourself in need of making compromises," Elizabeth retorted. "Seeing as we are the ones who generally propose compromise in the first place, which you gentlemen seem to regard with the same attitude as a bull with a red rag."

Somehow, within three sentences of that challenge, the conversation managed to come round to a spirited discussion of votes, university degrees, and equal responsibilities for women.

Marina listened, slowly munching her way through her breakfast, and began to see an interesting and quite logical explanation for the dream of last night.

It had to be a dream; none of the others had mentioned any unease at all, and they surely would. Even if they were cautious about speaking of magic in front of Sarah and Jenny, there were ways of saying things without actually *saying* them that amounted to a second language among the five of them.

No, it must have been a dream, and now Marina had a good idea of where it had come from.

She hadn't thought about it much, but she had known for the last several days that Elizabeth's return to her family was coming up shortly. How could she *not* be anxious about that, even though she knew that Elizabeth was going to come back? Her teacher was going to be gone, and not only was she not going to be getting new lessons in Water Magic, but if anything somehow went seriously wrong in her practicing, there would be no one in the household technically capable of putting it right again. The best they could do would be for Sebastian, the antagonistic Element, to put the whole mess down with sheer, brute force.

That could be very bad over the long run. The Elementals might take offense, and she'd be weeks in placating them.

So, that would explain all the unease, the tension, even the fear. And the feeling of something bad out there watching for her—well, dreams often showed you the opposite of what you were really feeling, and the fear came from the fact that *no one* would be watching for her with Elizabeth gone.

The anxiety as well—well, that was simply a straight reflection of the fact that with Elizabeth gone, she would be feeling rather lonely. For the first time she could remember, winter had not been a round of day after day, the same, with barely a visit or two to the village to break the monotony. Everyone had tasks that kept them involved except her. Posing might be hard work, but it wasn't intellectually stimulating. But with Elizabeth here, she'd had a friend and entirely new things to do.

It was all as simple and straightforward as that!

Relieved now that she had found a logical explanation for what must have been a simple bout of night-fears, she joined in the discussion—which, despite Uncle Sebastian claiming it was an argument, never got to the point of raised voices, much less to acrimony. Elizabeth even appealed to Sarah a time or two, though Sarah only replied with "I'm sure I don't know, ma'am," or "I couldn't rightly say, ma'am." And, essentially, all of the women knew deep down that Sebastian was firmly on *their* side in the case of the Cause. He was only arguing because one of his greatest joys was in playing devil's advocate. And another was to get Elizabeth sufficiently annoyed to exercise a talent for rather caustic wit that she rarely displayed.

At least, so long as it didn't interfere with his meals. The only reason that Elizabeth got in some fairly long speeches without being interrupted was because Uncle Sebastian was enjoying his broiled kidneys. Twice Sarah purloined her plate to rewarm what had gotten cold and unappetizing.

Finally, he cleaned his plate with a bit of toast, popped it in his mouth, and stood up. "You win, Elizabeth, as usual. You're right, I'm outnumbered, and besides, I am *not* going to waste this gorgeous light. You'll have to do without Marina this morning, Elizabeth—I've got a buyer for Werther and I mean to have the money in time to finance a really good Christmas. Come along, poppet—"

He gestured at Marina, who quickly rose from the table and followed him. She saw that determined, yet slightly absent look in his eyes and knew it of old. Werther *would* be finished—in very few days, if the weather held.

And Marina was going to be spending a great deal of time sprawled half on, half off that pallet, nearly upside down.

Oh well, she thought, suppressing a yawn as she fitted her upper torso within the chalk marks on the floor. *Uncle Sebastian's doing my legs this morning, since that's where the light is falling. So at least I'll get to make up my lost sleep today.*

By the time Elizabeth left, Marina had all but forgotten about her disturbed night. The few times she thought about it, she was glad she hadn't mentioned it; it would have been too, too embarrassing to be comforted and reassured over a nightmare. And in front of Elizabeth too—appalling thought!

She hadn't seen a sign of a single Sylph or any other Air Elemental since then, but they didn't much care for the cold, and she was too busy to summon one. The clear weather didn't hold, either, and they liked rain even less than cold. With Uncle Sebastian claiming her time during the day, feverishly painting his *Young Werther*, Elizabeth claimed the hours between sunset and bedtime. Which was only right, of course—after all, that was why Elizabeth was here in the first place!

The result was that when the day of departure arrived, Marina was able to build a shield two layers thick, with the outer layer looking just like the sort of aura that any ordinary person might have. What was more, she could shield a workspace, or even a smallish room, and within the room, she could make the shield permanent.

She still hadn't begun the next phase of her tutelage, which Elizabeth said would be the offensive and defensive uses of her power. That would have to wait; Elizabeth didn't want her to even think about such a thing until there was another Water Master physically present while she practiced.

The day of departure was gray, but not raining, so they all went to see her off, using both carts, and combining the trip with a Christmas shopping expedition to the village and perhaps beyond. When Elizabeth's train was safely gone, and the last glimpse of her hand waving a handkerchief out of the window was a memory, Marina and her aunt took one of the carts, and the uncles took the other. Uncle Thomas and Uncle Sebastian were in charge of arranging the Christmas feast.

"Make sure you get a gray goose, and not a white one!" Marina called after them as they set off on a round of the little village shop, the pub, and some of the farms. "The white ones are too fat!"

Uncle Sebastian waved absently; Uncle Thomas ignored them. Margherita sighed. "It's the same thing every year, isn't it?" she said to the pony's back-pointing ears. "Every year, I tell them, 'get a gray goose.' And what do they do every year? They get a white one."

"Maybe if you told them to get a turkey?" Marina suggested delicately.

"Then they'd bring back a pheasant, I swear." Margherita sighed again.

"Where first?" Marina asked, as Margherita took up the reins and glanced down the road after the uncles. Her aunt gave her a measuring look.

"Would you really, truly like a suit like Elizabeth's?" Margherita asked, a bit doubtfully. "Personally, I would feel as if I'd been trussed up like the Christmas goose in one of those rigs, but if you really want one—"

"Oh, *Aunt*!" Marina said breathlessly, hardly able to believe what she was hearing. Margherita had resisted, quietly, but implacably, every hint that Marina had ever given her about more fashionable clothing. Nothing moved her, not the most delectable sketch in the newspaper, not the most delicious description of a frock in one of Alanna's letters. "Do you think you'd really like that?" was one response, "It's not practical for running about outside," was another. And she couldn't help but agree, even while, the older she got, the more she yearned for something—just one outfit— that was truly stylish.

"All right then. It won't be a surprise, but it will be done in time for Christmas." Margherita's expression was a comical mix of amusement and resignation, as she turned the pony's head and slapped the reins on his back.

"But, where are we going?" Marina asked, bewildered, as

Margherita sent the pony out of the village, trotting along the road that ran parallel to the railway, into the west.

"Well, *I* don't have the skill to make you anything like that! And besides, we'll have to get you the proper corset for it as well; just compare what they're showing in advertisements with what you own. We won't find anything in Killatree; we might as well go to Holsworthy." Margherita smiled. "You've never had anything other than the gowns I made or ordinary waists and skirts from Maggie Potter; you'll have to be fitted, we'll have to select fabric, and we'll have to return for a final fitting."

"Oh." Marina was a bit nonplused. "I didn't mean to cause all this trouble—"

"Nonsense! A Christmas gift needs to be fussed over a bit!" Margherita laughed, and flicked her whip warningly at a dog that came out of one of the farmyards to bark at them. "It's not as if we were going all the way to Plymouth—although—" she hesitated. "You know, we could. We could take the train there, easily enough. The seamstress in Holsworthy is good, but she won't be as modish as the one that creates Elizabeth's gowns."

For a moment, Marina was sorely tempted. Plymouth! She had never been to Plymouth. She had never been to *any* big city.

But that was the rub; she had never been to any big city. After a moment, her spirit quailed at the thought of facing all those buildings, all those people. Not Plymouth; not unless she'd had time to get her mind around going there. And then—well, she'd want to stay there for more than a day. Which meant she truly needed to get herself mentally prepared for the big city.

"I'd like something simpler than Elizabeth's suit," she said, after thinking of a good way to phrase it. "After all, couldn't we do the ornamentation if I decide I want it later?

And I'd like that better. If you can't actually make the suit, I'd rather have your design for ornaments."

"We certainly could, Mari," her aunt said warmly, which made her pleased that she had thought of it. "You know, this was Thomas' suggestion for your Christmas present—and I suspect he had an ulterior motive, because it means that he won't be in the workshop from now until Christmas, trying to somehow craft something for you in secret *and* finish his commissions."

"Well, I can't blame him, since he's running out of space in my room to put the things he's made for me," Marina replied, casting an anxious tendril of energy toward the sky. Was it going to rain? They had umbrellas, but Holsworthy was more than twice as far away as Killatree.

No. We'll be fine. That was another lesson learned from Elizabeth; how to read the weather. Later she would learn how to change it, although that was dangerous. Little changes could have large consequences, and disturbing the weather too much could change convenience for her into a disaster for someone else.

So the pony trotted on, through the wet, cold air, along the road that smelled of wet leaves and coal smoke from the trains. Out in the pastures, sheep moved slowly over the grass, heads down, like fat white clouds—or brown-and-white cows raised their heads to stare at them fixedly as they passed. Jackdaws gave their peculiar twanging cry, and flocks of starlings made every sort of call that had ever echoed across the countryside, but mostly just chattered and squeaked.

In a little more than an hour, they reached the town of Holsworthy. It had a main street, it had shops, not the single, all-purpose little grocers, dry goods, and post office run by Peter Hunter and his wife Rosie. It even had a town square with a fountain in it, which had a practical purpose rather than an ornamental one. It provided water for anyone who didn't have it in their house, and for man and beast on the street.

Cobblestone streets led off the main road, with the houses and shop buildings clustering closely together, huddling together like a flock of chickens in a roost at night. Marina had been here before, usually twice or three times in a year. There was an annual wool fair, for instance, that they never missed if they could help it. Uncle Sebastian ordered some of his artistic supplies here from the stationer, and Uncle Thomas some of the exotic woods he used to make inlays. This was where Aunt Margherita got her special tapestry wool as well as her embroidery silks.

Of course, there were things that could not be bought in Holsworthy; for those, Sebastian or Thomas went to Plymouth, or even to London, perhaps once every two years.

"While we're here, oughtn't we to do other Christmas shopping, especially since Uncle Sebastian and Uncle Thomas aren't with us?" Marina asked, "I wanted to get them books, and there's a lovely bookshop."

"Exactly what I had thought." Margherita pulled the pony up to let à farm cart cross in front of her, then reined him toward the fountain. The pony, nothing loath, went straight for the basin and buried his nose in the water. Margherita and Marina got down out of the cart, and Margherita led the pony and cart to the single inn in town. It also had a stable, and the pony could wait there in comfort and safety while they did their shopping.

The sign on the shop and in the window read, "Madame Deremiere, Modiste." Now there was no Madam Deremiere, and had not been within the memory of anyone living in Holsworthy. Probably the lady in question had been an asylum seeker from the Great Revolution, or perhaps Napoleon. The current seamstress (also, by courtesy, called "Madame") was the apprentice of her apprentice, at the very least.

The first task before them, once the greetings and mandatory cup of tea had been disposed of, was the selection of material — and here, sadly, the selection was definitely *not* what it would have been in Plymouth. There was no emerald wool like that of the suit that Marina had coveted. The choice of fabric was, frankly, limited to the sort of thing that the well-to-do yeoman farmer's wife or merchant's wife would want, which tended to either the dull or the flamboyant.

There was, however, a wonderful soft brown wool plush that Marina could see Margherita had fallen in love with. She resolved the moment that her aunt's back was turned to purchase it and hide it in the back of the cart. In the colors that *she* preferred, there was a green velvet that was both utterly impractical and far too expensive, a pale green linen that was too light for a winter suit, and an olive green wool that had too much yellow in it. She was about to give up, when Margherita said, "But what about gray? Something soft, though, like that brown plush. Something with a firm hand, but a soft texture."

"I do have some gray woolens like that; I ordered them thinking that I might convince some of the ladies to commission me to tailor some little boys' suits, but nothing came of it," the seamstress replied, and went to the rear of her establishment.

Of the three choices, there was a woolen in a dove gray that Marina loved the moment she touched it. It was soft and weighty, a little like fine sueded leather. "Oh, that's merino, that is," the woman said. "Lovely stuff. Too dear for Holsworthy, though; if a lady of this town is going to spend that sort of money on a suit for her little boy, she'll go up a bit and have it done in velvet. Not as much difference in price, you see, when you're only using two yards or so."

"And how 'dear' would that be?" Margherita asked, settling in for a shrewd session of bargaining—Christmas present or no, she had never bought anything without a stiff bargaining session, and she clearly wasn't about to break that habit.

In the end, by pointing out a couple of odd places where a moth had gotten to the fabric, and making the case that since the lady was getting not only the price of the fabric but the commission to make it up, Margherita got her price. Then it was time to pick the design. Out came the pattern-books and sketches, and now Margherita excused herself. "I am not going to attempt to influence your choice, my dear," she said with a smile. "I want you to pick what *you* want, not what you think I think you should have. And I know I'll try to influence you, so I'll return in an hour or so."

And with that, she picked up her gloves and donned her cloak, and left Marina alone with the seamstress.

"And what do you want, miss?" the seamstress asked, with a hint both of humor and just a little apprehension.

"Oh," Marina paused. "Lady Hastings, a friend of ours, had the most beautiful suit with a trumpet-skirt and a train—"

She saw the apprehension growing, and knew that her aunt had been right; this seamstress in a small town was not at all confident of her ability to replicate something that a person like Lady Hastings could purchase.

"And I thought, something *like* that, but much simpler," she finished. She looked through the first few pages of "walking suits" and "resort dresses" and suddenly her eye alighted on a design that was precisely what she wanted, a jacket fastening to the side instead of down the middle.

"Like this!" she said, laying her finger on it, "But without the trimming."

It was labeled as a "walking suit" as well; it had a lappet collar and a double skirt, and in the sketch, was trimmed quite elegantly and elaborately. But the lines were simple and very tailored, the skirt less of a train than Elizabeth's, and so a little old-fashioned, but to Marina's eyes it looked a little more graceful.

"Without the trimming. . . ." The apprehension was replaced by relief, as Marina watched the woman mentally removing soutache and lace, pin tucks and ribbon. "Yes, indeed, miss; that's a very good choice, and if you don't mind my saying so, it will look very well on you." She marked the sketch and laid the book aside with the fabric. "Now, let's get you measured."

It wasn't quite that simple. First, Marina had to be laced into the new-style corset that the suit required. And she had gone uncorseted for so long that the only one she'd had up to this point had been bought when she was fourteen and still looked brand new. She hadn't worn it more than once or twice, and both times she had needed help to get into it.

It was something of an ordeal, although the modiste helpfully taught her how to manage on her own. So at least when she got it home, she'd be able to get *into* it!

"I hope you aren't wanting a fifteen-inch waist, miss," the seamstress said frankly, looking from the corset in her hands to Marina in drawers and camisole and back again. "You'll never get it."

"I'm wanting to be able to move and breathe," Marina replied, feeling a certain amount of dread at the sight of the thing, all steel boning and bootlaces. "My aunt doesn't believe in tight lacing, and neither do I. I just want to look right in this new dress."

"Oh! Well, then you'll do all right," the woman laughed.

She unhooked the basque and handed the garment to Marina, who put it on, hooked the front back up again, one little steel hook at a time, and turned her back so that the seamstress could tighten the laces. "You'll be doing this with the wall-hook I told you about, miss," the modiste said, deftly pulling the laces tight, but not uncomfortably so. "Just have someone put one into a beam, and you won't need a lady's maid."

When the woman was done, it felt rather like she'd been encased in a hard shell, or was wearing armor. It wasn't uncomfortable, in fact, it made her back feel quite nicely supported, but she definitely wouldn't be able to run in a garment like this. But a glance at the mirror showed a gratifyingly slim figure, and if she didn't have a fifteen-inch waist, she didn't particularly want to look like a wasp, either.

The seamstress, measuring tape and notebook in hand, went to work.

She was *very* thorough. She measured everything three times, presumably to make sure she got the measurement right, and it seemed as if she measured every part of Marina's body. Wrists, the widest part of the forearm, biceps, shoulder-joint, neck. From shoulder to shoulder across the back and across the front. Bust, under the bust, waist, hips, just below the hips. From nape to center of the back. From nape of the neck to the ground. She even measured each calf, each thigh, and each ankle, though Marina couldn't imagine how she'd use those measurements, and said so.

"It all goes in my book, my dear," the woman told her. "Some day you might want a cycling costume, for instance, and I'll have the measurements right here."

Marina couldn't think of anything less likely, but held her peace as the seamstress unlaced her corset and helped her out of it. For the first time she realized just how very comfortable her aunt's gowns were.

But she still wanted that suit. Already in her mind, she was planning the trimming that she and her aunt would put on it. Black, of course—black would look wonderful on the gray wool.

She paid for the brown wool herself, out of the pocket-money her parents had sent before they went to Italy. After a quick survey of the street to make sure that Margherita was not on the way, she hurried across to the inn and hid her purchase under the old rugs they kept in the pony cart in case it became too cold. Then she hurried back to the seamstress, and was looking over sketches of garden-party dresses when her aunt returned.

"Well, how did it go?" Margherita asked.

"I'm finished," Marina said, with triumph. "Look, this is what I picked—without the trimming. I have some ideas—"

"Hmm! And so do I! That's a fine choice of design. Well done, poppet!" Marina beamed in Margherita's approval. "When should we return for the fitting?" she asked, turning to the seamstress.

"Not sooner than a week," the woman replied promptly. "Now, that suit rightly needs a shirtwaist—did you have anything in mind for that?"

"This, I think," Margherita told her, turning back to the shirtwaists and pointing out a simple, but elegant design with a high collar and a lace jabot that could be tied in many ways, or left off altogether. "Two in white cambric, and one in dove-gray silk, and we'll want enough extra fabric to make three jabots for each."

Marina stared. "But—Aunt—I thought my old shirtwaists—"

"Nonsense, a new suit demands new shirtwaists." Margherita bargained again, but with the unexpected sale of the brown wool plush, the seamstress was feeling generous, and let her have her way after only a token struggle.

They left the shop arm-in-arm and headed up the street.

"Luncheon first, I think," Margherita said, steering Mari in the direction of a teashop. "It's *our* day out, and I think we'll spend it like ladies. A proper lady's luncheon, and none of those thick ham-and-butter sandwiches your uncles want!"

Marina giggled, but wasn't going to argue. She could count the number of times she'd eaten in a teashop on the fingers of one hand; it was a rare treat, and she was bound to enjoy it.

"Well, Mari, are you happy with your present?" Margherita asked, when they were settled, with porcelain cups of tea steaming in front of them, and a tempting selection of dainty little sandwiches arranged on a three-tiered plate between them.

"Oh, Aunt—" Marina sighed. "I can't tell you how much!"

Margherita just smiled. "Well, in that case, I think we should complete the job. What do you say to a new hat, gloves, and shoes to go with it all? Your mother sent a real surprise, but I've hidden it, and you'll just have to wait."

Marina had no thoughts for future surprises in the face of present generosity. "But—Aunt Margherita—isn't all that—expensive?" she faltered.

Margherita laughed. "All right, I'll confess. This year I finally convinced your mother to entrust the purchase of at least some of your Christmas presents to me. Oh, don't worry, you'll be able to give your Uncle Sebastian his usual largesse of painting supplies, but I pointed out, providentially it seems, that you were getting older and probably would start to need a more extensive wardrobe than *I* could produce. And that your mother, not being here, could hardly be expected to purchase anything for you that would actually fit. So although some of this is from us, the rest will be from Alanna and Hugh."

"Ah." She nibbled the corner off a potted-shrimp sandwich, much relieved. "In that case—"

Margherita laughed. "I know that look! And I knew very well that you would be more tempted by the bookstore than the seamstress!"

She flushed. "But I *would* like a hat. And gloves. And shoes." Then, recklessly, "And silk stockings and corset-covers and all new underthings!"

"And you shall have them," Margherita promised merrily. "But I am very glad that your uncles are off on their own errands, because by the time this day is out, they would have perished of ennui!"

7

BOXING Day was one of Marina's favorite days of the Christmas season, second only to Christmas itself. Perhaps this was because she really enjoyed giving gifts—not quite as much as receiving them, but she *did* take a great deal of pleasure from seeing the enjoyment that her gifts gave.

Traditionally, Boxing Day, December 26, was the day when those who were better off than others boxed up their old clothing and other things and distributed them to the poor—or at least, to their servants or the tenants on their property. But the inhabitants of Blackbird Cottage had a kindlier version of that tradition. No secondhand, worn-out things were ever packed up in the boxes they put together; instead, in odd moments throughout the year, they all had projects a-making that were intended to make those who weren't likely to get anything on Christmas a little happier on Boxing Day.

Uncle Thomas carved kitchen implements and other useful objects of wood and horn, as well as wooden boats, trains, tops, and dolls. Uncle Sebastian painted the toys, constructed wonderful kites, and used his skill at stretching canvas to stretch parchment and rawhide scraped paper-thin over frames to be mounted in open windows. Not as transparent as glass, perhaps, but tougher, and his frames were actually identical to the old medieval "windows" that had been in use by the well-to-do in ancient times. They kept the winter wind out of a poor man's cottage better than wooden shutters, and at least permitted *some* light to shine within during the day. Aunt Margherita knitted scarves, shawls, and stockings with the ends of her skeins of wool. And it was Marina's pleasure to clothe the dolls, rig sails to the boats, and stitch female underthings and baby's clothing. There were always babies to be clothed, for the one thing that the poor never lacked was mouths to feed and bodies to clothe.

As for the underthings—well, she considered that a form of comfort for the heart, if not the body. She knew how much better it could make a girl feel, even if she was wearing second-hand garments, to have brand new underthings with an embroidered forget-me-knot border to make them special. Many a village girl had gone into service with a set or two of Marina's gifts proudly folded in her little clothing-box, knowing that she would have something none of the other maids she would serve with would have—unless, of course, they were from Killatree as well. And many a poor (but proud) village bride had gone to a laborer-husband with a carefully hoarded set of those dainty things in her dower-chest, or worn beneath her Sunday dress (if she had one) to serve as the "something new" on her wedding-day.

Small things, perhaps, but they were *new.* Not second-hand, not worn threadbare, not out of the attic or torn, stained, or ill-made. For no few of the parish poor, this was the only time in their lives they ever got anything new.

So, on Boxing Day, Marina and Margherita drove down

to the village with the pony-cart full of bundles of stockings and gloves, scarves and shawls, useful things and toys, heading down to the parson, who would see that their gifts were distributed to those who needed them for another year. This year, Uncle Thomas had added something to his carvings; Hired John's son had expressed an interest in learning carpentry, and the uncles had put him to making stools and boot-jacks. If the legs were a trifle uneven, that was quickly remedied; and those of his efforts that he didn't care to keep—and how many people could actually *use* twenty stools and boot-jacks?—went into the cart as well.

Marina wore the "secret" present from her mother and father—a magnificent beaver cape, warm and soft, like nothing she'd ever had for winter before. She needed it; the temperature had plummeted just before Christmas, and it had snowed. Christmas Eve had resembled a storybook illustration, with snow lying thickly on the ground and along the limbs of the evergreens. The snow remained, softening the landscape, but making life even harder for the poor, if that was possible.

Marina yawned behind her glove, while Margherita drove. She had a faint headache as well as feeling fatigue-fogged and a little dull, but she was determined not to let it spoil the day for her. The cold air did wake her up a little, but it hadn't eased the headache as she had hoped.

Well, Uncle Sebastian's gone for the day. When we get home again, perhaps I'll try taking a nap, since he won't need me to pose.

For the past several nights, she hadn't slept at all well. At first she'd put it down to pre-Christmas nerves; now she wasn't certain what it was. She was certainly tired enough when it came time to go to bed, and she fell asleep without any trouble at all. But she just couldn't stay asleep; she half-woke a dozen times a night.

It was nothing even as concrete as that dream she'd had of waking in the middle of the night—just a sense that something was awry, or something was *about* to go wrong, and that she should be able to decipher what was wrong and set it right if only she knew how. She would fall asleep perfectly content, and the feeling would ooze through her dreams all night, making them anything but restful.

It will all stop when Elizabeth comes back, she told herself, stifling yet another yawn. *And I will not let this ruin the day.* And when her aunt turned to look at her, she managed to smile with real pleasure.

The parson was supposed to be the one distributing all of the largesse of Boxing Day, but over the years the poor children of the village and the farm-cottages had come to learn just who it was that made those marvelous toys and came to see to their own distribution of Blackbird Cottage's contribution to the Boxing Day spoils.

Life had never been easy for the poor, but it seemed to Marina that in these latter days, it had become nearly impossible. Certainly in all of the volumes of history and social commentary she'd read over the years (and in certain liberal-minded newspapers that occasionally made their way into the house) the authors had said things that agreed with her assessment. The poor these days were poorer; their conditions harder, their diet worse, their options fewer, their hours of work longer for less return.

It had probably begun in the days of the Corn Laws and the Enclosure Act—every village used to have its common, and anyone who lived there had a right to graze a sheep, a goat, a cow, or even geese there. Villagers used to have the right to run a pig or two in the local gentry's forest, fattening on whatever it could forage. They had rights to gather fallen wood for their fires, fallen nuts for their larders, glean grain left behind after harvest. With that, and with their cottage gardens, common laborers on the gentry's farms could have enough extra—meat from fowl or beast, eggs, perhaps milk and butter and cheese, and the garden vegetables—so that meager wages could be stretched to make a decent living. But one by one, the commons were enclosed, leaving cottagers with nothing to feed their geese and hens, their sheep or single cow. Then the swine were chased from the now-fenced forests in favor of deer and rabbits that the lord of the manor valued more than the well-being of humans. With the forests fenced and guarded by gamekeepers, you couldn't gather fallen sticks or nuts without being accused of poaching, and the penalty for poaching was prison. Mechanical reapers replaced men with scythes and rakes who cared about leaving a bit behind for a widow or old man. And wages stayed the same . . . but somehow, the cottage rent crept upwards, though the cottages themselves weren't usually improved. And heaven help you if the breadwinner took sick or was hurt too badly to work—as happened far too often among farm laborers. Rights to live in a farm cottage were only good so long as someone in the family actually worked on the farm. If the husband died or became disabled and you didn't have an unmarried son old enough to take his father's place, you lost your home as well as your income. Then what were your options? Parishes used to have a few cottages for those who'd been thrown on the charity of the parish, but more and more those were replaced with workhouses where families were broken up and forced to live in male and female dormitories, and both sexes were put to backbreaking work to "repay" the parish for their hard beds and scanty food.

Things were not much better if, say, the breadwinner worked on the railway as a laborer. The wages were higher, but the work was more dangerous—and yes, there were railway workers' cottages, but if your man lost his job or was too sick or hurt to keep it—like the farm laborer, you lost your home as well as your income.

As for other sorts of laborers, well, they didn't even have cottage-rights.

There was no factory nearby, but Marina had read plenty about them—those "dark, satanic mills" vilified by William Blake, where men, women, and children worked twelve hour shifts in dangerous conditions for a pittance. Entire families had to labor just to earn enough for rent, food, and a little clothing. Yet more and more country folk were having to turn to factory and mill-work in the cities just to survive. The owners of great estates were finding it more profitable to turn their tenant-farmers out and farm their own property with the help of the new machines—there were more hands to work the land than there were jobs to give them.

Or so Marina surmised from what she had read; she only had experience of country folk and country poverty, which was certainly harsh enough. There wasn't anything to spare in the budget of a cottager for toys for the kiddies. Small wonder there was a crowd waiting at the parsonage, and a cheer went up at the sight of their pony-cart.

When the pony came up alongside the front gate of the parsonage and Marina and her aunt climbed down off the seat, the children surrounded them, voices piping shrill greetings. And very blunt greetings as well—children, especially young ones, not being noted for patience or tact. "Merry Chrissmuss, mum!" vied with "Gie' us a present, mum?"

For all their pinched faces and threadbare clothing, their lack of familiarity with soap and water, they were remarkably good about not grabbing. They waited for Marina and Margherita to throw back the blanket covering the toys, waited their turns, though they crowded around with plead-

ing in their eyes. Margherita took the little girls, and Marina
the boys—Margherita allowed the girls to cluster around
her, but the boys were rowdier, and soon began elbowing
each other in an effort to get closer to get the choicest goods.

Marina fixed them with a stern glance, which quelled
some of the shoving. "You've all done this before," she
said sternly. "I shouldn't have to tell you the rules, now,
should I?"

One cheeky little fellow grinned, and piped up. "No,
miss. We gotter line up. Littlest first."

"Well, if you *know,* why aren't you doing it?" she retorted—and like magic (actually, *not* like magic, for order
came immediately and without effort on her part) they had
formed the prerequisite line. Marina gave the cheeky lad a
smile and a broad wink, and reached for a wooden horse
with wheels for the youngest in line. She paid most attention, not to the boy to whom she was giving a toy, but to the
ones behind him. Eyes would light up when a particularly
coveted object appeared, and she tried to match child to toy.
All the children got kites except for the very smallest who
couldn't have managed one even by spring; Sebastian had
done very well this year in the kite department. That meant
that each child got two toys this year, instead of just one, so
this was going to be quite a banner year so far as they were
concerned. Boys also got a pair of mittens each, fastened to
each other by a braided string so that they couldn't lose one
of the pair unless they cut the string. Boys being boys, they
usually didn't bother to put them on, either.

Truly small children, toddlers too young to talk, were
usually in the charge of an older sister. It sometimes made
her worry to see girls not even ten with a baby bundled in a
shawl on their backs, but what could be done? If their mothers weren't working, they were probably taking care of an
infant, and someone had to watch the next-youngest.

In general, these toddlers were too young even for wooden dolls, but based on the number of babies in the previous year, Marina usually had enough soft cloth dollies (for the girls) and lambs (for the boys) to satisfy everyone.

Boys got their toys and ran off shouting with greed and glee; over on Margherita's side of the pony-cart, Marina's aunt was doing her own distribution. Besides the dolls and kites, girls each got woolen scarves that they could use as shawls; they seemed to cherish the bright colors and the warmth as much as the playthings.

It didn't take long to give out the toys, and when there were no more children waiting, there were still some toys left, which was a fine thing. There were probably kiddies too far from the village to get here afoot, especially through the snow; the parson would know who they were, and see to it that they got playthings, too. He wouldn't be as careful about matching toy to child as Marina and her aunt were, but he was a kindly soul, and he would see that the farthest-flung members of his flock were cared for.

Only when the children were gone did the parson come out and collect the boxes, with a broad smile for both of them. Marina suspected that he took note of the decided lack of secondhand and much-worn articles in *their* offerings, and respected and appreciated their sensitivity. "My favorite artists!" he exclaimed, hefting a box of kitchen implements, and nodding to the hired man to take up a stack of window-panels. "As ever, thank you. You ladies and your gentlemen are generous to a fault."

"As ever, it was a pleasure," Margherita replied, with a cheerful smile. "With Marina all grown up, we would miss the fun of seeing children with new toys if not for this."

"Happy hearts and warm hands; you do a fine job of tending to both ends of the child," said parson's wife, who came trundling up, a bundle of shawls, to take in a box of stockings.

"And we leave their souls in your capable hands," Marina laughed.

The parson caught sight of the stack of stools, and grinned. "Well, well. Have you managed to persuade John Parkin the Younger to contribute as well?"

"It wasn't a matter of persuading," Marina said, laughing, each laugh coming out in a puff of white on the still air. "We told him that if he supplied the materials when Uncle Thomas promised to teach him joinery, he could keep what he made—but if *we* supplied it, what he made would be going out on Boxing Day!"

"Now," Margherita smiled. "Don't make him sound so ungenerous. I think he quite liked the idea. He certainly wasn't averse to it."

"And he'll have a trade when he's through, which is more than his father has," the parson's wife pointed out, in that no-nonsense way that village parson's wives, accustomed to a lifetime of making do on the meager proceeds of their husband's livings, often seemed to acquire. "I don't see where *he* has anything to complain of!"

When the cart was unloaded, they declined the invitation to tea—the parson's resources were strained enough as it was—and took their places in the cart again. The pony was pleased to turn around, and made brisk time back to Blackbird Cottage.

But without warning, just as they passed the halfway point between the village and the cottage, something—happened.

Marina gasped, as she reeled back in her seat beneath the unexpected impact of a mental and emotional blow.

It was like nothing she had ever felt before; a sickening

plunging of her heart, disorientation, nausea, and an over-whelming feeling of doom that she could not explain.

She clutched suddenly at her aunt's arm, fought down a surge of panic, and invoked her strongest shields.

To no effect. In fact, if anything, the sensation of *dread* increased tenfold.

"What's wrong?" Margherita exclaimed, startled.

"I don't know—" Marina choked out. "But something *is*. Something is horribly, horribly wrong—"

The feeling didn't pass; if anything, it deepened, and she closed her eyes to fight against the awful plummeting feeling in her stomach, the rising panic.

"Hold on—I'll get you home," Margherita said, and slapped the reins on the pony's back, cracking the whip above its ears and startling it into a trot. Marina clung to her aunt as to a rock in a flood, struggling against fear, and completely unable to think past it.

"Oh no," the phrase, loaded with dismay, that burst from her Aunt's lips, made her open her eyes again. They were nearly home—they had rounded the corner and the wall and gate of Blackbird Cottage were in sight—

But there were strangers there.

A huge black coach drawn by a pair of expensive carriage horses stood before the gate. And the sight of the strange carriage made her throat close with a panic worse than anything she had ever felt before.

In the space of a single hour, Marina had been plunged into a nightmare. The problem was, she was awake.

She sat on the sofa in the once-familiar parlor that had seemed a haven of familiar contentment, between Aunt Margherita and Uncle Thomas.

But in the last hour, every vestige of what she had *thought* was familiar had been ripped away from her.

She sat, every muscle rigid, every nerve paralyzed, her stomach a knot and her heart a cold lump in the middle of her chest.

On three chairs across from them sat four strangers, three of them in near-identical black suits, all three of them with the same stern, cold faces, the same expressionless eyes. They could have been poured from the same mold. They were lawyers, they said. They had come here because of her. They were lawyers who, from this moment on, were in charge of her—and her parents' estate.

Estate.

For her parents, it seemed, had made their last trip to Tuscany. There had been a dreadful accident, which at the moment, mattered not at all to her. She couldn't think of that; it meant nothing to her.

What mattered was that the people she had called aunt and uncle all her life were nothing more than family friends—who, because they had no ties of blood, had absolutely no rights whatsoever with regard to her, and never mind that they had raised her.

She was being taken from the only home and people she had ever known, to go to a place she had only seen in her uncle's sketches. Oakhurst. Where total strangers would be in charge of her, telling her what to do, controlling her for the next three years. And she had no choice.

"The law," said the tallest and thinnest of the three, "Is not to be trifled with."

Her rigidity and paralysis broke in a storm of emotion. "But I don't understand!" Marina wailed, clinging to her Aunt's arm. "*Why* can't I stay? I've lived here all my life! I'm *happy* here! You can't—you *can't* make me go away! I won't go! I won't!"

Her face was streaked now with the tears that poured from her eyes; her eyes blurred and burned, and she wanted to get the pony-whip and *beat* these horrible men out of the house, out of *her* house, and drive them back to whatever clerkly hell they had come from. For surely no one who could say things like they had to her could come from anywhere other than hell. She was not trifling with anything—*they* were the ones who were trifling with her, treating her like a goose that could be bundled up in a basket and taken wherever they cared to take her and set down in a new place and never notice!

"I won't go!" she repeated, hysterically, turning to the fourth stranger in the room, and the only one standing. "I won't! You can't make me!"

The policeman from Holsworthy looked uncomfortable; he inserted a finger in the collar of his tunic and tugged at it, as if it was too tight. The three lawyers, however, were utterly unmoved. They could have been waxwork figures for all the emotion they displayed.

"We have explained that, miss, several times," the one who did all the talking—the tallest, thinnest, and coldest—said yet again. He spoke to her in tones that one would use with the feeble-minded. "With your parents dead intestate, that is, without leaving a will, and your nearest relative perfectly willing and able to assume guardianship, you cannot legally remain with—these people." He looked down his long nose at Margherita and Thomas. "They have no blood ties with you, and no legal standing. Whatever your parents may have meant by boarding you with them, it doesn't matter to the law. Your *legal* aunt is not only prepared to assume responsibility for you, she has sued to do so, and the court has agreed. That is the law, and you must obey it. This policeman is here to see that you do."

It was *very* clear from his expression that he did not

approve of her current situation; that he did not approve of artists in general, and her aunt and uncle in particular. That, in fact, he considered artists to be only a little above actors and thieves in social standing.

Marina searched her aunt and uncle's faces, and saw nothing there but grief and resignation—and fear. There was no hope for her from them.

If she had allowed her body to do what her mind screamed at her to do, she'd have been beating those horrible, horrible men with a broom—or jumping up and running, running off to hide in the orchard until she froze to death or *they* went away without her. Her heart pounded with panic, and her throat was so choked with tears she could hardly get any words out.

I'll call up magic! I'll call up Undines and Sylphs and I'll drive them away!

Oh yes; she'd call up magic—call up Undines that could not function out of water and Sylphs they could not see. And do what? If these—these *lawyers* had been mages, perhaps she could have frightened them—if they had been the least bit sensitive, perhaps she could have influenced their minds and made them go away. But it would not be for long. The next time there would be more lawyers, and more policemen. And there would be a next time. The law was not to be trifled with.

It was all so impossible—in a single moment, her life had been turned completely upside down, and *no one was doing anything to help her.* This *couldn't* be right! This just *couldn't!*

Her parents were dead.

How could it have happened? It seemed like something out of a Gothic novel—there had been a horrible accident in Italy—a boating accident, the lawyers said. They'd drowned. Oh, they were definitely dead, their bodies had washed up on the beach within a day, and there were dozens of people to identify them.

They hadn't left a will. How could they *not* have left a will? Aunt Margherita seemed stunned, too stunned even to think; she hadn't said a dozen words since the lawyers broke the news. But there was no will, and her guardians were not her *legal* guardians.

Somewhere in the jumble of lawyers, estate managers, and men of business had been someone who had known where *she* was, and when her real aunt—someone she had never even heard of until now—had been told of the accident, had been told that Marina was living here, she had taken charge of everything. *She* —Arachne Chamberten— had sent these lawyers to take her away.

Now this person that Marina had never heard of, never seen, and never wanted to see, was legally in charge of her, her property, her very life until she turned twenty-one.

And this person decreed that she must leave Blackbird Cottage and go to Oakhurst. *Immediately.* With no argument or opposition to be tolerated.

Aunt Margherita and Uncle Thomas sat there like a pair of stunned sheep. Of course they were in shock—it had *always* been clear to Marina that her aunt and uncles considered her real mother and father to be their dearest friends, even though they only had contact with them through letters anymore—but Hugh and Alanna were dead, and Marina needed them now!

And they might just as well have been waxwork figures for all the help they were giving her!

"I don't *want* to leave!" she wailed, looking desperately at the policeman, fixing on him as the only possible person that might be moved by an appeal.

"Sorry, miss," he mumbled, turning very red. "I know

you're upset-like. I mean, know it's a shock, to lose your parents like this—"

I don't care about that! she screamed inside. *Don't you understand? My real parents are here, and you're trying to take me away from them!*

But—she couldn't say that, much less scream it.

"Miss, it's for your own good," the policeman said desperately. "These gennelmun know their business, and it's for your own good. You oughtn't to be with them as isn't your own flesh and blood, not now. And it's the law, miss. It's the law."

Her throat closed up entirely, and she felt the jaws of a terrible trap closing on her; she understood how the rabbit felt in the snare, the mouse as the talons of an owl descended on it. *If only Uncle Sebastian was here! He would do something, surely* —But Sebastian was off in Plymouth and wasn't expected back until tomorrow—

There could not have been a better time for them to arrive, or a worse time for her. Her chest ached, and black despair closed down around her.

The lawyers had made it abundantly clear that they were not going to wait that long—that in fact, if Marina balked at going, the policeman that they had brought with them was perfectly prepared to stuff her into their carriage by force. She saw that in their eyes—and in his. He would apologize, he would regret having to manhandle her, but he'd do it all the same.

No escape—no escape—

They couldn't have gotten the Killatree constable to go along with this—kidnapping! she thought frantically. Which was probably why they had brought one from Holsworthy. A Holsworthy man wouldn't know them. A Holsworthy man wouldn't have to answer to all of Killatree tomorrow for helping strangers tear her away from Blackbird Cottage and her guardians.

"Pack the girl's things," said the second lawyer coldly — the first words he'd spoken so far — looking over Margherita's shoulder at Sarah and Jenny. "And hurry up about it. We have a long journey ahead of us."

"Ma'am?" Sarah said, looking not at the lawyer, but at Margherita.

"Do it," the third lawyer snapped, "Unless you'd care to cool your heels in gaol for obstructing us in our duty, woman."

Shocked, angry, Sarah's gaze snapped to the policeman, who turned redder still, but nodded, affirming what the lawyer had said.

Sarah made a choking noise, and Jenny turned white.

"But—" Marina's spirit failed her utterly, and she slid to the floor, sobbing, her heart breaking.

She remained dissolved in tears while Sarah and Jenny packed for her, huddled against the seat of the sofa. Margherita just held her, speechlessly, and Uncle Thomas sat, white-faced, as if someone had shot him and he hadn't quite realized that he was dead yet.

She sobbed uncontrollably while Hired John grudgingly loaded the trunks and boxes on the top of the waiting carriage. She wept and clung to Margherita, until the policeman actually pried her fingers off of her aunt's arm, and pulled her away, wrapping her cape around her, ushering her into the carriage, almost shoving her inside.

There was nothing in her mind now but grief and despair. She continued to weep, inconsolable, tears pouring down her cheeks in the icy air as the carriage rolled away, leaning out of the window to wave, hoping for a miracle to save her.

But no miracle came, and the horses continued to carry her away — away —

She continued to wave, for as long as she could see her aunt and uncle standing stiff and still in the middle of the road, until the road took a turning and they vanished from view.

Then her strength left her. She collapsed back into the corner of her seat and sobbed, sobbed until her throat was sore and her eyes blurred, sobbed until her eyes were dry, and her cheeks raw with burning tears.

Through it all, two of the three detestable lawyers sat across from her, the third next to her, with folded arms, and stony faces. If they felt anything, it certainly didn't show. *They* were the waxworks, with their cold faces and hearts of straw.

They might claim that they were lawyers—but they were more and less than that. As much as that policemen, they had been sent to make sure she didn't escape, to make sure she was delivered into captivity, a prisoner of her parents' lack of foresight and the implacable will of a woman who was a complete stranger.

And so she wept, as darkness fell, and the carriage rolled on, and her captors, her jailers, watched her with the cold eyes of serpents in the night.

8

THE carriage rolled on through the night, long past even the most fashionable of supper-hours; evidently the Unholy Trinity were taking no chances on Marina making a bolt for freedom. The carriage rattled over roads not improved by the snow, swaying when it hit ruts, which would have thrown her against her unwelcome seat-mate if Marina hadn't wedged herself into place. She continued to huddle in her corner, as far as possible from them, back to them, her face turned into the corner where the seat met the side of the carriage, aching legs jammed against the floorboards to hold herself there. By the time darkness fell, she was no longer weeping and sobbing hysterically, but only because she was too exhausted for further emoting. Instead, she stared dull-eyed at the few inches of window curtain in front of her nose while slow, hot tears continued to burn down her raw cheeks. After sunset, she could no longer see even the curtains. The lawyers didn't bother trying to talk to her; leaning forward to put their heads together, they whispered among themselves in disapproving tones, but said nothing aloud. Apparently it was enough for them that they had her in keeping.

They can't keep me from writing, can they? They can't stop me from sending letters—

Well, actually, they could, or rather, her Aunt Arachne could, just by refusing to allow her pocket money for postage. It was very clear from the Trinity's attitude that they had been completely appalled by the household that they had found her in. Evidently Margherita, Thomas, and Sebastian were considered disreputable at best, and immoral at worst.

The Trinity would not have come as they had and acted as they had done if her new guardian had any intention of allowing her contact with the old ones, that much was blindingly clear from the way she had been handled—or, rather, manhandled. Whatever they had expected when they arrived, her situation had evidently fed right into their prejudices and preconceptions. They had expected to find a loose, disreputable, eccentric household *quite* beyond the pale of polite society, and that was exactly what they'd seen. Which probably contributed to the speed with which they bundled her out of there . . . their narrow little minds must have been near to splitting, and they must have been frantic to get her away.

And if Aunt Arachne ever finds out I was posing for Uncle Sebastian, she'll use that as a further weapon against my family.

Given how quickly she'd been hustled away, she could well picture the absolute opposition to any attempt on *her* part to return. She could see no way that she could win back home—not until she was of age and could do what she wanted.

Horrible little respectable minds!

Three years—it seemed an eternity. She stared into the blackness in front of her nose and tried to think. What to do? Was there, in fact, anything that she could do?

No. And imprisoning me is going to be "for my own good." How can you possibly argue with that? Worse, everyone, absolutely everyone, would agree with them! Taking me away from "corrupting and decadent influences," because everyone knows what artists are like. More tears flowed down her face, and her throat and chest were so tight she had trouble breathing.

It took her a moment to realize that the carriage was slowing; a moment later, it came to a stop. A hand tapped her elbow peremptorily.

"Miss Roeswood, we have paused for a moment at a post-tavern," a cold voice said distantly, its tone one of complete indifference. "Have you any—ah—urgent requirements? Do you need food or drink?"

She shook her head, refusing to turn to look at him.

"Then each of us will take it in turn to remain to keep you company while the others refresh themselves," the lawyer said, and settled back into his seat next to her, springs creaking, while the other two clambered out of the coach. Since she was wedged into the corner furthest from the door, and facing away from it, all that she saw was the reflection of a little lamplight on the curtains as the door opened. There was a little, a very little, sound of voices from the tavern itself, then the door shut again. She might have been alone, but for the breathing of her unwelcome companion.

She wondered what they would have done if she had needed to use a water closet. *Probably escorted me to the door and locked me inside,* she thought bitterly.

Her guard was shortly replaced by one of the other two, who had brought food and drink with him by the smell of it. She wasn't interested in anything like eating; in fact, the strong aromas of onion and cold, greasy beef from his side of the carriage made her feel ill and faint. He ate and drank with much champing of jaws and without offering her any, which (even though she had refused to move and had indicated she had no needs) was hardly gentlemanly.

Her stomach turned over, and she put one hand to her throat to loosen the collar of her cape. Her head ached; her eyes were sore, her cheeks and nose felt as if the skin on them was burned or raw. She shut her eyes and tried to shut her ears to the sound of stolid jaws chewing away at a Ploughman's lunch and a knife cutting bits off the onion and turnip that were part of it.

They were not going to stop for long, it seemed. The second lawyer returned to the carriage as well in a few moments, and then, hard on his heels the third joined his compatriots. Once he was inside, the third banged on the roof of the conveyance by way of telling the unseen coachman to move on, and the carriage lurched back into motion again. They really weren't wasting any time in getting her away.

She rested her burning forehead on the side of the carriage and pulled her warm cloak tighter around her shoulders, not against the chill of the night, but against the emotional chill within the walls of the carriage. Were they going to travel all night?

Evidently, they were.

The next stop, a few hours later, brought the same inquiry, which she answered with the same headshake. It also brought a change of horses, as if this carriage was a mail coach. No expense was being spared, it seemed, to make sure she was brought directly into the control of her new guardian.

I hope she's paying these horrible men next to nothing. From the type of food they'd brought into the carriage—the cheapest sort of provender, a Ploughman's lunch of bread, pickle, onion, a raw turnip, and a bit of greasy beef or strong cheese—it seemed that might be the case.

I hope it turns to live eels in their stomachs. I hope the carriage makes them sick. She wondered, at that moment, if there was something she could do magically to make them ill, or at least uncomfortable. But she hadn't been taught anything like that—probably because Elizabeth wouldn't approve of doing something that unkind even to automatons like these three.

Her spirits sank even further, if that was possible, when she realized that she couldn't even use magic to communicate with her former guardians. She hadn't been taught the direct means. There were indirect means, messages sent via Elemental creatures, but *hers* weren't *theirs*. The Undines, in particular, wouldn't approach Uncle Sebastian—theirs was the antagonist Element.

But—what about Elizabeth?

Surely she could send to Elizabeth for help, with the Undines as intermediaries—

But not until spring. Not until the water thawed again. The Sylphs might move in winter, but not the Water Elementals, or at least, not the ones she knew. And she couldn't count on the Sylphs—in fact, she hadn't even seen any since that odd nightmare. She could call them, but they wouldn't necessarily come.

Hope died again, and she stopped even trying to think. She simply stared at the darkness, endured the pain of her aching head, and braced herself against the pitching and swaying of the carriage.

Eventually, snoring from the opposite side told her that somehow at least two of her captors had managed to fall asleep. She hoped, viciously, that the coach would hit a particularly nasty pothole and send them all to the floor, or knock their heads together.

But in keeping with the rest of the day, nothing of the sort happened.

Hours later, they changed horses again. By this time she was in a complete fog of grief and fatigue, and couldn't have put a coherent thought together no matter how hard she tried. And she didn't try very hard. In all that time she hadn't eaten, drunk, or slept, but this time when the rude tap on her shoulder came, she asked for something to drink.

One of them handed her a flask, and she drank the contents without thinking. It tasted like cold tea, heavily creamed and sugared—but it wasn't very long before she realized that there had been something else in that flask besides tea. Her muscles went slack; foggy as her mind had been, it went almost blank, and she felt herself slipping over sideways in her seat to be caught by one of the repellent lawyers.

Horribly, whatever it was didn't put her to sleep, or not entirely. It just made her lose all conscious control over her body. She could still hear, and if she'd been able to get her eyes open, she'd have been able to see. But sensation was at one remove, and as she went limp and was picked up and laid out on the carriage seat, she heard the Unholy Trinity talking openly, but as if they were in the far distance. And although she could hear the words, she couldn't make sense of them.

She heard the crowing of roosters in farmyards that they passed, and knew that it must be near dawn. And shortly after that, the carriage made a right-angle turn, and the sound of the wheels changed.

Then it stopped.

The lawyers got out.

She fought to open her eyes, to no avail.

Someone else entered the carriage, and picked her up as if she weighed nothing. She heard the sound of gravel under heavy boots, then the same boots walking on stone. It felt as if the person carrying her was going up a set of stairs, but though she tried once again to regain control of her body, or at least open her eyes, her head lolled against his shoulder—definitely a he—and she could do nothing.

A door opened in front of them, and closed behind them. "She drank it all?" asked a cool, female voice.

"Yes, mum," replied a male voice, equally dispassionate. One of the Trinity. Not the person who was carrying her, who remained silent.

"Good. Come, James, follow me."

The sound of light footsteps preceding them. Another set of stairs, a landing, more stairs. Another door.

She might not even be able to open her eyes, but there was nothing wrong with her nose. And by the scent of a fire with fir-cones in it, of beeswax candles and lavender, she was in a bedchamber now. "This is the young Miss Roeswood, Mary Anne," said the female voice. "She's ill with grief, and she's drunk medicine that will make her sleep. Undress her and put her to bed."

The man carrying her stooped—her head lolled back—and laid her on a soft, but very large bed, with a muffled grunt.

The light footsteps and the heavy went away; the door opened and closed again. Someone began taking off her clothing, as if she was an over-large doll, and redressed her in a nightgown. The same someone—who must have been very strong—rolled her to one side, pulled the covers back, rolled her back in place, and covered her over.

Then, more footsteps receding. The door opening and closing again. Silence.

The state she drifted into then was not exactly sleep, and

not precisely waking. She seemed to drift in a fog in which she could see and hear nothing, and nothing she did affected it. There were others in this fog—she could hear them in the distance, but she could never find them, and when she called out to them, her voice was swallowed up by the endless mist.

It was, to be truthful, a horrible experience. Not at all restful. A deadly fatigue weighed her down, a malaise invaded her spirit, and despair filled her heart.

Finally, true sleep came, bringing oblivion, and with it, relief from her aching heart, at least for a time.

She woke with a start, the very feel of the bed telling her that yesterday's nightmare had been no thing of dreams, but of reality, even before she opened her eyes. And when she did open them, it was to find that she was staring up into the ochre velvet canopy of a huge, curtained bed. She sat up.

The room in which she found herself was as large as any four of the bedrooms in Blackbird Cottage put together. It had been furnished in the French style of a King Louis—she couldn't think of which one—all ornate baroque curlicues and spindly-legged chairs. The paper on the wall was watered silk in yellow, the cushions and coverlet more of the ochre velvet. There was a fireplace with a yellow marble mantle and hearth directly across from the foot of the bed, and a woman with brown hair tucked under a lace cap, a thin-faced creature in a crisp black-and-white maid's uniform and a cool manner, sitting in a chair beside it, reading. When Marina sat up, she put her book down, and stood up.

"Awake, miss?" she asked, with no inflection whatsoever.

No, I'm sleepwalking, Marina thought with irritation. The headache of yesterday in her temples had been joined by one at the back of her head, and whatever vile nastiness had been in the tea had left her with a foul taste in her mouth. But she answered the question civilly enough. "Yes, I am now. How long have I been asleep?"

The maid allowed a superior smile to cross her lips. "You've slept the clock around, miss. It's midmorning, two days after Boxing Day. But it's just as well you were asleep," the woman continued, turning and going to a wardrobe painted dark ochre, and ornamented with gilded scrollwork. "Madam has had her modiste here to make you some clothing fit to wear, and she only finished the first few items and delivered them an hour ago. You're in mourning, after all, and you need mourning frocks. And those things you brought with you—well, they weren't suitable." A sniff relegated her entire wardrobe to something not worth using as rags, much less being "fit to wear."

But the maid's words could only lead Marina to one horrified conclusion. "You didn't throw them out!" she exclaimed. "Not my clothes!"

The maid did not trouble to answer. Out of the wardrobe came a black velvet skirt, severely cut with a slight train, and a heavy black silk blouse, high-necked, and trimmed at wrists and neck with narrow black lace. Out of the drawers of a chest next to it came white silk underthings, black stockings, a corset, black satin slippers. All these were laid out at the end of the bed, and no sooner had Marina turned back the coverlet and stood up, then the maid pounced on her.

There could be no other description. Before Marina could make a move to reach for anything herself, the nightdress was whisked over her head, leaving her naked and shivering, and the maid was holding up the drawers for her to step into.

Marina had always wondered what it was like to be

dressed by a lady's maid, and now she was finding out with a vengeance. It was exactly like being a doll, and the maid was just as impersonal about the job as a woman in a toy-shop clothing one of the toys for display. In fact, the maid was ruthlessly efficient; before Marina had time to blink, the corset was on her, she had been turned to face the bed, and the woman was pulling at the laces with her knee in the small of Marina's back! And she was pulling *tightly,* much more tightly than the dressmaker in Holsworthy.

"Stop!" Marina protested, as her waist was squeezed into a circumference two sizes smaller than it had ever endured before. "I can't breathe!"

"You've never been properly corseted, miss," sniffed the maid, tugging harder. "Or you'd know that a lady doesn't need to puff and wheeze like a farm wench in a field. Shallow breaths, miss. A lady looks as if she isn't breathing at all."

Giving a final tug, the maid allowed Marina to stand straight up again—indeed, the corset hardly allowed any other posture. The laces were tied; three stiff petticoats, the last one of rustling black silk, came next. Then a chemise. And finally, the shirtwaist and skirt.

Feeling faint from lack of air, Marina was steered to a chair beside a dressing table with a mirror above it, both painted in dark ocher and ornamented with those baroque gold curlicues. The maid deftly unbraided her hair, brushed it out just as ruthlessly as she had done everything else and with a fine disregard for any pain caused when she encountered tangles, and proceeded to put it up in one of the pompadour hair styles that Marina had seen only in newspaper sketches. She had always longed to see her own hair like this—the arrangements looked so soft, and so very smart.

She'd had no idea that getting her hair done up in the fashionable style would involve being stuck so full of sharp-pointed hairpins that she thought her scalp was bleeding from a dozen places before the maid was through.

The maid fastened a jet cameo at her throat, and a matching jet locket on a slender chain around her neck. "There," she said at last, implying *now you're fit to be seen.*

The person staring back at Marina from the mirror was no one she recognized. The face was drawn and very white, and huge violet eyes stared back at her, with faint blue rings beneath them. Her pallor was only accentuated by the black silk of her blouse. Her hair had been arranged in the upswept style most favored by the PBs, with their delicate heart-shaped faces. It didn't suit Marina Roeswood.

"I'll take you down to meet your aunt now, miss," said the maid. "I am Mary Anne, and I will be your personal servant here from now on."

Giving her no choice in the matter, apparently. Personal maid—or watchdog for her aunt?

My own personal maid. Why does it seem as if she's higher in consequence than I am?

Perhaps, in this household, Mary Anne was.

"What happened to my things?" she asked, in a small voice, cowed by the icy correctness of the maid's manner. "My clothing—my books, my instruments, and my music—"

Another of those superior sniffs, and the maid looked down her long nose at Marina. "Miss could not possibly expect to wear those—frocks—in public," Mary Anne replied. "Madam said explicitly that they would not do, they would not do at all. *Not* the sort of thing miss would wish to encounter Madam's friends while wearing. However, the rest of your things have been put away in your private parlor." She waved her hand vaguely in the direction of the door. "Now, if you will please follow me, Madam wishes to speak with you."

As if she had a choice.

She followed the maid, who led her through that door and into a sitting room furnished in opulent reds, with a Turkey carpet on the floor, the whole done up in the style of the early part of Queen Victoria's reign. Quite frankly, Marina couldn't think of a pair of rooms less likely to make a Water Master comfortable. The bedroom produced a heavy feeling, the parlor made her feel horribly warm. Together they made her feel stifled, smothered. The ceilings in these rooms were high, they must have been twelve feet or more, and yet she still felt closed in and overheated. And there wasn't a chance that she'd be allowed to redecorate, either. She longed for her wonderful little room in Blackbird Cottage with an aching heart.

They walked for a good five minutes, going down a floor and all the way across a series of ever-more-opulent rooms. At the other end of the enormous house waited Arachne Chamberten, her new guardian.

Mary Anne opened a final door and motioned to Marina to enter as she stood aside. Still breathless, still feeling that her high collar was much too tight, Marina went in, and the door closed behind her.

In the center of a (relatively) small red room, in the exact middle of a carpet figured in red and black that looked to Marina's frightened eyes like a bed of hot coals, was a large, highly-polished wooden desk of ebony. Behind that desk sat a stunningly beautiful woman. Her hair was as black and as glossy as the heavy black silk-satin of her gown. Her skin was as white and translucent as porcelain. When she looked up, her black eyes stared right through Marina, her red lips smiled, but the smile didn't seem to reach beyond those lips.

She stood, and held out both hands. "Ah, my niece Marina, at last!" she said, in a sultry voice, warm as velvet laid before a fire. "You cannot know how deeply I regret the rift your parents saw fit to make with me; I saw you only once, at your christening, and never again. You have certainly changed greatly since that time."

Marina felt her lips move stiffly into a parody of a polite smile as she walked forward. She extended one hand, intending only to offer a mere handshake to her aunt, but Arachne drew her forward, captured the other hand before Marina could snatch it out of reach, and guided her to a chair beside her own behind the desk. Having both her cold hands, with skin roughened by the work she did in the kitchen and around the house, imprisoned in Arachne's warm, milk-smooth ones, felt distinctly uncomfortable. She tried to stiffen her own spine, and confronted Arachne's knowing eyes. "What do you mean when you say 'the rift my parents saw fit to make with you?' I never heard of any rift," she protested.

"And you never heard a word of me, did you?" Arachne countered. "That is precisely what I meant. Your father, who was my brother, and your Roeswood grandparents who were *our* father and mother, chose to cut me off from the family because of my marriage to Allan Chamberten. Perhaps it would be more charitable to say that it was my—our—parents' fault, and poor Hugh, child that he was at the time, simply followed their example. So I bear him no ill will; I only wish that I had managed a reconciliation before this. But who could have foreseen that he and Alanna would come to such a tragic end?"

For a moment, Marina thought that she would reach for the black silk handkerchief tucked into the waistband of her skirt in what could only be a feigned show of grief. For if she had been so totally estranged from Hugh and Alanna, how could any grief she felt be anything but feigned?

But she did nothing of the sort. She only sighed, and smiled, and squeezed Marina's hands. "Well, you and I shall be remedying that wrong, will we not? I take my responsibility as your guardian quite seriously, you may be sure of that."

"But I *had* guardians!" Marina burst out, angrily. "I was very happy there! *Why* did you send those horrible men—and policemen!—to kidnap me away from them? *They* were the people my parents chose to take care of me, not you!" She tried to wrench her hands away, but Arachne's grip was so strong it couldn't be broken.

Arachne bestowed the kind of pitying look on Marina that might be given a naughty child who had no notion of what she was saying. "My dear child, please. You are—at last—old enough to understand just how foolish your parents were—and how selfish." She shook her head. "Just listen to me for a moment, please, and don't interrupt. Are you under the impression that I don't know what they did with you? Do you think that I am not aware that they simply deposited you in that hive of artists and left you there? That they never, not once, attempted to see you? That they never troubled to see to it that you received the kind of upbringing someone of your wealth and social position should have had? And why do you think that happened?"

Since those very questions had passed through her mind more than once (though not, perhaps, phrased in quite that way), Marina was held dumb, hypnotized by the questions, and by Arachne's eyes. She shook her head slightly.

"Now, *I* do not know, not for certain," Arachne said. "I know only what my inquiries have brought to light. Alanna is—was—sensitive. Overly so, perhaps. Certainly she was of a very nervous disposition, and your birth was hard on her—very, very hard. Something happened then that terrified her; I have been unable to discover what it was, but whatever the cause was, you, a mere infant at the time, were at the heart of it, and she sent you away, as far away from

her as she could manage among her acquaintances."
Arachne shrugged, and the silk of her skirt rustled as she
shifted in her chair. "I know that Hugh considered your
artists to be friends, which was . . . something of a mistake,
a social faux pas, in my opinion. I know that they were visiting at the time of Alanna's fright, and I suspect that when
the emergency occurred, your father would have given you
into the keeping of whomsoever volunteered to take you. I
do know you were literally shoved into Margherita Tarrant's
arms and sent away with whatever could be bundled up
quickly into the cart that brought them here. I know this, because I have found witnesses among the servants who saw it
happen. Presumably they were the only ones among the
group that was visiting that were willing to accept the responsibility of an infant. For whatever reason, Alanna
Roeswood could not bear the sight of you, and my brother
chose his wife's welfare over that of his daughter."

The words struck her as hard as a rain of blows from a
cane. Marina could only sit with her hands limply in
Arachne's. Her head spun; this made altogether too much
sense.

But what about those letters? All those letters?

"He should have found someone to care for you more in
keeping with your rank and station, but he didn't."
Arachne's lips thinned. "I am not one to speak ill of the
dead, but my brother, I fear, must have been weak of will.
He allowed our parents to override him in the matter of myself, and he allowed his wife to dictate to him in the matter
of you. I am sorry, my dear, but he could not have chosen a
worse set of people to care for you. Oh, I know that they
were fond of you—I know they did their best for you! But
they have allowed you to run wild, they never sent you to a
proper finishing school nor got you a governess to teach
you, and they exposed you to all manner of improper

persons and impossible manners. In the matter of your wardrobe alone—" Her lips thinned even more with disapproval "—well, the less said about that, the better. Except that those so-called 'artistic reform tea-gowns' might have been the mode—in a certain circle—years ago, but they most certainly are not now, and the mere wearing of them would expose you to the utmost ridicule."

Marina dropped her eyes, her ears burning with embarrassment, torn between an instinctive urge to protest and the fear that her aunt was right. No matter what Elizabeth had said.

"Fortunately, by the standards of society, you are still a child, and your reputation has not suffered the irredeemable damage it would have if you were only a year older," Arachne continued. "I hope that my brother had the sense to realize that; I more than hope, I know—indeed, some of the things among his papers informed me that he had laid plans to bring you home before your eighteenth birthday. And certainly, by now even poor Alanna must have realized her fears, her terrors, could not be attached to a grown young woman. So, in order to carry out his wishes, I merely brought them forward—realizing as I did, once his men of business told me where you had been deposited, that you could not be left there a moment longer without terrible damage to your reputation." Once again, she squeezed Marina's hands as Marina stared down at them. Marina raised her eyes to meet her aunt's again, and Arachne smiled as she had before. "I knew you would, you must object to this removal. I knew that the Tarrants would object as well—they could not be expected to see why they were so unsuitable, poor things. That was why I proceeded as I did, why I moved to obtain legal custody of your person, why I sent people to remove you so quickly, and why I did it in the rather—authoritarian—manner that I chose."

Authoritarian? That's a mild term for kidnapping and drugging!

"But I did it for your own good, dear," Arachne concluded, as Marina had known she would. "I have been in society; *you* have not. Your former guardians may believe that it is possible to live above or beyond the social laws, but it is not. Not unless you wish to live a lonely and miserable existence, estranged from your peers, shunned by your equals, despised by your superiors. If you don't *object* to living here as a hermit on this estate for the rest of your life, well and good—but I should think that you would far rather find doors opening to you in welcome."

She couldn't help it; for years now, Marina had read the social pages in the newspaper, drunk in the descriptions of the glittering parties, the events, the receptions. She had pored over the sketches and photographs, and wished that her sketch or photograph could be among them . . . not that she aspired to the status of a PB, but the exciting round of the social scene beckoned so beguilingly.

Arachne chuckled, as if she could read Marina's thoughts. "Well, niece, your parents might have shunned my company, but I can assure you that no one else looks askance at the source of my wealth. The day, thank heaven, is long past when those who were born to rank and wealth can sneer down their noses at those who merely acquired it through hard work. And let me put one more possible fear of yours to rest—I have no interest in your inheritance. I am probably worth twice what you are; I own three pottery manufactories outright, and am partner in a fourth. I am also accepted in the best company; and I have every intention of seeing that you are accepted there as well. But first—" she sighed theatrically "—it is just as well that you are in mourning and cannot be expected to appear in public for the

next year, because you will need to work very hard before
you are ready for that society."

Oh, really? Anger flared at her aunt's assumptions, and
Marina felt her chin jut out stubbornly. "I know Latin,
Greek, French, Italian, and German, ma'am," she objected,
anger making her speak in a formal and stilted manner. "I
am familiar with a wide spectrum of literature and enough
science to satisfy a university examiner. I have read every
London paper published for the past five years. I am hardly
ignorant."

"Do you know how to properly address a duke, a countess, or a bishop?" Arachne countered, sharpness coming into
her voice for the first time. "I am painfully aware that you
do not know how to dress—do you know what to do at a
formal dinner? Could you eat *ortolon* or escargot or lobster
without disgracing yourself? Can you compose the appropriate invitations for a garden party, a masquerade ball, and
a formal dinner? Do you know when it is appropriate and
when it is inappropriate to discuss politics? Could you sit at
dinner with the Archbishop of Canterbury on your left and a
professional beauty on your right, and entertain both with
your conversation?" As Marina sat there, eyes wide,
Arachne continued ruthlessly. "How much is it appropriate
to leave as a tip for the servants of your host at a shooting
party? Do you know how to decide which invitations to decline and which to accept, and how to do both in such a way
that your would-be hostess is neither left feeling that you are
fawning on her nor insulting her? You may have a great deal
of *knowledge*, child, but you have no *learning*. And you
have a great deal to learn."

Finally she released Marina's hands. "Never fear. I am
going to see to it that you are fit for society. By the time you
are out of mourning, you will be able to take your place
among polite society with confidence. Now, I have work to

do, and so do you." She rang a bell on her desk, and the maid Mary Anne opened the door promptly. She must have been waiting just outside. "Mary Anne will take you to the dining room, where you will begin your education with your luncheon."

Marina rose, feeling as limp as a stalk of boiled celery. Arachne picked up a paper from her desk and began to read it. Seeing no other option, Marina turned and followed the stiff back of the maid out of the room.

It seemed that lack of options was going to be her life for the foreseeable future.

But not forever, she promised herself. *But not forever. . . .*

9

ARACHNE felt that her first interview with her niece had gone quite well. She'd kept the girl off-balance, inserted some doubts in her mind — and despite the girl's protestations to the contrary, she was not particularly impressed with Marina's intelligence. On the whole, she was, well, naive. Which was exactly how Arachne wanted things to remain.

She had the upper hand and kept it throughout the conversation — and discovered within the first couple of sentences that, contrary to her expectations, evidently no one had told the child anything about the curse or her aunt. How and why that had come about, she could not guess, but it gave her an advantage that she had never dreamed of having. With no expectations to counter, no preconceptions about her captor, it would be child's play to manipulate the girl and her emotions.

Arachne was no fool; within a year she had known that her curse had somehow misfired, and that the child had been removed into hiding. After an initial campaign to find the girl failed utterly, she had sat back and reconsidered her options for an entire year.

She had concentrated on consolidating her financial—and magical—position for the first five years. At the end of that time, she had solidified her social position, ensuring that any odd tales or accusations would be dismissed as lunatic raving. She had competent overseers in place who were absolutely terrified of her, enabling her to take her immediate attention off her manufactories and simply let the money accumulate. She had a very great deal of that money. And she had an impenetrable magical sanctuary. If she had been able to baffle her brother and his Elemental Mage friends before, she would be completely invisible and invulnerable now.

That was when she insinuated one single agent of her own into the office of their legal man and had their will destroyed. Then she worked one single, very powerful spell, to make everyone who had ever touched that will forget that it had ever existed. With Hugh and Alanna certain that, no matter what happened to them, Marina was safe until her majority—with the instrument of that safety gone—Arachne had ten years, more or less, to allow her campaign to mature.

So she bided her time, installed her own spies in Devon and Tuscany, and awaited the opportunity to strike—not at the child, which they were expecting, but at Hugh and Alanna themselves. She'd had plenty of practice already. After all, she had already eliminated her own parents, and Alanna's, though by means more mundane than magical.

She had known that the moment Hugh and Alanna were gone, the legal men would contact *her*—and once they were gone, intestate, leaving Arachne the only possible legal guardian, the law would give Arachne access to everything. Then it was just a simple matter of going through the carefully saved letters; putting them under lock and key did no good when Arachne was the keeper of the keys. Then, before the Tarrants got word of the tragedy themselves and spirited the child away—pounce. Stun them with the news of the deaths of their friends, and snatch the girl away with the backing of lawyers and police—that was the plan, and it worked to perfection. More than perfection, she had anticipated that the girl would have been warned, and that she might have to resort to any one of a number of complicated schemes, and at the least she would have had a dreadful struggle keeping her under control, until she decided what was to be done about her. Instead—the chit knew nothing—and Arachne's task had just been simplified enormously.

After she called Mary Anne back into the room to take the girl in charge, she pretended to read an invoice while the footsteps receded into the distance. She wasn't the only one waiting; after a moment, the door into the next room creaked, and her son Reggie stepped through.

She put the invoice down, and smiled at him. She was quite proud of him; he took entirely after her, and not after her late husband, who had been a pale and colorless sort of chap, although he'd been as cunning as a fox when it came to business.

Not cunning enough, though. Not at all curious about her associates, and what he called her "little hobbies." Not at all careful about what he ate.

Reggie had inherited his cunning, which he turned to all manner of things, not just business. He had sailed through university, not troubling to make the effort for a First or Second because all he wanted was the degree. It wasn't as if he was going to have to earn a living by means of it, so he enjoyed himself—and made social contacts. A great many social contacts. He was greatly sought after for every sort of party; facile, well-spoken, beautifully mannered and hand-some, he made the perfect escort for any unaccompanied woman, and was guaranteed to charm.

Reggie could have any young woman he chose, to tell the truth, between his darkly stunning good looks and his—her—money. His only faults were that he was lazy and arrogant, and women were more than inclined to overlook both those flaws in the face of charm, wealth, and ravishing features.

"Well?" she asked, as he dropped carelessly down into the chair that the girl had just vacated.

"She'll do—once your people bend her into the proper shape of a lady." He examined his fingernails with care, then graced her with a dazzling smile. "Properly subdued, she'll be ornamental enough, for as long as we choose to keep her. But I confess, I *cannot* imagine why no one ever told her about you!"

"Neither can I," Arachne admitted. "And for a moment, I toyed with the idea that she was feigning ignorance. But that child is as transparent as crystal; she couldn't hide a secret if her life depended on it."

Reggie laughed, showing very white teeth. "Appropriate, considering how much her life does depend on your will. How long do you intend to keep her?"

"I don't know yet," Arachne admitted, with a frown. "I don't know why my curse has gone dormant, for one thing, and I don't intend to do anything until I know the answer to that. She looks perfectly ordinary, magically speaking, with little more power than Mary Anne, so it can't be her doing."

"Your brother?" Reggie suggested, with a nod at the painting above the fireplace of the former owner of Oakhurst—a painting that Arachne intended to remove as soon as she could find something else that would fit there. Perhaps that landscape painting of a Roman ruin that was in the gallery. It would do until she could have a view of one of her manufactories commissioned.

"Hugh and Alanna were Earth Masters, but no more, and not outstandingly powerful. I think not. Whatever the cause, it must have been something that Hugh and Alanna had done to her." She rested both elbows on the desktop, and propped her chin on one slender hand, watching him thoughtfully. "That, in itself, is interesting. I didn't think they'd know anyone who'd even guess what I'd done, much less find a counter to it. I confess, I'm intrigued . . . it's a pretty puzzle."

Reggie laughed again. "Perhaps that was why they sent her away in the first place. You know, you were right—it was useful to get that university degree in a science. Applying principles of science to magic, I can think of any number of theoretical things that could have been done to your curse. It occurred to me, for instance, that some sort of dampening or draining effect could account for the failure of the curse, and it might affect everything around her. You know, she might actually function as a kind of grounding wire, draining the magic of those around her."

Arachne studied him for a moment; sometimes he threw things out as a red herring, just to see if she pursued them into dead ends he'd already foreseen, but this time she thought he was offering something genuine. "An interesting thought. But then, why would other Elemental Masters be willing to take her in, if she'd be a drain on their power?"

"It depends entirely on how much they used their magic," he replied, steepling his fingers over his chest. "Not every Elemental Master cares about magic; some seem to be content to be merely the custodians of it."

She tapped her cheek with one long finger. "True. And the more deeply buried in rustication, the less they seem to care."

"Such as the artists in question," Reggie nodded. "My guess is, they used magic very little, not enough to miss its loss, considering that their real energy goes into art." He looked sideways at her, shrewdly. "And it also depends on how powerful they were to begin with. If the answer is, 'not very,' then they were losing very little to gain a great deal. I have no doubt that Hugh compensated them well to care for his daughter."

"Not as well as I would have thought," Arachne replied, thoughtfully. "Not nearly as well as I would have thought, according to the accounts. Unless he disguised extra payments in some way."

"Perhaps he did—or perhaps it was paid in gifts, or in favors, instead—clients for paintings, for instance. Or perhaps the Tarrants are merely good *Christians.*" The sneer in his voice made her smile. "And they considered it their *Christian* duty to raise the poor child, afflicted as she was with a terrible curse."

"Considering that the girl and the Tarrant woman were out on a Boxing Day delivery to the local padre when my men came for her, that may well be the case," Arachne admitted. "Until we're sure, though, that there is no such effect around her, we had better do *our* work well away from her."

That, of course, was so easily done that Reggie didn't even trouble to comment on it. They hadn't even begun to set up a workspace here at Oakhurst, and at the moment, it was probably wiser not to bother.

"I liked that little speech about your properties, by the way, mater," Reggie continued, watching her with hooded eyes. "It was all the better for having the ring of sincerity."

She had to laugh herself at that. "Well of course, it was sincere. I don't want or need Oakhurst. But you—"

"Which brings me to the next question, Mother Dear. *Are* we taking the marriage option?" There was a gleam in his heavy-lidded eyes that indicated he didn't find this at all displeasing.

"I think we should pursue it," she replied firmly. "There is nothing in any of our other plans that would interfere with it, or be interfered with by it. But it does depend on you exerting yourself to be charming, my sweet." She reached out to touch his hand with one extended index finger. He caught the hand and pressed a kiss on the back of it.

"Now that I've seen the wench, I'm not averse," he responded readily enough. "She's not a bad looking little filly, and as I said, once your people have trained her, she'll be quite comely. So long as there's nothing going on with her in that area of magic that physical congress could complicate, once wedded and bedded, we'll have absolute control over her." He looked at his watch. "Speaking of which—"

"Indeed," Arachne said warmly. "It *is* your turn, isn't it? Well, run along, dear; take the gig and the fast horses, and try to be back by dawn."

Reggie stood up, kissed his mother's hand again, and saluted her as he straightened. "I go, but to return. This little play, I fancy, is going to prove utterly fascinating."

Arachne studied the graceful line of his back as he strode away, and felt her lips curve in a slight smile. He was so very like her—it was a good thing he was her son, and not her mate.

Because if she had been married to him or had been his lover—well, he was so like her that she would have felt forced, eventually, to kill him. And that would have been a great pity.

Marina had never felt so lost and alone in her life. Nor so utterly off balance. Luncheon was an ordeal. And it was just as well that Marina had no appetite at all, because she would have been half sick before she actually got to eat anything.

The maid—or rather, keeper—led her to a huge room with a long, polished table in it that would easily have seated a hundred. It was covered at a single place with a snowy linen tablecloth, and she saw as she neared that there was a single place setting laid out there.

But *such* a place setting! There was so much silverware that she could have furnished everyone at a meal at Blackbird Cottage with a knife, fork, and spoon! There were six differently shaped glasses, and many different sizes of plates, some of which were stacked three high immediately in front of the chair. With the maid standing over her, and a manservant to pull out the chair, she seated herself carefully, finding the corset binding under her breasts and under her arms as she did so.

And the first thing the footman did when she was seated was to take away the plates that had been immediately in front of her.

After some fussing at a sideboard behind her—and she only surmised it was a sideboard, because she thought she heard some subdued china-and-cutlery sounds—he returned, and placed a shallow bowl of broth resting on a larger plate in front of her. At least, she thought it was broth. There was no discernible aroma, and it looked like water that oak leaves had been steeping in for a very short time.

If this is what rich people eat—I'm not impressed. She picked up a spoon at random.

But before she could even get it near the bowl, the maid coughed in clear disapproval. Marina winced.

Arachne had hammered her with questions about "could she properly eat" all manner of things that she had never heard of. It seemed that meals were going to be part of her education.

She picked up another spoon. Another cough.

At this rate, she thought, looking at the other five spoons beside the plated soup, *I'll never get any of this into my mouth. . . .*

The third try, though, was evidently the right one. Her triumph was short-lived, however. She leaned forward.

Another cough sent her bolt upright, as if she'd had a board strapped to her back. The cough warned her that a full spoon was also *de trop.* Evidently only a few drops in the bottom of the bowl of the spoon were appropriate, which was just as well, since she was evidently required to sit straight-spined and look directly ahead and not at what she was doing, as she raised the nearly empty spoon to her lips to sip—not drink—the soup. The spoon was not to go into the mouth; only the rim was to touch the lips. The broth, by now cold, tasted faintly of the spirit of the beef that had made it. And it was going to take forever to finish it.

Except that after only six or seven spoonfuls, the footman took it away, and returned with something else—

She blinked at it. Was it a salad? Perhaps—there seemed to be beetroot involved in it somehow.

A cough recalled her to her task—for it was a task, and not a meal—and she sorted through silverware again until she found the right combinations. And this time, coughs directed her through a complicated salute of knife and fork before she was cutting a tiny portion correctly.

Two mouthfuls, and again the food was removed, to be replaced by something else.

In the end, luncheon, an affair that usually took no more than a quarter of an hour at home, had devoured an hour and a half of her time—perhaps two hours—and had left her feeling limp with nervous exhaustion. She *had* gotten something like a meal, though hardly as full a meal as a real luncheon would have been, but the waste of food was nothing short of appalling! And there had been nothing, *nothing* there that would have satisfied the appetite of a healthy, hungry person. There was a great deal of sauce, of garnish, of fripperies of hothouse lettuce and cress, but it all tasted utterly pale, bland, and insipid. The bread had no more flavor than a piece of pasteboard; the cheese was an afterthought. Even the chicken—at least, she thought it was chicken— was a limp, overcooked ghost of a proper bird.

No wonder Aunt Arachne is so pale, she thought wearily, as the silent footman removed her chair so she could leave the table, *if she's eating nothing but food like this.*

Her headache had returned, and all she wanted was to go back to that stifling room and lie down—but evidently that was not in the program for the afternoon.

"Miss will be coming with me to the library," Mary Anne said, sounding servile enough, but it was very clear to Marina that there was going to be no argument about it. "Madam wishes me to show her to her desk, where she is to study."

Oh yes . . . study. After that interview with Aunt Arachne, Marina thought she had a pretty good idea just what it was that her aunt wanted her to study, and indeed, she was right.

Her keeper took her to the Oakhurst library; the house itself was Georgian, and this was a typical Georgian library, with floor-to-ceiling bookshelves on all the walls, and extra bookshelves placed at intervals within the room. There were three small desks and many comfortable-looking windsor chairs and two sofas arrayed about the room, and a fine carpet on the floor. There were not one, but two fireplaces, both going, which kept an otherwise chilly room remarkably warm and comfortable. Someone cleaned in here regularly; there was no musty smell, just the scent of leather with a hint of wood smoke. Placed at a library window for the best light was one of the desks; this was the one Mary Anne brought her to. On a stand beside it were several books that included *Burke's Peerage* and another on *Graceful Corre-spondence*; on the desk itself were a pen, ink, and several sorts of stationery. And a list. She supposed that it was in Arachne's hand.

She sat down at the desk; the maid—*definitely* keeper—sat on one of the library sofas. Evidently Mary Anne was not deemed knowledgeable enough to pass judgment on the documents that Marina was expected to produce. She picked up the list.

Invitations to various sorts of *soirees* to a variety of peo-ple. Responses to invitations issued (in theory) to her. Thank you notes for gifts, for invitations, after an event; polite little notes about nothing. Notes of congratulation or condo-lence, of farewell or welcome. Longer letters—subjects in-cluded—to specific persons of consequence. Nothing, she noticed, to anyone who was actually supposed to be a friend . . . but perhaps people like Arachne didn't have friends.

As soon as she picked up the slim volumes on corre-spondence, she realized that there literally was not enough information here to perform this particular task correctly. And *that* was when she began to get angry. Like luncheon, Arachne had arranged for defeat and failure. And she'd done it on purpose, because she already knew that Marina didn't have training in the nuances of society, no more than any simple, middle-class working girl.

But—*but*—Marina knew what that simple, middle-class working girl didn't. She knew how to *find* the information she needed. For this was a library, and a very big one which might very well contain other books on etiquette. Marina knew that her father's library had been cataloged, and re-cently, because Alanna had written about some of the old books uncovered during the process, and how they'd had to be moved under lock and key. So instead of sitting there in despair, or looking frantically for somewhere to start, leafing through stationery or *Burke's*, she got up.

Mary Anne looked up from her own reading, startled, but evidently had no direct orders this time about what Marina was supposed to do in here, other than remain in the room. When Marina moved to the great book on the center table — the catalog — she went back to her own reading, with a little sneer on her face.

Huh! So you don't know everything, do you? Marina thought with satisfaction.

Just as she had thought, because the person who had cataloged the library was very thorough, he had cataloged every book in the house and moved them here. This included an entire set of books, described and cataloged as "juvenalia, foxed, defaced, poor condition" filed away in a book cupboard among other similar items. No true book lover would *ever* throw a book out without express orders. *Besides, every true book lover knows that in three hundred years, what was "defaced" becomes "historical."*

Presumably young Elizabeth Tudor's governess had boxed her ear for defacing that window at Hatfield House with her diamond ring. Now no amount of money could replace it.

So, from the catalog, Marina went to the book cupboard where less-than-desirable volumes were hidden away from critical eyes in the farthest corner of the library. The cupboard was crammed full, floor-to-ceiling, with worn-out books, from baby picturebooks to some quite impressive student volumes of Latin and Greek and literature in several languages.

She stared at the books for a moment; and in that moment, she realized that she was so surrounded by familiar auras that she almost wept.

These were the books that Aunt Margherita, Uncle Thomas, and Uncle Sebastian had been taught from! And her parents, of course. If she closed her eyes and opened her mind and widened her shields enough to include the books, she could *see* them, younger, oh much younger than they were now, bent over desks, puzzled or triumphant or merely enjoying themselves, listening, learning.

A tear oozed from beneath her closed eyelid, and almost, *almost,* she pulled her shields in —

But no! These ghosts of the past could help her in the present. She opened her eyes. *Show me what I need,* she told the wisps of memory, silently, and began brushing her hand slowly along the spines of books on the shelves, the worn, cracked spines, thin leather peeling away, fabric worn to illegibility. She didn't even bother to read the titles, as she concentrated on the task she had before her, and the feel of the books under her fingertips.

Which suddenly stuck to a book, as if they'd encountered glue. There!

She pulled the book off the shelf and set it at her feet, then went back to her perusal. She didn't neglect even the sections that seemed to have only picturebooks, for you never knew what might have been shoved in where there was room.

When she'd finished with the entire cupboard, she had a pile at her feet of perhaps a dozen books, none of them very large, that she picked up and carried back to her desk. Mary Anne looked up, clearly puzzled, but remained where she was sitting.

Good. Because these, the long-forgotten, slim volumes of instruction designed to guide very young ladies through the intricacies of society at its most baroque, were precisely what she needed.

That, and a fertile imagination coupled with a good memory of Jane Austen's novels, and other works of fiction. Perhaps her replies would seem formal, even stilted, and certainly old-fashioned, but that was far better than being wrong.

Her handwriting was as good, if not better, than Arachne's; there would be nothing to fault in *her* copperplate. And she decided to cheat, just a little. Instead of actually leafing through the books to look up what she needed to know, she followed the same "divination" that had directed her to these books in the first place. She ran her hand along the book spines until her fingers "stuck," then took up that volume and turned pages until they "stuck" again.

After that, it was a matter of verifying titles with *Burke's*, and virtually copying out the correspondence from the etiquette books—with creative additions, as her whimsy took her. Not too creative though; she mostly adopted "personalities" from the books she had read for the various people she was supposed to be writing to.

When she was done, after a good four hours of work, she had an aching hand, but a feeling of triumph, only tempered by the fact that sitting for four straight hours in a tightly laced corset left her feeling half-strangled and longing for release.

She glanced over to her keeper, and saw that Mary Anne was still immersed in her novel. Her lips thinned.

I don't believe I'm going to reveal the secret of my success, she decided, and picking up her books, went back to the rear of the library.

But instead of putting the books back in the cupboard in which she'd found them—because it occurred to her that she might need them again—she concealed them among a shelf of geography books. Then she returned to the cupboard and sought out further books of instruction in manners, and did the same with them. In particular, she found a little book with pictures designed to lead a child through the maze of cutlery at a formal dinner that she actually hid inside another book, for retrieval later. She suspected that she would still have to learn these arcane rituals by doing them, but at least this way she would make fewer mistakes.

Only then did she select a novel herself from the shelves and retire demurely to her desk. And just at sunset, Arachne appeared.

When she saw that Marina was reading, her lips hinted at a smile. At least, Marina *thought* they did. But when she saw the neatly stacked and addressed envelopes in the tray, she definitely frowned.

One at a time, she picked them up, studied the address, opened the envelope and read what was contained inside, then discarded envelope and missive in the wastepaper basket beside the desk, saying nothing. Finally, she finished the last, dropped it on the top of the pile of discards, and turned a frosty smile on Marina.

"Well done," she said, in a tone that suggested—nothing. Neither approval, nor disapproval. "But I thought you were not aware of the rules of polite address? When I questioned you earlier, you gave me the impression that you had been raised—quite rustically."

Marina licked her lips. "I have—read a good many novels of society, Aunt," she said carefully. "And the books that you left with me guided me in the exercise that you set me."

Carefully chosen truth—provided that "the books left" included the entire library.

"Novels." Arachne gave her a penetrating look, tempered with veiled disbelief. "A clever use of fiction, niece, but you should be aware that the authors of these books are not always careful in their research. And most, if not all of them, are not or never were members of polite society."

"Yes, Aunt," Marina replied, bowing her head so that Arachne would not see her eyes.

"And now you must dress for dinner. Mary Anne?" Arachne swept out of the room, the train of her black silk skirt trailing on the floor behind her with a soft hiss. She was gone before the maid even responded to her peremptory summons.

Dress for dinner. Well, Marina had an idea what *that* meant. Novels were full of it. Apparently her aunt expected that even when there were only the two of them, dinner would be completely formal.

She followed the maid back to her room—through the oppressive sitting room, through the stifling bedroom, but the woman beckoned her onward, through a door on the opposite side of the room that she had not noticed.

Past that door was a dressing room and a bathroom. A surprising bathroom, the like of which, frankly, Marina had never seen before. It had been done up in the style of a Roman bath, as designed by a modern artist. And it was the first room in the house in which she could draw a free breath.

The bathroom was plumbed in the most modern fashion. There was a huge bathtub, a flushing water closet, and even a shower-bath in one corner. Mary Anne went to the bathtub and immediately began drawing a hot bath. Hot water came out of the bronze, fish-shaped spigot, which meant there was a boiler somewhere nearby.

The bathroom itself was decorated in Marina's colors, greens and aquas! Green muslin curtains hung at the windows, green mosaics of shells and seaweed decorated the walls and floor, even the tub was painted green, and the fixtures were green-patinaed bronze. Mary Anne stripped her of her clothing as she stared wide-eyed around her; the moment the corset came off and she could take a deep breath, she did so, feeling free for the first time that day.

When Mary Anne left, she quickly adjusted the temperature of the bath—the maid had run it too hot for comfort—and got into it before her keeper could return. The tub was enormous, far bigger than the baths they used in winter in Blackbird Cottage. She wanted to lay back at her ease in her own element, but if she did, the odious maid would probably insist on bathing her, or washing her hair for her.

So she began her own scrub, so that Mary Anne would not be tempted to lend a hand. And to avoid the rough-handed maid's "caresses" to her head, she let down her hair and washed it first, pinning it up atop her head, wet, when she was finished. Mary Anne hurried in when she heard the splashing, too late to interfere with the hair-washing; she frowned, perhaps because she'd been thwarted, but possibly because her mistress had given her no orders about what to do if Marina managed to act on her own.

"I wouldn't have washed my hair, miss," she said with unconcealed disapproval. "It being so near dinnertime and all."

But it wasn't—it wasn't even six o'clock, and formal dinner was never until eight. "I'll dry it in front of the fire," Marina said. "It dries very fast." And with that, she arose from the tub, donned the loose—thankfully loose!—dressing gown that Mary Anne hastily held out, took a brush from the dressing table and sat on a stool in front of the fire in the bedroom.

This is an Earth bedroom. Could it have been Mother's? She thought not; but—the sitting room was reds . . . Fire? Could it have been Thomas'? There was another room on the other side of the sitting room—if that one was a Fire room, it would make sense that the uncles would have been near to each other when they lived here. *And Uncle Thomas wouldn't have minded a sitting room in Fire colors.*

There was no trace of Thomas now, but just thinking that the room might have been his made it seem less stifling. She brushed out her hair herself, carefully working through the knots and tangles, and used a tiny touch of magic to drive the water out of it. She had no desire to incur Arachne's further disapproval by appearing at dinner with damp hair.

With a full hour remaining before dinner, somewhat to Mary Anne's astonishment, her hair was dry and ready to be dressed, and so was she.

Her hour of freedom was over. It was time to be laced back into her imprisoning corsets.

Black again, of course; this time a satin skirt with a train, a black silk blouse with the same high neck as before, but this time a quantity of black jet bead trimming. Mary Anne pinned her hair up in a more formal style, with a set of black jet combs ornamenting it. *Pinned* was the word; once again, Marina wondered that there wasn't blood trickling down her scalp.

But Mary Anne did not conduct her to dinner when the gong rang; instead, she excused herself, leaving Marina to find her own way down. Which she did; it wasn't *that* difficult. Georgian houses like Oakhurst weren't the kind of insane mazes that houses that had been built up over hundreds of years turned into.

Dinner was not quite as difficult as luncheon, although it was just as uncomfortable. Arachne was already there, although she hadn't been waiting long. The footman seated Marina; Arachne was served first, Marina second. Arachne sat at the head of the table, Marina down the side, some distance away from her aunt. At least Mary Anne with her disapproving coughs was not in attendance.

When the footman served the first course, before she

reached for a utensil, she heard a discreet sound from him, more of a clearing of his throat, hardly loud enough to hear. And before the footman took the tureen away, she noticed that he was pointing at one of the spoons with his little finger.

She took it up, glanced at him; he smiled, only for a second, and very faintly. Then his face resumed its proper mask, and he retreated to the sideboard.

She had an ally!

She watched his hands through the rest of the meal, aware that her aunt was waiting until *she* picked up an implement before reaching for the appropriate bit of silverware herself. And as they moved through the courses, and her aunt began to develop a tiny crease between her brows, it suddenly occurred to her that if she didn't want Arachne to guess that she was being coached and had a friend here, she'd better make a mistake.

So she did—the next course was fish, and even though she actually *knew* what the fish-knife and fish-fork looked like, she reached for the ones she'd used for the salad.

"Marina," Arachne said dryly, "If you don't want to be thought a bumpkin, you had better use *these* tools for the fish course in future." She held up the proper implements.

"Yes, Aunt," Marina said subserviently, reaching for the right silverware, with a sidelong glance at the footman and a very quick wink when Arachne's eyes dropped to her plate. The footman winked back.

The food was still pallid stuff. And there was still an appalling waste of it. But at least at this meal, Marina got hot food warm, and cold food cool. And despite a general lack of appetite, enough of it to serve.

And the fruit and cheese at the end were actually rather good. Arachne regarded her over the rim of her wineglass.

"After dinner, when there is company, in general the

company gathers in the sitting room or the card room for conversation or games. Perhaps music—I believe you brought instruments?" This time she only raised her brows a trifle, and not as if she found this fact an evidence of her rustication.

"Yes, Aunt," she said. "I play Elizabethan music, mostly."

"Pity; that's not anything considered entertaining for one's guests these days," Arachne said, dismissively. "I don't suppose you have much in the way of conversation, either."

Marina kept her thoughts to herself; in any case, Arachne didn't wait for an answer. "I will be teaching you polite conversation, later, when I have your affairs in hand. I don't suppose you can ride."

"Actually, I had use of one of the local hunt master's jumpers, Aunt." It gave her a little feeling of triumph to see the surprise on Arachne's face. "I didn't hunt often, and mostly only when he needed someone to keep an eye on an unsteady lady guest, but he kept his favorite old cob retired on our land."

"Well." Arachne coughed, to cover her surprise. "In that case . . . my modiste is coming with more garments for you tomorrow. I'll order proper riding attire for you; your father's stable isn't stunning, but it's adequate. I'm sure you'll find something there you can mount." Her expression turned thoughtful. "Actually, riding and hunting are two elements of proper conversation you can make use of at nearly any time; keep that in mind. And books, but they mustn't be controversial or too modern *or* too old-fashioned—unless, of course, you are speaking to an older lady or gentleman, in which case they will be pleased that you are reading the books of their youth. Tomorrow you will meet my son,

Reginald. I have instructed him to see that you are not left at loose ends."

I would like very much to be left at loose ends, thank you, she thought, but she answered with an appreciative murmur.

"I'm pleased to see that you are no longer hysterical; I hope you realize how childish your reaction was to being removed from what you must see was an unsuitable situation," Arachne concluded, putting her glass down.

"Yes, Aunt."

"And I hope you are properly grateful."

"Yes, Aunt." *I'm grateful that I haven't lost my temper with you yet.*

"Excellent. I believe that we have reached a good understanding." Arachne rose; the slight tug on her chair by the footman warned Marina that she should do the same. "As I said, I have tasks to complete; I suggest that you improve your mind with a book in your sitting room before bed. I will see you at breakfast, Marina."

"Yes, Aunt," she replied obediently, and Arachne flowed off in the direction of the office in which Marina had first found her, leaving Marina to her own devices.

10

WITHIN an hour, Marina learned that she had more than one ally among the staff.

The second one appeared once the formidable Mary Anne had undressed her with the same ruthless efficiency she showed when getting her dressed, and left her, dressing-gowned and night-gowned for the night, with her hair in a comfortable braid, and instructions to ring for one of the downstairs maids "if you need anything." The tone implied that there was nothing she should need, and her attitude was quite intimidating, except for one thing. Apparently, Mary Anne was above being summoned once her mistress was put to bed for the night, and on the whole, at this point Marina was inclined to take her chances with anyone that Mary Anne considered an inferior.

Once Mary Anne was gone, Marina moved into the sitting room, with a single book of poetry she had found on a table there for company, until the corridor beyond the door was very quiet indeed. Then, barefoot (because the slippers that had been supplied to her had very hard leather soles that would have clattered on the parquet floor) she tiptoed down to the library, ascertained that there was no one there, and retrieved those books of etiquette that she had hidden there. And as an afterthought, collected some real reading material, as well as some duller books that she could use to hide her studies in. Somewhere in her rooms were the books she had brought with her; when she'd arranged these on the shelves, she'd look for her own things, and with any luck, there'd be enough books there to make looking through them too tedious for the very superior Mary Anne.

Moving silently, her feet freezing, she quickly made her way back to her rooms, where she put her finds on the shelves in the sitting room. She worked quietly among the ornaments she found on the shelves, putting the books up without disarranging them, in the hopes of making it appear that the books had always been there. She guessed that no one in Arachne's household realized that all the books had been collected in the library; Mary Anne had seen her using books there this afternoon, she would assume that the books were still there and not look for them here. She was still setting back vases and figurines when the sound of the door opening made her jump and turn quickly, guiltily.

But the person in the door wasn't her aunt, nor the supercilious Mary Anne; it was a young woman in a very much plainer version of Mary Anne's uniform—the black skirt, but of plain wool, the black shirtwaist, unadorned—and a neat white apron, rather than the black silk that Mary Anne sported. A perfectly ordinary maid—with a round, pretty, farm girl's face, and wary eyes.

"I come to see if you needed anything, miss," the girl whispered, as if she was not quite sure of her welcome.

In a response that Marina could not have controlled if she'd tried, her stomach growled. Audibly.

And the little maidservant broke into an involuntary grin, which she quickly hid behind her hand.

"I suppose it wouldn't do any good to ask for something to eat," Marina said, wistfully assuming the negative. "I don't want you to get in any trouble with the cook or the— the housekeeper? I guess there's a housekeeper here, isn't there?" She sighed. From what she'd heard from old Sarah, the housekeepers in great houses held the keys to the pantry and kept strict tally of every morsel that entered and left, and woe betide the staff if the accounting did not match.

The girl dropped her hand and winked. "Just you wait, miss," she said warmly, and whisked out the door.

Marina finished shelving her books, hiding the ones she didn't want anyone to find. By the time the maid returned, she was in a chair by the fireplace with a book in her hands, having mended the fire and built it up herself, warming her half-frozen feet. The girl seemed much nicer than Mary Anne, but there was no telling if she was just another spy for her aunt. Let her think that Marina had only been looking for something to read.

The girl had left the door open just about an inch, and on her return, pushed it open with her foot. She carried with her a laden tray, which she brought over to Marina and set down on the little table beside her. Marina stared at the contents with astonishment.

"Mister Reginald, he likes a bit to eat around midnight, so the pantry's not locked up," the girl said cheerfully. "My Peter, he told us downstairs about your luncheon. And supper. And Madam's special cook—" she made a face. "Miss, we don't think much of that special cook. Only person that likes his cooking is Madam; it isn't even the kind of thing that Mister Reginald likes, so he's always eating a midnight supper. So I thought, and Peter thought, you mightn't like that cooking much either, even if you hadn't got more than a few bites of it."

"You were right," Marina said with relief at the sight of a pot of hot chocolate, a plate of sliced ham and real, honest cheese—none of that sad, pale stuff that Arachne had served—a nice chunk of hearty cottage loaf—and a fine Cox's Orange Pippin apple. "I feel like I haven't eaten in two days!"

"Well, miss, I don't much know about yesterday, but according to my Peter, you haven't had more than a few mouthfuls today at luncheon and dinner, and no breakfast at all. Just you tuck into that! I'll wait and take the plates away." She winked conspiratorially. "We'll let that housekeeper think that Mister Reginald's eating a bit more than usual."

Since Marina was already tucking in, wasting no time at all in filling her poor, empty stomach, the little maid beamed with pleasure. "If you really don't mind waiting," Marina said, taking just long enough from her food to gulp down a lovely cup of chocolate, "You ought to at least sit down." She paused a moment, and added, "I'm sure I oughtn't to invite you, according to Aunt Arachne."

"Madam is very conscious of what is proper," the maid said, her mouth going prim. But Marina noticed that she sat right down anyway. She considered Marina for a moment more, then asked, "Miss, how early are you like to be awake?"

Oh no—surely Madam wakes up before dawn, and I'm supposed to be, too, she thought, already falling into the habit of thinking of her aunt as "Madam"—"Oh—late, if I'm given the choice," she admitted, shamefacedly. "No earlier than full sun, seven, even eight."

"You think that late?" the maid stifled a giggle. "That Mary Anne, she won't bestir herself before ten, earliest, and

Madam keeps city hours herself. We-ell, miss, what do you say to a spot of conspiracy between us? Just us Devon folk—for we can't be letting Mister Hugh—" and here she faltered, before catching herself, and continuing resolutely. "We can't be letting Mister Hugh's daughter fade away to naught. I'll be bringing you a proper breakfast sevenish, and a bit of proper supper after that Mary Anne has took herself off of a night. So you won't go hungry, even if that Mary Anne has got a bee in her bonnet that you ought to be scrawny."

Marina was overwhelmed, and couldn't help herself; this was the first open kindness she'd had since she'd been kidnapped—was it only yesterday? She began to cry.

"Oh miss—there now, miss—" The maid plied her with a napkin, then ran into the bedroom and fetched out handkerchiefs from somewhere, and dabbed at Marina's cheeks with them. Very fine cambric they were too, her aunt certainly wasn't stinting her in the matter of wardrobe. "Now miss, you mustn't cry—Mister Hugh and Missus Alanna wouldn't like that—"

For a moment, Marina was tempted to tell her the truth, all of it; but no, this girl would never understand. "I'm—alone—" she managed, as the maid soothed her, sitting beside her and patting her hand. That was true—true enough. Not the whole truth, but true enough.

She didn't cry herself sick this time, and perhaps it was the best thing she could have done, though it was entirely involuntary, for by the time that she cried herself out, she knew that she had friends here, after all. She also knew, if not everything there was to know about the "downstairs" household, at least a very great deal. She knew that the maid was Sally, she was going to marry the footman Peter one day, that Arachne had dismissed the upper servants—the chief cook (replaced by her "chef"), the housekeeper and butler, her own personal maidservant, the valet.

Of course, the maidservant and the valet were still stranded in Italy, poor things. The other servants weren't even sure they would be able to get home, for Arachne had left orders that Marina's parents were to be buried in Italy where they had died.

"'Where they so loved to live,' that was what Madam Arachne said. And it isn't my place to say," Sally continued, in a doubtful whisper, "But it did seem to me that Mister Hugh and Missus Alanna loved it *here*. This is where the family was all buried, and I know Mister Hugh felt strong about his family."

But Arachne couldn't replace all the servants—trained city servants weren't very willing to move to the country, not without a substantial rise in wages. So a substantial number of the lower servants were the same as had served Marina's parents, and they remembered their kind master and mistress. Although they knew nothing about Hugh's sister, except that she'd fallen out with her parents over her choice of husband, that counted more against her than her blood counted for her.

And although they were very circumspect with regard to Arachne and her son, they were all very sympathetic to Marina, *especially* after seeing the ordeals she was undergoing at the hands of Arachne and Mary Anne. *She* was Devon-bred as well as born, almost one of them, even if she did come from over near to the border with Cornwall. If they didn't know why she'd been sent away, at least she hadn't been sent far; she wasn't a foreigner, and she didn't have *any* airs.

And one and all, these downstairs servants hated Mary Anne.

"Fancies herself a superior lady's maid, she does," Sally

sniffed. "Too good to eat with us, has her meals with the butler and housekeeper, if you please. And it isn't as if Madam
Arachne doesn't have her own maid, for she does, a French
woman. Well, things have changed for us." She sighed pen-
sively. "But miss, we'll take care of you, don't you worry. If
Madam Arachne wants you to be made a lady like her, we'll
help you out, till there isn't nothing you don't know. There's
Peter, he served with Lord Bridgeworth, and *he* knows all
the right things—and it wasn't as if Mister Hugh and Missus Alanna weren't gentry. We'll help you, for you're *ours,*
and we won't ever forget that!"

Marina swallowed down another lump in her throat and
a spate of hastily suppressed tears with her hot chocolate.

"Thank you," she said, hoping she put the gratitude she
felt into those simple words.

By the warm smile on Sally's face, she did.

Morning brought Sally with a proper breakfast tray—the
kind of hearty breakfast Marina was used to getting at
home—from thick country bacon to hot, buttered toast.
There was only one thing missing, oat porridge, which was
just as well, since she would have felt homesick on seeing
it, guilty if she hadn't eaten it, and miserable if she did. Sally
waited while she ate, and whisked the tray away, leaving her
to go back to sleep again if she chose.

Which was a confirmation this was all being done in secret, abetted by a conspiracy among the lower servants, the
ones who remembered her parents.

For some reason, they did not trust her aunt to treat her
properly. Why? She couldn't think of any reason why
Arachne would mistreat her on purpose—she was clearly a
very cold woman, but she seemed determined to do her duty
to Marina. Even if her idea of her duty was not what Marina

would have chosen for herself. She wasn't stinting on wardrobe, that was sure. The clothing that she'd had made for Marina was of first quality and highest workmanship.

But servants saw and heard everything. Probably they were only worried that she was so unhappy and was being bullied. In any case, life was going to be much easier with the kind of help they had already offered, and she was not going to betray them by any carelessness on her part.

So she made sure that there was no sign that anyone had been in her rooms, and tucked herself back up in her bed, dozing until the odious Mary Anne appeared to wake her by pulling back the curtains and making a great clattering of noise with the breakfast-tray that *she* had brought.

It was breakfast for an invalid. A nauseated invalid. Or someone afraid of getting fat. Weak tea, and four pieces of cold toast.

With a silent prayer of thanks for Sally's foresight, Marina drank a cup of the tea, but before she could eat more than a single piece of the toast, Mary Anne insistently dragged her out of bed and into her clothing. "Madam's modiste is here, and miss must be measured again and select fabrics and patterns," the maid ordered. "Madam is also selecting clothing, and miss must not monopolize the modiste's time, nor keep her waiting."

This was said as Mary Anne was lacing up her corset, and as Marina suddenly remembered a trick that one of the ponies used to employ, of blowing himself up so that his girth couldn't be tightened. And it occurred to her at that moment that if she could just manage the same trick, herself—

So she secretly took in the deepest breath that she could, and instead of trying to draw herself up, hunched herself over, sticking her stomach out as far as she could manage and obstinately tensing the muscles of her midsection against the tightening of the corset-laces. Mary Anne tugged and pulled, but to no avail; when she gave up and tied the laces off, tying a modest bustle on the back of the corset and pulling the first of the three petticoats over Marina's head, Marina was able to straighten up without feeling as if she was going to faint from lack of air. Her corsets were only a little tighter than she would have tied them herself. Not as comfortable as no corset at all but not a torture either.

There was nothing to show that Mary Anne had been doing any rummaging about among the books that Marina had put on the shelves last night, but that was not to say that she wouldn't later. For now, the modiste was waiting in the sitting room, a patient little woman with sad eyes and gray hair, done up in a severe, but impeccably tailored, gray wool suit and matching hat, modestly ornamented with a ribbon cockade. She had swatches of fabric piled up beside her on one side of the couch, and pattern books on the other. Her eyes brightened at the sight of Marina; perhaps she had expected another martinet like Madam, or someone so countrified as to be impossible to outfit, with freckles, gap-teeth, and enormous feet that had never seen anything other than boots. In the midst of this florid room, the modiste looked like a little pile of ashes.

For that matter, I probably look like an unburned bit of coal.

"I will leave you with Miss Eldergast," said Mary Anne loftily, and turned to the modiste. "Miss Eldergast, you have your instructions upon what is suitable for the young lady from Madam, so I will return for you in one hour."

Both of them looked reflexively at the clock upon the mantelpiece, which was just showing half past ten. Then, as Mary Anne sailed out of the room with a self-important air, Marina smiled at the modiste.

"Why don't you show me what is suitable for the young

lady, Miss Eldergast," Marina said, with some humor, "And we'll pick something or other out."

"Well, you're in deep mourning, of course," the dressmaker said hesitantly, "So these are the samples I brought—"

"Black, black, and black, of course." Marina sighed, picked up the stack of swatches, and sat down next to Miss Eldergast, putting them in her lap. She added bitterly, "And it matters not at all that I never knew my parents; the sensibilities of society must not be outraged."

Of course, I could be in mourning for the happy life I had in Killatree.

Miss Eldergast hesitated, somewhat taken aback. "Yes, yes, of course," she said hastily, clearly trying and failing to find some polite response to Marina's bald statement. "Now, if you could choose from among *these* for a riding habit and walking skirts—"

It didn't take very long to make her selections; although the choice of fabric was wider and the number of patterns Miss Eldergast was able to execute much larger than the dressmaker in Holsworthy was able to offer, there were only a limited number of ways in which to dress in "black, black, and black." What was suitable for the young lady, at least according to Madam Arachne, was the strictest possible interpretation of mourning, without even the touch of mauve, lavender or violet that as a young unmarried woman she should have been able to don without offending anyone.

I shall look like Queen Victoria before this is over. Or one of those melancholy women who are would-be Gothic poetesses.

Still, there was no doubt that Madam was equipping Marina generously, and in the height of fashion, the only exception being that everything suitable had high necks and high collars. Not that this would be too onerous in the winter, but when summer came, black and high collars were going to be difficult to bear.

Time enough to worry about that when the time comes, she told herself. For now, heavy silk blouses and shirtwaists, unlike the very plain things that she'd been dressed in so far, were going to be made exactly to her measure and ornamented lavishly with lace, ribbon, and flounces. Beautifully soft skirts and jackets were getting braid, tucking, ruffles, beading—

It would have taken a harder heart than Marina had not to be enchanted by the clothing that the dressmaker had planned for her. Madam Arachne had only given orders as to the color and general design, not to the specifics, nor to the amount to be spent. So the modiste was going to create garments similar to the kind that Madam Arachne herself wore—lavish, and stylish.

And I hope that Madam doesn't contradict that plan.

"Have you any preferences as to what I deliver first, miss?" the modiste asked at last, packing up their selections with care.

"Unless Madam says differently, the riding habit, please," Marina begged. "I'm dying for some exercise."

The dressmaker smiled wanly. "Indeed, miss?" she responded, just as Mary Anne returned. The maid gathered the poor little woman in without a single word, polite or otherwise, to Marina, and took her off, leaving Marina alone.

This was her chance; she walked across the room to a door she had noticed behind a swag of ornamental drapery, and tried the knob. The door swung open easily.

The room revealed was, indeed, another bedroom, this one with all the furnishings under sheets. But the sheets didn't hide the carpet, walls, or the curtains on the bed, which were even more flamboyantly scarlet than in Marina's sitting room. Not a feminine decorating scheme, either; this was a distinctly masculine room. And now that she thought about it, the sitting room and her own room had been given ruffles and flourishes that, taken away, also left a distinctly masculine appearance in the room.

This single glance told her what she had wanted to know. If ever there was a room utterly suited to a young male Fire Master, this was it. So these rooms must have once been the home of her uncles Sebastian and Thomas!

She closed the door, and let the swag of drapery fall back to hide it with a feeling of satisfaction. And if the surroundings she found herself in were at odds with her own preferences and her Element—now she no longer felt so stifled and overheated by them. How could she? Here, more than anywhere else (unless she discovered her Aunt Margherita's room) she was closer to the people she'd known than she had been since she'd been taken away from them.

Until, that is, I see if Sally can manage to smuggle letters out for me. With friends among the lower servants, what had seemed impossible yesterday was no longer. There was still the matter of obtaining postage, but if she got her hands on some money. . . .

Well, meanwhile, she needed to make concerted efforts to please Madam Arachne; the sooner it appeared to her new guardian that Marina was settling in and being obedient, the sooner opportunities to act on her own would appear.

After some hunting, she found her instruments, her music, her needlework, and her books tucked away in a cupboard in the sitting room, no longer in the boxes or baskets that they had been packed into. While she waited for the odious Mary Anne to come fetch her for another luncheon ordeal, she began shelving her books among the ones she had purloined from the library.

As she did so, she couldn't help but notice that some

books she would have expected to have with her were not there.

The missing books were an odd assortment; Greek and Latin philosophers, essays by some of the Suffragrists that Elizabeth admired, and some weighty history books. The problem was, since Marina had not seen these books packed, she could not say for certain that she'd actually had them with her—Jenny and Sarah had been overwrought, and there was no telling what they had and had not packed. The books had been in her room and should have been boxed—but those horrid lawyers had been in a great hurry, and they might not have waited for everything.

Still . . . novels and poetry were there, including the scandalous poetry of Byron and sensational books by other notorious authors, and some rather daring, if frivolous, works in French. What was missing were books that were—well—*serious* in tone.

She didn't quite know what to make of that. Why take away serious literature and leave the frivolous, even the demi-scandalous?

On the other hand, it wasn't as if there was anything among them, except the essays, that she probably couldn't find in the Oakhurst library.

Still, if someone had gone through her books, discarding some just as her entire wardrobe had been discarded, it was very likely that someone would continue to monitor her reading. Which meant that perhaps she had better hide her etiquette books a little better. Maybe no one would take them—but Mary Anne seemed determined to see her humiliated.

Why? Well, there was a very obvious reason—as long as Marina remained a naive and socially inept bumpkin, Mary Anne was guaranteed a position. Trained as a lady's maid she might be, but Marina could not imagine any real lady putting up with the woman's airs for very long. If novels were to be believed, a proper lady's maid was silent, invisible, and kept any opinions she might have to herself.

If Marina ever got to the point where Madam Arachne was satisfied with her, Mary Anne would probably find herself out of a position.

And she certainly will when I am twenty-one!

Unless, of course, she could sufficiently cow her charge to make her think that Mary Anne could not possibly be dispensed with.

So—the removal of the "serious" books might be on Madam's orders, to ensure that Marina concentrated on learning social graces and didn't bury her nose in a book. But Mary Anne would find it in her best interests to remove anything that would help Marina do without her. Having confiscated books once, she certainly wouldn't hesitate to do it again.

Definitely, Marina had better hide her latest acquisitions.

Where? Not in among her clothing—Mary Anne would be sure to find them there. And the first place anyone would look for hidden treasures would be under the bed or the mattress.

In my *room*—

The thought was parent to the deed; within a moment, she had gathered up her purloined books and whisked them into Sebastian's old room. She shoved them under the mattress, smoothed over the dust-cloth, and hurried back to the sitting room. When Mary Anne returned, she was putting her instruments and music away.

"Do you suppose there would be a music stand I could have here?" she asked the maid diffidently.

"You should practice in the music room, miss," Mary Anne replied with a frown. "That's what it's for. You wouldn't want to disturb people with your practicing."

So, music practice was among the permitted activities—though who she was going to disturb was a mystery, since she hadn't seen anyone but servants except Madam since she arrived, and this wasn't the servants' wing.

Well, perhaps Madam was planning to entertain soon, which would put guests in this wing. *Hmm. She must have taken my parents' suite.* It would, of course, be the largest and best-appointed. Somehow she couldn't imagine Madam settling for anything less.

And I certainly wouldn't want that suite. This is cavernous enough for me, thank you.

"Yes, but changing temperatures are very bad for lutes," Marina replied. "The necks crack very easily. It shouldn't be in a room that doesn't have a constant fire in it in winter." This, of course, was not true—but Mary Anne wouldn't know that.

The maid sniffed. "I'll have someone find a stand," she said, as if conferring a great favor. "In the meantime, miss, it's time for luncheon."

Marina followed the maid to the dining room again; she was glad to see Peter there, but even happier that she'd had a chance to study one of those etiquette books last night. The number of supercilious coughs was far fewer, and if the food was just as bland and tasteless as before, at least she got a bit more of it this time.

Madam joined her at luncheon as well; Marina could only watch her covertly, marveling that she actually seemed to enjoy what was set before her—as much as Madam Arachne ever appeared to enjoy anything.

Halfway through, Madam cleared her throat delicately. "I should like you to meet my son Reginald this afternoon," she said, as Marina looked up quickly. "He can help immeasurably in instructing you in polite conversation. And as we have a gramaphone, he can also teach you to dance properly. I am assuming you have never learned?"

She shook her head. "Only country dances, Madam," she replied truthfully. "And not often."

"Well, you're not completely ungraceful; I think he can manage," Madam Arachne said coolly. "Mary Anne, please show miss to the music room when luncheon is over."

"Of course, Madam," the maid said, with a servility she had not demonstrated until this moment.

Luncheon was very soon deemed to be over, with the arrival of a blancmange; since Marina detested blancmange, she toyed with her portion and was not displeased to have it taken away when Madam rose and left to go back to whatever it was that she was doing. Work, presumably. Something to do with the estate, perhaps. Accounts. Whoever reigned over Oakhurst would have to be an estate manager as well as the head of the household; there were the tenant farms to manage as well as the home farm, and the household accounts to run.

Or perhaps she was dealing with her own businesses — after all, hadn't she said that she had three pottery manufactories? Or was it four? Marina could not imagine Madam leaving the details of her businesses to anyone other than herself.

Another trek through the house brought them to the door of the music room, which had a fire in the fireplace, but which, by the chill still in the air, had not had one there for long. There was a harp, shrouded in a cover and probably out of tune, and a piano in the corner, a grouping of sofas and chairs about the fireplace, and an expanse of clear floor for dancing. There was also, more prominently, an expensive gramophone on a table of its own, and records shelved beside it.

Mary Anne simply left her there to her own devices; she

thought about examining the recordings for the gramophone, but if the device was Reginald's rather than belonging to the house, the young man might resent her touching it. So instead, she examined the harp. As she had expected, it had been de-tuned, but by the amount of wear on it, someone had been used to playing it often.

Mother, probably. Marina didn't really remember if Uncle Thomas had ever said anything about her mother playing the harp, but it was the instrument of choice for young women of her mother's generation.

"Not a bad instrument, but I'd rather play the gramophone," said a careless-sounding male voice from the door. She turned.

And there he was, leaning indolently against the doorframe. Posed, in fact. There was no doubt that Reginald was Madam Arachne's son; he had her pale coloring, black hair, and finely chiseled features—but where it was impossible to decide what Madam Arachne felt about anything, Reginald wore a look of sardonic amusement and an air of general superiority as casually as he wore his impeccably tailored suit. "Hello, cuz," he continued, sauntering across the room and holding out his hand. "I'm Reggie."

"Marina," she replied, not particularly wanting to offer *her* hand, but constrained to by politeness. *He's going to kiss it instead of shaking it,* she thought grimly. *He'll make a flourish out of it, to impress me with how Continental he is.*

And he did exactly that, taking the half-extended hand and kissing the back of it, letting it go with a mocking little click of bootheels.

"So, the mater thinks we ought to have a turn or two around the ballroom," he continued. "I understand you don't dance?"

"Only country dances," she repeated reluctantly, as he cranked the gramophone and selected a recording, then mounted it on the machine, dropped the needle in the groove, and held out his hand to her imperiously as a waltz sounded from the horn.

"You don't dance," he repeated, dismissively. "Well, I'm reckoned handy at it; you need have no fear, fair cuz. Just do what I do, only opposite and backwards." His eyebrow raised, drawing her attention to his cleverness.

Annoyingly enough, he was a good dancer, and didn't make her feel as if she had no more grace than a young calf. In fact, if it hadn't been for the not-altogether-hidden smirk of superiority he wore, she might have enjoyed herself. He was not only a good dancer, he was a good instructor. She was good at country dances, and her skill carried over into the popular and ballroom dances that he showed her.

Fortunately, the other half of the program—that polite conversation he was supposed to be teaching her—didn't require much on her part except to listen attentively and murmur vague agreement while *he* talked.

And how he talked—she had to wonder how much of it was true and how much boasting.

Not that it mattered much; whichever it was, so far as she was concerned, his general attitude was so detestable that she was hard put to conceal it from him—and she did so in the only way she could think of. She stared fixedly at him as if she hung on his every word, while all the time trying to work out how she could get away from him.

In the end, she didn't have to; Mary Anne arrived to announce the advent of teatime, and Reggie sprang to his feet with an oath that wasn't quite muffled enough.

"You won't catch me sipping that cursed stuff!" he laughed rudely. "Well, cuz, I'll be off; I'll have my tea down in the village pub. I expect this will be a regular meeting for us from now on. Mater wants you to be ready for the gay old social whirl as soon as you're out of mourning, don't you know. So, I'll be giving you my coaching for a while." He laughed. "Now, don't you go pretending you haven't learned anything just so you can keep the lessons going! The mater isn't fooled that easily."

She dropped her eyes to hide the contempt she felt for his assumption that she would do anything just to be in his company. "I won't," she murmured.

"There's a good gel," he said, patting the back of her hand. "Well then, I'll be pushing off, and I'll see you tomorrow."

And as Marina followed Mary Anne to wherever her aunt was holding court among the teapots, she found herself resolving to learn these new dances in record time. The sooner she learned them, the sooner she'd be rid of Reggie, and by her way of thinking that could not possibly be soon enough.

"**M**ADAM Arachne, I'll be going to church tomorrow," Marina announced over dinner, as the soup was cleared away. By the second day, she had begun calling her aunt by that name, and since the woman didn't object—

I can't call her Aunt, I just can't. Aunts were nothing like this cold woman, who held the household at Oakhurst in such an iron grip that the servants leaped to obey her. Aunts were warm and loving, and were more likely to indulge a niece than correct her.

"I suppose I'll need a carriage? It seems rather far to walk—I could, easily enough, but it's an hour to the village at least. I don't suppose I could ride—I'd have to stable the horse, and I'm not sure where in the village I could do that. . . ." The riding-habit had just been delivered today, too late for her to go out for a ride. So far, she'd been out of the house itself only twice, both times for a walk in the gardens. She supposed that they were lovely—and she certainly detected the now-fading magic of an Earth Master in the robust health of all of the plantings. But the gardens weren't her half-wild orchard, and the only water in them was a tame—and at the moment, inactive—fountain. It was all very lush, but very planned and mannered—reflective of the woman of all those letters.

None of this was much like Margherita; Margherita's magic was cozier, more domestic; and at the same time, wilder—Alanna's broad and wide, and controlled. Marina could only compare her mother's magic to that of the goddess Demeter, a thing of ordered, rich harvests and settled fields.

And her own? She didn't know—except that it wasn't *tame*.

She wasn't sure why, but she felt very uneasy about using any magic of her own here at Oakhurst.

What was it about this place here, Oakhurst, that made her so afraid—yes, *afraid*—and made her hide her power behind those masking shields that Elizabeth had taught her?

She glanced at Arachne from under her lashes, waiting for a response to her announcement, and realized that it wasn't *Oakhurst* that made her feel as if she dared not work magic—after all, it was plain enough that magic had been worked in plenty here. No, her unease was centered around using magic *near her aunt.* Not that Arachne showed any signs of magic herself, nor did Reggie, nor the supercilious Mary Anne. But Elizabeth had taught her when to trust her instincts, and her instincts told her that any magic use should be kept under heavy shields and never, ever, where Arachne or her people were.

Which was everywhere, it seemed, within the walls of Oakhurst.

Tonight, not only was Madam Arachne present at dinner, so was Reginald. At Marina's announcement, which he evidently found surprising, his eyebrows rose.

"It is too far to walk, and it would be in poor taste to display yourself at a church service in a riding habit," Madam admitted, without betraying any expression. "But is this really necessary?"

Marina's chin rose, and she looked her aunt directly in the eyes. A confrontation of sorts—a testing. "Yes, Madam, it is," she said, and did not elaborate on why. Let Arachne assume it was because she was religious. That might even confuse her a bit, for she surely wouldn't expect a religious upbringing out of pack of wild artists!

It was just an excuse to get out of the house and grounds, and she knew it, although in Killatree she and the other inhabitants of Blackbird Cottage had been regulars at the village church, except when the weather was particularly foul. She *was* curious about the village from which Oakhurst took its name; as much to the point, the people of the village were probably curious about her, the daughter that no one had ever seen. She might as well go to church where they could look their fill at her. It would be better and more comfortable to have her first encounter with them in the church than in the village street. And besides—there was one inhabitant of the village that Madam could not possibly object to. The vicar was the one man in a village whose position allowed him to cross class lines. He was as welcome a guest at dinner in a great house as he was at tea in the smallest, lowliest farmer's cottage. Once Marina actually introduced herself to him, he would have to pay a visit. And at the moment, she didn't care if he was the most boring old snob imaginable, he would at least keep Madam's corrections to a minimum just by his presence.

"Well, you might as well go if you really want to, and let all the gossips and clatter-tongues look their fill at you," said Madam dismissively, in an unconscious echo of Marina's own reasoning. "At least they will know that you haven't got two heads, or devil's hooves, or any of the other non-sense that has probably been mooted about in the teashop and the pub. I will order the carriage for you."

"Thank you, Madam," Marina said, lowering her eyes to her plate—which was promptly whisked away. Not that she minded; this course looked like chopped pasteboard and mayonnaise, and tasted about the same. She had figured out by now that there were no more than two or three dishes in a meal that she found palatable, and she took care to get exactly the right implements for them and to eat them quickly when they appeared. Usually she got at least half of the portions set in front of her that she *wanted* to eat, if she managed to maneuver bites around Madam's mandatory polite conversation.

That, and her hearty breakfasts and midnight feasts supplied by Sally, kept her from feeling as if she was going to starve to death any time soon. Perhaps when spring and summer arrived, she could convince her aunt to let her have picnic luncheons or teas out of doors.

But I suppose that will only happen if they're in fashion.

"What was that telegraph about, that you ran off so quickly today?" Arachne asked her son, who was eating his portion of the next course with a distinct lack of enthusiasm.

"Another one of the paintresses left the Okehampton works—or, as their foreman said, 'disappeared,' " he said, setting his fork aside. "That's two this week, and there's been some talk that somehow we're responsible for the disappearances. The manager reckoned I'd better come deal with the talk before it got out of hand. He was right; not only did I have to talk to the girls—all of them, not just the paintresses—but every one of the shop foremen cornered me before I left. They all wanted to know if there was any truth to the talk that for some reason we'd gotten rid of her and hushed it up."

"Talk?" Arachne said sharply. "We're the ones who've been injured! Doesn't it occur to those people that it takes *time* to train a paintress? Why would we want to be rid of *trained* ones? It costs us time and money when one of the little ingrates decides to try her prospects elsewhere."

"That's what I told them," Reggie replied with a shrug. "And eventually they all admitted what I'd already known—" He gave a sharp glance at Marina, who was pretending great interest in her plate. "Once those girls start the easy life of a paintress, they start getting airs. *You* know what I mean, Mater."

Arachne laughed, and actually looked fully at her niece. "This, Marina, is *not* considered polite conversation. For one thing, it is about the inner workings of our business, and it is not polite to discuss these things in front of those who are not involved in the business themselves. For another— well, the petty lives of little factory girls with money to spend who find that they have become interesting to men are not appropriate subjects for conversation at any time."

"Yes, Madam," Marina murmured.

"However, this is something that Reginald and I *must* discuss, so— well, remember that this sort of thing is not to be brought up in public."

"Yes, Madam," Marina agreed, softly.

She turned back to Reggie. "Now, there has to be some reason why these foremen were convinced we had anything to do with these girls running off," Arachne continued, fixing her son with a cool gaze. "You might as well tell me what it is."

Reggie groaned. "Never could get anything by you, Mater, could I? Some pesky Suffragists brought in their pet female doctor and commenced whinging about the entire painting room, especially about the paints and glazes, saying we're poisoning the girls and that's why they disappear. Some of the men were daft enough to listen to her."

"Suffragists!" Arachne's voice rose incredulously. "What possible quarrel can they have with me? Am I not a woman? Have I not, by my own hard work and despite the machinations of men who would see me fail, turned my single manufactory into four? Do I not employ *women*? And at good wages, too!"

Reggie just shrugged. "How should I know? They're mad, that's all. They say the lead in the glazes—the woman *doctor* says that the lead in the glazes—poisons the girls, makes them go mad, and we know all about it. So when they start becoming unhinged we have them taken away."

"Pfft!" said Arachne. "A little lead is what makes them so pretty—just like arsenic does, everyone knows that. I've never heard that a little lead ever did more than clear up their complexions, but now some ill-trained woman doctor says it is dangerous and—" She shrugged. "Who gave her this medical degree? No university in England, I am sure! No university in England would be so foolish as to grant a woman a medical degree!"

"I don't know, Mater—"

She fixed him with an icy stare. "I trust you made it very clear to the men that these accusations are groundless and that this so-called doctor is a quack and a fraud."

"I made it very clear to the men that it is easy enough to replace them if they stir up trouble and spread tales, Mater," Reggie told her, with that smirk that so annoyed Marina.

"Well done." Arachne thawed a trifle, and smiled. "Now we have disposed of the *impolite* conversation, perhaps we can discuss other things." With no more warning than that, she turned to her niece. "Well, Marina? What shall we discuss?"

Her mind went blank. She couldn't remember the topics

that Arachne had indicated were appropriate. "Why shouldn't a woman be a doctor, Madam?" she asked, the first question that came into her head.

But Arachne raised an admonitory eyebrow. "Not appropriate, child," she replied. "That particular question comes under any number of inappropriate topics, from politics to religion. Polite conversation, if you please."

"Um—" She pummeled her brain frantically. "The concerts in Bath? The London opera season?"

"Ah. The London opera season. That will do nicely." Arachne smiled graciously. "Now, since you have never been to London, and in any case, you cannot go to the opera until you are out of mourning, what could you possibly say about the London opera season?"

"I could—say that—ask the opinion of whomever I was with," she said, groping after further conversation. "About the opera selections—the tenors—"

"Very good. It is not wise to ask a gentleman about the sopranos, my dear. The gentleman in question might have an interest in one of them that has nothing to do with their vocal abilities." She turned to Reggie. "So, what do you think of our London Faust this year? Shall I trouble to see it?"

That gained her a respite, as mother and son discussed music—or rather, discussed the people who had come to see the music, and be seen there. Marina had only to make the occasional "yes" or "no" that agreed with their opinions. And when mother and son disagreed—she sided always with the mother.

It seemed politic.

The carriage rolled away from the gates of Oakhurst with Marina in it, but not alone. Mary Anne was with her, all starch and sour looks, sitting stiffly on the seat across from

Marina. Just to make the maid's day complete, Marina had taken care to get in first, so as to have the forward-facing seat, leaving Mary Anne the rearward-facing one.

I should have expected that I wouldn't be allowed out without my leash-holder, she thought, doing her best to ignore the maid's disgruntled glances, watching the manicured landscape roll by outside the carriage window.

Mary Anne had not been the *least* little bit pleased about going to church. She didn't even have a prayerbook—but last night, a quick raid of the schoolbook cupboard in the library had supplied a pair of not too badly abused specimens, which she presented to the seriously annoyed woman for choice. Marina, of course, had her own, with her other books, a childhood present from Sebastian, with wonderful little pen-and-ink illuminations of fish, ocean creatures, and water plants. And had *it* turned up missing, there would have been a confrontation. . . .

So here she was, everything about her in soberest black except that magnificent beaver cloak. She'd no doubt that even the cloak would have been black, had her aunt thought about it in advance, and considered that she might actually want to show her face in the village this Sunday.

Saint Peter's was nothing particularly outstanding in the way of ecclesiastical architecture—but it wasn't hideously ugly or a jumble of added-on styles, either. And it was substantial, not a boxy little chapel with no graces and no beauty, but a good medieval church in the Perpendicular style with a square tower and a fine peal of bells, which were sounding as they drove up. It was a pity that the interior had been stripped by Cromwell's Puritans during the Reformation, but there—the number of churches that hadn't been could be counted on one hand, if that. It had nice vaulting, though, and though it was cold, at least she had that lovely warm beaver cape to keep her comfortable

during the service. The poor young vicar looked a little blue
about the nose and fingertips.

The Roeswoods were not an old enough family to have a
family pew, but Marina was shown straight up to the front
and seated there, giving everyone who had already arrived a
good look at her as she walked up the aisle with Mary Anne
trailing behind. And of course, the entire village could regard
the back of her head at their leisure all through the service.

For the first time, Marina's keeper was at a complete loss.
Mary Anne appeared not to have set foot in a church since
early childhood. Somewhat to Marina's bemusement, she
made heavy work of the service, fumbling the responses, not
even knowing the tunes of the hymns. Marina could not
imagine what was wrong with the girl—unless, of course,
she was chapel and not church—or even of some odd sect
or other like Quakers or Methodists. And Marina had the
feeling that, given Arachne's autocratic attitudes, it wouldn't
have mattered if the maid had been a devotee of the Norse
god Odin and utterly opposed to setting foot in a Christian
church—if Mary Anne wanted to keep her place, to church
she would go every time that Marina went.

*I hope—oh, I hope she can't ride! If she can't ride—and
I can avoid Reggie—I might be able to ride alone. Or if not
alone, at least with someone who won't be looking for my
mistakes all the time.*

She even went so far as to insert that hope into her
prayers.

After the service—the organist was tolerably good, and
the choir cheerful and in tune, if not outstanding—Marina
remained in the pew while Mary Anne sat beside her and
fumed. If the maid had been given a choice, she would have
gone charging straight down the aisle the moment the first
note of the recessional sounded, Marina suspected. Mary
Anne had made an abortive attempt to rise, but when Ma-

rina didn't move, she'd sat back down, perching impatiently on the very edge of the pew, which couldn't have been comfortable.

Having gone to this sort of church all her life, however, Marina knew very well that it was no good thinking that you could get out quickly if you were in the first pew. Not a chance . . . not with most of the village, including all of the littlest children and the oldest of the elderly, between you and the exit. Today, with Marina Roeswood present—well, all of those people would be lingering for more long looks at the mysterious daughter of the great house.

So she sat and waited for the aisle to clear, and only when a quick glance over her shoulder showed her that there were just a few folk left, lingering around the door, did she rise and make her leisurely way toward the rear of the church.

And once at the door, it was time, as she had known, for another delay, which clearly infuriated Mary Anne. But it was a delay that Marina was not, under any circumstances, going to forego *or* cut short.

"And *you* must be the young Miss Roeswood," said the vicar—sandy-haired, bare-headed—stationed at the door to greet his parishioners as they left. He reached for her black-gloved hand, as she held it out to him. "I wish that we had gotten this first meeting under better circumstances," he continued, fixing his brown eyes on her face in a way that suggested to her that he was slightly short-sighted. "My name is Davies, Clifton Davies."

"The *Reverend* Clifton Davies, I assume," Marina put in, with a hint of a smile. *Cornish or Welsh father, I suspect, but born on the Devon side of the border. He doesn't have quite the lilt nor the accent.*

"Yes, yes, of course," the vicar laughed deprecatingly. "I'm rather new in my position, and not used to being the

'Reverend' Davies—but the village has welcomed me beyond my expectation."

"So both of us are new to Oakhurst—I shan't feel so
completely the stranger," Marina replied, and as Mary Anne
smoldered, continued to make conversation with the young
Mr. Davies. In no time at all she had learned that he was as
fond of chess as she was—"And you must come to the vicarage to play!"—passionate about music—"Although I
cannot play a note, sadly"—and unmarried. Which ac-
counted for the amused glances of the parishioners lingering purposefully about the door. Well, those were for the
most part older parishioners. She rather thought that if any
of the young and unmarried women had been lingering,
she wouldn't have been getting amused glances. They
would think her a rival, and a rival with advantages
they would never have. If she told them that she was not,
they would never believe her.

But she was delighted to discover that Mr. Davies was
well-spoken, friendly, intelligent. And the more that Marina
spoke with the young vicar, the better she liked him.

Finally Mary Anne had had enough. "Excuse me, Miss
Marina, but I think I had better fetch the carriage," the
woman said, interrupting the vicar in mid-sentence, then
pushing past her charge as the young man looked after her
with a bemused glance.

"I suppose I've monopolized your time unforgivably—"
he began with a blush.

"You have done no such thing," Marina replied with
warmth, then seized her chance. "Mr. Davies, I should like
very much to visit you, and play for your enjoyment or have
a chess game with you, but my Aunt Arachne has some very
strict notions about my behavior. Please send me or *us* actual invitations for specific days and times, so that she cannot put me off and must either be rude and decline, or

gracious and accept. Please come up to Oakhurst Manor to visit—teatime would be ideal!"

"Forgive me, but you sound rather desperate," the vicar said hesitantly, warily.

"I am—for intelligent company, and conversation that isn't confined to the few topics considered appropriate among the fashionable elite!" she said, allowing him a brief glimpse of her frustration. Just a flash—but Clifton Davies was not at all stupid, and very, very intuitive. She saw something like understanding in his eyes, a conspiratorial smile, and he gave her a quick nod.

"In that case, I believe I am overdue to make a call upon your aunt—and you," he said, with a little bow over her hand. Then he released it, and stepped back, and turned to another of his flock. It was all perfectly timed, and she turned away, hiding a smile of satisfaction, to make her way up the path to the waiting carriage and the fuming Mary Anne. Now she would have a reason to come to the village; now there would be an outsider in Oakhurst to free her from the endless round of supervision and etiquette lessons.

And she just might start to get a decent tea now and again, with the vicar coming to call.

"And how did you find the little vicar?" Arachne asked over luncheon—how *could* anyone make roast beef so bland?— with a very slight smile.

Mary Anne told her how long I stayed talking to him, she realized at once. "I found him polite and well-spoken, who composes an intelligent sermon and delivers it admirably," she replied casually. "And although he did not know my mother and father well, he wished to properly express his condolences and asked me to convey them to you as well, Madam. He intends to pay a call here soon, to impart them in person, and tender his respect to you and welcome you here."

"Ah." Arachne gave her a measuring look. "And did he say anything else?"

"That he plays chess and hopes that one of us will indulge him in a game," she said truthfully. And added, "I expect that he will want one or both of us to help in church charity work. That is what my mother used to do, all the time. She used to write to me about it, pages and pages."

There was a spark of something in Arachne's eyes. "Really? That surprises me. I would not have expected Hugh's wife to be so closely concerned with village life."

"She enjoyed doing it; she enjoyed being able to help people," Marina replied. "I suppose—I should do something too, but—I don't know what. There's an obligation, you see, responsibilities between the house and the village. We're responsible for a great deal of parish charity, either directly, or indirectly." Since Arachne had not interrupted her, she assumed that this must be appropriate conversation and continued. "I'm not good with sick people—my mother used to take food and other comforts to sick people. Perhaps you should, Madam."

"I think that there are better uses of our time," Arachne said, dismissively. "We can send one of the servants with such things, if the vicar wishes the custom to continue. Still . . . if it is the custom. . . ."

Marina actually got to finish her course in peace, as Arachne pondered this sudden revelation of the linking of house and village. Evidently it had not occurred to her that there could be such a thing.

"You, I think, will be taking the responsibility of our obligation to the village," Arachne said into the silence. "I am sure Mr. Davies will know what is best for you to do. It will give you something constructive to do with your time."

Since that was exactly what Marina had been hoping she would say, she simply nodded. Another reason to be out of the manor!

"You will, of course, direct the servants to do as much as possible in your stead," Arachne added. "The responsibility of directing them will be good for you."

She stifled a sigh. *Oh well—I'll still have some chances to get away from here, if not as many as I had hoped for.*

Still—still! She had gotten away, if only for the duration of the church service. She had made a friend of the vicar, and now there would be an outsider coming here. The bars of the cage were loosening, ever so slightly.

When Arachne was finished with luncheon, she did not immediately leave. Instead, she fixed Marina with an oddly penetrating look, and said, "Come with me, please, to the drawing room." She smiled; it did not change the expression of her eyes. "We haven't spoken of your parents, and I think it is time that we did so."

Obediently, Marina rose when Arachne did, and followed her to the drawing room, which was between the library and the smoking room and connected with both. She knew the plan of the house now; she was in the north wing and Arachne and Reginald were in the south; in between lay the central portion of the house which contained the entry hall and the other important rooms. Most of the servants were also quartered in the north wing, all except for Madam's personal maid, Reggie's valet, and Mary Anne.

Like most of the house, this was a finely appointed, but comfortable room—not one designed for a particular Elemental Mage, either, so at least Marina didn't feel stifled. The furnishings were from the middle of the last century, she suspected; they didn't have the ornate quality of those more recently in vogue. Arachne took a couch with its back to the window, which perforce made Marina take a chair that faced it. With the light behind her aunt, she could not easily see Arachne's face.

"How often did your mother write to you, child?" Arachne asked, as Marina settled uneasily into her chair.

"Once a week or so, except when she and my father were in Italy; less often then," Marina replied, trying to keep her tone light and conversational. "She told me what she was doing, about the books she had read, the friends who had visited. Not when I was a child, of course," she amended. "Then she told me mostly about her garden, and made up stories to amuse me. At least, I think she made them up, although they could have been stories from the fairy tale books she read as a child."

"What sort of stories?" Arachne asked, leaning forward. *I wonder why she's so interested?*

"Oh, fairy tales and myths, about little creatures that were supposed to live in her garden, gnomes and fauns and the like," she replied with a slight laugh. "Entirely whimsical, and perhaps that was the problem, why I never cared much for them. I was not a child much given to whimsy."

She thought that Arachne smiled. "No?"

"No. I preferred the myths of Greece and Rome—and later, the stories about Arthur and his knights and court and the legends of Wales and Cornwall," she said firmly. "And serious things; real history, Shakespeare and adult books. And poetry, which I suppose, given that I lived with artists, was inevitable, but the poetry I read was mostly Elizabethan. I was a serious child, and mother didn't seem to understand that." She chose her words with care. "Oh, just for instance, she seemed to think that since I lived with the Tarrants, I should be a painter, when my real interest is music. She would send me expensive paints and brushes, and I would just give them to Sebastian Tarrant—and *he* would buy me music."

"An equitable arrangement. How very businesslike of you." Arachne chuckled dryly, a tinkling sound like broken bits of china rubbing together. "And when you were older, what did your mother write about then?"

"What I've told you—mostly about her everyday life. Her letters were very like journal entries, and I tried to write the same to her, but it was difficult for me." She shrugged. "I think, perhaps, that she was trying to—to bring us together again. To make us less than strangers."

"I believe you could be right." Arachne shook her head. "Poor Alanna; I knew her even less than you, for I did not even have the benefit of letters, but all I have gleaned since I arrived here makes me think that she must have been a seriously troubled young woman. I begin to wonder if the estrangement between my brother and myself might have been due in part to her."

"Surely you don't believe that my mother would have wanted to come between a brother and sister!" Marina exclaimed indignantly. "That doesn't sound anything like her!"

"No, nothing of the sort," Arachne replied, unruffled by the outburst. "No—but I must wonder if—if my brother was afraid that if I saw her, I would—" She shook her head again. "No, surely not. But if I saw that he had bound himself to someone who was—not stable—well, he must have realized that I would urge him to—"

"Madam, you must know that my parents' behavior seriously puzzles me, but that I really did not know them," Marina said, sitting up straighter. "If you have any guesses that would explain why I was sent away, I would be interested to hear them, and I assure you, I am adult enough to deal with them in a mature manner."

Oh, very pompous, Marina. On the other hand—I'm tired of being treated like I'm still in the nursery.

Arachne paused. "You know that I told you how your mother seemed to have a—a breakdown of her nerves following your birth. Now, when you tell me of these letters of hers, well—what if she was not telling you whimsical tales as a child? What if she actually thought she saw these creatures in her garden?"

Marina for a moment could not believe what her aunt was trying to tell her. "Are you suggesting that she lost her wits?" Her voice squeaked on the last word, making her exclamation a little less than impressive.

"It would fit the facts," Arachne said, as if musing to herself. "My brother's refusal to see, speak, or even write to me, their reclusiveness, the fact that he sent you away. He could have been protecting you—from *her.*"

It was a horrible thought. And one which, as Arachne pointed out, did fit the facts.

And it would explain why the uncles and my aunt wouldn't tell me why I'd been sent away. And why the reason was never, ever brought up in those letters.

Now, Marina knew that the little whimsical creatures that her mother had described really did exist—and had lived in her garden. But just because an Elemental Master was able to work magic and see the creatures of her element, it did not follow that she was sane . . . in fact, Elemental Masters had been known to become deranged by the very power that they wielded. Especially after a great stress, such as a death, an accident—or childbirth.

So what if that *had* happened to Alanna? Then Hugh would have wanted to get the infant Marina as far away from her as possible—*he* was protected against anything she might do, magically, but a baby would not be. And who better to send her to than the Tarrants, whose power could block Alanna's?

It all made hideous sense. "I have to wonder if you are

right, Madam Arachne," she said slowly. "It does explain a number of things. In fact, it is the only explanation that fits all of the facts as I know them."

She felt a horrible guilt then; here, all this time, she had been blaming her parents for sending her away, when they were protecting her, and in the only way possible! And those letters, filled with anguish and longing—had they come from a mother who *dared* not bring her child home lest she harm it? What worse heartbreak could there be?

Without Marina realizing it, Arachne had bent forward, and now she seized Marina's hand. "It is only a theory, child. Nothing more. And I know—I *know*—that if nothing else, your mother must have been quite well and in her full wits when they went to Italy this year. I am certain, as certain as I am of my own name, that your parents intended to bring you here after your eighteenth birthday. Everything that I have found in their papers points to that."

When I would be able to protect myself, even if mother wasn't quite right yet. She nodded. "I think, from the letters I got, that you are right."

Arachne released her hand. "I hope I haven't distressed you, child. I didn't intend to."

"I'm sure not—" Marina faltered. "But you have given me a great deal to think about."

Arachne made shooing motions with her hands. "In that case, dear child, perhaps you ought to go to your room where you can think in peace."

Marina took the hint, and rose. "Thank you. I believe that I will."

But as she turned to leave, she caught sight of her aunt's expression; unguarded for once.

Satisfaction. And triumph. As if she had won a high wager.

12

MARY Anne did not ride. Mary Anne was, in fact, afraid of horses. It was all very well for them to be at one end of a carriage, strapped in and harnessed up, while she was at the other, but she could not, would not be anywhere near one that was loose or under saddle. And for once, not even Arachne's iron will prevailed. When confronted with the order to take to saddle, Mary Anne gave notice. Arachne rescinded the order. Or so Sally had told Marina, in strictest confidence.

Supposedly a groom was detailed to ride with Marina for her safety. Supposedly, in fact, a groom was to lead her horse (as if she was a toddler on a pony) in a parody of riding. In actuality, the stableman took one look at her firm and expert seat, her easy control of the reins, and the way in which she could handle every beast in the stables (not that there were any horses that Marina would call troublesome) and snorted with contempt at the very idea. "I'm short-handed enough as 'tis," he said, " 'thout sending out one on fool's errands. The day Hugh Roeswood's daughter needs to be in leading-strings is the day they put me to pasture."

So Marina (whether or not Arachne was aware of it) rode alone, and for the last week, she had gone out every day for at least an hour.

She was learning the paths and the lanes around Oakhurst slowly, for the horse that the stableman assigned to her was a placid little mare, disinclined to move out of a walk unless there was a powerful incentive. But the old hunter that Marina used to ride at Blackbird Cottage was the same, and on the whole, she would rather ride a sedate and predictable horse than a spirited, but unpredictable one.

She took great pleasure in her riding habit, of black wool and trimmed with fur, not the least because it came with a riding-corset that allowed her almost as much freedom as going uncorseted. She needed it; she needed her riding-cloak as well, for it was cold, with snow lying deeply on the fields, and especially in the lee of the banks and hedges. There might be more snow some time soon, though for now, nothing much had come from the cloud-covered sky.

Her rides had taken her down to the vicarage on two visits so far—not too often, and only by invitation, which Mr. Davies had been punctilious about sending up to the house after his teatime visit the Monday afternoon following her foray to church. In fact, she would be going there today on a third visit, this time with a peculiar bag slung over her shoulder.

She'd seen this bag in the gun room—dragged there by Reggie so that he could boast about previous triumphs in the field—and rather thought it was a falconer's game bag. Whatever its original purpose in life, it was now a carryall when she went riding, as it sat very nicely on her hip and was large enough to carry almost anything. Today it held copies of her embroidery patterns, tracing paper, her spare pricking-wheel, and pounce bags of chalk and charcoal.

Whenever Margherita (or Sebastian, at her behest) had created an embroidery pattern, Marina had made a copy; she had an entire portfolio of them now. The vicar had asked for her suggestions for items for the parish booth at the annual May Day Fair on her first visit. She suspected that he hoped for items from Oakhurst for the jumble table, but she knew that her mother had contributed a great many white elephants over the years to little purpose. Marina had a better idea, and had asked him to gather the materials—and people—she needed to make it work.

When she arrived at the vicarage, she left her horse tied up at the gate, for she didn't expect to be very long. At her request, the vicar had gathered the women of the Parish Society together, and at her entrance into his rather bare parlor, a dozen pairs of curious eyes turned toward her. She smiled, and received some smiles, some nods, and one or two wary looks in return as he introduced her.

Following her instructions, he had arranged for a worktable in the middle of the room, and supplied some scrap fabric, which lay atop it. The worktable looked to be purloined from the kitchen and the ladies of the parish sat around it on a motley assortment of chairs, none new, most ancient. A cheerful fire in the fireplace warmed the air sufficiently that they had dispensed with their coats and cloaks, but all had kept their bonnets on, and a wide variety of hat ornaments bobbed in her direction.

"Good afternoon, ladies!" she said cheerfully. "I'm sure you know that I'm Marina Roeswood. I hope you don't mind my putting myself forward like this; Mr. Davies thought, because I was fostered with the Tarrants of Blackbird Cottage, who are well-known artists, I might have some

original ideas for the goods for this year's parish booth—
and as a matter of fact, I do."

With no further preamble, she took her supplies from the
falconer's bag and proceeded to show the women how a professional seamstress, embroideress, or modiste transferred
an embroidery pattern from paper to fabric. They watched
with amazement as she ran the pricking-wheel over the pen-
ciled design, then laid the now-perforated paper on a piece
of fabric and used the pounce-bag along the lines of the design, tapping it expertly and firmly on the paper.

"There, you see?" she said, removing the paper to show
the design picked out in tiny dots of white chalk. "Now, the
last step is to baste the lines of the design before the chalk
brushes off, and there you are! On dark fabric, you use a
chalk-bag; on light, a charcoal-bag. And this system allows
you to use the pricked pattern over and over, as many times
as you like, doesn't mark the fabric, and is a great deal less
fussy than sewing over the paper pattern."

The vicar proclaimed himself astonished. The
women—the wives and daughters of the shopkeepers and
the well-to-do farmers—were delighted. As with most am-
ateur embroideresses, they had either stitched through a
paper pattern, forcing them to use it only once, or had
drawn their patterns inaccurately on the fabric itself when
the fabric was too dark or thick to use as tracing paper.
Many a fine piece of cambric or silk had been ruined this
way when the marks made by the pencil wouldn't come
out—many lovely designs had been executed off center or
lopsided.

"And these are all very new and fashionable designs,
similar to the ones that Messrs. Morris & Co. is producing,
but quite original," she told them, spreading out the sheets
of patterns before their eyes. "My Aunt Margherita Tarrant
is known all over England for her art-embroidery, and has

produced lovely things with these designs for some of the
best homes in London and Plymouth."

That won them over, completely, and with these new designs and tools, there was great excitement over what manner of things might be made. Marina helped them to parcel
out patterns, tracing them so that more than one copy could
be dispensed, and running the wheel over them since there
was only the one wheel to share among the lot of them. As
they worked, they were happily discussing fire screens,
cushions, antimacassars, and any number of other delights.
No one else would have anything like this in the three other
parish booths from the churches that regularly had booths at
the May Day Fair. Every one of these ladies would make
something that she would like to have in her own home. In
fact, it wouldn't surprise Marina in the least to discover that
each would make two projects at a time—one to sell and
one to keep. As that cheerful fire further warmed the room,
the ladies warmed to Marina—who had, of course, seen exactly the items that had been originally made with these patterns, and was ready to offer advice as to materials and color
schemes. Mr. Davies beamed on them all impartially; from
the scent of baking, his old housekeeper was making ginger
biscuits to serve the ladies for tea.

But the spicy scent perfumed the air in a way that shook
her unexpectedly with memories of home, and suddenly, she
couldn't bear to be there—among strangers—

"Have I left you with enough to occupy you, ladies?" she
asked, quickly, around a rising lump in her throat. "For I believe my guardian will be expecting me back—"

By this time, the gossip was flying thick and fast as well
as discussion of fabrics and colors and stitches, but it
stopped dead at her question. The ladies looked at one another, and the eldest, old Mrs. Havershay, took it upon herself to act as spokeswoman. "Thank you, Miss! We're ever

so much obliged to you," she said, managing to sound both autocratic (which she was, as acknowledged leader of her circle) and grateful at the same time.

"Oh, thank *you*," she replied, flushing. "You've no idea what a good time I've had with you, here. I hope—"

But she couldn't have said what she hoped; they wouldn't have understood why she wished she could join their sewing circle. She was gentry; they were village. The gap was insurmountable.

As the others discussed projects, love affairs, and business of the village, one of the younger—and prettier—of the daughters helped her gather her hat, cloak, and gloves and escorted her to the door. "Thank you, Miss Roeswood; we were all dreading what sort of crack-brained notion the vicar might have had for us when he told us you were going to show us your ideas for the booth," she said, and hesitated, then continued, "and we were afraid that he might be letting—ah—kindliness—get ahead of him. He's a kindly gentleman, we all like him, but he's never done a charity booth before."

"He's a very kind and very pleasant gentleman," she agreed readily. "And don't underestimate him, because he's also quite intelligent. As you've seen, sometimes a new idea is better than what's been traditional."

"True, miss, and even though some folks would rather we had our old vicar back, well, he was a good man, but he's dead, and they aren't going to get him back, so at least Mr. Davies is one of us, and they ought to get to like him as much as us young ones. But please—some of us—"

Marina gave her a penetrating look, and she seemed to lose her courage, and blurted, "—we've been wondering about what you think of our vicar, what with making three visits in the week, and—"

She clapped her hand over her mouth and looked appalled at what she had let slip. Marina just chuckled.

"You mean, have I any designs on him myself, hmm?" she whispered, and the girl turned beet red. She couldn't have been more than fifteen, and surely had what schoolgirls called a "pash" for the amiable young man. Marina suddenly felt very old and worldly wise.

"My dear Miss Horn, I promise you that my only interest in our good vicar extends to his ability to play chess," she said soberly. "And his ability to compose and deliver an interesting, inspiring, and enlightening sermon," she added as an afterthought.

"Oh." The girl turned pale, then red again, and ducked her head. Marina patted her hand, and turned to go.

The meeting with the ladies had taken less than an hour; she hadn't expected it to take much longer, truth to tell. The cold air on her cheeks made enough of a distraction to get her tears swallowed down, and she mounted her horse feeling that she had done her duty, in more ways than one. If Arachne expected her back as soon as she finished, well, she was going to take her time, and never mind the cold.

"And she believed it?"

Arachne smiled; Reggie's expression could not be more gratifying, compounded as it was of equal parts of astonishment, admiration, and envy. He leaned back into his chair in her personal sitting room, a lush and luxurious retreat furnished with pieces she had taken from all over the house when she first arrived here, and smiled. "Mater," he continued, "That was brilliant! I never would have considered suggesting to Marina that her mother was a candidate for a sanitarium."

"It honestly didn't occur to me until I was in the middle

of that conversation with her," Arachne admitted. "But the child is so utterly unmagical—and seems to have been brought up that way—that when she was describing the letters her mother sent her about the Elemental creatures in the garden I suddenly realized how insane such tales would seem to someone who was not a mage." Her hand unconsciously caressed the chocolate-colored velvet of her chair. "Ah, that reminds me—you *have* cleared out the miserable little fauns and such from the grounds, haven't you?"

Reggie snorted. "A lamb sacrificed at each cardinal point drove them out quickly enough. All sweetness and light, was your Hugh's precious Alanna—the Earth Elementals she had around here couldn't bear the first touch of blood on the soil."

Arachne smiled. "When we make this place ours, we shall have to use something more potent than lambs. And speaking of lambs—"

He quirked an eyebrow. "I have two replacements safe enough, both with the magic in them, both just turned ten."

"Two?" She eyed him askance.

He sighed. "Besides the one that I took off to die, I lost a second that was carried off by a relative. Pity, that. She had *just* come to realize what was going to happen to her with that much lead in her. Her hands were starting to go. But the ones I've got to replace them are orphans off the parish rolls, and both are Earth, which should bolster our power immensely in that element."

Arachne smiled. "Lovely," she purred. "You are a wonderful pupil, dear." She raised her cup of chocolate to her lips and sipped, savoring the sting of brandy in it.

"You are a wonderful teacher, Mater," he replied slyly, and her smile broadened. "Fancy learning that you could steal the magic from those who haven't come into their powers. I wouldn't have thought of that—" He raised his glass of wine to her in a toast.

"It was others who thought of it before I did," Arachne admitted, but with a feeling of great satisfaction. "Even if none of them were as efficient as I am."

"That's my mater; a model of modern efficiency. You took one ramshackle old pottery and made it into four that are making money so fast you'd think we were coining it." He chuckled. "And in another six months?"

"There is a fine deposit of porcelain clay on this property, access to rail and water, near enough to Barnstaple for cheap sea shipping, plenty of water. . . ." She flexed her fingers slightly as if they were closing around something she wanted very much. "And cheap labor."

"And it is so very quiet here," Reggie prompted slyly. "Well, Mater, I'm doing my part. I'm playing court to the lit-tle thing, and I expect I'll have her one way or another by the summer, if your side doesn't come in. Have *you* discov-ered anything? Just between the two of us, I'd as soon not find myself leg-shackled; it does cut down on a fellow's fun, no matter how quiet the little wife is." He shrugged at her sardonic expression. "There's the social connections to think about, don't you know. They don't mind winking at a bit of jiggery-pokery when a fellow's single, but once he's married, he daren't let 'em find out about it, or they'll cut him."

She smiled, but sourly. "Ah, society. Well, once married, you needn't stay married to her long."

He frowned at that; the sulky frown he had whenever he was balked. "I'd still rather you found a way to make that curse of yours work," he told her crossly. "Folk start to talk if a fellow's wife dies right after the wedding. And this isn't the middle ages, you know. There's inquests, coroners' ju-ries, chemical tests—"

"That will do, Reggie," she said sharply. "At the moment, we have a number of options, which include you remaining married to the girl. She doesn't have to die to suit our purposes. She only needs to sicken and take to her bed." She allowed a smile to cross her lips. "And no one would censure you very strongly for a few little peccadilloes if you were known to have an invalid wife."

"Hmm. And if I had an—institutionalized wife?" he ventured, brightening. "A wife who followed—but perhaps, more dangerously—in the footsteps of her mother?"

She blinked. "Why Reggie—that is not a bad notion at all! What if we allowed some rumors about Alanna to spread down into the village? What would Marina think, having heard of her own mother's fantasies, if she began seeing things?"

"A mix of illusions created by magic and those created by stage-magic?" he prompted further, a malicious smile on his lips. "Your expertise—and mine? Why, she might even be driven to suicide!"

She laughed aloud, something she did so rarely that she startled herself with the sound. "Ah, Reggie! What a team we make!"

"That we do, Mater," he agreed, a smile spreading over his handsome face. "That we do. Now—I believe I have every detail set for tonight, but just go over the plans with me once again."

The mare, whose unimaginative name was Brownie, was probably the steadiest beast that Marina had ever seen. And she knew these lanes and paths far, far better than Marina did. At the moment, they were on the lane that ran along the side of another great estate called Briareley Hall, a pounded-dirt track studded with rocks like the raisins in a cake, wide enough for a hay wain pulled by two horses, with banks and hedgerows on either side that went well above Marina's head even when she was in the saddle. The bank itself, knobby with the roots of the hedge planted on it, came as high as Marina's own knee. The road was in shadow most of the day because of the hedgerows, and snow lingered in the roots of the hedgerow and the edges of the road no matter how bright the sun elsewhere. Brownie knew that she was on her way home, back to stable and oats and perhaps an apple, so her usual shambling walk had turned into a brisk one—nearly, but not quite, a trot. Marina was thinking of a hot cup of strong tea in the kitchen to fortify herself against the insipid tea she would get with Madam. She had ridden this route often enough to know that there was nothing particularly interesting on it, as well. So when Brownie suddenly threw up her head and shied sideways, she was taken completely by surprise.

Fortunately, the little mare was too fat and too indolent by nature to do anything, even shy, quickly or violently. It was more like a sideways stumble, a couple of bumbling steps in which all four feet got tangled up. Marina was startled, but too good a rider to be thrown, though she had to grab the pommel of the sidesaddle and drop the reins, holding on for dear life and throwing all of her weight onto the stirrup to brace herself against the sidesaddle. Her stomach lurched, and her heart raced, but she didn't lose her head, and fortunately, neither did Brownie.

When Brownie's feet found purchase again, the mare slung her head around and snorted indignantly at the thing that had frightened her.

Sweet heaven—it's a person—it's a girl!

A girl, huddled into the roots and frozen earth at the foot of the hedgerow. And one glance at the white, terrified face of that girl huddled at the side of the road sent Marina flying out of the saddle that Brownie's antics hadn't been able to budge her from.

The girl, dressed in nothing more than a nightgown and dressing-gown, with oversized slippers half falling off her feet, had scrambled backward and wedged herself in among the roots and the frozen dirt and weeds of the bank. Marina had never seen a human so utterly terrified in her life.

If her mouth hadn't been twisted up in a silent scream, if her eyes hadn't been so widened with fear that the whites showed all around them, she would have been pretty.

But she was thin, so very thin, and her skin was so pale the blue veins showed through. Too thin to be pretty anymore, unless your taste ran to the waiflike and skeletal.

All of that was secondary to the girl's terror, and instinctively, as she would have with a frightened animal, Marina got down on her knees and held out one hand, making soothing sounds at her. She heard Brownie snort behind her, then the unmistakable sound of the horse nosing at the sere grasses and weeds among the roots.

Good, she won't be going anywhere for a while, greedy pig.

"It's all right, dear. It is. I'm a friend." she said softly, trying to win past that terror to some kernel of sanity. If one existed.

From the way the girl's eyes were fixed on something off to Marina's right, Marina had a notion that the child wasn't seeing *her,* but something else. A tiny thread of sound, a strangled keening, came out of her throat; the sound of a soul certain that it was on the verge of destruction.

Except, of course, there was nothing there. At least, Marina thought there was nothing there.

Just to be sure, Marina stole a glance in the direction that the girl was looking, and made *sure* there was nothing of an occult nature there. Just in case. It was always possible that the girl herself had a touch—or more than a touch—of Elemental Magery about her and could *see* such things.

But there wasn't; nothing more alarming than sparrows in the hedges, no magic, not even a breath of power. Whatever this poor creature saw existed only in her own mind.

Marina crept forward a little; even through the thick wool of her skirt and three petticoats, she felt the cold of the frozen ground and the pebbles embedded in it biting into her knees and the palm of the hand that supported her. "It's all right, dear. I'll help you. I'll protect you." Her breath puffed out whitely with each word, but the girl still didn't seem to notice she was there.

Then—all at once, she did. Her eyes rolled like a frightened horse's, and the girl moved her head a little; it was a jerky, not-quite-controlled movement. And at the same time, her right hand flailed out sideways and hit a root, hard, hard enough to scrape it open. Marina gasped and bit her lip at the thought of how it should hurt.

The girl didn't react, not even with a wince. Exactly as if she hadn't even felt it.

There's more wrong with her than I thought. There's something physically wrong with her. As if it's not bad enough that she's seeing monsters that aren't there!

She heard a horse trotting briskly along the lane, coming from the direction in which she'd been riding. Purposeful sounds; whoever was riding or driving knew where he was going.

Good—maybe that's help.

A light breeze whipped a strand of hair across her eyes and chilled her cheeks. She didn't take her eyes off the girl, though. There was no telling whether or not the poor thing was going to bolt, or try to, any moment now. And dressed as she was, if she ran off somewhere and succeeded in hiding, she wouldn't last out the night. Not in no more than a nightgown, dressing gown and slippers.

The hoofbeats stopped; Marina risked a glance to the side to see who, or what, had arrived. *Even if it isn't help—surely if I call out for assistance, whoever it is will help me try to catch her.*

A horse and cart waited there, just on Marina's side of the next curve in the road. A tall, muscular gentleman, hatless, but wearing a suit, was walking slowly toward them, looking entirely at the girl. But the words he spoke, in a casual, cheerful voice, were addressed to Marina.

"Thank you, miss, you're doing exactly the right thing. Keep talking to her. Her name is Ellen, and she's a patient of mine. I'm Dr. Pike."

Marina nodded, and crooned to the girl, edging toward her as Pike approached from the other side. As long as they kept her between them, she didn't have a clean escape route.

Marina tried to catch the girl's eye again. "Ellen. Ellen, look at me—"

The wandering eye fell on her, briefly. Marina tried to hold it. "Listen, Ellen, some help has come for you, but you mustn't run away. Stay where you are, Ellen, and everything will be all right."

The newcomer added his voice. "Ellen! Ellen, child, it's Doctor Andrew—I've come to take you back—" the man said. Marina risked a longer look at him; he was rather . . . square. Square face, square jaw, blocky shoulders. He'd have looked intimidating, if it hadn't been that his expression, his eyes, were full of kindness and compassion. He made the "tch-ing" sound one makes to a horse to get its attention, rounded his shoulders to look less intimidating, and finally the girl stopped staring at her invisible threat. Her head wavered in a trembling arc until she was looking at him instead of her hobgoblins. He smiled with encouragement. "Ellen! I've come to take you back, back where it's safe!"

Now at this point, Marina was ready for the girl to screech and attempt to flee. By all rights, that "I've come to take you back" coupled with the appearance of her own doctor should make her panic. "I've come to take you back" was the sign that one was going to go "back" into captivity. And in Marina's limited experience, the doctors of those incarcerated in such places were *not* regarded as saviors by their patients. She braced herself, and prepared to try to tackle the girl when she attempted to run.

But evidently that was not the case this time.

With a little mew, the girl lurched out of her position wedged against the roots and stumbled, weeping, straight toward the newcomer.

It was more apparent than ever that there was something physically wrong with her as she tried to run to him, and could only manage a shambling parody of the graceful movements she should have had. But the thing that struck Marina dumb was that the girl did regard her doctor as a sort of savior.

She tumbled into the doctor's arms, and hid there, moaning, as if she was certain that he and he alone could shelter her from whatever it was she feared.

Marina could only stare, eyebrows raised. *Good gad,* she thought. *Good gad.*

As gracefully as she could, Marina got back up to her feet and walked—slowly, so as not to frighten the girl all over again—toward the two of them.

The girl hid her face in the doctor's coat. The doctor's attention was fully on his patient; Marina got the distinct impression that an anarchist could have thrown a bomb at him and at the moment he would have only batted it absently away. She was impressed all over again by the manner in which he soothed the girl, exactly as any sensible person would soothe a small child.

He looked up, finally, as she got within a few feet of the two of them, and smiled at her without a trace of self-consciousness. "Thank you for your help, miss," he said easily, quite as if this sort of thing happened every day.

She sincerely hoped that was *not* the case.

"I don't know how I could have helped you," she replied, with a shrug. "All I did was stop when my horse shied, and try to keep her from running off down the lane. I was afraid that if she found a stile to get over, she'd be off and hiding, and catch her death."

"You didn't ride on and ignore her, you didn't rush at her and frighten her further, you actually stopped and got off your horse, you even went down on your knees in the road and talked to her carefully. If that's not helping, I don't know what is. So thank you, miss. You did exactly as one of my own people would have done; you couldn't have done better than that if I'd trained you myself." He smiled warmly at her, with gratitude that was not at all servile. She couldn't help smiling back at him, as he wrapped his own coat around the girl. "I'm Andrew Pike, by the way. Dr. Andrew Pike. I own Briareley Sanitarium just up the road."

Now she recognized who and what he was—her mother had written something about the young doctor the summer before last—how he had spent every penny he owned to buy old Briareley Hall when it came up for sale, and as much of the surrounding land as he could afford from young Lord Creighton, of whom there was gossip of high living in London, and perhaps gambling debts.

So this was the doctor who had benefited by Lord Creighton's folly. His intention—which he had fulfilled within the month of taking possession—had been to establish his sanitarium for the treatment of mostly mental ills.

He apparently hadn't been able to afford most of the farm-land, which had been parceled out; he still had the grounds and the gardens, but that was all that was left of the original estate.

According to her mother, Dr. Pike, unlike too many of his ilk, who established sanitariums as warehouses for the ill and the inconvenient, actually attempted to cure people entrusted to his care. And it seemed that he had had some success at curing his patients. Not all, but at least some of the people put in his hands walked out of his gates prepared to resume their normal lives after a stint behind his walls.

"I have heard of you, Dr. Pike," she said, as these thoughts passed through her mind in an eye blink. "And I have heard well of you, from my late mother's letters." She gave him a look of speculation, wondering what his reaction was going to be to her identity. "Since there's no one here to introduce me, I trust you'll forgive my breach of etiquette, even if my aunt wouldn't. I am Marina Roeswood."

She watched as recognition and something else passed across his face. Sympathy, she thought. "Miss Roeswood, of course—may I express my condolences, then? I did not know your parents beyond a nodding acquaintance."

Somehow, she didn't want his sympathy, or at least, not on false pretenses. "Then you knew them better than I did, Doctor Pike," she said forthrightly, sensing that this man would be better served with the truth rather than polite fiction. "As you must be aware, or at least, as you would learn if you make even casual inquiries in the village, I was raised from infancy by friends of my parents, and I knew them only through letters. To me, they were no more real than—" She groped for the appropriate simile.

"—than creations of fiction?" he suggested, surprising her with his acuity and quick comprehension. "Nevertheless, Miss Roeswood, as John Donne said in his poem, 'No man is an island, complete in himself—' "

"And 'Every man's death diminishes me.' Very true, Dr. Pike, and well put," she bowed her head slightly in acknowledgement. "And I do mourn for them, as I would for any good folk who were my distant friends."

But not as much as I mourn to be separated from my aunt and uncles. She couldn't help the involuntary thought; she wondered, with a pang of the real despair that she couldn't muster up for her own parents, how long it would be before she could even get a letter to them.

The girl Ellen made an inarticulate cry of horror, turning to point at nothing off to the side of the road, and any reply he might have made was lost as he turned to her. And then came the next surprise.

She watched in astonishment as a glow of golden Earth magic rose up around him, a soft mist that clung to him and enveloped both him and his patient. And when she looked *closely,* she was able to make out the shields layered in a dozen thin skins that enclosed that power cocoonlike about them.

She felt her mouth dropping open.

What—

Brownie snorted into her hair, startling her. She snapped her mouth shut before he could notice her reaction.

Good gad—an Earth Master! Here! Why had Alanna never mentioned that the doctor was an Earth Master?

Because she didn't know?

Had her parents ever even met Dr. Pike face-to-face? She didn't recall a mention of such a meeting, if they had. But surely they would have noticed another Earth Master practicing his magics practically on their doorstep!

Maybe not. Those shields were good ones, as good as anything Elizabeth Hastings was able to create. Maybe better; they were like thin shells of steel, refined, impeccably crafted. So well-crafted, in fact, that she hadn't actually seen them at first.

I'm not sure I'd have seen him raising power if I wasn't used to seeing Earth Masters at work.

And Alanna seldom left Oakhurst, except on errands to the poor of the village. It wasn't likely she'd have encountered Dr. Pike on one of those.

She heard more horses approaching, as the girl responded to the healing power of the Earth energies Doctor Pike poured into her by sighing—then relaxing, and showing the first evidences of calming.

Another cart, this one slightly larger and drawn by a pair of shaggy Dartmoor ponies, stopped just behind Dr. Pike's; and three people, two men and a woman, carefully got out.

They were perfectly ordinary, and what was more, they didn't seem to notice anything different about Dr. Pike as they approached him. If they had been mages themselves, they would have waited for him to dismiss the energies he had raised before reaching for the girl—which they did, and Marina had to stifle a call of warning.

"Wait a moment," he cautioned, just before their fingertips touched the outermost shield. "Let me get her a bit calmer first."

Let me take this down before you do me an injury, you mean, Doctor. But he was as quick to disperse the unused power as he had been to raise it in the first place, and within moments, his shields had contracted down to become one with his very skin.

Oooh, that's a neat trick! I wonder how he does it?

"Here, Ellen, look who's come to take you back home," he said, carefully putting two fingers under her chin, and turning the girl's face toward the attendants.

Once again, although Marina would have expected her to

react with fear, the girl Ellen smiled with relief and actually reached out for the hands of one of the men and the woman. More than that—she spoke. Real words, and not animal keening or moans.

"Oh, Diccon, Eleanor—I'm sorry—I've had one of my fits again, haven't I?" There was sense in her eyes, and although her hands trembled, her words indicated that whatever had turned her into a mindless, fear-filled creature had passed for the moment.

"Yes, Miss Ellen," the man said, sorrowfully. "I'm afraid you did. And we was stupid enough to have left you alone with the door unlocked."

Her tremulous laugh sounded like it was a short step from a sob. "Well, don't do that again! I'm not to be trusted, remember?"

But Doctor Pike patted her shoulder, and said admonishingly, "It isn't you that we don't trust, child. It's the demons in your mind."

Ellen only shook her head, and allowed herself to be bundled into blankets and a lap robe in the cart and carried off.

Doctor Pike watched them go, then turned to Marina.

"That poor child is one of my charity patients," he said, and his voice took on a tinge of repressed anger. "Her cousin brought her here—the poor thing worked in a pottery factory as a painter, and she'd been systematically poisoned by the people who make their wealth off the labor and deaths of girls just like her!"

For a moment, she wondered why he was telling her this—did he know about Arachne and her manufactories?

But how could he? The villagers didn't know; they all thought, when they thought at all, that Arachne must own something like a woolen mill. Surely Dr. Pike had no idea that she had heard about the dangers of the potteries from the other side of the argument.

And I'd believe the doctor a hundred times over before I'd believe Madam.

The doctor continued, the angry words spilling from him as if they had been long pent up, and only now had been able to find release. "They use lead-glazes and lead-paints—the glaze powder hangs in clouds of dust in the air, it gets into their food, they breathe it in, they carry it home with them on their clothing. And it kills them—but oh, cruelly, Miss Roeswood, cruelly! Because before it kills them, it makes them beautiful—you saw her complexion, the fine and delicate figure she has! The paintresses have a reputation for beauty, and they've no lack of suitors—" He laughed, but there was no humor in the laugh. "Or, shall we say, men with money willing to spend it on a pretty girl. They might not be able to afford an opera dancer, or a music hall performer, but they can afford a paintress, who will be at least as pretty, and cost far less to feed, since the lead destroys their appetite."

She shook her head, sickened. Yes, she knew something of this—because her Uncle Sebastian had warned her about the danger of eating some of his paints, when she was a child. And there were certain of them, the whites in particular, that he was absolutely fanatical about cleaning off his hands and face before he went to eat.

Yes, she believed Dr. Pike.

His voice dropped, and a dull despair crept into it. "Then it destroys everything else; first the feeling in their hands and feet, then their control over their limbs, then their minds. And there is nothing I can do about it once it has reached that stage."

No, he can't heal what has gone wrong when the poison is still at work inside the poor thing! But—what if it was flushed out? Can Water magic combined with Earth do what Earth alone cannot? She felt resolve come over her like armor.

"Perhaps you cannot," she said, making up her mind on the instant. "But—perhaps together, you and I can."

With that, she raised her own shields, filled them for just a moment with the swirling green energies of water. Then she sketched a recognition-sigil that Elizabeth had taught her in the air between them, where it hung for an instant, glowing, before fading out.

And now it was his turn to stare at her with loose jaw and astonished eyes.

13

MARINA moved back to Brownie and pulled the reins out of the hedge where she'd tossed them. A small hail of bits of twig and snow came down with them. She took her time in looping the reins around her hand and turning back to face the doctor.

He bowed—just a slight bow, but there was a world of respect in it. She was very glad for a cold breeze that sprang up, for it cooled her hot cheeks.

"It seems I must reintroduce myself," he said, then smiled. His smile reached and warmed his eyes. "Andrew Pike, Elemental Master of Earth."

She sketched a curtsy. "Marina Roeswood, Elemental Mage of Water," she replied, feeling oddly shy.

Now he looked puzzled. "Not Master? Excuse me, Miss Roeswood, but the power is certainly within you to claim that distinction. And forgive my asking this, but as one mage to another, we must know the strengths of each other."

"The strength? Perhaps. But not, I fear, the practice," she

admitted, dropping her eyes for a moment, and scuffing the toe of her riding boot in the snow. "I only began learning the magics peculiar to my Element a few months ago, and then—" She looked back up. "Doctor Pike, this is the first time since I was taken from the place that I considered my home that I have been able to even think about magic without a sense of—well, nervousness. I can't think why, but there is something about my aunt that puts me on my guard where magic is concerned. I thought it was only that I didn't know her, and I am chary of practicing my powers around those who are strangers to me, but now I am not so sure."

He regarded her thoughtfully, holding out his hand, but not to her—a tiny glow surrounded it for a moment, and she was not surprised to see his horse pace gravely forward until its nose touched, then nudged, his hand. He caressed its cheek absently.

"I don't know anything about the magicians of this part of the country," he admitted. "Is *she,* perhaps, the antagonistic Element of Fire?"

"She's not a magician at all, so far as anyone can tell. I have never seen anything about her that made me think that was not true. And again, I thought *that* might be the reason for my reluctance, because I have been taught to be wary around those who do not have the gifts themselves—but even in the privacy of my own rooms, I cannot bring myself to summon the tiniest Elemental."

"Still—if she is the antagonist Element, but has been equally reluctant to practice around you because of possible conflicts that could only complicate your situation with her?" he persisted.

She frowned at him. "Possible, but there are no signs of it, none at all. As for the antagonistic Element, I've lived with my Uncle Sebastian all my life, and the worst clash we ever had was over which of us got the last currant bun at tea." She tilted her head to one side, as his expression turned thoughtful.

"In that case—could it simply be that you resent your aunt's interference in your life?" he hazarded, then shook his head. "You must forgive me again, but I am accustomed to asking very uncomfortable questions of my patients. Very often the only way for them to begin recovery is to confront uncomfortable, even painful, truths."

"I thought of that, but—" she would have said more, but the sound of another horse's hooves approaching from the direction of Oakhurst made her bite off her words. *Curse it*—she thought, knowing immediately that it must be one of the servants, or Reginald, or even Arachne herself come looking for her. "Dr. Pike, I spend every Wednesday afternoon with the vicar playing chess," she said hurriedly, thinking, *All right—it was only* one *Wednesday, but surely I can turn it into a regular meeting.* And she had no time to say anything more, for around the corner came Reginald, riding one of the hunters, a big bay beast with a mouth like cast iron and a phlegmatic temperament. Riding easily, too, which she would not necessarily have expected from someone she thought of as a townsman. His riding coat and hat were of the finest cut and materials, but she would not have expected less.

"Marina!" he called, his voice sounding unnecessarily hearty, "I thought I would ride down to meet you. Is there anything the matter?"

"Nothing at all, Reggie," she said smoothly. "This is Dr. Pike of the Briareley Sanitarium. We've had a chance encounter—Dr. Pike, this is my cousin, Reginald Chamberten."

"It was something less convenient for Miss Roeswood, I am afraid," Doctor Pike said, as cool and impersonal as Marina could have wished. "One of my patients took unauthorized leave, and Miss Roeswood here was kind enough to detain her long enough for my people to arrive, persuade her that all was well, and take her back."

Reggie's eyebrows assumed that ever-so-superior angle that Marina had come to detest. "Well, Doctor, you'll have to do better about keeping control of your patients! Dangerous lunatics running about the neighborhood—"

But Pike interrupted him with an icy laugh. "What, a little girl, frightened out-of-doors by a loud noise? Hardly dangerous, Mr. Chamberten. I do not keep dangerous patients, only those whose delicate nerves are better served by pleasant surroundings in the quiet of the countryside. And, sadly, a few who are, alas, in no condition to take notice of anything, much less leave their beds."

"Hmm." Reggie looked down his handsome nose at the doctor, and seemed to take a great deal of pleasure in being his arrogant worst. "Still, patients escaping—frightening young ladies—"

"I was hardly frightened, Reggie," Marina objected, suddenly tired of her cousin's little games. "I was far more concerned that the poor child didn't run off into the fields and come to grief. Even Brownie was more indignant than startled when she popped up under her hooves." Reggie's eyes narrowed, and she decided that it was politic to say no more. Instead, she put her foot in the stirrup and mounted before either man could offer her help. No small feat in a corset and long skirts—and into a sidesaddle; delicate young ladies accustomed to fainting at the least exertion couldn't do it. She thought she saw a brief flash of admiration in Dr. Pike's eyes before he returned to his pose of cool indifference.

"Still, letting your patients run off like that strikes me as careless," Reggie persisted.

"When the patients are themselves unpredictable, it is difficult to imagine what they are going to do in advance," the doctor replied in a tone of complete indifference. "That is one of the challenges of my profession. And if you will excuse me, I had better get on with my business so that I can get back to them. Thank you again, Miss Roeswood. A pleasure to meet you. Good day, Mr. Chamberten." With that, he hopped into his little gig and sent the horse briskly down the road toward the village.

"The cheek!" Reggie muttered, glaring after him.

"He's a doctor, cousin," Marina retorted, tapping Brownie's flank with her heel, and sending the horse back toward Oakhurst. "I believe arrogance even to the point of rudeness is required of them, like a frock coat. Otherwise they lose that air of the omniscient."

Reggie stared at her for a moment, then burst out with a great bray of a laugh, startling his horse. "Oh, well put, little cuz," he said, in tones that suggested he would be patting her head if he could reach it. "Now, the reason I came down here in the first place was because the mater and I had an early tea, and we're going to be going off for a day or two. Not more than three. Business, don't you know, a bit of an emergency came up—we'll be taking the last train tonight. Mater's left orders with the servants to take care of everything, and Mary Anne has been put in charge of them, so you won't have to trouble your pretty little head about anything."

She turned wide eyes on him. "That is very kind of her," she said, wondering if she sounded as insincere as she felt. The only possible benefit to all of this was that Mary Anne might consider it enough to oversee her behavior at mealtimes and leave her alone the rest of the time. She thought about asking whether she would still be allowed to ride out, and then decided that she *wouldn't* ask. If she didn't say anything, Arachne might forget to forbid her.

Reggie smiled down at her from his superior height. "I

suppose that old pile of Oakhurst seems rather overwhelming to you, doesn't it, cuz?" he laughed. "Bit different from that little cottage in Cornwall."

"It's not what I was used to," she murmured, dropping her eyes to stare at Brownie's neck.

"I should think not. Well, you just let us take care of it all for you," he said in that voice that drove her mad. She made monosyllabic replies to his conversation, something that only seemed to encourage him. Evidently, despite direct evidence to the contrary, he considered her timid.

But at least his monologue gave her plenty of information without her having to ask for it. Something had come up in the course of the afternoon that required their personal attention having to do with the factory near Exeter; they had called for tea and ordered the servants to pack, then Reggie had been dispatched to the Rectory to fetch Marina back. The carriage would take them to the nearest station to catch the last train, and there was some urgency to get there in order to make the connection. It sounded as if there hadn't been time for Arachne to issue many orders; in order to get to the station in time, they would have to leave immediately.

So it proved; when Marina and Reggie rode through the gates, the carriage, the big traveling one that required two horses, was already at the door, and one of the grooms waited to take Reggie's horse. Arachne seemed both excited and annoyed, but more the former than the latter. "Amuse yourself quietly while we're gone, Marina," she called, as Reggie climbed out of the saddle and into the carriage. "We'll be back by Saturday at the latest."

Then the coachman flicked the reins over the horses, and the carriage rolled away before she could issue any direct orders to Marina or anyone else.

For a moment she sat in her saddle as still as a stone. She was quite alone for the moment. She was on a fresh horse.

And the two people with authority to stop her from leaving were gone. *I could ride right down to the village and past. I could go home—*

Oh yes, she could go home. But if she did that, it would be no more than a week at most, and probably less, before Arachne appeared again at Blackbird Cottage with her lawyers and possibly more police, and she would be perfectly within her rights to do so.

I could only make trouble for Margherita and Sebastian and Thomas. The police, at the least, would not be happy, not happy at all.

What could Marina claim, anyway, as an excuse for escaping from her legal guardian? That her aunt was somehow abusing her with the lessons in etiquette, and the bizarre meals they shared? Arachne ate the same food, which was presumably wholesome, if unpalatable. And as for the etiquette, it could be reasonably argued that Marina was ill-educated, even backward, for her position in life. She had never gone to school, never had a proper nurse, nor a governess, nor tutors. She had never been exposed to the sort of society that her parents moved in. She was certainly ill-equipped to function in the social circles in which Arachne moved. That she didn't particularly *wish* to function in that social strata was of no purpose—her inherited wealth and rank as a gentleman's daughter would require her to do so. Anyone in authority would see Marina's rebellion as a childish tantrum, the result of having been spoiled by her erstwhile guardians, a reaction to the discipline that she badly needed.

This could be in the manner of a test on Arachne's part to see if she would behave herself when left on her own.

So instead of turning Brownie back out the gates and away, she guided the horse toward the stable and allowed the groom to help her down. As she expected, Mary Anne was waiting for her right inside the door.

"You need to change for tea, miss," the maid said, with her usual authoritarian manner, quite as if nothing whatsoever had changed. But something had—Mary Anne no longer had the authority of her mistress to back her. And—perhaps—had not been given any directions.

So we will start with something simple, I think, as a test.

"Did Madam leave any orders about what my meal menus were to be?" she asked, in a calculated effort to catch the maid off guard. She tilted her head to the side and attempted to look cheerful and innocent—not confrontational. She did not want to confront Mary Anne, only confound her.

"Why—no—" Mary Anne stammered, caught precisely as Marina had hoped.

"Ah. Then before I change, I had better take care of that detail for the rest of the day, or the cook will never forgive me." She smiled slightly, which seemed to put the maid more off balance than before. She detoured to the library, and quickly wrote out a menu for high tea, dinner, and for good measure, breakfast in the morning. And not trusting to Mary Anne, she took the menus to the cook herself, with the maid trailing along behind, for once completely at a loss. Only then did she permit the maid to bear her off to her room to be changed into a suitable gown. But Mary Anne was so rattled, she forgot completely to exchange the riding corset for a more restrictive garment, and the tea gown, designed to be comfortable and loose-fitting, went on over her petticoat and combinations without any corset at all. Marina was almost beside herself with pleasure by the time she sat down—in the empty parlor, of course—to the first truly satisfying meal that she had eaten since she arrived.

And thanks to her books and the other help she had been

getting from Peter, despite Mary Anne's glum supervision, she poured, selected, and ate with absolute correctness. Good strong tea to begin with, not the colored water she had been drinking. And real food, with flavor to it. Oh, it was dainty stuff, for a *lady,* not the hearty teas of Blackbird Cottage—but it was such a difference from what she'd been having with Arachne.

It was probably exactly the same food that downstairs ate for their tea, just sliced and prepared to appear delicate— dainty little minced-ham, deviled shrimp, and cheese sandwiches; miniature sweet scones, clotted cream and jam; and the most amazing collection of wonderful little iced cakes and tartlets.

And those hadn't been conjured up on the instant. But they certainly hadn't been making appearances at the teas she had been having.

Arachne's been eating on the sly, that's what. She has that miserable excuse for tea with me, then goes off to her own sitting room and has a feast.

Well, Arachne wasn't here to complain that her cakes were gone, and the cook could make more. Marina sipped her tea and nibbled decorously while she watched birds collecting the crumbs that the cook scattered for them in the snow-covered garden outside the parlor windows, ignoring the silent presence of Mary Anne. Left to herself, of course, it would have been a book by the fire, a plate of cakes, and a pot of tea—but she conducted herself as if she had company. There would be no lapses for Mary Anne to report; there was not a single scornful cough. At length, she rang for Peter to come take the trays away and Mary Anne went off to her own splendidly solitary tea while Marina remained in the library with a final cup of tea, a book, and the fire.

Dinner was delightful, though it required a change into corset and dinner gown. And Mary Anne was so rattled by then that she retired without even undressing her charge. Marina just rang for Sally to help her with the corset, then sent everyone away. So, attired in a warm and comfortable dressing gown and her favorite sheepskin slippers, she should have been ready to settle down beside the fire for a night of reading.

But two things stopped her. The first was that this absence gave her an unanticipated opportunity. She could write letters tonight without the fear that she would be caught at it. She sat down at her desk in her sitting room, and laid out paper, envelopes, and pen and ink—then stopped.

How to get them delivered? There was still that problem; she hadn't had so much as a single penny of money since she arrived here, and she had the distinct feeling that if she asked for any, Arachne would ask her what she wanted it for, since all her wants and needs were supplied.

She chewed on her lower lip for a moment. There were probably stamps in Arachne's desk and more in the one in the room used as an office for the estate manager.

But she counts them. I know *she does. She's the sort that would.*

The same probably held true for the pin money kept in the desk in the estate office. Probably? No doubt; pin money would provide an even greater temptation to staff than stamps, and Arachne had no real hold of loyalty over most of the servants, as demonstrated by their quiet support of Marina, and there was no trust there. So, she probably counted it out three times a day; no use looking for postage money there.

But—I wonder—does it need to be by a physical letter?

Arachne was not here—and if ever there was a chance to contact Elizabeth by means of magic, this would be it—

For a moment, excitement rose in her—if she could call

up an Undine or a Sylph, she could get messages to Elizabeth directly, perhaps even within the hour!

But, suddenly, she knew, she *knew,* that was wrong. That if she tried, something horrible would happen. It was *just* like the night she thought she had dreamed, when the Sylph gave her that warning, when she had been so very frightened. If she used magic here, even though Arachne was gone—it would be bad.

No. No.

A chill swept over her at the mere thought of invoking an Elemental here. She suddenly felt unseen eyes on her.

It might not be Arachne—it might be someone else entirely. But now that Marina was out of Blackbird Cottage, she was out from underneath protections that Thomas, Sebastian, and Margherita had spent decades building. It might only be that whoever or whatever was hunting for her now knew where she was and was watching her because she was living openly at Oakhurst, and with only the personal magical protections she herself had in place. Watching her—why? She was beginning to have an idea why Arachne might want to isolate her from all her former friends, but why would some stranger be watching her?

Well, that made no sense. Not that anything necessarily made obvious sense unless you had all the facts. *Still, I cannot imagine why some stranger would wish to spy on me, much less wish me harm.*

Ah, but thinking of Arachne, there might be another explanation for the feeling of an unseen watcher about. *What if Madam is a magician after all? Just—not the kind of magician I know about?*

She wondered. Elizabeth had told her to trust her instincts, and right now, those instincts warned her that she was not unobserved. If Arachne was a magician, Arachne would be able to tell if she worked magic. At the moment, the only magic that Marina was practicing was passive, defensive, protective; not only would it not draw attention to her, it was designed, intended, to take attention away from her.

She could have left something here as a sort of watchdog. And if I arouse the watchdog's interest . . . she'll find out what I was up to, and she'll discipline me for it.

Arachne would only have to forbid the servants to give her access to riding to punish her, and it would be a terrible punishment from her point of view. And as to why Arachne might want to keep her away from all her former friends— that was simple enough. Marina was not so naive as to think that Reggie was devoting so much of his time to her because she was attractive to him. Maybe Arachne didn't need Oakhurst or Marina's fortune, but a fashionable man-about-town like her son was an expensive beast to support. Granted, Reggie did seem to have some interest in working at the potteries, but still. . . .

On the other hand, if Arachne could get Marina married to her son, it would be her wealth that he was playing with, not Arachne's. And if he wrecked someone else's fortune, Arachne would not particularly care. In fact, it might be a way of bringing him to heel—if he overran himself and had to come to his mama for financial help, Arachne could impose all sorts of curbs and conditions on him.

The only way for Arachne to be sure that Marina would fall into her plans, would be to keep her niece here, completely under Arachne's thumb, until Reggie managed to wheedle her into matrimony.

So it will have to be real letters. For which I need postage. There must be another way of finding the money for two stamps!

If only—so many little boys were inveterate collectors of stamps—if *only* the uncles or her father had ever been

remotely interested in such things, she would probably have
found a stamp-album among the old school books with one
or two uncanceled specimens among the ones carefully
steamed off of the letters that arrived at the house!

Then it occurred to her; this house had a nursery that
hadn't been touched since the five children left it, except to
clean out the books from the schoolroom. And little children
tended to collect and hide treasures. With luck, she could
find them—heaven knew she had hidden enough little treasure boxes herself over the years. And with further luck,
there might be a penny or two amongst the stones and cast-
off snakeskins and bits of ribbon.

The thought was parent to the act; she put the writing implements away and got resolutely up from the desk.

This entailed an expedition armed with a paraffin-lamp,
but now she knew approximately where everything was,
courtesy of Sally. After opening a couple of doors that
proved to open up onto disused rooms other than the old
nursery—the nurserymaid's room, a linen closet, and the
old schoolroom—she found El Dorado—or at least, the
room she was looking for. Aside from being much neater
than any five real children would leave such a room, it was
pretty much as it must have looked when they were still
using it. She put the lamp on the nursery table and went to
work.

She found six caches before she decided that she was finished: one inside the Noah's Ark, two under the floorboards,
two out in plain sight in old cigar boxes and one in a cupboard in the dollhouse. When she'd finished collecting
ha'pennies, she had exactly fourpence. Quite enough to buy
postage for two letters. But by that point, it was very late,
she was chilled right through, and she decided to take her
booty and go to bed. *Must make sure and ask that they send
more postage in their return letters,* she told herself sleepily,

as she climbed into her warm bed after hiding her "treasure" in a vase. *I think like the rest of the mines in Devon, my copper-field is exhausted . . . though at least I haven't left any ugly tailings.*

Arachne stared out the window of their first-class carriage into the last light of sunset, and wondered how wretched a mess awaited them when she and Reggie got to Exeter. She prided herself on her efficiency, but there were some things that no amount of efficiency could compensate for.

Such as an accident like the one that had just occurred at the Exeter pottery.

Right in the middle of her discussion with Reggie, a telegram came. One of the kilns had exploded that morning. At the moment she didn't know what the cause had been, although she intended to find out as soon as she and Reggie arrived.

The railway carriage swayed back and forth, and the iron wheels clacked over the joins in the rails with little jolts— but the swaying and jolting was nothing compared with the discomfort of the same trip by carriage, and this first-class compartment was much warmer.

An explosion. These things happened now and again; water suddenly leaking into a red-hot kiln could cause it, or something in the pottery loaded into it—or sabotage by anarchists, unionists, or other troublemakers. If it was the latter, well, she was going to find *that* out quickly enough, and it wouldn't take clumsy police bumbling about to do so, either. A few words, a little magic, and she would know if there was someone personally responsible. If there was, well—whoever had done it would wish it had been the police who'd caught him, before he died.

The main problem so far as she was concerned was that

the kiln had been one of the ones where the glazes were fired, and three of her paintresses had been seriously injured, two killed outright.

Reggie would take care of the physical details tomorrow, but tonight—he and she would have to salvage what they could from the three injured girls.

At length, long after sunset, the train lurched into the Exeter station, and came to a halt with a shrieking of brakes and a great burst of steam. Reggie opened the compartment door, but the cachet (and money) attached to a first-class carriage got them instant service—one porter for luggage, another to summon a taxi. Little did he guess he would need to summon two. Their luggage went to the hotel with orders to secure them their usual rooms, but they went straight to the pottery.

At the moment, Arachne's sole concern, as they rattled along in a motor-taxi, was the tiny infirmary she kept for the benefit of the paintresses. If the other workers wondered about this special privilege, they never said anything, perhaps because the paintresses were given the grand title of Porcelain Artist and got other privileges as well. They needed the infirmary; after a certain point in their short careers, they grew faint readily, and this gave them a place to lie down until the dizziness passed off. Being paid by the piece rather than by the hour was a powerful incentive not to go home ill, no matter how ill they felt.

She'd telegraphed ahead to authorize sending for a doctor; if the girls could be saved, it would be better for her plans.

The taxi stopped at the gates, and Arachne stepped out onto the pavement without a backward glance, leaving Reggie to pay the fare. She went straight to her office; from the gate to the office there was no sign that anything had gone wrong; the sound of work, the noise of the machinery that ground and mixed the clay, the whirring of the wheels, and the slapping of the wet clay as the air and excess water was driven out of it continued unabated under the glaring gaslights—which was as it should be. Accidents happened, but unless the entire pottery blew up or fell into the river, work continued. The workers themselves could not afford to do without the wages they would lose if it shut down, and would be the first to insist that work went on the moment after the debris was shoveled out of the way.

The main offices were vacant, and unlit but for a single gaslight on the wall, but her managers knew what to leave for her. Her office, a spacious, though spartan room enlivened only by her enormous mahogany desk, was cleaned three times daily to rid it of the ever present clay-dust. This occurred whether she was present in Exeter or not, so that her office was always ready for her. Reggie caught up with her as she entered the main offices and strode toward her private sanctum. By the light shining under the door, someone had gone in and lit the gas for her; she reached for the polished brass knob and pulled the door open, stepping through with Reggie close behind her.

The doctor—one she recognized from past meetings, an old quack with an addiction to gin—stood up unsteadily as she entered. He had not been sitting behind the desk, which was fortunate for him, since she would have left orders never to use him again if he had been.

A whiff of liquor-laden breath came to her as she faced him. "Well?" she asked, shrewdly gauging his level of skill by the florid character of his face and steadiness of his stance. He wasn't that bad; intoxicated, but not so badly as to impair his judgment.

He shook his head. "They won't last the week," he told her. "And even if they do, they'll never be more than bodies propped in the corner of the poorhouse. One's blinded, one's lost an eye, and all three are maimed past working, even if their injuries would heal."

He didn't bother to point out that they probably wouldn't heal; the lead-dust they ate saw to that. The lead-poisoned didn't heal well.

She nodded briskly. "Well, then, we'll just let them lie in the infirmary until they die. No point in increasing their misery by moving them. Thank you, Dr. Thane."

She reached behind her back and held out her hand. Reggie placed a folded piece of paper into it, and she handed the doctor the envelope that contained his fee without looking at it. He took it without a word and shambled off through the door and out into the darkened outer office. She turned to Reggie, who nodded wordlessly.

"We might as well salvage what we can," Arachne said, with grudging resignation. "Tomorrow I'll find replacements. I'll try, at any rate."

"We're using up the available talent, Mater," Reggie pointed out. "It's going to be hard to find orphans who can paint who are also potential magicians—"

She felt a headache coming on, and gritted her teeth. She couldn't afford weakness, not at this moment. "Don't you think I *know* that?" she snarled. "Of all the times for this to happen—it could take days to find replacements, they probably won't be ideal and—" She stopped, took a deep breath, and exerted control over herself. "And we can burn some of the magic we salvage off these three to help us find others. We might as well; it'll fade if we don't use it."

"True enough." Reggie led the way this time, but not out the door. Instead, a hidden catch released the door concealed in the paneling at the back of the office, revealing a set of stairs faced with rock, and very, very old, leading down. "After you, Mater."

They each took a candle from a niche just inside the door,

lit it at the gas-mantle, and went inside, closing the door behind them. The stairs led in their turn to a small underground room, which, if anyone had been checking, would prove by careful measuring to lie directly beneath the infirmary.

At the bottom of the stairs was a landing, and another door. Arachne took one of the two black robes hanging on pegs outside the door to this room, and pulled it on over her street clothing. Only when Reggie was similarly garbed did she open this final door onto a room so dark it seemed to swallow up the light of their candles.

She went inside first, and by feel alone, lit the waiting black candles, each as thick as her wrist, that stood in floor-sconces on either side of the door. Light slowly oozed into the room.

It was a small, rectangular room, draped in black, with a small altar at the end opposite the door; it had in fact *been* a chapel, a hidden Roman Catholic chapel that dated back to the time of the eighth Henry, before it became what it was now.

It communicated with an escape tunnel to the river—the doorway now walled off, behind the drapery on the right—and its existence was the reason why Arachne had built this factory here in the first place. It wasn't often that one could find a hidden chapel that was both accessible and had never been deconsecrated.

It still was a chapel—but the crucifix above the altar was reversed, of course. This place belonged to another form of worship, now.

Arachne went to the wall where a black-painted cupboard waited that held the black wine and the special wafers, while Reggie readied the altar itself. She smiled to herself, in spite of their difficulties; if it was rare to find a chapel of the sort needed for a proper Black Mass, it was even rarer to find someone who was willing to go through the seminary and ordination with the express purpose of being defrocked just so he could celebrate it.

Clever Reggie had been the one to think of going to the Continent and lying about his age, entering a Catholic seminary at the age of fifteen, being ordained at eighteen—and being defrocked in plenty of time to pass his entrance examinations and be accepted at Cambridge with the rest of the young men his age. It had taken an extraordinary amount of work and effort. But then again, Reggie had enjoyed the action that had gotten him defrocked quite a bit. Enough that he hadn't minded a bit when it had taken him several tries to actually be caught in the act by the senior priest of his little Provence parish.

He had made *quite* certain there could be no forgiveness involved. Bad enough to be caught *in flagrante delicto* with a young woman of the parish. Worse, that the act took place in the sacristy, with her drunk and insensible. But when the young woman was barely pubescent—and feebleminded—and especially put in his charge by her trusting parents—and to cap it all with defiance of the priest, saying boldly that it was no sin, since the girl wasn't even human— well.

The old man had excommunicated him there and then, and had gone the extraordinary step of reporting his behavior to Rome to have his judgment reinforced with a papal decree.

Had all this happened by accident, it would have been impossible to hush up, and would have ruined Reggie.

But he and Arachne had been planning it from the moment he was old enough to understand just what it was that his mother was doing in her little "private bower." He had gone to France under an assumed name. No one ever knew he had even left England.

As for Arachne, she had been planning to *somehow* find

a true partner from the moment she found those old books at the sale of the contents of a Plymouth townhouse.

She closed her eyes for a moment, and savored the memory of that moment. Those books—they might have been waiting for her. It had only been chance that led her to be in Plymouth *that* day, to go down *that* street to encounter a sale in progress. Had her parents known what she'd brought home, hidden among the poetry books, they'd have died from horror. Or else, they'd never have believed, magicians though they were, that anything like the Black Mass truly had existed, far less that their daughter, their pitied, magicless daughter, was learning how to steal what she had not been born with.

That Reggie was only too happy to fall in with her plans had been the keystone that had allowed her to realize her plans in a way that fulfilled all her hopes and the wildest dreams she had dared to imagine.

And this had brought them both prosperity built from the beginning on the power drained from her poisoned and dying paintresses; power that no Elemental Mage would ever detect, for it was so far outside the scope of their experience.

She had gone beyond anything described in those books, in no small part because the Satanists who had written them had been so lacking in imagination. Yes, the *potential* power gained by sacrificing children was great—but their souls were lost to the Opposition, which was a loss as great as the gain. Why sacrifice infants, when the power generated by girls just at adolescence was so much stronger? Why sacrifice those whose souls were clean when one could engineer the corruption of potential victims, and gain not only the power from the death, but from the fall, and the despair when, at the last, they realized their damnation?

And why "sacrifice" them by knife or garrote or sword,

when one could still be the author of their deaths by means
of the way in which they earned their livings, and do so with
no fear of the law? It was the slow, dull blade of lead that
killed these sacrifices, making them briefly beautiful and
proud (another sin!) and then stealing strength, intelligence,
will, even sanity. And no one, not the police, not her social
peers who gathered at her parties, not the government, not
even the other workers, guessed that she was slowly and deliberately murdering them. In fact, no one thought of her as
anything but a shrewd businesswoman.

Sometimes, now and again, she wondered if other,
equally successful industrialists, were pursuing the same
path as she. Certainly the potential was there. So many children, working such long hours, among so much dangerous
machinery—the potential sacrifices were enormous. Weaving mills, steel mills, mines—all were fed on blood as much
as on sweat. She wondered now and again if she ought not
to expand her own interests.

No, I think I will leave that to Reggie. This is what I know.
She decanted the black wine into the chalice; arranged the
black wafers on their plate.

But her ways were so much more—efficient—than the
hurried slaughter of the unbaptized infants purchased from
their uncaring, gin- or opium-sodden mothers in some slum.

Not that she *hadn't* done all that in the beginning. It was
all she had been able to do, until she had married Chamberten, seen his pottery firsthand, and realized the *other uses*
that could be made of it. And now and again, at the Great
Sabbats, she had gone back to the traditional ways. But it
was always better to be on the right side of the law whenever possible; it made life so much less complicated.

"Ready?" Reggie asked. She smiled again. And turned to
face her priest and son, with the instruments of their power
in her hands, ready and waiting, for him.

14

ANDREW Pike arrived back at Briareley in a moderately better mood than when he had parted from the Roeswood girl and her insufferable fiancé. He *assumed* the man was her fiancé. He couldn't imagine any man acting so—proprietary—if he didn't have a firm hold over a woman.

He'd been so angry at the blighter—*Reginald. Reginald Chamberten. What does she call him? "Reggie, dear?" He looks like a Reggie—money, looks and arrogance enough for five*—that he had just driven poor little Pansy at a trot most of the way on the long way around to Briareley's front gate. He couldn't have turned her, of course; there wasn't enough room on that lane to turn a cart. But the bright sun, the cold wind in his face, his own good sense, and the unexpectedly positive outcome of his anxious chase after poor Ellen put him back in an equable mood by the time he reached the last crossing and made the turn that would take him to the gates. Pansy sensed the change in his mood and slowed to a walk.

He stopped being angry, and allowed himself to laugh at
the foolishness of even bothering to *be* angry at the arrogant
young jackanapes. Why should one overbearing idiot with
delusions of grandeur get his temper aroused? No reason, of
course. What was he to Reggie, or Reggie to him? Nothing.

So those are the neighbors. The girl was all right. No,
that was being ungenerous. The girl was fine. Look at how
she had stopped and managed to soothe Ellen—and she'd
practically volunteered herself and her magic to help him
with her.

*Earth and Water . . . the problem I've had is that if I
could get that damned poison confined in* lumps, *I could get
it out of her. And I could heal some, at least, of the damage.
But I can't suck it out of her blood, and that's the problem.
But a Water Master can actually purify liquid—and blood
is a liquid.*

· The girl—*Marina. Must put the name to her*—had said
she wasn't a Master. Yes, but she was the one who'd said she
could help. So she must be able to do *that,* at least, and for
his purposes it didn't matter if she thought she was a Master, so long as she had mastered the aspect of her Element
that would let her clean out the poison. She had the power to
do whatever she needed to; that much was very clear. Perhaps it was the will that was lacking to make her a Master;
she certainly hadn't stood up to that arrogant blockhead
who'd turned up to claim her. With a touch on the reins, he
guided the gig between the huge stone pillars at the head of
the drive, past the open wrought-iron gates. Pansy's head
bobbed as they came up the long graveled drive. The jolting
of the gig ended as soon as the wheels touched the drive—
hundreds of years of graveling and rolling went a long way
toward making a stretch of driveway as flat and hard as a
paved street in London. He looked up and caught sight of
the house through the leafless trees.

House? What a totally inadequate word for the place. It was an amazing pile of a building, parts of it going all the way back to Henry the Third, and it was no wonder that its former owner had let it go so cheaply. If it hadn't been for magic, *he* would never have been able to make the place habitable. But it was amazing what a troupe of Brownies could and would pull off, given the reason to.

Odd little beggars, Brownies. Lady Almsley claimed they must be Hindu or Buddhist, the way they worked like the very devil for anyone who really, truly deserved the help, and were off like a shot if you tried to do something to thank them. "Building up good karma, or dogma, or whatever it is," Lady Almsley said in her usual charming and decaptively muddle-headed manner. "I get rather confused with all those mystical things — but it just quite ruins it for them, steals all of it away, if you pay them for what they do, or even try to thank them."

Of course, they couldn't abide Cold Iron, not the tiniest particle of it, and he'd had to remove every nail and iron hinge in the place before they could move in to work. Thank God most of the place was good Devon stone, and the woodwork had mostly been put together the old-fashioned way, with wooden pegs instead of nails. Even so, he'd spent all of his time moving one room ahead of the busy little beggars, pulling nails and whatnot, and hoping what he took out didn't mean parts of his new acquisition were about to come tumbling down on his head.

Hearing what it was he was going to do with it though — that had pretty much insured that every Brownie not otherwise occupied on the whole island of Logres turned up to help. One month; that was all it had taken for the Brownies to do their work. One single month. Two months of preparation by him just to give them a place to start, and the one month keeping barely ahead of them. He never would have believed it, if he hadn't seen it with his own eyes.

He suspected that they had had help as well; Brownies weren't noted for forge-work, and every bit of ironmongery had been replaced with beautifully crafted bronze and copper. They didn't do stonework so far as he knew, but every bit of stone was as good or better than new, now. All the wet rot and dry rot—gone. Woodwork, floors, ceilings, roof, all repaired. Every draft, hole and crack, stopped. Chimneys cleaned and mended. Stone and brickwork retucked (and who had done *that?* Gnomes? Dwarves? Surely not Kobolds—though not *all* Kobolds were evil-minded and ill-tempered). Slates replaced, stones made whole, vermin vanished. He'd asked one of the fauns how they did it, he'd gotten an odd explanation.

"They remind the house of how it was, when it was new."
Though how one "reminded" a house of anything, much less how that could get it repaired, he could not even begin to imagine. Sometimes the best thing that an Elemental Master could do was to bargain with the Elementals themselves, then step back and allow them to determine how something was accomplished.

All right, none of it was major repair, it was all just little things that would quickly have required major repair if they'd gone on. The problem was, with a mismatched barn like this one, there were a great many of those little things; probably why the original owner hadn't done anything about them. When the money got tight, it was always the little bits of repair that got put off and forgotten. Tiny leaks in the roof that never gave any trouble became gaping holes, missing slates let in hordes of starlings and daws, cracks widened, wood rotted—then gave way.

Thank heavens I was able to step in before the trickle of small problems turned into a flood of disaster.

He could never have paid to have it all done in the normal way, no one could have. Not even one of those American millionaires who seemed to have pots and pots of money to throw about. It hadn't been *just* his doing; every Earth Master he knew had called in favors, once word had gotten around of what he was up to. *Bless 'em, for they're all going to be doing their own housekeeping for the next ten years, doubtless.*

For that was what Brownies usually did; household repair was just part of that. Mind, only the most adamantly Luddite of the Earth Masters still had Brownies about— people who lived in remote cottages built in the Middle Ages, genuine Scottish crofters, folk on Lewis and Skye and the hundred tiny islands of the coast. Folk who cooked with copper and bronze pots and implements, and kept—at most—a single steel knife in the house, shielded by layers of silk. Now they would be doing their own cleaning and mending for a time.

And by the time their Brownies returned, they'd probably have gotten used to having Cold Iron about, and all the conveniences and improvements that Cold Iron meant, and the Brownies would never come back to their homes. The price, perhaps, of progress?

Makes one wonder. I cannot even imagine doing without Cold Iron, steel. Well, think of all the screws and nails, the hinges and bits and bobs that are absolutely integral to the building alone! Let alone iron grates in the fireplaces, the stove and implements in the kitchen, all the ironmongery in the furniture! It was only this one time, for this one reason, that I was able to. And very nearly not even then. It had been an exhausting three months, and one he hadn't been entirely certain he would survive.

Already there was so much Cold Iron back in the place that the creatures who were most sensitive couldn't come

within fifty miles. Small wonder few people saw the Oldest
Ones anymore, the ones the Celts had called the Sidhe; there
was no place "safe" for them on the material plane anywhere near humans.

He drove Pansy around to the stables—ridiculous thing,
room for twenty horses and five or six carriages in the carriage house—driving her into the cobblestone courtyard in
the center of the carriage house to unharness her, getting her
to back up into the gig's bay so he wouldn't have to push it
into shelter by hand. Another advantage to being an Earth
Master, his ability to communicate with animals.

With the gig's shafts resting on the stone floor of the
carriage-bay, he gathered up the long reins so that Pansy
wouldn't trip on them and walked her to her stall in the stables. He supposed it was ridiculous for the chief physician—and owner!—of the sanitarium to be unharnessing
and grooming his own horse but—well, there it was, Diccon was still in the manor, probably looking after some other
chore that needed a strong back, and *he* wasn't going to let
Pansy stand about in harness, cold and hungry, just because
he was "too good" to do a little manual labor.

And Pansy was a grateful little beast. So grateful that she
cheered him completely out of any lingering annoyance
with that arrogant *Reggie Chamberten.*

But how had a girl like that gotten engaged to someone
like him? They were, or seemed to be, totally incompatible
personalities. Unless it was financial need on her part, or on
her family's. Stranger things had happened. Just because
one owned a manor, that didn't mean one was secure in the
bank. Look what had happened to Briareley.

He went in through the kitchen entrance—a good, big
kitchen, and thanks to the Brownies, all he'd had to do was
move in the new cast-iron stove to make it perfect for serving all his patients now, and the capacity to feed the many,

many more he hoped to have one day. Right now, he had one cook, a good old soul from the village, afraid of nothing and a fine hand with plain farm fare, who used to cook for the servants here. Red-faced and a little stout, she still moved as briskly as one of her helpers, and she was always willing to fix a little something different, delicate, to tempt a waning appetite among his patients. Helping her were two kitchen maids; a far cry from the days when there had been a fancy French cook for upstairs, a pastry cook, and a cook for downstairs *and* a host of kitchen maids, scullions, and cleaning staff to serve them.

"Where is Eleanor?" he asked Mrs. Hunter, the cook.

"She's still with that poor little Ellen, Doctor, but Diccon recks the girl will be all right. He's took up a hot brick for her bed, and a pot of my good chamomile tea." Mrs. Hunter beamed at him; she approved of the fact that he took charity patients along with the wealthy ones—and she approved of the fact that he was trying to *cure* the wealthy ones rather than just warehousing them for the convenience of their relatives. In fact, Mrs. Hunter approved of just about everything he had done here, which had made his acceptance by Oakhurst village much smoother than it would have been otherwise. Not that the folk of Devon were surly or standoffish, oh, much to the contrary, they were amazingly welcoming of strangers! During his early days here, when he'd gotten lost on these banked and hedged lanes time and time again, he'd found over and over that when he asked for directions people would walk away from what they were doing to personally escort him to where he needed to go. Astonishing! So much for the stereotype of the insular and surly cottager.

Not in Devon. In Devon, if one got lost and approached a cottage, one was more apt to find oneself having to decline the fourth or fifth cup of hot tea and an offer of an overnight bed rather than finding oneself run off with a gun and snarling dogs.

But nevertheless, there was a certain proprietary feeling that villagers had for the titled families of their great houses and stately homes. They tended to resent interlopers coming in and buying out the families who had been there since the Conquest. Mrs. Hunter smoothed all that over for him.

"Thank you, Mrs. Hunter," he said, and passed through the kitchen after a deep anticipatory breath redolent of rabbit stew and fresh bread. That was one good thing about buying this place. It wasn't poaching when you set rabbit wires on your own property. It wasn't poaching when you had your own man shoot a couple of the red deer that came wandering down into your back garden. There was some lovely venison hanging in the cold larder. Frozen, actually, thanks to the cold winter. Every little bit of money saved was to the good at this point. Money saved on food could go toward the wages of another hand, or perhaps even having gas laid on. At this point, electricity was not even to be thought of; there wasn't an electrified house in the entire village. Someday, perhaps, the wires would come here. And just perhaps, by the time they did, he would have the money put away to have the house wired.

First, though, would come extra wages for extra help.

Because until he could afford to hire another big, strong fellow like Mrs. Hunter's son Diccon, he didn't dare take potentially dangerous patients.

From the downstairs he took the former servants' stair upstairs, into the house proper.

What the family hadn't taken or sold in the way of furnishings, he had mostly disposed of as being utterly impractical for their purposes. A pity, but what was the point of having furnishings too fragile to sit on or too heavy to shift?

Damned if he was going to tear down woodwork or paint

anything over, though—even when the effect was dreadful. Some day, someone might want to buy this barn and make it a stately home again. Too many folk didn't think of that when they purchased one of these places and then proceeded to cut it up.

Besides, for all I know, the ghosts of long-gone owners would rise up against me if I touched the place with impious hands. When you were an Elemental Master, such thoughts were not just whimsy; they had the potential to become fact. Having angry spirits roaming about among people who were already mentally unbalanced was not a good idea.

Particularly not when those people were among the minority who were able to see them as clearly as they saw the living.

Andrew had elected to make diverse use of the large rooms on the first floor. The old dining room was a dining room still, a communal one for those patients who felt able to leave their rooms or wards. The old library was a library and sitting room now, with a table for chess and another for cards; the old music room that overlooked the gardens was now allotted to the caretakers, where they could go when not on duty for a chat, a cup of tea, or a game of cards themselves. But the rest of the large rooms were wards for those patients who need not be segregated from the rest, or who lacked the funds to pay for a private room, or, like Ellen, were charity cases. Needless to say, the patients ensconced in the former bedrooms upstairs were the bread-and-butter of this place.

He checked on the two wards before Ellen's carefully, since it was about time for him to make his rounds anyway, but all was quiet. In the first, there was no one in the four beds at all, for they were all playing a brisk game of faro for beans in the library. In the second, the patients were having their naps, for they were children.

Poor babies. Poor, poor babies. Children born too sensitive, like Eleanor, or born with the power of the Elements in them; children born to parents who were perfectly ordinary, who had no notion of what to do when their offspring saw things—heard things—that weren't there. He looked for those children, actively sought for them, had friends and fellow magicians watching for them. If he could get them under his care quickly enough, before they really *were* mad, driven to insanity by the tortures within themselves and the vile way in which the mentally afflicted were treated, then he could save them.

If. That was the reason for this place. Because when he began his practice, he found those for whom he had come too late.

Well, I'm not too late now. Here were the results of his rescue-missions, taking naps before dinner in the hush of their ward. Seven of them, their pinched faces relaxed in sleep, a sleep that, at last, was no longer full of hideous nightmares. They tended to sleep a lot when they first arrived here, as if they were making up for all the broken unrest that had passed for slumber until they arrived here, in sanctuary at last.

He left them to their slumbers. It wasn't at all the usual thing for children to be mental patients.

Then again, he didn't have the usual run of mental patients; when *his* people were "seeing things," often enough, they really *were* seeing things.

That was why he'd had no difficulty in getting patients right from the beginning. Once word spread among the magicians, the occultists, and the other students of esoterica that Dr. Andrew Pike was prepared to treat their friends, relations, and (tragically) children for the traumatic aftermath of hauntings, curses, and other encounters with the supernatural, his beds began to fill. He got other patients when mundane physicians referred them to him, without knowing what it was they suffered from but having seen that under certain circumstances, with certain symptoms, Andrew Pike could effect a real cure.

It wasn't only those who were born magicians or highly sensitive who ended up coming to him. Under the right—or perhaps wrong—circumstances, virtually anyone could find horror staring him in the face. And sometimes, it wasn't content just to stare.

There were a few of the adult patients who were under the judicious influence of drugs designed to keep them from being agitated, which tended to make them sleep a great deal; those were the ones back in their beds after tea. The rest of the patients were in the parlor, reading or socializing. He didn't like drugging them, but in the earliest stages here, sometimes he had to, just to break the holds that their own particular horrors had over them.

Ellen was on the third ward, and was fast asleep when he got there. Eleanor, the female ward nurse, was with her, sitting beside her bed, and looked up at the sound of his footsteps. She kept her pale hair pulled tightly back and done in a knot after the manner of a Jane Eyre, and her dark, somber clothing tended to reinforce that image. Eleanor seldom smiled, but her solemn face was not wearing that subtle expression of concern that would have told him there was something wrong.

Well—more *wrong than there already is.*

"She'll be fine for now, Doctor," Eleanor said without prompting. "She got chilled, but I don't believe there will be any ill effects from it. We got her warmed up quickly enough once we got her back here." She stroked a few stray hairs from Ellen's brow, and her expression softened. "Poor child. Doctor, we mustn't allow that boy Simon Ashford around her. She can see what he sees, of course; they seem peculiarly sensitive to one another. That's what frightened her. I've already told Diccon not to let the child near her, but not why, of course."

"I'll make a note of it." Eleanor was invaluable; one of his former patients who had decided to stay with him as a nurse and assistant when he'd helped her out of the hell that her inability to shut out the thoughts of others had thrown her into. Pike had been the only doctor at the asylum where she'd been who had understood that when it sounded as if she was answering someone that no one else could hear—she really was speaking to another person, or trying to. She was another of those cases of extreme sensitivity to the thoughts of others that came on at puberty—and thank heavens, one he had gotten to in time. It had been getting worse, and before very long, all of the voices in her head would have driven her mad.

For a time, she had been in love with him. He had allowed it long enough to be sure that her cure was permanent, then he had used just a little magic, the opposite of a love charm, to be certain that she fell out of love with him again. A very useful bit of magery, that charm, for it was inevitable that most of his female patients, and even a few male, fell in love with him. In fact, there was one school of thought among the Germans that such an emotional attachment was necessary for the patient's recovery, that only someone who was beloved could be trusted with the most intimate secrets. Whether that was true or not, Andrew wasn't prepared to judge; it was his duty to see that he did everything humanly possible to cure them, no more, and no less. Let others formulate theories; he worked by observation and used what was successful. He had more than enough on his hands, balancing magic and medicine, without worrying about concocting theories of how the mind worked!

He wished, though, that Eleanor could really find someone for herself. The regret that she hadn't came over him as he watched her with Ellen; she was a nurturer, and she loved the children here. She seemed very lonely; well educated, she would have probably become a teacher had she not her unfortunate background.

"Who was that girl?" Eleanor asked, rising and smoothing her pearl-gray apron as she did so. "The one that helped us, I mean."

"That, it seems, was the young Miss Roeswood that the village has been buzzing about." He raised an eyebrow at her, and she made a little "o" with her mouth. Eleanor was a Methodist by practice, so of course she went to chapel, not church, and had missed the exciting appearance of the mysterious young heiress at Sunday services two weeks ago.

"But—what a *kind* young woman she is!" Eleanor exclaimed. "Not that her parents were bad people but—"

"But I cannot imagine, from what I heard of her, seeing Alanna Roeswood on her knees in the snow, trying to keep Ellen from running off into the fields," Andrew replied with a nod. "Visiting the sick with soup and jelly, yes. Delivering Christmas baskets. Sending bric-a-brac to the jumble sale. But not preparing to tackle a runaway madwoman to keep her from freezing to death in the woods." He thought about asking Eleanor if she had seen anything of Marina's magic, but realized in the next instant that of course, she wouldn't. *She* wasn't a magician, only a sensitive. If she wished to, she might be able to hear the girl's thoughts, but only if the girl herself dropped the shields that she must have had to have avoided immediate recognition by Andrew himself.

This Marina Roeswood might claim she wasn't a Master, but all her shields were as good as anything he had ever seen.

"If Ellen is well enough," he suggested, "Why don't you help me finish the rounds?"

Eleanor got to her feet without an objection. "Certainly, Dr. Pike," she replied. "Will I need my notebook?"

"I don't think so," he told her, and smiled. "I certainly hope that young Ellen is our last crisis for a while."

With Eleanor following behind, Andrew finished checking on the patients in the other wards, and took a quick look in on the library. The card game was still going briskly, and Craig, one of his little boys who was very close to being discharged, had engaged Roger Smith, one of the oldest patients, in a spirited chess match. Andrew and Eleanor exchanged a quick smile when they saw that; Roger was going to be discharged tomorrow, and he loved chess as much as Craig disliked it, so this must be Craig's idea of a proper farewell present for the old man.

Craig was one of the few children here who was an "ordinary" patient, brought here by a parent because of a life-threatening breakdown brought on by strain. Young Craig had been a chess-prodigy; his father had trotted him around Britain and three-fourths of Europe, staging tournaments in front of paying audiences with the greatest of chess masters, before his health and mental stability collapsed under the strain. He'd literally collapsed, and it was a good thing he'd done so in Plymouth, and that, for once, his mother had been with him as well as his father. She took over when the father simply tried to shake the boy into obedience—and consciousness!—again. When Craig couldn't be awakened, the father vanished, and she started looking for someone to help her child.

Small wonder Craig hated chess now—and, in fact, on Pike's suggestion was going to pretend that all of his knowledge of the game had vanished in his breakdown. His mother, on recommendation from one of Andrew's colleagues, had brought him to Briareley, hoping to find someone who would treat her son as a child and not a broken machine that needed to be fixed so it could resume its job.

But it was a measure of how much he had recovered that he was willing to treat the old man who had read him fairy tales to send him to sleep every night for the past six months to the game that gave *him* such pleasure.

"He's a good boy, Doctor," Eleanor said softly.

"Yes," Andrew replied, feeling a warm smile cross his lips. "He is. God willing, that beast that calls himself a father will leave him alone now."

They took the wide, formal stairs up to the second floor, and the private rooms.

Here, the patients were a mix in the opposite direction from the ones in the wards. Most of these folk were not magicians or extraordinarily sensitive. Andrew's establishment was slowly gaining a reputation among ladies of fashion as a place to recover from nerves.

And "nerves" was an umbrella that covered a great many things.

Now, Andrew would *not* accept the sort of nerves that came from too much liquor, or from indulgences in drugs. For one thing, he could not afford the sort of round-the-clock watching such patients required. For another, their problems would make life difficult for his other patients. For a third, well, he'd need half a dozen Diccons to make sure everyone was safe.

Nor did he accept—although it was always possible that a set of circumstances would occur that would cause him to make an exception—the sort of nerves that produced an inconvenient infant in nine months' time.

But if too many debutante-parties and the stress of being on the marriage-market sent a young lady into hysterics or depression—if too many late nights and champagne and tight corseting did the same to her mother—if the strain of too much responsibility sent a young widow into collapse—

Well, here there were quiet, well-appointed rooms, simple but delicious food, grounds where one could walk, lanes where one could drive, and no one would bother you with invitations, decisions, noise, bustle, or anything else until you were rested. A week, a month, and you were ready to go back to the social whirl.

And no one acted as if your problems were so insignificant that you should feel ashamed of your weakness. And if Andrew's establishment was doing no more than providing a kind of country spa rather than real treatment for serious problems for these women, well, why not? Why shouldn't he have the benefit of their money?

If, however, there was a serious problem, unlike a spa or other fashionable resort, Andrew was going to spot it, and at least attempt to treat it.

So he and Eleanor completely bypassed one wing of guest rooms that had been converted into patient rooms. The ladies housed there had no need of him or his services; they were quite satisfied to see him once a day, just after a late breakfast.

He did stop at several other rooms, though. Three were cases of real depression, and aside from seeing that they got a great deal of sunlight (which seemed to help), and slowly, slowly seeing what healing magic might do, there wasn't a lot that seemed to make a difference to them.

At least he wasn't dousing them with cold water baths six times a day, or tying them to beds and force-feeding them, or throwing them into those horrors called general wards.

There were four cases of feeble-mindedness, one of whom could barely feed himself. Two unfortunates who had fallen from heights onto their heads, who were in similar case. One old demented woman. All of these could have been warehoused anywhere, but at least they had family who cared that they were treated decently, kept clean, warm, and well-fed, and that no one abused them. For this, they paid very well indeed, and Dr. Pike was very grateful.

And he had one poor soul who really *was* hearing voices in his head that didn't exist, not on any plane. He didn't know what to do with that fellow; nothing he tried seemed to work. There was something wrong in the brain, but what? And how was he to fix it, even if he could discover what was wrong?

That man, though he had never shown any inclination to violence, was locked in a room in which the bed and chair were too heavy to move, and in any case, bolted to the floor so that he couldn't use them to break the window. There was an ornamental iron grate bolted over the window on the inside. And the poor man was never allowed a candle or an open fire; there was a cast-iron American stove in the fireplace in his room, and Andrew could only hope that the voices in his head would never tell him to try to open it with his bare hands.

He was the last visit this afternoon; all was well, and Andrew heaved a sigh of relief as he always did.

"Have your tea, Eleanor," he told her. "I'm going to go help Diana Gorden with her shields."

She smiled faintly. "Very well, Doctor. Don't forget to eat, yourself."

"I won't," he promised.

And of course, promptly did.

15

MARINA stared at the four small objects in the palm of her hand; there was no confusion about what she was seeing, as sunlight flooded the room. In her hand lay what were supposed to have been four ha'pennies that she had just poured out of the vase. Well, she'd thought they were ha'pennies last night when she'd put them *in* the vase.

But when she'd tilted them out this morning, it was painfully clear that they were nothing of the sort. They were, in fact, four "good conduct" medals of the sort given out at Sunday School, *sans* ribbon and pin. They were copper, they did feature the Queen's profile, and they were the size of a ha'pence. But not even the kindest-hearted postmaster was going to exchange these for a stamp.

I must have been more tired than I thought. I just looked at these things last night, saw the Queen's head, and thought they were coins. Or maybe it was just that I was working by the light of one candle. Oh, conkers. I'm back where I started.

She sighed. She'd have wept, except that with Madam and Reggie still gone, she had plenty of things to leaven her disappointment. She had a real breakfast, Miss Mary Anne had been told that, in absence of any tasks that Madam had left for Marina to do (there were none, since Madam had left in such a hurry) Marina was going out to ride this morning *and* this afternoon.

Mary Anne sullenly attired her in her riding habit and left, ostensibly on some other task that she had been assigned. In reality, since no one seemed to have authority over Mary Anne but Madam, that was unlikely. Marina strongly suspected that the girl would be back here to snoop as soon as her putative mistress was gone, though. She'd probably go through every bit of Marina's belongings while she had the chance.

Well, I'd better dispose of these. . . . She put them in the very bottom of her jewel case. If Mary Anne found them, she would assume that they were further evidence of Marina's faithful churchgoing, which was all to the good; church activities were high on the list of appropriate things for young ladies of even the highest ranks to do.

A quick note on menu-paper to the cook took care of luncheon, tea and dinner, and Marina was out into the cold, flinging her cloak over her shoulders, her hat pinned jauntily on her head at an angle that was quite out of keeping with one in mourning.

This time, instead of placid old Brownie, Marina asked the groom to saddle the iron-mouthed hunter Reggie usually rode, an extremely tall gelding named Beau. She had a notion that he was all right, despite Reggie's assertions that "he's a rum 'un," and to make sure she started off on the best of terms with him, she brought a bread crust smeared in jam from breakfast. He laid back his ears when he saw the groom approaching with the saddle, but pricked them forward again when it was Marina, not Reggie, who approached.

She held out the crust, which he sniffed at, then engulfed with good appetite, using lips more than teeth. That was a good sign. As he chewed it, she ventured to scratch his nose. He closed his eyes and leaned into the caress, then made no fuss about being saddled and bridled. He stood steady as a rock beside the mounting-block (he was so tall she needed to use one) and then stepped out smartly when she barely nudged him with a heel. She hadn't even got halfway down the drive before figuring out that although his mouth was insensitive, he neck-reined beautifully. And his manners were impeccable.

"Well, you're just every inch the gentleman, aren't you?" she asked, as his ears swiveled back to catch what she said. He snorted, quite as if he understood her, and bobbed his head.

He had a silken fast walk, and because his legs were so long, a surprisingly comfortable trot. *No odds that's why Reggie bagged him,* she thought. *I ought to see if I could teach him to "bounce" on his trot; that'd serve Reggie right.*

Ah, but Reggie would probably just take it out on the horse, which wouldn't be fair to Beau.

She had a particular goal in mind for this morning, while Madam was still away; she had gotten Sally to tell her the way to Briareley, and she was not going to wait for Dr. Pike to decide whether or not he was going to contact her at the vicarage. She was going to come to *him.* This would probably be her only opportunity to go to Briareley ever; Madam might be back this very afternoon, and would never permit Marina to make such a visit. It would be highly improper— they hadn't been introduced, Briareley was no longer a place where one might ask for a tour of the house, *she* should not be visiting a man unescorted. The notion of paying a visit to a sanitarium where there were madmen—well, a daring young man might well pull such a thing off on a lark, but no woman would even consider such a thing. Marina was breaking all manner of social rules by doing this.

But this was not a social visit—this was Magician to Magician, and as such, did not fall under any of the chapters in Marina's book of etiquette.

I did look, though, she thought whimsically, *I tried to find even a mention of Magician to Magician protocol. But there wasn't anything there on the subject. So the "Young Lady's Compleate Guide to Manners" isn't as complete a guide as it claims to be.*

The hunter trotted along briskly, while she was engrossed in thought. Etiquette aside, she needed to be very careful with what she did and did not say and do around this man. After all, she knew nothing about him, except that he had a good reputation in the village. Now, that was no bad thing; the village saw a great deal, and gossiped about it widely.

But that didn't mean that the village saw everything; the fact that he hadn't betrayed himself as an Earth Master proved that.

Magicians were only human, as Elizabeth had been at pains to point out. They could be brave—or cowards. Noble—or petty. Altruistic—or selfish.

Marina had a long talk with Sally over breakfast; she knew already that Doctor Pike had more than charity patients—he catered to ladies of wealth and privilege who suffered from nervous exhaustion. Treatment for these special patients amounted to a bit of cosseting, flattering attention to their symptoms, some nostrums, and being left undisturbed—or pampered—as their whims dictated. And these women were probably paying a great deal of money to have that much attention given them by a sympathetic, handsome, young physician. So, whatever else Dr. Pike was, he was clearly willing to pander to them in order to get those handsome fees.

Not the altogether altruistic and idealistic physician he might have seemed from his treatment of the runaway girl.

Caution is in order, I think, in how much I believe about him. And caution in how much I tell him about myself. But if nothing else, I will make arrangements to help him with that girl.

The hunter's head bobbed with effort as he climbed a hill; at a walk, not a trot; this was a steep bit of lane. She could just imagine the hay-wains laboring up here—the poor horses straining in their harness as they tried to get themselves and their load up to the top of this rise. Add to that the rocks and ruts, what a hideous climb it must be.

Or perhaps not; it wasn't quite wide enough for a loaded wain, which must have relieved quite a few farm horses over the years.

And then they reached the top; the horse paused for a breath, and she reined him in, looking around for a moment. And paused, arrested by the view.

On her left, the hill dropped steeply away from the lane, giving her an unparalleled view of the countryside. The top of the hedge along the edge of that field was actually level with her ankle, the slope dropping off steeply at the very edge of the lane and continuing that way for yards. The hills and valley spread out below her in a snow-covered panorama, ending in distant, misty hills, higher than the rest, blue-gray and fading into the clouds on the horizon, that *might* be the edge of Exmoor.

Now, it was to be admitted that no one traveled from across the world—or even across England—to see the views of Devon countryside. There was nothing spectacular here in front of her, no snow-covered peaks, no wild cliffs and crashing waves, no great canyons, wilderness valleys.

But spectacle was not always what the heart craved, although the soul might feast on it. *Sometimes you don't want a feast. Sometimes you just want a cozy tea in front of the fire.*

She rested her eyes on the fields below, irregularly-shaped patches of white bordered by the dark gray lines of the leafless hedges, like fuzzy charcoal lines on a pristine sheet of paper. The wavering lines were sometimes joined, and sometimes broken, by coppices of trees, the nearer looking exactly like Uncle Sebastian's pencil-sketches of winter trees, the farther blurred by distance into patches of gray haze, containing the occasional green lance-head of a conifer. Some of those white patches of ground held tiny red-brown cattle, scarcely seeming to move; presumably some held sheep, although it was difficult to make out the white-on-white blobs at any distance. Sheep on the high ground, cattle on the low, that was the rule. Farmhouses rose up out of the snow, shielded protectively by more trees, looking for all the world, with their thatched roofs covered in snow, and their walls of pale cob or gray stone, as if they had grown up out of the landscape. Thin trails of white smoke rose in the air from chimneys, and in the far distance, barely discernible, was the village, a set of miniature toy-buildings identifiable by the square Gothic tower of St. Peter's rising in their midst.

There was a faint scent of wood smoke from those far-off hearth fires; a biting chill to the air that warned of colder winds to come, and a scent of ice that suggested she might want to be indoors by nightfall. The blazing sun of early morning was gone; muted by high mare's-tail clouds with lower, puffier clouds moving in on the wind.

Jackdaws shouted metallically at one another from two coppices, and a male starling somewhere nearby pretended it was spring with an outpouring of mimicked song. So had this valley looked for the last two hundred years. So, probably, would it look for the next hundred, with only minor additions.

It slumbered now, beneath its coverlet of snow, but Marina did not need to close her eyes to know how it would look in the spring when it came to vivid life. Green—green and honey-brown, but mostly green—would be the colors of the landscape. The vivid green of the fields would be bisected by the dark-green lines of the hedges; the farmhouses would disappear altogether behind their screening of trees—or would, at most, look like mounds of old hay left behind after harvest beneath the graying thatch. When walls showed at all, the cob would glow with the sunlight, the stone pick up the same mellow warmth. The hillside fields would be dotted with the white puffs of sheep, the valley fields holding the red-brown shapes of cattle moving through the knee-deep grass, heads down, intent on browsing as though the grass were going to vanish in the next instant. And everywhere would be the song of water.

For although there were few lakes, and fewer rivers, this was a land of a thousand little streams, all gone silent now under the snow, but ready to burst out as soon as spring came. They burbled up out of the hills, they babbled their way across meadows, they chuckled along the lanes and laughed on their way to join the great rivers, the Tamar, the Taw, the Torridge, the Okement, the Exe.

And over and around the sound of the waters would be the songs of the birds—starling and lark, crow and wren, jackdaw and robin, bluetit and sparrow, nightingale, thrush—all of them daring each other to come encroach on a territory, shouting out love for a mate or desire for one. Between the songs of the waters and the birds would be the lowing of cattle, the bleating of sheep, and all the little homely sounds of farm and land made soft by distance.

The sky would be an impossible blue, gentle and misty, with white clouds fluffy as newly-washed fleeces sailing over the hills on their way to the next valley.

And the air would be soft with damp, full of the scent of green growing things, of moss and fern, and the sweet fragrance of fresh-cut grass and spring flowers. It would touch the cheek in a caress that would negate the knife-flick of winter's wind, the unkindly wind that knew no softness but that of snow.

Marina heard all of these things in her memory, as she saw them in her mind's eye, as she felt them, as sure as the ground beneath her horse's hooves, his muscular, warm neck under her gloved hand. In all seasons, under all weathers, she knew this land, not so different from the place where she had grown up, after all—its waters flowed in her blood, its stones called to her bones. Not sudden, but slow and powerful, she felt that call, and the answer within her, to protect, to serve, and above all, to cleanse.

Not that this land needed any cleansing.

Unbidden, the answer to that thought came immediately. *Yet.*

For there was a girl poisoned, polluted, lying sick in a room not a quarter mile from here, representative of how many others? And worse, of how much poison pouring into the air, the water, and the soil? And where was that blight? It couldn't be far; if Ellen was a charity patient, the relative who had brought her to Andrew Pike must be poor as well, and unable to afford an extended journey. Would it spread? How could it not? Disease, cancer, poison—all of them spread, inexorably; it was in their nature to spread. Some day, the poison would touch this place.

She clenched her jaw, angry at her aunt, at all of the short-sighted fools who couldn't see, wouldn't see, that what poisoned the land came, eventually, to poison *them*.

What was wrong with them? Did they think, in their arrogance, that their money would keep them isolated from the filth they poured out every day? Was their greed such that the cost didn't matter so long as it was hidden? Or were they willfully not believing, pretending that the poison was somehow harmless, or even beneficial? She'd seen for herself how some people had eagerly bought the copper-tailings from the mines and the smelters to spread on their garden paths, because what was left in the processed ore was so poisonous that no weed could grow in it. It never occurred to them that the same gravel was poisonous enough to kill birds that picked bits of it up—or babies that stuck pieces of it in their mouths to suck. Willful ignorance, or just stupidity? In the end, it didn't matter, for the damage was done.

But it wasn't difficult to keep land and water and air clean! Any housewife knew that—if you just took proper care—and took it all the time.

But the people responsible for Ellen's condition didn't care for the wisdom of the housewife; that much was clear enough. Theirs was the wisdom of the accounting book, the figures on the proper side of the ledger, and never mind a cost that could not be reckoned in pounds and pence.

For a moment, her heart sank, but her resolve strengthened. *I will do what I can,* she vowed silently, though to what, she wasn't sure. *I will do all that I can. Because I must.*

If anything answered, there were no dramatic signs, yet she felt as if something *had* heard her vow, found it good, and accepted it. And she turned her horse's head away, down the hill, and toward Briareley, determined to begin that endless task with one single girl.

There was no stableman at Briareley, no servant arrived to hold her horse and take it away when she rode up the drive toward the imposing front entrance—Georgian, she thought, with four huge columns holding up the porch roof—at the top of a long staircase of native stone made smooth as marble. A Georgian front, Tudor wings, and heaven only knew what else behind them. And no servants for all of this pile.

This, however, was not unexpected; from Sally, she had heard that the doctor cut as many corners as possible, and keeping a stablehand about just to care for a horse and two ponies was a great waste of wages when a man-of-all-work was what was really needed. So Marina sat up in her saddle and looked carefully at the drive; saw the wheel-ruts leading off to the side of the house, and followed them. As she expected, they led her to a wide doorway into a square court-yard open to the sky. Along two sides were stalls for horses, along two were bays for carriages and other vehicles. There was, thank heavens, a mounting-block in the center.

She made use of it, then led the horse to an unoccupied stall. It was also utterly bare; she couldn't do much about the lack of straw on the ground, but she did take off his bridle, throw a blanket over him, and leave him a bucket of water. He'd had his breakfast before she rode out, and if Dr. Pike was as careful with money as he seemed to be, she didn't want to pilfer oats or hay without permission.

She considered going around to the kitchen entrance—but this was a formal visit, after all, and she wasn't an expected and casual arrival. So, patting her hat to make sure it was still on straight, she walked back around to the front.

She felt very small as she trudged up the staircase, wondering what long-ago ancestor of the original owners had deemed it necessary to cow his guests before they entered his home. Someone with a profound sense of his own

importance, she reckoned. Compared with this place, Oakhurst, which had seemed so huge when she first arrived, was
nothing.

*When he gets staff for this hulk, and has it full of patients,
he'll bowl over people who come to see if this is where loony
Uncle Terrance should be put.*

It was a pity that a place like this, absolutely overflowing
with history, should have to be made into a sanitarium. But
what else was to be done with it? Let it molder until the roof
fell in? Turn it into a school? Who else would want it? People like Arachne, with new money out of their factories,
built brand new mansions with modern conveniences, and
didn't care a tot about history. There were only so many
American millionaires about, and most of them wanted
fancy homes near London, not out in the farmlands of
Devon. What was the point (they thought) of having money
enough to buy a huge old castle if there was nobody around
to see it and admire it?

Except, of course, the local villagers, who had seen it all
their lives.

And what was the point of living out where there was
nothing to see and do? Nothing, as American millionaires
saw it. They loved London, London sights, excitement, theater, society.

It came as no surprise to her that there was no one in the
entrance hall, although there was a single desk set up facing
the doors there. The enormous room, with magnificent
gilded and painted plaster-molding, cream and olive and
pale green, ornamenting the walls and ceiling. She paused to
listen, head tilted to one side, and followed the echoing
sounds of soft voices along the right side of the building.

I thought this place was supposed to be in poor repair?
That was the first thing she noticed; none of the signs of neglect that she had expected, no stains on walls or ceilings be-

traying leaks, no cracks, no rot or woodworm. In fact, although gilt was rubbed or flaked off from plasterwork here and there, and paint and wallpaper fading, the building appeared to be sound.

She walked quietly—she'd had practice by now—but her footsteps still echoed in the empty rooms. Not even a scrap of carpet to soften the wooden floors!

Perhaps the financing of repair work is where all the Doctor's money is going. If that was so, she was inclined to feel more charitable. It would take a great deal of society money to pay for repairs to a place like this one.

And it appeared that the huge rooms here had been made into wards. As she entered the third, this one featuring painted panels of mythological scenes up near the ceiling, she found people there. A modern cast-iron stove with a fireguard about it had been fitted into the fireplace, rendering it safer and a great deal more efficient at producing heat, and two folk who were not in their beds dozing sat in a pair out of the motley assortment of chairs around it. There were roughly a dozen beds, three occupied, and one brisk-looking young woman in a nurse's cap and apron and light blue smock who seemed to be in charge of them; when she saw Marina, she nodded, and walked toward her.

"I beg your pardon, miss," the nurse said, as soon as she was near enough to speak and be heard, "But the old family no longer owns this home. This is Briareley Sanitarium now, and we do not give house tours, nor entertain visitors, except for the visitors to the patients."

"I know that," she replied, with a smile to soften it. "I'm Marina Roeswood, and I'm here on two accounts. I would like to speak to Dr. Pike, and I would like to enquire about the poor girl who was—"

How to put this tactfully?

"—out in the snow yesterday. Ellen, I believe is her name?"

"Ah." The young woman seemed partially mollified. "Well, in that case, I suppose it must be all right." She looked over her shoulder, back at the patients. "Miss, I can't leave my charges, and there's no one to send for to take you around. I shall tell you where to find the doctor, or at least, where to wait for him, but you'll have to promise to go straight there and not to disturb the patients in any way. Do you understand?"

"Perfectly." Again she smiled, and nodded. "It's possible that one of them might approach me; would it hurt anything if I try to soothe him and put him back in a fireside chair? I think I can feign to be whomever I'm thought to be."

"We don't have many as is inclined to delusions, miss, but—yes, I think that would be the thing to do," the nurse replied after a moment of thought. "There isn't a one as is dangerous—or we couldn't be as few of us for as many of them as there is."

Marina thought she sounded wistful at that. Perhaps she had come from a larger establishment; Marina hoped she didn't regret the change.

"Now, you turn right around, go back to the hall, across and to the back of the room. Go through that door, and keep going until you find the Red Saloon, what used to be the billiard room. It's Doctor's office now, and you wait for him there. He'll be done with his rounds soon, and I'll try to see he knows you're here."

"And Ellen?" she asked.

"Not a jot of harm done her, poor little lamb," the nurse said sympathetically. "But that's what happens, sometimes, when you take your eyes off these folks. Like little children, they are, and just as naughty when they've got a mind to it."

She looked back over her shoulder again, and Marina took the hint and turned and went back the way she had come.

Following the nurse's instructions, she found the Red Saloon without difficulty, complete with medical books in the shelves and empty racks where billiard cues had once stood. It still boasted the red figured wallpaper that had given it its name, and the red and white marble tiles of the floor, as well as a handsome white marble fireplace and wonderful plasterwork friezes near the ceiling. It was not hard to imagine the billiard-table and other masculine furniture that must have once been here. Now there was nothing but a desk, a green-shaded paraffin lamp, and a couple of chairs. She moved toward one, then hesitated, and went over to the bookshelves to examine what was there and see if there was anything she could while away her time with.

Medical texts, yes. Bound issues of medical journals. But—tucked in a corner—a few volumes of poetry. Spencer. Ben Jonson. John Donne.

Well. She slid the last book out; the brown, tooled-leather cover was well-worn, the pages well-thumbed, the title page inscribed *To Andrew, a companion for Oxford, from Father.*

She took it down, and only then did she take a seat, now with a familiar voice to keep her company.

She looked up when the doctor came in, and extended her hand. "Well, we meet again, Dr. Pike," she said, as he took it, and shook it firmly. "I won't apologize for visiting you without invitation, although I will do so for borrowing this copy of one of my old friends."

She held up the book of poetry, and he smiled. "No apologies necessary," he replied, and took his seat behind his desk. "Now, why did you decide to come here?"

She took a deep breath; as she had read Donne, encountering with a little pain some of his poems on the falseness of women, she had determined to be as forthright and blunt as she dared. "You know, of course, that I'm not of age?"

He raised an eyebrow. "The thought had occurred to me. But I must say that you are extremely prepossessing for one who is—?"

She flushed. "Almost eighteen," she said, with a touch of defensiveness.

"It is a very mature eighteen, and I am not attempting to flatter you," he replied. "Do I take it that this has something to do with your age?"

"I have a guardian, as you may know—my father's sister, Arachne Chamberten. My guardian would be horrified if she knew how much freedom I am accustomed to," she said, wishing bitterly it were otherwise. "Furthermore, my guardian doesn't know that I'm here and she isn't going to find out. She and her son have gone to deal with a business emergency in Exeter, and they can't be back until this evening at the earliest. Madam Arachne has very, very strict ideas about what is proper for the behavior of a girl my age." She couldn't help herself, she made a face. "I think she has some rather exaggerated ideas about how one has to act to be accepted in society, and the kind of people that one can and can't know."

"Ah?" he responded, and she felt her cheeks getting hotter.

"I mean, she thinks that if I fraternize with anyone who isn't absolutely on the most-desired guest-lists, I would be hurting my future." Her blushes were cooled by her resentment. "I think she's wrong. Lady Hastings doesn't act anything like Madam, and I'm sure *she* is in the best circles."

"I wouldn't know," Dr. Pike said dryly. "I don't move in those circles myself. Oh, they may come to me when they need me, but they wouldn't invite me to their parties."

She felt heat rushing into her cheeks again. "The point is,

I did promise to help you with that girl, and since my guardian is probably going to have my wretched cousin riding with me at any time I'm *not* going to church or the vicarage, this was the only time I was going to be able to arrange things with you. *I* think, if you can manage it, that we ought to bring her there. I think the vicar would understand, he seems a very understanding sort—"

The doctor seemed, oddly enough, to fix first on what she'd said about the odious Reggie. "Your cousin? Don't you mean, your fiancé?"

She stared at him blankly. "*What* fiancé?"

"The gentleman who came to get you—"

Reggie. He thought she was engaged to *Reggie*. What an absolutely *thick* thing to assume!

"Good gad!" she burst out. "Whatever possessed you, to think the Odious Reggie was my *fiancé*? I'd rather marry my horse!"

He stared at her blankly, as she stared at him, fuming. Then, maddeningly, he began to chuckle. "My apologies, Miss Roeswood. I should have known better. I should have known that you would have more sense than that."

She drew herself up, offended that he had even given the thought a moment of credence. *Not one ounce of credit to my good sense, not* one. *Couldn't he see from the first words out of my mouth that I would have less than no interest in a beast like Reggie?*

He probably thought that, like any silly society debutante, she would be so swayed by Reggie's handsome face that she'd ignore everything else. "I should hope so," she said, stiffly. "I should think anyone but the village idiot would have more sense than that. Now—"

She was irrationally pleased to see him blush.

"—perhaps we can talk about your patient, and how I am to be able to help her after today."

"I think that you are right, if getting away from your—escort—is going to be so difficult. The vicarage is the only solution, Miss Roeswood," the doctor replied. "And I believe that we can manufacture some sort of reason to bring you and Ellen together there on a regular basis. But first, well, I would like to see if you can do anything for her, before we make any further plans."

She nodded; that was a reasonable request. "Why not now?" she asked. "I came prepared to do just that."

"Come along then," he replied, waving his hand vaguely toward the door.

"I have her in a ward that has other Sensitives in it," he told her, as she followed him. "We won't have to hide anything." Now with a patient to treat, he was all business, which was a great deal more comfortable a situation than when he was assessing her personally. She was not altogether certain that she liked him—

But she didn't have to like him to work with him.

"That should make things easier then," she replied, just as they reached Ellen's ward, this one in an older part of the house, wood-paneled and floored with parquetry-work, with only six of the austere iron-framed beds in it. The poor thing looked paler than ever, but she recognized Marina easily enough, and mustered up a smile for both of them.

The doctor looked around and addressed the other four women currently in the ward. "Ladies, this young woman is another magician," he said softly, just loud enough to carry to all of the people in the room, but not beyond. "She is going to help me try a new treatment for Ellen, so don't be surprised by anything you see."

One looked fearful, but nodded. The other three looked interested. Marina surveyed the situation.

"Shields first, I think," she said, and with a nod from the

Doctor, she invoked them, spreading them out as she had been taught from a center-point above Ellen's bed.

"Hmm," the doctor said, noncommittally, but Marina thought he looked impressed. "Why shields?" he asked, so exactly like Sebastian trying to trip her up that she felt her breath catch in memory.

"Because, Doctor, not *every* Elemental is friendly," she replied. *Nor are all other magicians,* she thought, but did not say. "Now, if lead-poisoning works like the arsenic-poisoning I treated some birds for, it will take more than one go to get the filth out of you, Ellen," she continued, deciding that she was not going to make conversation over the girl's head as if she wasn't there. "I don't know, but I *think* that the poison is in your blood and the rest of you as well, and when I flush it out of your blood, some of it comes out of the flesh to replace it. So this will take several treatments."

Ellen nodded. "That makes sense," she ventured; a quick glance upward at the doctor proved he was nodding.

"I think you've gotten things damaged; that's something *I* can't do anything about. All I can do is try and force the lead out. And the first thing I want you to do—is drink that entire pitcher of water!" She pointed at the pitcher beside the bed, and Ellen made a little gasp of dismay.

"But miss—won't I—" a pale ghost of a blush spread over the girl's cheeks.

"Have to piss *horribly*?" she whispered in Ellen's ear, and the girl giggled at hearing the coarse words out of a lady. "Of course you will, where do you think I'm going to make the poison go? And I want it *out* of you, without causing any more harm. So, water first, then let me go to work."

Ellen drank as much of the water as she could hold without getting sick; Marina groped for the nearest water-source and found one, a fine little river running along the bottom of Briareley's garden too strong for the ice to close up. And with it, a single Undine, surprisingly awake and active. A wordless exchange flashed between them, ending with the Undine's assent, and power, like cool water from an opened stopcock, flowed into her in a green and luminescent flood.

Ah. She drank it, feeling it course through her, filling her with a drink she had missed more than she knew. With fingers resting just over the girl's navel, Marina closed her eyes, and went to work.

It *was* largely a matter of cleansing the blood, which looked to Marina like a polluted river with millions of tributaries. But it all had to go where *she* lurked, eventually, and she was able to "grab" the poison and send it where *she* wanted it to go, whether it wanted to or not. It didn't want to; it was stubborn stuff, and wanted to stay. But she was not going to let it, and the green fires of water-magic were stronger than poison.

About the time that Ellen stirred restlessly and uncomfortably under her hand—needing to empty out all that poisoned "water," before she burst—Marina ran out of energy—the personal energy she needed to control the Water Energy, not the Water Magic itself. Reluctantly, she severed the connection with the little stream, and opened her eyes.

"I think that's all I can manage for now," she said with a sigh.

"I know 'tis all *I* can—" Ellen got out, and Marina was only *just* able to get the shields down before the girl was out of bed and staggering towards a door that probably led to a water closet.

I hope it leads to one quickly—poor thing!

"Poor Ellen!" Dr. Pike got out, around what were clearly stifled chuckles.

"Poor Ellen, indeed," Marina said dryly. She didn't elaborate, but she had noted a distinct lack of comprehension among the male of the human species for the female's smaller . . . capacity. It had made for some interesting arguments between Margherita and Sebastian, arguments in which the language got downright Elizabethan in earthiness, and which had culminated in a second WC downstairs in Blackbird Cottage.

"Allow me to say that was quite what I wished I could do for her," the Doctor added ruefully. "It was quite frustrating. I could *see* the poison, but I couldn't make it go away; it was too diffuse, too widely spread through the body, and nothing like a wound or a disease."

"Well, we Water powers have to be good for something, I suppose," she replied, feeling cautiously proud of herself. "How long—?"

"Just about an hour and a half. I would like to invite you to luncheon—" he began, but stopped when she shook her head.

"I would very much like to accept, but even I know that is behavior that is simply unacceptable in a single girl my age," she said regretfully. "And Madam would be certain to hear of it. Servants cannot keep a secret like that one—for you know, if there is any appearance of familiarity between us, it will be blown out of all proportion and gossiped about interminably. So long as my only ostensible reason for being here was to look in on Ellen, all's well."

He grimaced. "I suppose you are right—and if you are to get to your own luncheon without enraging your cook by being late, you should leave within the quarter-hour. How often are you at the vicarage?"

"Every Wednesday for chess, but—" she hesitated. "I suspect that you and the vicar can contrive more occasions. He knows that I play instruments; perhaps he could 'arrange' practices with the choir or a soloist? Or I could even teach a Bible class." She had to laugh at that. "Though I fear I know *far* more Shakespeare than the Bible!"

"How often do you think you could contrive to get away, that's the real question, I think." He folded back the blankets on Ellen's bed, and held out his hand to assist her to stand. "At most, do you think you could manage Monday, Wednesday, and Friday?"

"Possibly. Let's try for Friday, at first. Madam always seems to be extra busy that day." She was glad of his hand; she was awfully tired. Though that would pass, it always did. He smiled at her, quite as if he understood how tired she must be.

Well of course he does, ninny, he does all this himself! What a relief to have someone with whom she could discuss magic openly.

"I suppose it isn't going to hurt anything to tell you that I'll be able to let the vicar in on the real reason why I'll bring Ellen down on Friday," he was saying, as he let go of her hand so he could escort her to the front door. "He'll tell you himself, soon enough. He's a Clairvoyant Sensitive, and a bit of an Air Magician. Not much—and it mostly gives him that silver tongue for preaching, more than anything else." He chuckled at her startled glance. "Oh, you wouldn't know it, not just to look at him. His shields are as good as or better than yours; they have to be."

"But that couldn't be better!" she exclaimed. "Oh, thank goodness we aren't going to have to concoct some idiotic excuse like—like you and Ellen wanting me to teach you Bible lessons!"

"And trying to come up with a reason why it had to be done in private, in the vicarage—yes, indeed. Next time, though, the vicar and I will save you a bit of work and we'll do the shield-casting." If she hadn't been so tired, she'd have resented the slightly patronizing way he said that.

Bit of work, indeed! Oh, I suppose it's only a bit *of work for a Master!*

But she was too tired to sustain an emotion like resentment for long, and anyway, she could be over-reacting to what was, after all, a kindly gesture.

"Excellent," was all she said, instead. "The more of my personal energies I can conserve, the longer I can spend on Ellen."

By this time, they had reached, not the front door, but the kitchen. "This way to the stables is shorter," he said, hesitating on the threshold, as a red-cheeked woman bustled about a modern iron range set into a shockingly huge fireplace (what age was *this* part of the house? Tudor? It was big enough to roast the proverbial ox!) at the far end of the room, completely oblivious to anything but the food she was preparing for luncheon. "If you don't mind—"

"After all my railing on the foolishness of Madam's society manners?" she retorted.

He actually laughed. "Well struck," was all he said, and escorted her across the expanse of spotless tile—the growling of her stomach at a whiff of something wonderful and meaty fortunately being swallowed up in the general clamor of pots, pans, and orders to the two kitchen-maids. Then they were out in the cold, crisp air, and the stable was just in front of them.

It turned out to be a good thing that Dr. Pike had escorted her; when they reached the stall where she'd put Beau, she was feeling so faint with hunger and weariness that her fingers would have fumbled the bridle-buckles, and she would never have been able to lift the sidesaddle onto the gelding's back. But he managed both without being asked, and then, without a word, put both hands around her waist and lifted her into place!

She gaped down at him, once she'd hooked her leg over the horn and gotten her foot into the stirrup. He grinned back up at her. "I'm stronger than I appear," he said.

"I—should think so!" she managed.

His grin broadened. "I'm glad to have surprised *you* for a change," he told her, with a suspiciously merry look in his eyes. "Now, you're near-perishing with hunger, so the sooner you can get back to Oakhurst, the better. I'll look forward to seeing you at the vicarage; if not on Wednesday, then you'll get an invitation from the vicar for *something*. Fair enough?"

"Perfect," she said, feeling that it was a great deal more than excellent. If the man was maddening, at least he was quickly learning not to assume too much about her! And she had the sense that he could be excellent company, when he chose. She finished arranging her skirts, and tapped Beau with her heel. "I'll be looking forward to it, Doctor!" she called, as he moved out at a fast walk, evidently as ready for his own stable and manger full of hay as she was for her luncheon.

"So will I!" she heard with pleasure, as she passed out of the yard and onto the drive. "That, I promise you!"

16

MARINA had thought that she could predict what Arachne was likely to say or do, but Madam was still able to surprise her. "I have ordered more riding habits for you," Madam said over breakfast, the day after she and Reggie returned on the afternoon train.

A telegraph to the house had warned of their coming yesterday morning, and gave orders to send the coach to the station, giving the entire household plenty of time to prepare for their return. Which was, sadly, *before* supper, so Marina had needed to go to the cook and ask her to prepare Madam's usual supper. And she appeared at that meal dressed, trussed up, coiffed, and entirely up to Madam's standards. But she had eaten supper alone; Madam had gone straight to her room and did not emerge that evening.

She was summoned to a formal breakfast, though, and steeled herself for rebuke as she entered the dining room. Madam, however, was in a curious mood. She had a sated, yet unsatisfied air about her. The moment that Madam opened her mouth to speak, Marina had cringed, expecting a rebuke.

Instead—just a comment. A gift, in fact! Marina wasn't certain whether to thank Arachne or not, though.

She decided to opt for muted appreciation.

"Thank you, Madam," she murmured.

Arachne nodded, and made a vague, waving motion with one hand. She spoke very little after that initial statement; Reggie not at all, until finally Marina herself decided to break the silence.

"I hope that you put things to rights in Exeter, Madam?" she said, tentatively. "I am sure that you and my cousin are able to cope with any difficulties."

Reggie smirked. Madam, however, turned her head and gave her a measuring look. "I believe that we have set things in order," she said, "And I trust you have kept yourself in good order as well."

"In absence of tasks, Madam, I went riding, for it is marvelous good exercise, and healthy," she replied demurely. "And I read. Poetry, for the most part."

"Browning?" Reggie asked, between forkfuls of egg and grilled sausages. "Keats?"

"Donne," she replied demurely.

"Mary Anne informed me of your rides," Madam said. "And I fear that you will soon look shabby in the same habit day after day. This is why I have ordered more, and I believe we will try some different cuts. Perhaps Mrs. Langtry can become famous and admired for wearing the same dress over and over again, but I believe no one else could."

"Mrs. Langtry is a noted beauty, Madam. I should not presume to think that I could follow her example." She applied herself to her breakfast plate, grateful that there was very little that Madam's orders could do to ruin breakfast foods—and that, by its nature, breakfast was a meal in which there were no courses as such to be removed. So with Peter attentively—but quietly—seeing to her plate, she was actually enjoying her meal.

Except for the tea, which was, as always with Madam, scarcely more than colored water.

"I understand that you are planning to visit the vicar this afternoon? Something about a Bible-study class?" Madam continued, with a slight, but very superior, smile. "You must take care that you are not labeled as a bluestocking."

"There can be nothing improper about taking comfort in religion," Marina retorted, hoping to sound just the tiniest bit stuffy and offended. Reggie thought she wasn't looking, and rolled his eyes. Madam's mouth twitched slightly.

"Not at all, my dear." Madam chided. "It may not be *improper,* but it is—" she hesitated "—boring."

"And of course, one shouldn't be boring," Reggie said solemnly, though there was no doubt in Marina's mind that he was laughing at her behind his mask. "I'm afraid it is an unpardonable social crime."

"Oh." She did her best to appear chastened, and noted the satisfaction on both their faces. "Then I shan't mention it to anyone. It won't matter in the village."

"The village matters very little," Madam pronounced. "But I believe your time would be better spent in some other pursuit."

Marina contrived a mulish expression, and Arachne sighed. Reggie didn't even bother to hide his amusement.

"You're going to turn into a laughingstock, cuz," he said. "People will snicker at you behind your back, call you 'the little nun' and never invite you to parties. Turn it into a Shakespeare class instead—or a poetry society. Try and instill some culture into these bumpkins. People might think you're mad, but at least they won't call you a bore."

She set her chin to look as stubborn as possible. "Perhaps I shall," she said.

Reggie laughed. Madam hid a smile.

Marina had to pretend to be very interested in her plate in order to hide her own triumph. Madam hadn't forbidden her to go to this "Bible study class" and that was all that was important. Let Reggie laugh at her; the more that he thought she was a bore, the less time he'd spend with her.

"No riding off this morning, though, cuz," Reggie reminded her, wagging a finger at her. "Dancing lessons. You're shockingly behind. You *might* be invited to parties even if you're a bluestocking, as long as you can dance."

She escaped with a sigh of gratitude after luncheon, and claimed Beau.

The closer she got to the village, the lighter her heart became. When she was within sight of the vicarage, she felt—

Almost normal. Being dragged away from Blackbird Cottage *hadn't* been the end of the world. Madam was a tyrant—and a terrible snob—but there were advantages to being under her care.

The wardrobe, for one. She had never had so many fashionable gowns. Granted, they were all in black, but still—and being all in black, it would be a fine excuse next year, when her year of deep mourning was over, to order another entire wardrobe!

Then there were the half-promises of going to London. The theater—the music—and the amusements of society. The things she had read about in the social pages of the Times and wished she could attend them herself.

And there was the matter of a coming-out ball. She would *never* have had a coming-out ball with Margherita—for one thing, their village wasn't exactly the sort of place where one held coming-out parties, and for another, the Tarrants weren't the sort of people who held them. But given

Madam's near-worship of society, there was no way that the Chambertens would *not* hold a coming-out ball for their ward. If they didn't, it would look very strange indeed. They would probably put it off until next year, rather than this, because of her mourning, but she would *need* that long to get used to all of the clothing and the manners, not to mention learning the dances.

A coming-out ball! Just like all the ones she had read about! The prospect was almost enough to make up for everything else.

As for the everything else—things were by far and away not as wretched as they had first seemed. Now that she had a safe place away from Oakhurst where she could work magic, she *could* send a message to Elizabeth and to Sebastian, Margherita, and Thomas. She didn't need a stamp; all she needed was time and energy.

Now that she knew that she *could* contact them, the frantic feeling, the fear that she'd been completely uprooted, was fading. This was more like—well, rather like being away at school, with a horribly strict headmistress. And the same wretched food that all the books like *Jane Eyre* described! But there were none of the other privations, and if Jane could survive her school, surely Marina could sort this experience out without immediate help.

Besides, I've been here for weeks now, and there hasn't been a single Undine or Sylph that has tried to speak to me—so they must be certain I'm all right. Even if the others couldn't raise Air or Water Elementals to send to her, Elizabeth certainly could. Perhaps they had scryed, discovered she was all right, and decided to wait for her to contact them.

But what if they hadn't? What if they thought she had forgotten them once she had some inkling of the social position she held, the wealth she would eventually command?

What if they thought she was ashamed of them? Madam seemed to think she *should* be, after all—

—perhaps I can ask the doctor or the vicar to help me. After all, once I make them understand my situation, we could use letters, as I planned. They can send me postage. Oh, what a ridiculous position she was in! A wardrobe worth hundreds of pounds, and she hadn't a penny for a stamp! Looking forward to a coming-out ball, yet so strictly confined she might as well be in a convent!

Riding about on the back of a high-bred hunter, and knowing that if I took him farther than the village, I'd be so close-confined that a convent would be preferable.

She shook the mood off; there was work to be done.

There would be no leaving Beau tied up at the gate today, not since she was planning on spending at least two hours working on Ellen. Instead, she brought him around to the rear of the vicarage where there was a little shed that held the moor pony that the vicar hitched to a cart to do his errands. There was a second stall with just enough space in there for Beau as well, although she had to take his tack off him outside, since there wasn't enough room for her in the stall too. Beau gave her an incredulous look as she led him in, as if to object. Strongly. She couldn't understand animals the way Uncle Thomas could, but she could almost hear him speaking. *"You intend for me to lodge here? Me? A hunter of impeccable bloodline? Next to that?"*

"Don't be as much of a snob as Madam," she told him severely.

He heaved a huge sigh, and suffered himself to be led into the stall and offered hay. It was perfectly good hay, as good as he'd get in his own stall at Oakhurst, but he sniffed it with deep suspicion.

"Now don't be tiresome," she scolded, and shut the half-door on him. "If you can't learn to enjoy the company of ordinary folk, I leave you to the Odious Reggie's good graces from now on, and we'll see whom you prefer!"

She left him sighing over his hay, and went around to the front of the vicarage to tap on the door.

To her immense surprise, it was Dr. Pike who opened the door of the vicarage at her second knock. "Good gad!" she blurted. "What are you doing here?"

He laughed, looking much more amiable than he had at the sanitarium, and held the door open. "That's a fine greeting! Where else should I be but here at the appointed time?"

She blushed, then got annoyed with herself. Who was this fellow, that he made the color rise in her cheeks so often? But it was a rude thing to say.

I really have to be more careful. Having to curb my tongue around Madam is making things break out when I'm around anyone else.

She apologized immediately. "I beg your pardon—I'm always just bleating out whatever is in my head without thinking about it. What I *meant* was, your horse and cart are nowhere to be seen—"

"That's because my poor horse would hardly fit in there with that monster you ride and that little pony of the vicar's. My horse and cart are doing the weekly errands for the sanitarium, the good Diccon having carried Miss Ellen in here for me, and will return for us at a quarter before five." He grinned. "That will give us time for you to rest after helping Ellen, and have a nice strong cup of tea."

She moved into the little white-wainscoted hallway and he closed the door behind her.

Then, unexpectedly, he shook his head. "What am I saying? My dear Miss Roeswood, I intend to assist you to the level of my strength, and as your partner in this enterprise, I will be as much in need of that strong cup of tea as you.

Probably more, as I have often noted that my female patients seem to have more stamina than the male."

As my partner *in this enterprise*! Feeling pleased and immensely flattered, Marina followed him into the vicarage.

"How is Ellen coming along?" she asked anxiously, as he led the way past the parlor that the Ladies' Friendly Society had used, past what appeared to be a study, and into the back of the house.

"She was much better for a little, then relapsed—" he said, looking back over his shoulder at her. "Ah, I see that you are not surprised."

"That *is* what happened to the arsenic-poisoned birds I treated," she replied. "But I don't know why. I had to purge them several times before they got better and stayed better."

"I believe that I do, or I have a good guess. You purge the blood of the poison, which causes the victim to feel better. But that creates a—a kind of vacuum in the blood, so the tissues release some of what they hold back into the blood again, and the patient relapses." He flung open a door on a narrow little room, painted white, and hung with prints of country churches, with white curtains at the tall, narrow windows. "And here we are!"

Ellen lay in an iron-framed bed much like her own back at Briareley, propped up with pillows like a giant doll. She smiled to see Marina. "Lord love you, Miss, I wasn't sure you'd be able to come! That Madam—"

"Is a terror, but she thinks this is a Bible-study class," Marina interrupted, getting a startled laugh from the girl "So, I suppose we had all better have the vicar expound on a verse before we all go home again, so that it isn't a lie."

"Then I will take for my text, 'Even as ye have done it unto the least of these, ye have done it unto Me,'" said Davies, who was kneeling beside the fire and putting another log on. "And for an original and radical interpretation, you may wax eloquent on the point that I feel—quite strongly—that the text means actions both for good *and* ill."

"Oh my—have we a reformer in our midst, Clifton?" asked the doctor, taking Marina's cloak and draping it over a peg on the wall beside his own.

"You do. But on the whole, I prefer to be a subversive reformer. They get a great deal more accomplished than the ones who shout and carry placards and get themselves arrested." Mr. Davies stood up, and smiled, quite cheerfully. "Which is one reason why, for instance, that I am providing a space for you and Miss Roeswood to work in."

"We can talk all about subversion and theology when I have no more strength to spare for magic," Marina said firmly. "It is always possible that Madam will send to fetch me at any point on some pretext or other—she didn't forbid me, but she did not altogether approve of my interest in Bible studies."

Doctor and vicar turned astonished expressions on her, but it was the vicar who spoke first. "Whyever not?" he asked. "I should think it would be entirely proper for a young lady of your age."

"She says it is because I will turn into a bluestocking and a bore," Marina replied with relish. "Although it is possible that she has got wind of those radical opinions of yours, so I believe I will not voice them, if you don't mind, vicar. Well, shall we to work?"

Ellen made a face, and began drinking water—Dr. Pike must have remembered everything from the last time, for there was a full pitcher on the little table next to her. There were three chairs of faded upholstery, indeterminate age and much wear in this room besides the bedside table and the bed; Marina was offered the most comfortable-looking of the three, and took it, on the grounds that *she* was the one who was going to be doing most of the work. And besides, she was burdened with corsets; they weren't. She closed her eyes, and put her right hand out toward Ellen. The girl took it, and laid it on the covers over her stomach, folding her own hands over it.

"Shields please, vicar," she heard Dr. Pike say, and heard the vicar whisper something in Latin. His voice was too soft to make out the words, but she rather thought it was a prayer. Then his shields swept smoothly through her—she felt them pass, like a cool wave—and established themselves, settling into place with a swirl and a flourish, into ever-changing and fluid shields that looked much like Elizabeth's, except for being a slightly deeper shade and blue instead of green.

A second set spun up at that perimeter, very like Uncle Thomas' craftsmanly constructions, but more organic and alive. This variant of Earth was the *living* Earth, a tapestry of intertwining life, rich and flavored with the feel of sun on a freshly-turned furrow, the taste of (oddly enough) warm milk and honey, and the scent of new-mown hay. But it was the same rich, golden-brown of Uncle Thomas' magic, and the shields rose up like a powerful buttress behind the fluidity of the vicar's.

She sighed; they were perfectly *lovely* things, and she wished she could study them. But time was passing; she needed a source of power.

And found it immediately, a spring that supplied the vicarage well. There were lesser Elementals here, though no Undines—not surprising, really, since it was directly below a human-occupied building, and despite the lovely shields, she could tell that Clifton Davies was not really strong enough to attract the attention of powerful Elementals. She tapped into it, and let the full force of it flow into her hands and out again.

She sensed the doctor probing what she was doing at one point when she was so deep into her task that she wouldn't have noticed a bugle being blown in her ear. He was very deft—and he made a brief attempt to join his personal energies to hers. But it came to nothing, as she had already known would happen, and he withdrew, turning instead to the task of healing what he could of the harm done to Ellen by the poison.

Then she lost herself in the intricacy and sheer delight of the task—she had seen Margherita similarly lost in the intricacy of a tapestry or an embroidery piece, and supposed it must be much the same thing. *Some to make and some to mend,* her aunt had always said when she lamented her inability to create. Well, there was joy enough in both.

Then, as ever, she felt her strength run out, and came back to herself with an unpleasant jarring sensation. At almost the same moment, she felt the two sets of shields come down again. She opened her eyes, and took away her hand, and was pleased to see that now there was some faint color in Ellen's cheeks. But she didn't get to admire them for long, because the girl struggled to her feet with Dr. Davies' help, and was out the door as Marina sagged back into the comfort of the old wingback. Poor Ellen! She hoped the vicarage had an indoor WC.

"About that cup of tea," she suggested, feeling very much in need of it.

"We can manage a bit better than that," Davies said, and held up his hand when she opened her mouth to protest. "Now I know you are reluctant to be a drain on my larder, but there are two things you don't know about the state of it. First, I am a single man living here, not one burdened with a family, and although a country parson doesn't see much in the way of monetary help, he is certainly well-endowed with the gifts of the farmers in his parish. And they have been granting me those as if I *did* have an enormous family, and would take it very hard if I were not to make use of it. Second, Miss Roeswood, I am a *single* parson—singularly single, as the saying is. Not a day goes by when some young lady or other—equally single—doesn't gift me with a little offering that is, I must suppose, intended to impress me with her kitchen skills." He chuckled. "If I ate all of these things I should be as round as a Michaelmas goose, and a good corn-fed one at that. My housekeeper would probably be mortally offended at this unintended slur on her skills, if she wasn't so pleased that she hasn't had to do any baking herself since Christmas. Some of this supplies the Parish groups with refreshments, but by no means all of it. So, the long and short of it is, I can and will provide the means for a sumptuous high tea every time you bring Miss Ellen here."

She held up both hands. "I yield to the honorable opposition," she said, and he went off to some other part of the house, returning with Ellen leaning on his arm.

The housekeeper arrived after Ellen had been settled back in the bed, with an enormous tray stacked with plates of sandwiches and cakes, and Marina's mouth began to water at the sight of it all. This was *not* ladylike fare! Good, honest ham, egg, and cheese sandwiches, and decent-sized cakes, just like she used to eat at the cottage when Margherita made a high tea!

"Doctor, will you pour?" Davies asked genially. "I know that's supposed to be the lady's job, but frankly, the lady's hand is shaking too much and I don't want tea slopped all over my saucer. Now, what will you have, Miss Roeswood?"

"For starters, I'd like to dispense with the formality, at least while the four of us are together," she replied, telling her protesting stomach that it did not want one of everything. "Marina, please, from now on, vicar. And the same for you, doctor. Other than that—some sandwiches, tea with two, and milk, please."

"Then it will be Andrew and Clifton," the doctor said, handing her a cup of good strong tea, with plenty of sugar and just a touch of milk. "At least in private. We don't want to give rise to any of those rumors you warned me of—and quite properly too—at Briareley."

"Hmm." The vicar made up a plate for Marina at her direction. "A very good point," he said, handing it to her. "Your guardian mustn't be given any excuse to forbid our meeting. Ellen, I am afraid it is beef broth and milk-pudding for you, my child."

She accepted both with no sign of discontent. "I'd on'y lose anything stronger," she said with good humor. "Oh, I feel so much better, though! I know I'll feel bad again, but—"

"But it won't be *as* bad as it was before," Andrew told her. "And every time we do this, it will be a little better, until we've purged all of the poison out of you and I've healed what I can."

Ellen smiled, but the smile faded. "Pardon my asking, but—then what?" she said reluctantly. "What'm I to do then? Go back to painting?"

"Good gad, no!" the doctor and the vicar exclaimed at the same time. Andrew made a "go ahead" motion to the vicar.

"You'll come to work for one of us, Ellen, if you want to," Davies said. "I must warn you though, that it's no gilded life here. You'd live here and eat here, but I couldn't afford much in wages, and it is likely to be hard work."

Ellen was shaking her head. "I got no skill at it, sir, begging your pardon. I never been trained in service."

"Then you'll work for me—which is very little better, but you can start training as a nurse little by little as you get healthier," Andrew told her. "Like Eleanor—you see, nurses are readily come by, but nurses who are Sensitives, or even magicians, are far, far, rarer. I could use you to work with the children. Would you like that?"

Ellen brightened immediately. "That'd suit me, yes it would! That'd suit me fine!"

"It's settled then." Both men seemed satisfied with the outcome, and certainly for someone who was a Sensitive, there really was no better place to work than Briareley, however poor the wages might be.

Well—Blackbird Cottage. But she'd have to do heavy work, just like Jenny, and I doubt she'll ever be able to do that again. But Marina made a mental note to talk seriously with Margherita when she finally got back in touch about supplying a place or two for other former charity patients of Andrew's who were more robustly built.

"If that doesn't work for you, I expect I'll need a lady's maid eventually, Ellen," Marina put in. "I'd rather have someone who I know that can learn what to do than have someone who might be beautifully trained but whom I don't know that I'd have to trust. But—" she sighed. "That will have to wait for three years, until I'm of age. Until then, I have less charge over Oakhurst than you do! Madam has charge of everything. Including me." She finished the last bite of an exquisite little Bakewell tart, and grimaced. "I don't even get to say what I have for tea—which is why I have made such a disgusting pig of myself over the sweets today!"

Ellen put her empty bowls aside. "Miss, I've been wondering—who's this Madam? Why's she such a hold over you, miss?"

"She's my guardian, worse luck," Marina sighed, and began to explain her situation to the girl. Which, of course, ran right counter to everything she'd seen in etiquette books, or been taught by Arachne. Ellen was a mere factory girl, an absolute inferior; Marina a lady of privilege. Marina should have addressed her by her last name only, and really, should not even have noticed her, much less be laying out her entire life for her scrutiny.

Madam would have the vapors. If Madam ever does *have the vapors. Which I doubt, actually.*

She got as far as her first interview with Madam, when Ellen interrupted her. "Now, miss—I *know* your Madam Arachne! I wondered, when I first heard you call her that, and I do! 'Twas her pottery I worked at, in Exeter! 'Twas there I got poisoned by all the glaze-dust, or at least, that's what Dr. Pike says!"

Up until this moment, Arachne's potteries had been nothing more than an abstract to Marina—something that hadn't any real shape in her mind, as it were. Oh, she had thought, if she had thought at all, that they were—like a village pottery, only larger. She hadn't even had a mental image, nor put together Andrew's rant about the lead-poisoning with what made her guardian's fortune. Now, though—

"Good gad," she whispered.

Ellen held out her trembling hand and frowned at it. "She's real particular, Madam is. Picks her paintresses herself. And she does make sure that the girls is taken care of for when the shakes start. Gives us a lay-down room so we can take a bit of a rest and still get the quota done. And she sees to it other ways. If you know what I mean." She looked more than a little embarrassed, when the vicar and Marina shook their heads dumbly.

Andrew saved the girl from having to answer. "Let me handle this, Ellen." He turned to Clifton and Marina. "I think I might have told you already, but if I haven't, well— the lead kills the girls' appetites and has an effect on the complexions. Ironically enough, their skin becomes as pale and translucent as porcelain—well, just like Ellen's is now.

So, they are thin and pale, ethereal and delicate; they have to stay clean and neat because they're on show for visitors."

"Madam gives us a wash-up room, and she gets a second-hand clothes woman who gets stuff from the gentry to come around and give us good prices," Ellen put in. "And if we ain't got enough, she has it laid by for us, and takes a shilling a week out of our wages."

Andrew made a helpless gesture. "There you have it. Clean, well-gowned, and if they had any looks at all before, they become pretty. If they were pretty before, they become beautiful. Men who are looking for—companionship—"

Clifton turned beet-red. Marina tilted her head to the side; wide and uncensored reading, and Elizabeth's influence had given information on what came next, if not personal experience. "Men looking for pretty mistresses may go looking among the paintresses, you mean? Ellen, is that what you meant when you said that Madam sees that the girls are cared for?"

Ellen nodded. "She lets visitors come right in the painting-room," she admitted. "Lets 'em palaver with us girls, and so long as the quota gets done, nobody says anything. So when they can't paint no more, they'll have maybe someone as is interested in other things they can do."

"Monstrous!" Davies burst out, red-faced now with anger. "Appalling!"

"Well, what else are they supposed to do? Petition Madam to take care of them?" Andrew looked just as angry, but tempered with resignation. "Good God, Clifton, what would that get them? Nowhere, of course—she's the one who's poisoned them in the first place! What relations are going to care for them? Ellen's second-cousin is the only person that has ever brought one of these paintresses to the attention of a doctor, and that is in no small part because the cousin discovered Ellen's magical potential was being drained away from her by a person unknown. That is *one* case, out of how many potteries?"

"Quite a few, I would venture to say," Marina offered, feeling an odd sort of dislocation—ethically, she was as appalled as the vicar, emotionally she was as horrified. But intellectually—she couldn't find it in her heart to blame any girl who took such a step toward ensuring whatever future she had was comfortable. "But I suspect that would be because those doctors are disinclined to see a patient without being paid. Actually, Andrew, that's not quite true— Madam and Reggie were discussing something about a female doctor, a suffragist, who was campaigning on behalf of the paintresses at one of her potteries. But I don't know which pottery that was, so I can't tell you if there's anyone trying to do anything about the place where Ellen worked."

"I'm glad to hear that, but it's irrelevant to the situation we were discussing," Andrew pointed out. "So Clifton, what exactly *are* these girls to do with themselves before they die? Eke out the remaining miserable days of their lives in the poorhouse? Or spend them in comfort by selling their bodies while the bodies are still desirable?"

The vicar hung his head, his color fading. "I don't know, Andrew. A hard choice, in a hard life."

"They say that Madam letting them men in, makes sure all the paintresses gets a chance to get set up—and they *do* just go off, sometimes without giving notice," Ellen observed, with a hint of sardonic amusement at the vicar's reaction. "Girls get a lot of men coming 'round. We all figured soon or late, you get one as is willing to take care of you proper. And until you do, you get nice presents, lovely dinners, get taken to music-halls. . . ."

Marina had a good idea that Ellen must have had her

share of those things from the way she spoke of them, wistfully, even knowing what she knew now, with regret.

It isn't just their bodies that Madam is poisoning, she thought, suddenly. She locked gazes with both Andrew and the vicar, and saw that they were thinking the same thing.

But it was still hard to believe. The immediate thought was that surely, surely, Arachne Chamberten didn't actually know what her pottery was doing to the girls who worked there. Surely anyone who did would change things!

But then she remembered that discussion—that most "unacceptable" discussion—over the dinner-table. No, Arachne knew. She might pretend that she didn't, but she knew. And Arachne didn't seem to think of the lower orders as being—well—*human.* She didn't care what happened to them, so long as there was a steady supply of them at cheap wages.

When their hands start to shake, she'd rather have them out selling their bodies anyway, to make room for new ones.

"Difficult as this may seem to you, Ellen's situation is worse yet, Clifton," the Doctor said grimly. "Or *was.* One of the reasons that her cousin whisked her away from that vile place so quickly was that besides being poisoned, she was being drained, magically."

"What?" Marina and the vicar exclaimed together, aghast. "But—how? Why? By whom?" Davies had the wit to ask, as Marina just stared.

"I don't know. There definitely was some sort of tie to her when she was brought to me, something that was acting as a drain on her personal and emotional energies, but one that I didn't recognize, and one I couldn't trace back." Andrew shrugged. "Not that I didn't want to, but I was too busy trying to save her life at the time. I just cut it, cauterized it, and dismissed it from my mind. Now, though—" He paused. "Clifton, you can work through the Church to see that the physical aspects of this disgusting situation are dealt with—but if there is an occult aspect to it, I think we ought to look into it. There was only myself before—frankly, trying to get other Masters to help in something as vague as this would be like persuading cats to swim."

"Now you have two more of us," the vicar said, with a lifting of his chin and a touch of fire in his eyes. "And Ellen is going to be all right."

"If you don't mind helping us with this," Andrew replied, slowly. "The only problem I can see is that the tie isn't there anymore."

Ellen gave him a stern look. "Don't be daft," she said, forthrightly. "Begging your pardon, but the on'y places I ever went was the pottery and out with—men. And them men came to the pottery. So?"

"QED," Andrew said ruefully. "You're right, Ellen. The place to look is the pottery. If this business involves more girls than just you, it could be the symptom of something much worse." He scratched his head ruefully. "This is where I have nothing to go on but vague premonition—"

"But the premonitions of an Elemental Master are as important as an ordinary person's certainties!" Marina and the vicar said in chorus—then looked at each other—and at Ellen's puzzled expression—and chuckled weakly.

"All right. If *you* agree that my premonition is not nonsense—well, I just think that this is important."

Something I can do! Finally, something only I can do! "And—" Marina said, with a sudden smile. "I think I can get in there. Easily, and with no one suspecting a thing. There's just one problem."

"What is it?" Andrew asked, immediately. "I'll help you with it!"

"I wish you could, but you are the *last* person who would

be of any use," she replied, with a rueful laugh. "The problem is, to do so I'll have to spend at least two days in the inescapable company of the Odious Reggie!"

And at the sight of his expression, she could only shake her head.

17

SEQUESTERED in her office, with orders not to be disturbed, Arachne fixed her son with an ice-dagger stare. "What," she asked, in the coldest voice she could muster, "are you doing about winning that girl?"

For a long while, the only sound was that of the fire in the fireplace behind her, crackling and popping. Arachne licked her lips, and thought she tasted the least little hint of blood on them.

She didn't have to elaborate her question; there was only one girl that he was supposed to be winning, after all. He squirmed a little in his chair; not a good sign. Reggie only squirmed when he was trying to be evasive. When he was lying, he looked directly into your eyes, and produced his most charming of smiles. When he was telling the truth, he didn't smile, he looked completely sober, and didn't try to charm. She wondered if he realized that. Perhaps not; he was not as experienced as she was in reading expressions and the nuances of behavior.

"She's a bore, Mater," he said, sideslipping the topic—or trying to. "She's a bluestocking and a bore. I wrack my brain to tell her amusing stories, and she talks about literature; I try to make love to her, and she asks me about votes for women or politics."

She frowned. "That is not what I asked. The girl is normal enough. She certainly has a craving for fine feathers, she's young, and I'm sure you can turn her head with flattery if you exert yourself; she's not that different from the little trollops you amuse your idle hours with. You ought to be able to charm her without thinking twice about it."

He couldn't meet her eyes. Her frown deepened.

"Clearly, you have gotten nowhere. Clearly, you are not even trying," she stated. "Reggie, this is important. You *have* to get that girl under your control. You have to win her; it's imperative to have her your creature."

"It's damned hard to flatter someone who isn't listening," he muttered, casting a resentful glance at her from under long eyelashes that most women would sell their souls for. Though there seemed to be plenty of women who would sell their souls to have Reggie himself. Just—not the one that mattered, it seemed. "Furthermore," he continued, "I should think it would make more sense for you to work on that curse of yours. After all, if the little wretch just dies, the problem will be solved."

If she answered that, she'd be on the defensive—and it was always her policy to be on the offensive, not the defensive. She glared at him, the "it's all your fault" look. "Try harder," she ordered. "Put some imagination into it, instead of using all the tricks that work on girls with more sophistication. She might be intelligent, but she is *not* sophisticated. You might take her somewhere, show her some sight or other. From all I can tell, she never ventured out of that tiny village of hers—take her to Exeter for an excursion!"

Reggie groaned. "Damn, Mater, what the *hell* is there in Exeter worth looking at?"

"That's not my business," she told him, exasperated at his willful lack of imagination. "It's yours. *Find* something. A conservatory. Theater—there has to be a music hall, at least. The shops—the cathedral—a concert. Even a pantomime is going to be something she's never seen before!" Her eyes narrowed. "She's spending every Wednesday *and* Friday at the vicarage, and I'm not entirely certain that it's chess and piety that take her there. That vicar is young and single. Did it ever occur to you that he might be your rival for her affections?" She raised an eyebrow. "He certainly seems to be setting the hearts aflutter in the village."

"A vicar?" To her great annoyance, Reggie snorted. "Not bloody likely! Not that vicar in particular—he looks like a bag of bones, and he's all prunes and prisms. Miss Marina may be a bore, but I've never seen a bore yet that didn't have repressed passions seething under the crust. No stick in a dog collar is going to be *my* rival for her."

Arachne's exasperation overflowed. Arrogance was one thing, but this—this was blind stupidity itself. "Then do something about those repressed passions! Rouse her somehow! Go take her slumming and tell her it's the fashion to do so, *I* don't care, as long as you impress her."

"Yes, you do," he said sullenly, his eyes smoldering with things he didn't dare express, at least to her face. "If I were to take her slumming and she managed to slip away from me and back to those artists of hers, you'd have my hide."

He was right about that, at least. "Yes," she replied grimly. "I would. And don't think that you can get out of this by helping her on her way, either. Don't even give her the chance to acquire a single stamp. Because the moment she gets in communication with them, they'll tell her enough about me—and you, by extension—that she won't trust us.

No matter how circumspect they are, they can still make the case that Alanna sent her away to hide her from me, and there were six witnesses there to back them up."

"Even without talking about magic?" he asked skeptically.

"Especially without talking about magic. Elizabeth Hastings can turn black into white if she puts her mind to it, and all they have to do is send the girl to her. Then where will we be? Damn it, boy, all they have to do is smuggle her over to the Continent and hide her there until she's twenty-one for her to have complete control of her property, unless you manage to get her married to you! Do you want her property or not?"

She did not want to consider what would happen with Marina on the Continent, and it wouldn't take waiting until she was twenty-one, either. If the curse didn't take effect by the time Marina was eighteen—and if Arachne herself was not in physical contact to nullify or even cancel it—it not only could backfire against the caster, it *would*. She had worked that much out, at least. Not that she was going to tell Reggie any of that. What he didn't know, he couldn't use for leverage against his mother. He was getting altogether too independent lately.

No, the blasted Tarrants wouldn't have to hide the girl until she was twenty-one; the eighteenth birthday would suffice. Shuttling her around France in company with a gaggle of schoolgirls would do the trick—she'd never be able to find one schoolgirl tour among all the ones traipsing around Provence and Paris.

"I had intended," she said smoothly, "to use the girls from the Exeter works to make the curse work again. I *tried* to do that. The accident put paid to that plan, rather thoroughly. They were too damaged; there wasn't enough power in them. None of the others are strong enough or ripe enough, nor will they be for at least a year."

Reggie shrugged, striving to look indifferent, and managing only to look arrogant. He was getting altogether too like his mother for her comfort. Altogether too like. Ambitious, manipulative, sly. . . . "Do what you did to set the curse in the first place. Find *me* a sacrifice. The proper sort."

"I've tried," she admitted, nettled that she'd needed to admit anything. "A single virgin child of Master potential is difficult enough to obtain; it was only a fluke that I managed to get my hands on four and only because they were all from the same family! And if you had any notion how long I waited with that curse heavy on my hands, until Hugh got himself an heir—"

Now it was Reggie's turn to frown, and his brows knitted in confusion. "Four? You shouldn't need four, not for enough power to reinstate an existing curse. A single child should do, so long as it's mage-born and virgin. His Infernal Majesty should—" At her dubious expression, his frown deepened, and he blinked, slowly, as if some entirely new thought had crossed his mind. "Mater—don't you *believe?*"

He sounded—shocked. As shocked as any good Christian would have been to learn that she was a Satanist. Well, now it was coming out; her son, whom she had raised and trained to be her helper, had finally grasped the idea that his mother was a skeptic. How had he missed it? How had she raised a believer? "I have never seen anything to make me believe—or disbelieve," she said reluctantly. "The rites give me power; that was all I have ever cared about. It's power I take from the weaker creatures that I sacrifice, so far as I can tell, and not from any other source; what odd's that? It's still power, it works, and it gives me what I want. Belief doesn't enter into it, nor does it need to."

She'd have laughed at the expression on his face, if she

hadn't known that would make him turn against her. What a joke! To think that she, a skeptic above all else, had raised up a pious little Satanist! Could Satanists *be* pious? A true believer, at any rate, and she wondered how, as careful as she had been with him, she had missed the signs of it developing.

And how far had he gone down that road? Did he go so far as to keep a shrine to the Dark One in his room? Oh, probably not; of all the servants, only Mary Anne and his valet were aware of anything unusual in the household, and Mary Anne only because she had discovered Reggie's secret when she first became his mistress. She had, in fact, been an actress, and a clever one at that—but not a good one. Good enough to get the secondary parts, but never the leads; graceful enough to ornament the stage, but nothing else. So she augmented her status and income with gentlemen, and she managed to snare Reggie. But she had plans, she did—plans for a comfortable old age, having seen far too many of her kind tottering around as street whores, without even a room to take a customer to. She was not satisfied with all the accompanying privileges and presents of being Reggie's regular, for she wanted something more in order to keep her mouth shut. Clever girl; you couldn't eat a dinner twice, if the man didn't keep paying for your flat you had to find a way to pay for it yourself or be out in the street. Presents of flowers were worthless—presents of jewelry always pawned for less than they cost. She wasn't in love with Reggie. It was entirely a mercenary relationship with nothing in it at all of affection.

That something more that Mary Anne wanted was a permanent position—involving no more work than she'd put in on stage, at the same rate of pay as a star turn—in the household, whether or not she was in Reggie's bed. She was shrewd enough to know that Madam was not about to pay her for doing nothing, but she was perfectly willing to perform something as minimal as assisting Madam's own maid, for instance. And the other privilege she wanted was her own separate apartment for as long as she stayed with the household.

Things became a little more complicated with the move to Oakhurst, for Reggie insisted on having her along. Well, she kept Reggie satisfied, and that took some imagination and athletic ability, and her presence at Oakhurst was probably the only thing keeping Reggie here at all. The Oakhurst household did not know what Mary Anne's position was, and Arachne had not wanted them to discover it. In light of Mary Anne's stage experience, Arachne had decided that playing lady's maid to the girl fit the criteria of "no more work than she'd put in on stage" and she'd proved herself useful in that regard as well.

But that was beside the point, given this new revelation. That Reggie actually believed and worshipped, now, that was something that Arachne would not have even guessed at until this moment. How had he gotten that way, and what was the cause? Surely there must have been a cause.

Yet so far as she knew, he had never seen anything during a rite that she hadn't seen. There had never been any manifestations of lesser demons or devils, much less His Infernal Majesty himself at a single Black Mass, however perfectly performed. The only things that had appeared when summoned were the physical manifestations of Elementals—the nastier sort of Elementals, that is; Lamias, Incubi, Trolls, Hobgoblins, Manticores, all the inimical fauna of a fabulous bestiary. Never a hint of a devil. Not a single demon in the classical sense of hellspawn. Plenty of things that fed on negative energies, on pain and despair, on sorrow and fear, but not a single creature that was itself despair.

Her eyes narrowed as she regarded him with speculation.

Could it be that he had been holding rites on his own? *And* had gotten unexpected results? Had he accomplished things he had not troubled to tell his mother?

Could he, in fact, have gone so far as to invoke a devil and make a classic pact?

If he had, that put another complexion on this conversation entirely.

"I suppose—" he said finally, and she didn't much like the expression, or rather, lack of it, in his face and hooded eyes. "—I suppose you're right. It's not belief, it's results that count."

She countered his mask with one of her own. "And in the realm of results, it would be best to have every option ready to put into motion," she purred. "I am by no means out of plans, yet. And I am by no means limited to the ones we have already discussed."

She was, in fact, perfectly prepared to perform the Great Rite with her own son, if everything fell apart and she needed to do so to protect herself from the backlash of the curse—though she had a notion that she would have to drug or otherwise disconnect Reggie's mind from his body to accomplish that particular feat. Even her unshockable son might consider that going a bit too far.

Well, that was what she had her own pet doctors and chemists for. A little of this, a smidgen of that, and a glass of that brandy he was so fond of, and he'd be seeing and hearing what she chose, and doing exactly what she wanted.

Yes, and what was more, she was equally prepared to channel that backlash through him if she had to. Especially if he was getting above himself. If she was going to have to eliminate him, she certainly wouldn't waste his potential. He could be eliminated, and it wasn't likely that when the body was found, anyone would ever suspect her hand behind the death. Someone else could be trained; the valet, perhaps. She'd done without an Infernal Celebrant before, and she could do so again, awkward though it might be.

And less effective.

That was the problem with the Satanic rituals; so *damned* misogynistic, so *infernally* patriarchal.

Perhaps . . . when all this was sorted, she ought to pay someone to research the rites of the Magna Mater, or the goddess Hecate, or some other goddess of black powers. Perhaps endow three or four scholarships, or even get someone to search the proscribed sections of the Vatican library and abstract the appropriate texts. Then she wouldn't need any Celebrant but herself.

No time for that now, though. The days and weeks were ticking past; March was half over, and spring would be here too soon. Already the snow was gone, and cold rain had taken its place. Then summer, and the birthday. . . .

"Woo the girl, and win her if you can," she ordered. "If *nothing* else, it will make inheritance easier if you're married to her when the curse takes her. There will be no nonsense about probate courts and dying intestate and a minor; you'll already have it all, no questions, no hesitation."

"A good point." He grimaced, and seemed to revert to his usual indolent self—though having seen the Believer behind the mask, Arachne was never going to trust to that mask again. "All right, Mater, I'll do what—I'll do the *best* that I can."

"I'm sure you will," she replied as he rose and walked out of the room. Though at that moment, she was not *at all* certain that he would.

After all—if she died in the backlash of the curse, he stood to inherit all that *she* owned. And then, if he chose, he could have his freedom to live his life as he chose, or his pick of heiresses, couldn't he?

For all she knew, if he actually had made a pact, that would be the sum of it.

Treachery, treachery. It might all come to which of them betrayed the other first.

Marina was wracking her brains, trying to come up with a reason, any excuse at all, to get Reggie and Arachne to take her to the pottery at Exeter. She'd considered feigning some mysterious female illness, considered a toothache that would require a visit to a dentist. But both those ploys could involve having her ruse exposed as such, and would involve—particularly in the case of the dentist—a certain amount of pain. If she wanted books, well they could be ordered, and the same for the shoes she actually needed.

She'd even gone so far as to make a handwritten list of plausible approaches last night, but nothing seemed particularly inspired. She was still turning things over in her mind as she followed Mary Anne to breakfast the next morning, trying on this idea, then that, and coming up with nothing.

Still, when she discovered that Madam was not down to breakfast that morning, leaving her alone with Reggie, it seemed as though the opportunity to approach him directly was too good to let slip. So she listened to his interminable boasts and pointless stories with wide-eyed patience, then, after a description of some petty triumph in business, she sighed theatrically.

At least he managed to pick up on that, although he was utterly obtuse to the fact that she was bored silly with him. "Why the sighs, fair cuz?" he asked, with an empty grin. "Do my triumphs on the field of commerce so entrance you? Or is it just that, like a good little feminine creature, you've no head for business and would like me to change the subject?"

It was about as good an opening as she was ever likely to get. "Actually, in a peculiar way, it's partly both. I *am* fascinated by your enterprises," she replied, making her eyes wide, and looking at him with great seriousness. "Since I'm part of your family now, I've come to the conclusion that I really ought to see your business, first hand, so I can understand it when you discuss it. Oh, Reggie! *Could* you take me to the pottery at Exeter?" She made her voice turn wheedling, though she cringed inside to hear herself. "Please? That is the closest one, isn't it? I should *so* like to see it, and even more, to see you in charge of all of it! It must be thrilling, like seeing a captain command his warship!"

Good gad, am I really saying this tripe?

For a moment, he looked so startled that she had to swallow an entire cup of tea in three gulps to keep from laughing aloud. "Are you serious, cuz?" he said incredulously. "Do you really want to see the pottery and watch me at work?"

"Absolutely," she replied, looking straight into his eyes. "More than wanting to see it, I feel that I must see it, and that I can never properly understand you or Madam unless I see you in command of it all. Could you take me? Perhaps on your next business trip?" She actually stooped so low as to bat her eyes at him, and tried not to gag.

"By Jove, I not only could, but this will fit in with my plans splendidly!" he exclaimed with such glee that she was startled. "Just yesterday Mater was saying that I ought to take you to some place bigger than Oakhurst and let you see the sights; maybe do a trifle of shopping, I know how you little creatures love to shop—"

She stifled the urge to strangle him and concentrated on looking overjoyed with the prospect of a day away from the house and the village. It wasn't that hard to do, given the promise of "a little shopping." Perhaps she could manage to get hold of some money in the process.

"I would like that above all things, so long as I can also see the pottery," she said, gazing at him with feigned adoration. "Oh, Reggie, you are *so* good to me, and I know I must bore a worldly fellow like you to distraction. I can't help it, I know I'm too serious, and so horribly provincial. I must seem like such a bumpkin to a man of the world like you."

"Oh no—you have other things to distract me with, fair cuz," he flattered, with such complete insincerity that she wondered why every woman he met didn't see through him immediately. "Well then, this is Saturday—I'll send Hibdon down to reserve a first-class compartment on the first train down to Exeter Monday morning and the last returning Monday night. We'll be up at dawn, catch the train and have breakfast on it, be in Exeter by ten. We'll trot you about the shops, a handsome little luncheon, perhaps a little more shopping, then we'll off to the pottery. I'll do my duty to the old firm, don't you know, then we'll catch the train, have a good tea on it, and be back here in time for a late dinner!" He laughed then, and winked at her. "I know that won't be nearly enough shopping for you—you ladies don't seem to want to do anything but shop, but maybe you'll take pity on a poor fellow and let me make a promise to take you up again another time."

She simpered, and dropped her eyes, to avoid having to look at him. "Oh, cousin Reggie, I really have very simple tastes. I would like to see a bookshop, and I haven't nearly enough gloves, and perhaps a hat—"

He guffawed—there was no other word for it. "A hat? My dear cuz, I have never yet seen a woman who could buy *a* hat! If you manage that feat, I will fall dead in a faint!"

I just wish you'd fall dead, she thought ungenerously, but she managed to fake a giggle. "Shoes, too," she added as an afterthought. "And riding boots, at least. Mine," she added with genuine regret, "are a disgrace."

"That's enough to fill a morning and an afternoon. Gloves, hats, books—romances, I'll be bound, or poetry—and shoes. Hands, head, heart and—" he grinned at his own cleverness, "—*soles.*"

She did the expected, and groaned and rolled her eyes at the pun. He looked pleased, and chuckled. "I'll tell the Mater; she'll be cheered. She thinks you ought to see the big city—well, something bigger than a village, anyway. Maybe we can go down for a concert or recital or whatnot after this, if the sight of all those people in one place doesn't give you the collywobbles."

"I shall do everything on my part to avoid the collywobbles," she promised solemnly. She managed to be flatteringly good company until he finished his breakfast, then went off to whatever task he had at hand. She finished hers, then took herself off to the long gallery for her newest lessons, which were occupying her mornings now.

The long gallery was a painting and statue gallery, with windows looking out on the terrace on one side, and the artworks on the other. To show off the art, the walls had been painted white and had minimal ornamentation. And now, during autumn, winter, and early spring, the ornamental orange trees in their huge pots from the terrace were kept at the windows inside. The highly polished stone floor echoed with every footstep, and a glance at the rain-slick terrace outside made Marina shiver.

Mary Anne was conducting these lessons, but Marina had hopes that they would be over relatively soon, since she was mastering them more quickly than the dancing lessons. And for once, the wretched girl was actually being helpful instead of superior. It didn't seem as though one ought to need lessons in how to move and walk once one was past babyhood, but as Marina was discovering, it wasn't so much "how to walk" as it was "how to walk gracefully."

The first mistake in her carriage that Mary Anne had corrected had been that Marina always swung her right foot out and back when she moved—she wasn't sure *why*, or how she had gotten into the habit, but now she understood why it was that she was always stubbing the toes of her right foot on things she *should* have passed right by. Then Mary Anne had made her shorten her stride and slow down by tying a string between her ankles, so that she couldn't take a long stride and was constantly reminded by the string not to.

Yesterday, at the end of the lesson, the string had come off so that Mary Anne could view her unimpeded progress.

Today, Mary Anne ordered her to walk the long gallery with a proper stride without the string. She began, taking steps half the size of the ones she was used to, and feeling as if she was taking an age to traverse the distance.

"Now, mind, if you're in a great hurry, and there's no one about to see you," Mary Anne said, as she reached the other end of the Gallery, "then go ahead and tear about with that gallop of yours. But if there's anyone who catches you at it, they'll know in an instant that you're a country cousin."

Eh? "What on earth do you mean by that?" she replied— pitching her voice so that it carried without shouting, which had been Madam's personal lesson for the afternoons when she wasn't at the vicarage.

"You can't race about a townhouse like that without tripping over or running into something," the maid replied smugly. "Nor on a city sidewalk. You have to take short strides in a city; dwellings are smaller, there's much less space and more people and things to share it. Why do you think people talk about going to the country to 'stretch their legs'?"

"I hadn't thought about that," she admitted.

"I'm not going to put a book on your head, though Madam said I should," the maid said thoughtfully, watching her as she approached. "That's only to keep your chin up and your shoulders back. I must say, for someone tossed about in a den of artists, you have excellent posture."

"My uncles used to have me pose for ladies' portrait bodies and busts, so that the ladies themselves only had to sit for the faces," she said, giving a quarter of the truth. "And I posed for saints, sometimes—Saint Jeanne d'Arc, for one. You can't slouch when you're posing for something like that. They have to look—" she pitched her voice a little differently now, making it gluey and unctuous, like the utterly wet individual who had commissioned a Madonna and Child once, when she was very small and posing as Jesus as a young child, with Margherita standing duty as Mary "—drrrrawn up, my child, drrrawn up to Heaven by their faith and their hair—"

For the first time in all the weeks that she had been afflicted with the maid's presence, Mary Anne stared at her—then burst out laughing. Real laughter, not a superior little cough, or a snicker.

"By their hair?" she gasped. "By their hair?" Tears rolled down her face to the point where she had to dry her eyes on her apron, and she was actually panting between whoops, trying to get in air. Marina couldn't help it; she started giggling herself, and made things worse by continuing the impression. "As if, my child, they are suspended above the mortal clay, by means of a strrrrring attached to the tops of their heads—"

"A string?" howled Mary Anne, doubling over. "A string?"

When she finally got control of herself, it seemed that something had changed forever, some barrier between them had cracked and fallen. "Oh," the maid said, finally getting a full breath, the red of her face fading at last. "Thank you for that. I haven't had such a good laugh in a long, long time." She dabbed at the corners of her eyes with her apron. "Imagine. A *string*. Like a puppet—" she shook her head. "Or suspended by their hair! What fool said that?"

"A fool of a bishop who got his position because he was related to someone important," she replied, with amusement and just a touch of disgust at the memory. "Who knew less about real faith than our little vicar down in the village, but a very great deal about whom and how to flatter. But my u—guardian Sebastian Tarrant needed his money, and he did a lovely painting for the man, and since it was for a parlor, *that* is how he painted it. To be ornamental, just as if it was to illustrate something out of King Arthur rather than the Bible. Sebastian said he just tried to tell himself that it was just an Italian bucolic scene he was doing, and it came out all right."

She smiled at the memory. She could still remember him fuming at first over the sketches that the Bishop rejected. *"Damn it all, Margherita! That pompous ass rejected my angels! Angels are supposed to be* powerful, *not simpering ninnys with goose-wings! The first thing they say to mortals is* 'Fear not!' *for heaven's sake! Don't you think they must be saying it because their very appearance is so tremendous it should inspire fear? The angels he* wants *don't look like they're saying* 'Fear not!', *they look like they're saying,* 'There, there'. . . ."

"Mary Anne," she said, sitting down—insinuating herself into the chair, as the maid had just taught her—"I know that you aren't comfortable going to church with me. I don't see why you should still have to, honestly—in the beginning, yes, when I might have done something foolish like crying to the vicar about how horrid my guardian was and how she was mistreating me, but not now. Why don't you ask Madam to be excused?"

The maid gave her a measuring look. "I believe that I will, miss. And you are correct in thinking that Madam assumed you might do something foolish. There was, after all, no telling how you'd been brought up out there—nor what you'd been told about Madam."

Oh yes; something has fallen that was between us. She is never going to be a friend, but she's not my enemy anymore.

"Well—" she shrugged. "What child likes a strict tutor? But the child has to be readied for business or university, and *I* have to be readied for society. I know a great deal from books, and nothing at all about society."

There. That's noncommittal enough.

Mary Anne unbent just a little more. "A wise observation, miss. And may I say that thus far you have been a good pupil, if rebellious at first."

Marina smiled and held out her hand to the maid. "I promise to be completely cooperative from now on, even if I think what you're trying to teach me is daft." She lowered her voice to a whisper as the astonished maid first stared at, then took her hand in a tentative handshake. "Just promise to keep the fact that I posed for saints a secret. Reggie and Madam already think I'm too pious as it is."

"It's a promise, miss." The handshake was firmer. "Everyone has a secret or two. Yours is harmless enough."

"And I'd better practice walking if I'm not to look like a country-cousin Monday in Exeter." She got to her feet— *ascending,* rather than heaving herself up—and resumed her walk up and down the Gallery.

But she couldn't help but wonder just what that last remark of the maid's had implied.

Everyone has a secret or two. Yours is harmless enough.

18

To Marina's immense relief, all she had to do was act naturally on the trip to Exeter to keep Reggie amused. It was, after all, her first train ride, and she found it absolutely enthralling—they had their own little first-class compartment to themselves, so she didn't have to concern herself about embarrassing rather than amusing him. The speed with which they flew through the countryside thrilled her, and she kept her nose practically pressed against the glass of the compartment door for the first half of the journey. By the time she had just begun to tire—a little, only a little—of the passing countryside, it was time to take breakfast, and for that, they moved to the dining car.

This, of course, was another new experience, and she looked at the menu, and fluttered her eyelashes and let Reggie do all the ordering for her. Which he did, with a great deal of amusement. She didn't care. She was having too much fun. Eating at a charming little dining table with lovely linen and a waiter and all, while careening through the countryside at the same time, was nothing short of amazing. Mind, you did have to take care when drinking or trying to cut something; there was certainly a trick to it. For once, there was an advantage to wearing black!

The enjoyment continued after they disembarked from the train, though the sheer number of people pouring out of their train alone was bewildering, and there were several trains at the platforms. In fact, it seemed to her that there were more people on their train than were in the entire village of Oakhurst!

And they all seemed to be in a very great hurry.

For once, the Odious Reggie was extremely useful, as he bullied his way along the platform, with Marina trailing in his wake. Literally in his wake; he left a clear area behind himself that she just fitted into. The engine at rest chuffed and hissed and sent off vast clouds of steam and smoke as they passed it, and she followed the example of the other passengers and covered her nose and mouth with her scarf until they were off the platform.

The Odious Reggie continued to prove his utility; he took her arm as soon as they were out of the crush. She didn't get much chance to look at the terminal, though; he steered her through a mob of people who streamed toward the street. Once there, he commandeered a hansom cab and lifted her into it.

"Head, heart, hands, or soles first?" he asked genially, once he was safely in beside her. She could only shake her head in bewilderment.

"Lightest first, then, since I'm likely to end up as your beast of burden." He tapped on the roof with his umbrella, and a little hatch above their heads opened and the driver peered down at them through it.

Evidently Reggie knew exactly where to go, too. He rattled off a name, the hatch snapped shut, and they were off, the horse moving at a brisk trot through streets crowded with all manner of vehicles—including motorcars. Marina couldn't help it; she stared at them with round eyes, causing Reggie still more amusement.

"Soles" proved to be Reggie's first choice; the cobbler. This was for the very simple reason that the shoes would have to be sent, being "bespoke," or made to Marina's measure. She chose riding boots, two pairs of walking shoes, and at Reggie's urging, a pair of dancing slippers. When she protested that she had no use for such a thing, he laughed.

"Do you think I'm going to let you keep treading on my toes in what you're wearing now?" he said, making her blush. "Dancing slippers, m'gel. My feet have had enough punishment. If you're going to keep treading on them, let it be with soft slippers."

From there, they went to the glover—which was a thing of amazement to her, that there was an establishment that sold nothing but gloves—and she got a full dozen pairs, all black, of course, but of materials as varied as knitted lace and the softest kid-leather. Reggie overruled her completely there, when she would only have gotten one satin pair and one kid. He'd gone down the entire selection in black, picking out one of everything except the heavy wool, and two of the kid.

Then the milliner. And at that establishment, Reggie excused himself. She had conducted herself with dispatch—or at least, as much as would be allowed, given that the cobbler took all the measurements necessary to make a pair of lasts to exactly duplicate her feet—but here she stopped in the entrance and just stared.

Hats—she had never *seen* such hats, except in pictures. Enormous cartwheel picture-hats, hoods, riding hats, straw hats, little bits of netting and feathers that could hardly be *called* a hat, plain, loaded with everything under the sun.

"I'll be back in an hour, m'gel," Reggie said, patronizingly. "I expect by that time, you'll have just gotten started."

By that point, an attentive young woman in a neat skirt and shirtwaist had come up to them. "Whatever she wants, and put it on Madam Arachne Chamberten's account," he told the assistant, and took himself off, leaving Marina in her hands.

Marina shook herself out of her daze, and determined that, although it was unlikely she was going to escape with only the single hat she had promised Reggie, she was going to keep her purchases down to only what she needed. She faced the eager assistant. "I'm in full mourning," she said firmly. "So we will not be purchasing anything frivolous. I need a riding hat. And a foul-weather hood, or something of the sort—"

"Yes, indeed, miss," the assistant said with amusement, sounding fully confident that the very opposite was going to happen.

No you don't— she swore to herself, despite the fact that her eyes kept going to a particularly fetching straw for summer.

When Reggie returned, she was waiting for him—with only a single hatbox. Granted, there were three hats in it, but she had managed to select items that fit together neatly so as to all fit in a single box. It had been a narrow escape, but she'd done it.

"*One* hat?" Reggie asked incredulously, staring at the box. "*One* hat? You're escaping this Aladdin's cave with *one* hat?"

"No," she admitted. "Three small ones."

"It's one box. It counts as one hat. My heart fails me!" He clutched theatrically at his chest, and the assistants giggled over his antics, stopping just short of flirtation with him— probably because the milliner's eye was on them.

"Off to the bookshop, then," he said, "Then luncheon at the Palm Court, and the old firm, then homeward bound." He scooped up her, her hat- and glove-boxes, and carried them all off to the waiting cab.

If there was one blot on the day so far, it was that Madam seemed to have accounts everywhere, and not a single actual penny had changed hands, so Marina hadn't been able to say something like "Oh, I'll take care of it while you visit the tobacconist," and keep back a shilling or so for herself.

The same case proved to hold at the bookshop—which was the biggest such establishment that Marina had ever seen, and had actual *electric* lights, which had been turned on because of growing overcast that threatened rain. She tried very, very hard not to stare, but it was extremely difficult, and she couldn't help but wish for such a thing at Oakhurst.

Not that it was going to be possible for years, even decades yet. Electricity hadn't come anywhere near the village, which didn't even have gas lighting either. It would be paraffin lamps and candles for some time, she suspected.

"Electric lights," she said wistfully. "What a magical invention!"

"We've gas at the pottery," Reggie said, giving close attention to the electrical lamps, which burned away the gloom with steady light not even gas could rival. "I wonder if this is more efficient, though. I believe I'll look into it."

Since he seemed more interested in the lamps than in books, she left him there, and penetrated deep into the recesses of the closely set shelves. Bewildered, she was not, but dazzled, she was. It was one thing to encounter a wealth of books in a private library like that of Oakhurst—such collections were the result of the work of generations, and (not to put too fine a point upon it) a great many of the resulting volumes stored in such libraries were of very little use to anyone other than scholars. Often enough you couldn't, daren't read them, for fear of them crumbling away, the pages separating as you tried to turn them. But here were twice or three times that number, all of them eminently readable, in modern editions, brand new. A feast—that was what it was! A feast for the mind. . . .

It was consideration of how much she could carry and not anything else that led her to limit her selection. She decided that since she wanted some volumes anyway, there was no harm in feeding Reggie's assumptions about her. So in her chosen stack there was some poetry, and some novels, and some very interesting volumes that Elizabeth had recommended, books that raised an eyebrow on the clerk who was tallying them up. He didn't say anything though, and Reggie was deep in another flirtation with a lady wearing one of those frothy confections of lace and velvet that made her wilt with envy, knowing how silly *she* would look in it, at the front of the store. And when he finally did make his way to the till, he picked one of the books up and looked at the title with no sign of recognition, anyway.

"Madam Arachne Chamberten's account," he said as usual. "Have the parcel made up with this young lady's name on it and send it to the station to catch the afternoon train to Eggesford. The four-fifteen, that would be. Have the porter stow it in our compartment. And here—" he handed over the hat- and glove-boxes. "Send these along with it, there's a good fellow."

"All but this—" Marina said, taking one of the poetry books out at random, mostly because it was small and fit in her reticule. Just in case, she wanted to have something with her to read. Reggie might choose to abandon her someplace for a while.

The clerk bowed, Reggie grinned, and she tucked the book into her bag. "Yes, sir," the clerk said, briskly. "Marina

Roeswood, Oakhurst, by way of the four-fifteen to Egges-ford." He wrote it all down on a card that he tucked into the front cover of the topmost book, and handed off the lot to an errand boy. Reggie handed the lad a half crown by way of a tip as Marina bit her lip in vexation. The boy grinned and averred he'd take care of it all personally.

Then there was nothing for it, but to let Reggie sweep her off into yet another cab, which disgorged them on the premises of an hotel. The Palm Court proved to be its restau-rant, which must have been famous enough in Exeter, given the crowds of people. Not merely middle-class people, ei-ther; there wasn't a single one of the ladies there who wasn't be-gowned and be-hatted to the tune of several tens of pounds, judging by the prices that Marina had noted today. She felt so drab in her black—at the next table was a woman in a wonderful suit of French blue trimmed in pur-ple velvet, with a purple silk shirtwaist and a huge purple velvet rose at her throat, cartwheel hat to match. She felt raw with envy, even though you had to have a neck like a Greek column to wear something like that flower at the throat, not an ordinary un-swanlike neck like hers. Then Reggie spoiled everything when the waiter came and he ordered for her, be-fore the waiter could even offer her a menu, quite as if she hadn't a will (and taste) of her own.

Marina got a good stranglehold on her temper and smiled as the waiter bowed and trotted away. "I've never had lob-ster salad, Reggie," she said.

"Oh, you'll like it, all ladies do," he said vaguely, as the waiter returned with tea and a basket of bread and rolls. He chose, cut, and buttered one for her. Was this supposed to be gallantry?

She decided to take it as such, or at least pretend to, and thanked him, even though it was a soft roll, not the hard sort with the crunchy crust that she preferred.

She did actually enjoy the lobster salad when it came, although it wasn't the meal she'd have chosen on a cold day. Fortunately, it turned out to be one of those things that she did know how to eat, although she had waited for its appearance with growing dread, not knowing if this meal was a sadistic ploy on Reggie's part to discomfit her in public. But Reggie was either inclined to treat her nicely today, or else had been ordered to be on his best behavior, because other than taking complete charge of everything but the actual choice of hats and books for the entire day, he'd treated her rather well.

Perhaps it's because I haven't objected to all those flirtations, she thought, watching him exchange another set of wordless communications with a lady two tables over, whom he evidently knew of old. *There was the glover's girl, the milliner's apprentices, the lady at the bookshop—and now here.* Whatever the exchange portended, however, must not have been to his benefit, as the lady shortly after welcomed another gentleman to her table with every evidence of pleasure, and Reggie applied himself to his saddle of mutton with an air of having been defeated.

The defeat must have been a very minor one, though, as he was all smiles again by dessert.

"All right, m'gel," he said, when the bill was settled, to the waiter's unctuous satisfaction, "It's off to work for us! Let's collect our traps and hie us hence."

All the pleasures of the day faded into insignificance at that reminder of what she was here for in the first place. And as they collected their "traps" from the cloakroom girl and piled into yet another cab, Marina tried to prepare herself to hunt—even though she didn't really know what she was looking for.

❁

Andrew Pike drummed his fingers on the desk-blotter, stared into nothing much, and tried not to worry too much about Marina. After all, it wasn't as if she was going to open herself up to anything dangerous just by passive observation. And it wasn't as if they'd had any evidence that either her guardian or the Odious Reggie (how he loved that nickname!) were the ones responsible for the occult drain on Ellen. It was just as likely that the pottery had been built on the site of some ancient evil, and that the presence of someone with Ellen's potentials had caused it to reach out and attach itself to her. For heaven's sake, it was equally possible that she'd *done* something unconsciously that awoke the thing! It was equally likely that one of her so-called gentleman friends had done it, figuring the girl was ignorant, and perfectly willing to drain her and throw her away when he was satisfied. After all, the rotters were equally willing to do the same sort of thing physically.

Still.

Still, just because Madam hasn't shown any signs of otherworldly abilities, that doesn't mean she doesn't have them.

Andrew was not a Scot—he was from Yorkshire, actually—but he had taken his medical degree in Scotland, where there was a strong occult tradition—which was how he'd come to find another Earth Master to teach him beyond what his Air Mage mother had taught him in the first place. And up there, he'd encountered a number of—interesting fragments. There had been rumors among the Scots Masters for centuries, for instance, that perfectly ordinary folk, without any discernible magical abilities, could *steal* magic from others by frankly unpleasant means. Yes, and use that magic too, even though they were effectively working blind. Some of those fragments attested that a cult of Druids were the ones who practiced this theft, some that it was a splinter of the Templars that really did worship the old god Baphomet

as was claimed, and some—well, the majority actually—
said it was Satanists. A group of Satanists recruited and
taught by the infamous Gilles de Rais to be exact, who then
came to England when he was caught in his crimes and
brought the teachings with them. The trouble was, no one
had any proof—and it was a difficult proposition to track
down what was essentially a Left-Hand Path magician when
he didn't look like a magician, didn't have shields like a magician, and could not be told from ordinary, non-magical
folk.

And as it happened, neither Madam nor her son looked
like magicians, had shields like magicians, or seemed in any
way to be anything other than ordinary, non-magical folk.

He had many questions that were bothering him at this
point, of which one was why, exactly, had Marina not been
living here with her parents? No one in the village knew—
although there were stories that something terrible had happened shortly after the child's christening that had sent
Marina's mother into "a state." Coincident with that, it
seemed, the child was sent away.

Why was it that no one had seen or heard anything of this
sister of Hugh's for years? Interestingly enough, it was common knowledge that Madam had had a falling-out with her
parents over her choice of husband, and had not been seen
at Oakhurst ever again until the Roeswoods died so tragically. But why, after the parents were dead, had brother and
sister not made some attempt to reconcile? Unless Hugh
Roeswood was of the same mind as his parents about
Arachne. But then, why not have a will, just in case, to prevent Arachne from ever having anything to do with the
Roeswoods? But if the rift was so insurmountable, why had
Arachne claimed the girl and taken her directly into her
household? Why not just leave her where she was, washing

her hands entirely of her? No law could force her to become Marina's hands-on guardian.

It was all fragments that instinct told him should fit together, but which didn't.

He wished that he'd had more uninterrupted time to talk to her. He wished that Clifton Davies had discussed more of her past and less of chess-moves and music with her. Merely mentioning her mother seemed to make her wary, as if there was something about her mother that she didn't much want to think about.

Though what it could be—if there was anything—he was hanged if he could imagine!

Well, old man, there is one route to find out what you can about her that you haven't taken.

Not that he hadn't thought about it—but magicians as he knew them up in Scotland were odd ducks. Insular, self-protective, and inclined to keep things close to their chests. Those that had formed groups tended to look a little suspiciously on outsiders, and if anyone was an outsider here, it was definitely Dr. Andrew Pike, with Clifton Davies from the Welsh Borders a close second. Still—

They're sending their sick to me, and mage-born children of ordinary parents when they find them in trouble. So I might not be so much of an outsider that I can't get information out of these Devonian mages after all. It'd serve me right to discover that the only reason no one's told me anything is because I didn't ask.

Fauns would be the best messengers, he reckoned. They weren't at all troubled by cold weather—didn't go dormant to sleep until spring like some Earth Elementals. They went everywhere there was a patch of wildwood, and every Earth mage *he* had ever seen had a patch of wildwood somewhere about. That was one reason why they didn't much like being in cities, truth to tell. When he got done sending out *his* messengers, he could get Clifton to send out—oh, Sylphs, he supposed. They were the Air Elementals he was most familiar with, though perhaps there was something else that was more suitable. Then . . . hmm. Who did he know that he could trade on favors to help him with Water and Fire?

Oh, good Lord—two of the children, of course! Naiads hung about Jamie Cooper like bees around a honey pot, and Craig Newton was always talking to Salamanders in the fire. He couldn't send messengers from those two Elements, of course; the children didn't command anything at the moment, and now that he'd gotten them over their fears that they were going mad, his main job was to shield them from the nastier Elementals of their types until they could protect themselves. But he could ask them to ask their Elementals to do the favor, and if the creatures didn't lose interest or get distracted by something else, they probably would.

But—send out his own Elementals, first, and see where that got him.

The one good and reliable thing about Fauns was that unlike Brownies, they were pitiably easy to bribe with things from the human world. Unfortunately, they were also scatterbrained. But as long as they could lick their lips and taste the honey he'd give them, and as long as their little flasks held the wine he'd offer them, they'd remember, and they'd keep to the job.

After a quick stop in the kitchen for a peg of the *vin ordinaire* that the departing family had deemed too inferior to take with them or to try and sell, a big cottage-loaf, and a pot of honey, he bundled himself up in his mackintosh and went out into the wet, tying his hood down around his ears.

It was a wild day, one of the "lion" days of March, full of wind and lashings of rain, and he was glad that there hadn't been two fair days in a row, for weather like this would doom any buds that had been coaxed out before their time.

Mercedes Lackey

He bent his head to the rain and trudged down to the bottom of the garden, then beyond, into the acres that had once been manicured parkland but had been allowed to fall into neglect. Near the edge of the property he owned was a coppice that had grown up around what had once been a tended grove of Italian cypress, and in the center of that grove was still a marble statue of Pan in one of his milder moods— Pan, the musician, boon companion of Bacchus, not Great God Pan of the wilderness and Panic fear. Even without casting a shield-circle and doing a formal invocation, such a setting was still potent to bring and hold the little fauns (and he sometimes wondered if they were homesick for the warmer winds and cypresses of Italy that they came so readily here).

He shoved his way into the grove, past a couple of gorse bushes grown up like rude boys pressing on the edge of the circle of cypress trees. Something about this spot had suited the cypresses; they had grown tall and thick in this place, and what had once been a circle of graceful, thin, green columns with marble benches at their bases facing the statue that stood at the south-point of the circle, was now a green wall. He edged himself sideways between two of the Italian cypresses, whose dark green, brackenlike branches resisted him for a moment, then yielded.

Then he was within the tiny grove itself, a disk of rank, dead grass, protected from the wind and so marginally warmer than the space outside it. There was Pan, staring down at him with a benign, slightly mischievous grin, holding his syrinx just below his bearded lips. The benches were all toppled, shoved over by the roots and thickening trunks of the cypresses. The marble of the statue was darkened with grime in all the crevices, which had the effect of making it look more like a living creature rather than less. The hair was green with moss, a green which in this light looked black, and the eyes had been cleverly carved so that they seemed to follow whomever walked in front of it.

Here was relative warmth, peace, no Cold Iron, the trees of the Italian peninsula and wilderness. Only two things were lacking to bring the Fauns—food, and drink.

He pulled the cork from the bung-hole of the cask, and dribbled a little on the plinth that Pan stood upon, tore off a bit of bread, dipped it in the honey, and laid it at Pan's feet. Ideally, he'd have had olive oil as well, but that comestible was a bit difficult to come by in the heart of Devon.

"You could have brought butter," said a piping voice at his elbow. *"We've gotten used to butter. Cheese, too, we like cheese."*

"Next time, then I will," he replied, looking down into the slanted, goatlike golden eyes of the little faun. The shameless little faun, without even a loincloth to cover his privates. Unlike Pan's—which in the statue were modestly screened by an enormous fig leaf. Fortunately, fauns were not as priapic in nature as the god of whom they were the votaries and earthly representatives.

"It would only get wet," the Faun pointed out cheerfully. *"Have you ever worn a wet leather loincloth? Misery."*

"You have a point," he admitted. "And I have a favor to ask."

He sensed more of them all around him, some in hiding, some stealing up behind him. The faun at his elbow sniffed at the wine-smell longingly, his nose twitching. *"They don't make wine here,"* he complained. *"Only cider. It's very good cider, really excellent cider, but we're* tired *of cider."*

"So this should be very welcome," he responded, putting the cork back in the bunghole, and carefully placing the cask, bung-end up, on the ground. He added the loaf of bread and the jar of honey beside it. "I'm trying to find anyone who knows the Water Mage up the hill and would be willing to talk to me. The girl-mage, not the man."

"Not the Christ-man in the village?" This was another faun, who practically quivered with eagerness as his nose filled with the scent of bread and wine.

"No, the young lady who lives in the big house now—"

"We can't get near," complained a third, drumming on the ground with one hoof. *"They drove us out of the garden and closed the bounds! She made us welcome there, the gentle She with sad eyes, but they drove us out when they came!"*

That would have been Madam and her son—small wonder. He'd seen the garden now, manicured to a fare-thee-well, and bristling with wrought-iron ornaments. Madam apparently liked wrought-iron trellises and arbors, lamp-posts and what not. Taming the wildness and planting iron everywhere would have made the fauns flee as fast as they could.

"You don't have to try and go near her to catch her scent; she has come to me once, and many times to the Christ-man," he said patiently. "Besides, to look for those who know her, you do not need the scent. You only need the name. Names are like scent to men."

"Both is better," said the first, *"But we can do this, if we can find her scent. Did she do magic there, too?"*

Fauns needed a great deal of simple explanation, sometimes. "Yes, she did—Water magic, for she is a Water Mage. Her scent will be there, where the Christ-man dwells, with their magic mingled with mine. And her name is Marina Roeswood." He stepped away from his offerings, just in case any of the Cold Iron he was wearing in tiny bits all over his person troubled them. Fauns were fairly robust about that, but it didn't hurt to be certain. "To the fruit of the vine, the harvest of the field, be welcome," he added, the litany that allowed them to take what he had placed there.

A half-dozen of them swarmed his offerings like locusts, and a moment later, they were all gone but the one that had first addressed him. That one stood hipshot, still looking up at him.

"Marina Roeswood, blood of Earth, born of Water," the faun said. Andrew nodded, though he hadn't the faintest idea what it meant. *"Good. We will send askings, for as long as we remember."*

"Then remember this, too. I will continue to bring Vine and Harvest here every two days for the next six, so if you have anything to tell me, there will be more to share." He smiled to see the faun's eyes widen. "And since you have gotten accustomed to butter and cheese, there will be some of that, as well."

"Butter is good," the faun said meditatively. *"And cheese. I think remembrance will run long, if you come every two days."*

Fortunately, there was a bit left in the original cask of *vin ordinaire,* and no one at the sanitarium drank wine.

Isn't that a line out of Bram Stoker's novel? "I never drink . . . wine. . . ."

Odd thought, that. But it was the truth at Briareley. The staff was Devon born and bred, except for Eleanor, and your true Devonian wouldn't look at wine when there was cider about. Old fashioned fermented cider, that is, the stuff that had a kick like a mule, and was stronger than anyone outside the county usually suspected.

He didn't drink wine, either, as a rule. A glass of whisky by preference, if he felt the taste for spirits coming on—that was where Scotland had rubbed off on him. Otherwise, tea was his drink. And he'd never seen Eleanor touch a drop of spirit even when offered it; tea for her as well. So the fauns could have the wine and welcome to it.

"Vine and harvest, bee-sup and butter and cheese, all to come if we bring word. We will remember, Earth Master," the faun said, with a stamp of his hoof to seal the bargain.

Then Andrew was once again alone in the clearing, with only the knowing eyes of Pan upon him, the faint purple stain and the bit of bread still on the plinth. The fauns would not take that bit of an offering to their god; a bird or a mouse might steal it, but that was Pan's will.

He saluted the god with no sense of irony, and turned to push his way back out of the grove and into the workaday world again.

Marina sat at a desk in one of the inner offices and trembled. She had never been so glad of anything in her life as she was glad of the fact that Reggie had left the tour of the pottery to one of his underlings—and that business conferences with his managers had kept him pent up in his office all afternoon. Because it took her all afternoon to recover from what she found in the painting-room.

It had been bad enough to discover that the pottery was a blight, a cancer, a malignant spring spewing poison into the land, the water, the very air. Everyone and everything around here was poisoned, more or less—the clay-lees choked the Exe where the runoff entered it, and no living thing could survive the murky water, not fish nor plant. Clay clogged the gills and smothered the fish, coated the leaves of water-plants and choked them. The clay choked the soil as well—and the lead from the glazes killed what the clay didn't choke. Even the air, loaded with lead vapor and smoke from the kilns, was a hazard to everything that came in contact with it. But those were the least of the poisons here.

The rather dull young clerk who took her around didn't even notice when the blood drained out of her face and she grew faint on the first probing touch of the paintresses and their special environs. The girls themselves were too busy to pay attention to her—she was only a female, after all. There weren't any of their gentleman friends there at the time, but Marina had the idea that they'd been chivvied out long enough for her to take her look around, and would pop out of hiding as soon as she was gone. So there was no one to notice that she clutched at the doorpost and chattered ridiculous questions for a good fifteen minutes before she felt ready to move on.

Thank heavens that was the end of the tour, she thought, shuddering. The clerk had tucked her up in one of the managers' offices with apologies that he couldn't put her in Madam Chamberten's office, because it was Madam Chamberten's orders that it was locked up unless she was expected. She waved him away and asked for a pot of tea, then changed her mind and left it untouched when she realized how much lead must be in the water. She didn't want to go into Madam Chamberten's office. Not when—that sinkhole of evil lay so close to it.

So instead, she propped her forehead on her hand and pretended to read her poetry book, strengthening her shields from her inner reserves, and trying to make them as invisible as all her skill could. One touch, one single touch had told her all she needed to know.

Ellen was by no means the first, nor the only girl with untapped magic-potential that had been drained. Every girl in that painting-room was being drained, and more than being drained, was being *corrupted.* Oh, it was insidious enough; and really, Marina could not imagine how Ellen had escaped permanent harm. It began with being brought into the painting-room, with flattery as the poison worked its fatal changes and made the girls beautiful, with pretty dresses made available to them, and cosmetics in the form of the glaze-powders. Then the temptations began in the form of the men who visited, and their presents, invitations, the stories of good times and pleasure from girls who had been here a while. There were two of those girls whose sexuality was so robust and honest that they actually got no spiritual harm from yielding to that temptation. They enjoyed themselves to the hilt, taking what was offered and laughingly thrust away anything that was perverse, that was the wonder of it. But the rest were tempted to do things they felt in their hearts were wrong, saw themselves as fallen— because they saw themselves as fallen, they became fallen, grew hard, and then—

And then realized with horror that they were dancing with death, as the first signs of trouble came on them. Understood that they were doomed, and saw themselves as damned by their own actions, and despaired.

And that cesspit, that sinkhole hidden beneath the floor of the painting room, drank it all in and stored it up, aged and refined it, then distilled it in a dark flame of pure evil.

And then what?

She didn't know. Something came and tapped off the unwholesome vintage, more poisonous than the lead dust that floated in the air of that place. It was power, that wine of iniquity; power stolen from the girls, from their magic, from their guilt, from their despair. Three separate vintages blended into a deadly draught that something or some*one* drank to the dregs.

And she had a horrible feeling that she knew who that someone was.

The office door opened, and she looked up. "Ready to

go?" asked Reggie, with obscene cheer. "We have a train to catch!"

She set her mouth in a false smile, and got up. "Of course," she replied, and managed to step quite calmly into the coat he held out for her.

He caught up her hand and all but propelled her out of the offices and down to the street to the inevitable cab. A glance at the station-clock as they arrived showed the reason for his haste; they were cutting it fine, indeed, and she broke into an undignified run beside him as they dashed for the train.

It was only as the train pulled out of the station and she settled into their compartment and caught her breath—taking care that she put her face in shadow, where her expression would be more difficult to read—that Reggie finally spoke to her again.

"Well, cuz, did you learn all you wanted to?" he asked genially.

And she was very, very glad for her caution, because she was certain that her eyes, at least, would have betrayed her, as she answered him.

"Oh yes, Reggie," she said, exerting every bit of control she had to keep her voice even. "I certainly did. More than I ever dreamed."

19

MARINA had never been so sure of anything in her life as she was that Reggie and his mother were behind the dreadful evil beneath their pottery.

And yet within the hour, Marina was sitting across from Reggie in the dining car, a sumptuous tea laid out on the table between them, listening to him chatter with bewilderment.

"Good for me to show the face every so often there," he said, after she had sat across from him, numb and sick, trying to get as far from him as she could and still be unobtrusive. "Never on a schedule, of course. Unexpected; that way they can't play any jiggery-pokery. Mater gives me a pretty free hand there—well, except for that emergency, I don't think she's set foot in the place for a year. So the running of the place is my doing."

Madam hasn't been there for a year? How could that be possible? That sinkhole didn't have that sort of capacity, and it must have been tapped off several times in the last year. Could Reggie be tapping it?

Surely not—"Of course, when things happen like kilns blowing up, Mater wants to get right in there; in her nature, you might say. But the Exeter works are half mine, and she reckoned it was a good place for me to get m'feet wet, get used to running things." He grinned at her, as pleased as a boy making the winning score at rugby.

Surely not Reggie—

That sort of seething morass couldn't be handled at a distance—yet Madam couldn't have tapped it. So if she wasn't tapping that unhealthy power, who was?

Surely not Reggie. Not possible. No matter what Shakespeare said, that a man could "smile and smile and still be a villain," evil that profound *couldn't* present a surface so— banal.

And besides, there was nothing, not the slightest hint of power, evil or otherwise, about him! Nor, now that she came to think about it, was there anything of the sort about Madam.

She had followed him out of the compartment at his urging as contradictions overwhelmed her and left her confused and uncertain. The touch of his hand on her elbow left her even more uncertain. There was *nothing* in that touch. No magic, no evil, nothing to alert her to danger. Perfectly, solidly ordinary, and no more odious than the Odious Reggie usually was, in that he took possession of her arm as if he had already taken possession of her entire person and was merely marking his claim to her.

It was so baffling it made her head ache, and she sought comfort in the familiar rituals of teapot and jam jar. Although the teapot was heavy silver, and the jam jar not a jar at all, but a dish of elegant, cut crystal, the tea tasted the same as the China Black from Aunt Margherita's humble brown ceramic pot with the chipped spout, and the jam not quite as good as the home-made strawberry she'd put up with her own hands. Still, as she poured and one-lump-or-twoed, split scones and spread them with jam, the automatic movements gave her a point of steadiness and familiarity.

". . . jolly fine deposit of kaolin clay under the North Pasture," Reggie was saying, showing almost as much enthusiasm as he'd had for his flirtations with all those strange young women today. "With Chipping Brook so deep and fast there, we've got water-power enough for grinding, mixing, anything else we'd want. Plenty of trees in the copse at the western edge for charcoal to fire the kilns—plenty of workers in the village—the road to the railroad *or* going up north to the sea for cheap transport—there's nothing lacking but the works itself!"

Chipping Brook? North Pasture? My North Pasture? Her scattered thoughts suddenly collected as she realized what he'd been babbling about for the past several minutes.

Putting a pottery—another of those poisonous blots—in the North Pasture beside Oakhurst. On her land. Spewing death into her brook, her air—devouring her trees to feed the voracious kilns, turning her verdant meadow into a hideous, barren scrape in the ground.

And taking the villagers, people I know, or their children, offering them jobs and then poisoning them with lead dust and overwork.

"I think I can do without that, Reggie," she said, attempting to sound smooth and cool, interrupting the stream of plans from her cousin. "Your potteries are astonishing, and surely must be the envy of your peers, but I haven't the interest or the ability to run one, and I prefer the North Pasture as it is. I certainly have no desire to live next to a noisy factory, which is what I would be doing if you put a pottery in the North Pasture."

"Well, cuz, obviously you don't have to live next to it—there are hundreds of places you could live!" Reggie said with a fatuous laugh as the train sped past undulating hills slowly darkening as the light faded. "Why live at Oakhurst, anyway? It's just an old country manor without gas, much less electricity, and neither are likely to reach the village in the next thirty years, much less get to the manor! A London townhouse—now *there's* the ticket!"

She winced inwardly. That much was true, too true. But she wasn't about to admit to him that she would very much have liked to have the option to modernize within her own lifetime. "Nevertheless, Oakhurst is my inheritance, to order as I choose, and I do not choose to have it turned into a factory, so you can put that notion out of your mind," she said sharply—so sharply that he was clearly surprised and taken aback.

Oh dear. She softened her posture immediately and smiled winsomely. "Silly man! I haven't even gotten to know the place, and already you want to change it entirely! Haven't you come to know me well enough by now to know that given any other choice, I would still live here? I like the countryside, and Oakhurst is particularly beautiful. Surely there are cities enough where you can put another factory without ruining my peace and quiet and my views!"

Reggie regained that superior smirk. "I forgot, cuz, you're just a little country-cousin at heart," he said condescendingly.

"I'm afraid so," she admitted, lowering her gaze and looking up at him through her lashes. "After my trip today, I am only more confirmed in my notions, I must admit. Exeter was exciting but—there were so many *people!*"

She might have despised herself for being so manipulative; might, except for all that was at stake. She could not, would not allow another diseased blight to take root here. She would fight it to the last cell of her body.

"You'll change your mind," he said, dismissing her and her concerns out of hand. "Especially when you're out, when you've had a real London season, when you're going to parties and balls and the theater—you'll like cities so much you'll wonder how you ever thought a pasture worth bothering your pretty head about. Heh—and when you start seeing how much of the ready it takes to buy all those gowns and froofahs and things you ladies are so fond of, you'll realize just how much good a factory could do your pocketbook. Can't be seen in the same frock twice, don't you know. You can't support a lively Town style on farm rents. It needs a lot of the ready to be in the mode."

We'll see about that, she thought grimly. If the choice was between fine feathers and the preservation of this land—she would be willing to make a regular guy of herself in London. She would do without that promised London season! No gown, no string of balls, nothing was worth despoiling Oakhurst, raping the land, poisoning the waters.

The real question was—since she had no direct control of her property, how was she to keep Reggie from plunging ahead with his plan no matter what she wanted? She had no doubt that Madam would be only too happy to give ear to this idea, and Madam was the one who was making the decisions at the moment, where Oakhurst was concerned.

"Oh, Reggie, you can't want to make me miserable!" she pouted. "That pottery just gave me the awfullest headache, and I just know I'd have nothing but headaches with one of those things right in the next field!"

"But you wouldn't be here, you'd be in London," he tried to point out, but she sighed deeply and quivered her lower lip.

"Not all the time! And how can I have house parties with

a *factory* in the next field? People don't come to house parties to see factories, they come to see views, and to shoot — and oh, everyone around here of any consequence will just hate us, for the shooting will be quite spoilt for miles around!"

That actually seemed to get through to him, at last, and he looked startled. Encouraged, she elaborated. "Oh, we'll be a disgrace! My season will be a disaster! *No one* will want to be seen with the girl who had the audacity to drive all the game out to the moor!"

"Well — not to the moor, surely —" he ventured, looking alarmed.

She turned an utterly sober gaze upon him. "I'm the country-cousin, remember? Oh, do *trust* me, Reggie, all it will take is for your factory to drive the red deer out of this neighborhood — or worse, the pheasants! — and we will be entirely in disgrace and everyone who is anyone will know what we'd done and who's to blame! You just wait — wait and see how your London friends treat you when shooting they were counting on isn't *there* anymore! Not everyone goes to Scotland, you know — people depend on Devon and Surrey for their sport!"

That turned the trick; he promised not to do anything about his plans until she knew she would want to live in London and not at Oakhurst, after all — and until he had made certain that there were no notable shoots anywhere around the vicinity.

"But you just wait, little cuz," he laughed, as he escorted her back to their compartment. "Once you've had a taste of proper life, you won't care if I blow the place up if it buys you more frocks and fun."

She settled herself in the corner under one of the ingenious wall-mounted paraffin lamps that the steward had lit in their absence. He dropped onto the seat across from her

beneath the other and opened his paper. She took out her poetry book and stared at it, turning the pages now and again,
without reading them.

*"You won't care if I blow the place up if it buys you more
frocks and fun."* Callous, unfeeling, greedy, selfish—but is
that evil? *Evil enough to account for that horror beneath
Exeter? Or is it just plain, ordinary, piggy badness?* It didn't
equate, it just didn't—evil wasn't bland. Evil didn't worry
about ruining its reputation by running off the game. Evil
probably would be perfectly happy to ruin anything.

If not the son, what about my first *thought, the mother?
She's the only parent he's had for ever so long, so she's had
the only hand over him—he should reflect her.* Madam was
cold, yes. Selfish, yes. Utterly self-centered. *And she's all
business and money and appearances. Still. That doesn't
add up to horror either.* Evil should slaver and gnash its
teeth, howling in glee at the rich vein of nourishment beneath Madam's office. It shouldn't wear stylish suits and
smart frocks and give one strenuous lessons in etiquette.

There was only one possible conclusion here. There *had*
to be something else behind the cesspit of vileness back
there in Exeter.

And she would be hanged if she could figure out who
was feeding off of it. Or what.

My head hurts. She felt a sinking sort of desperation. Out
of her depth, unable to cope. Too much was happening at
once, and on such wildly disparate levels that she couldn't
begin to imagine how she was to deal with it all. *I am out,
completely out, of ideas or even wild guesses.* She stared at
her poem, unseeing, as the railway carriage rocked from
side to side. *Someone else will have to solve this mystery.
They* can't *expect me to solve it—all they asked me was to
see if there was anything there, after all . . . come to that,
they never asked me, I volunteered to look.*

She told herself to breathe deeply, and calm down. No one was expecting her to do anything—except herself. And anyway, it wasn't her outlook to actually do anything about it either! Hadn't Dr. Pike and Mr. Davies virtually volunteered to be the ones to track this thing down to its cause and eliminate it? She was only seventeen, after all, and no Master of her element! She wasn't anywhere ready to go charging off, doing battle with vile magics!

They simply can't expect me to do anything about this! It would be like sending me out into the desert after the Mad Mullah, for heaven's sake—with only my parasol and a stern lecture to deliver! At some point, Marina, she continued, lecturing herself in her thoughts, *You simply have to let someone else* do *things and allow that you can't.*

Well, there was one thing at least that she could do— and that was to let the proper people know about the—the vileness.

And another—to keep that poison away from Oakhurst.

She didn't have any more time to think about it, though, for the train was pulling into the station, and Reggie was making all the motions of gathering up their things.

Reggie opened the door and helped her out onto the platform. The carriage was waiting for them, the coachman already taking up the parcels from the shops and stowing them away as they approached; they were inside and on the way within minutes. The coach rattled over cobblestones, passing the lights of the town, then jolted onto a dirt road; a crack of the whip, and the horses moved out of a fast walk into a trot. The coachman seemed in a monstrous hurry, for some reason; perhaps he sensed yet another wretched March storm coming, for he kept the horses moving at such a brisk pace that Marina was jounced all over her seat, and even Reggie had to hang on like grim death.

"I'll be—having a word—with our driver—" he said between bounces. "Damn me! See if I—don't!"

But the moment he said that, the reason for the rush became apparent, as the skies opened up and poured down rain.

This was a veritable Ark-floating torrent, and no wonder the coachman had wanted them to get out and on the road so quickly. It drummed on the coach roof and streamed past the windows, and Reggie let out a yelp and a curse as a lightning bolt sizzled down with a crash far too near the road for comfort. There was a sideways jolt as the horses shied, but the coachman held them firm and kept them under control.

The coach slowed, of necessity—you couldn't send horses headlong through *this*—but they were near home now. The lights of the village loomed up through the curtains of rain; not much of them, no streetlights at all, just the lights over the shops, and the houses on either side of the road all veiled by rain—a moment of transition from road to cobbles and back again, splashing through enormous puddles. Then they were past, the lights of the village behind them, and they were minutes from Oakhurst. Over two hills, across the bridge, climbing a third—

Then the lights of Oakhurst appeared through the trees and just above them, although the rain was showing no signs of slackening off. Marina peered anxiously through the windows; lightning pulsed across the sky, illuminating Oakhurst in bursts of blue-white radiance. The coach slowed as they neared the front and pulled up as close to the door as possible, and servants with umbrellas dashed out into the downpour to shelter both of them inside and fetch the parcels.

To no avail, of course, with the rain coming as much sideways as down; Marina was soaked to the skin despite the umbrella held over her. Once inside the door she was swiftly separated from Reggie by Mary Anne and chivvied off to her own—warm!—room to be stripped and regarbed from the skin outward. For once Marina was glad, very glad, of the tendency of her room to be too warm for her taste, for she was cold and shivering, which combined with her headache made her ache all over. The flames in her fireplace slowly warmed her skin as Mary Anne rubbed her with a heavy towel then held out undergarments for her to step into.

"Madam's got a bit of a surprise for you," Mary Anne said, lacing her tightly into a brand new corset, which must have been delivered that very day. "Seems she found something in the attics she thinks you'll fancy. She must have been that bored, to send someone to go rummaging about up there. Been raining all day, though, so perhaps that was it."

"I didn't even know there was an attic," Marina ventured, wondering if she dared mention her splitting head to Mary Anne. She decided in favor of it. "Now I wish I hadn't asked Reggie to take me to that pottery—I've such a headache—"

Mary Anne tugged her rustling silk trumpet skirt over her head with an exclamation of distaste. "I shouldn't be surprised!" she replied. "Nasty, noisy, filthy places, factories. I'll find a dose for you, then you're to go straight to Madam. She's in the sitting-room."

The dose was laudanum, and if it dulled the pain, it also made her feel as if there was a disconnection between her and her thoughts, and her wits moved sluggishly. It occurred to her belatedly that perhaps she shouldn't have taken it so eagerly.

Well, it was too late now. When she stepped out of the door of her room, she moved carefully, slowly, more so than even Madam would have asked, because her feet didn't feel quite steady beneath her. She was handicapped now.

But I must look at her—really look *at her,* she reminded herself. *I* must *know for certain if she has anything to do with that vileness.* It seemed days, and not hours ago, since this morning, weeks since her encounter with what lay under the pottery, months since she had vowed to investigate. She had gone from utter certainty that Madam was behind it to complete uncertainty. She kept one hand pressed to her throat, trying to center herself.

As she passed darkened rooms, lightning flashed beyond the windows; the panes shook and rattled with rain driven against them and drafts skittered through the halls, sending icy tendrils up beneath her skirt to wrap around her ankles and make her shiver. The coachman had been right to gallop; it was a tempest out there. It was a good thing that it had been too cold for buds to form; they'd have been stripped from the boughs. The thin silk of her shirtwaist did nothing to keep the drafts from her arms; she had been warm when she left her room, and she hadn't gone more than halfway down the corridor before she was cold all over again.

The sitting room had a blazing great fire in it, and by now Marina was so chilled that she had eyes only for that warmth, and never noticed Madam standing half in shadow on the far side of the room. She went straight for the flames like a moth entranced, and only Madam's chuckle as she spread her icy hands to the promised warmth reminded her of why she was here.

"A pity the horses were slow," Madam said, as Marina turned to face her. "Reggie has been complaining mightily and swearing I should replace them."

"I don't think any horses could have gone faster in the dark, no matter how well they knew the road, Madam," she protested. "Before the rain started, Reggie was angry that he was going so fast, actually. And the coachman could hardly have made the *train* arrive any sooner," she added, in sudden inspiration.

"True enough." Madam's lips moved into something like

a smile, or as near as she ever got to one. "True, and reasonable as well. So, my dear, you have begun to think like a grown woman, and not like an impulsive child."

Marina dropped her eyes—and took that moment to concentrate, as well as she could through the fog of the drug, to search her guardian for any taint of that terrible evil.

Nothing. Nothing at all. Magic might never exist at all for all of the signs of it that Madam showed. Never a hint; marble, ice showed more sign of magic than she.

Not possible then— She didn't know whether to be disappointed or glad. "Mary Anne said you had found something you wished me to see, Madam?" she said instead.

"Not I—although I guessed that it might exist, given who and what the people your parents had sent you to stay with were." The words were simple enough—but the tone made Marina look up, suspecting—something. What, she didn't know, but—something. There was something hidden there, under that calculating tone.

But as usual, Madam's face was quite without any expression other than the faintest of amusement.

"So," she continued, looking straight into Marina's eyes, "I asked of some of the older servants, and sent someone who remembered up to the attic to find what I was looking for. And here it is—"

She stepped aside and behind her was something large concealed beneath a dust-sheet. The firelight made moving shadows on the folds, and they seemed to move.

Madam seized a corner of the dust cover and whisked it off in a single motion.

The fire flared up at that moment, fully revealing what had been beneath that dust-sheet. Carved wood—sinuous curves—a shape that at first she did not recognize.

"Oh—" Of all of the things that she might have guessed

had she been better able to think, this was not one of them. "A cradle?"

"*Your* cradle, or so I presume," Madam said silkily. "Given your name and the undeniable *marine* themes of the carving. Not to mention that it is clearly of—rather unique design. An odd choice for a cradle, but there is no doubt of the skill of the carver."

Marina stepped forward, drawn to the bit of furniture by more than mere curiosity. Carved with garlands of seaweed and frolicking mermaids, with little fish and naiads peeking from behind undulating waves, there was only one hand that could have produced this cradle.

Uncle Thomas.

She had seen these very carvings, even to the funny little octopus with wide and melting eyes—here meant to hold a gauzy canopy to shield the occupant of the cradle from stray insects—repeated a hundred times in the furnishings in her room in Blackbird Cottage. All of her homesickness, all of her loneliness, overcame her in a rush of longing that excluded everything else. And she wanted nothing more at this moment than to touch them, to feel the silken wood under her hand. With a catch at her throat and an aching heart to match her aching head, she wanted to feel those familiar curves and take comfort from them.

Madam stepped lightly aside as her hand reached for the little octopus, moving as if it had a life of its own.

A lightning bolt struck just outside the sitting-room windows; she was too enthralled even to wince.

Something bright glinted among the octopus's tentacles. Something metallic, a spark of wicked blue-white.

She hesitated.

"Lovely, isn't it?" Madam crooned, suddenly looming behind her. "The wood is just like silk. Here—" she seized Marina's wrist in an iron grip. "Just feel it."

Marina didn't resist; it was as if she had surrendered her will to her longing for this bit of home and everything else was of no importance at all. She watched her hand as if it belonged to someone else, watched as Madam guided it towards the carving, felt the fingers caress the smooth wood.

Felt something stab through the pad of her index finger when it touched that place where something had gleamed in the lightning-flash.

Madam released her wrist, and stepped swiftly back. Marina staggered back a pace.

She cried out—not loudly, for it had been little more than a pinprick. She took another step backward, as Madam moved out of her way.

But then, as she turned her hand to see where she had been hurt, the finger suddenly began to burn—burn with pain, and burn to her innermost eye, burn with that same, poisonous, black-green light as the evil pit beneath Madam's office!

She tried to scream, but nothing would come out but a strangled whimper—stared at her hand as the stuff spread like oil poured on water, as the burning spread through her veins like the poison it was—stared—as Madam began to laugh.

Burning black, flickering yellow-green, spread over her, *under* her shields, eating into her, permeating her, as Madam's triumphant laughter rang in her ears and peals of thunder answered the laughter. She staggered back one step at a time until she stood swaying on the hearthrug, screams stillborn, trapped in her throat, which could only produce a moan. Until a black-green curtain fell between her and the world, and she felt her knees giving way beneath her, and then—nothing.

❖

Reggie stepped out of the shadows and stared at the crumpled form of Marina on the hearthrug. "By Jove, Mater!" he gasped. "You *did* it! You managed to call up the curse again!"

Arachne smiled with the deepest satisfaction, and prodded at the girl's outstretched hand with one elegantly clad toe. "I told you that I would, if I could only find the right combination," she said. "And the right way to get past those shields she had all over her. Not a sign of them from the outside, but layers of them, there were. No wonder she didn't show any evidence of magic about her."

"So you knew about those, did you?" Reggie asked, inadvertently betraying that *he* had known about the shields—and had not told his mother. Arachne hadn't *known,* she had intuited their presence, but she hadn't *known.* She'd simply decided that they must be there, and had worked to solve the problem of their existence.

So how had he known about them, when nothing she had done had revealed their presence?

"Well, it was obvious, wasn't it?" she prevaricated. "I decided to take a gamble. It occurred to me that shields would only be against magic, not something physical—and that no one would think to shield her *beneath* the surface of her skin."

She watched him with hooded eyes. He frowned, then nodded, understanding dawning in his face. "Of course—the physical vehicle—the exposed nail—delivering the curse past the shield in a way that no one would think of in advance. Brilliant! Just brilliant!"

She made a little sour *moue* with her lips. "It won't do for you to forget that, Reggie dear," she said acidly. "I *am* far more experienced than you. And very creative."

Would he take that as the warning it was meant to be?

He stiffened, then took her hand and bowed over it. "Far

be it from me to do so," he replied. But his face was hidden, and she couldn't see the expression it wore.

Resentment, probably. Perhaps defeat. Temporary defeat, though—

"But surely that wasn't all," he continued, rising, showing her only an expression as bland and smooth as Devon cream. "If that was all, why all the rigmarole with the cradle?"

"Because the vehicle had to be something that was within the influence of the curse when I first set it, of course," she said, with a tone of *as you should have figured out for yourself* covering every word. "That was why the cradle—and why I had that little octopus-ornament removed. I wanted metal as the vehicle by preference, and the nail holding the octopus in place was perfect. At that point, it was easy to have it reversed and driven up and out to become the vehicle."

"Brilliant," Reggie repeated, then frowned, and bent over Marina's form. "She's breathing."

Arachne sighed. "She's not dead, sadly," she admitted, meditatively. "The curse was warped, somehow; it sent her into a trance. I did think of that—I have her spirit trapped in a sort of limbo, but that was the best I could do. But she will be dead, soon enough. She can't eat or drink in that state."

The solution was simple enough; call the servants, have her taken to her room, allow her to waste away. How long would it take? No more than a few weeks, surely—less than that, perhaps.

Reggie's jaw tightened. "Mater, we have a problem—" he began.

"Nonsense," she snapped. "What problem could there be?"

"That someone is likely to think that we poisoned her—"

"Then we call a doctor in the morning," she said dismissively.

"And if we let her waste away, that people will say that we did so deliberately!" he countered angrily. "There will be enquiries—police—even an inquest—"

She felt anger rising in her. "Then get a doctor for her now!" she responded, throttling down the urge to slap him. Here she had done *everything,* and he had the cheek to criticize her! Why shouldn't he stir himself to deal with these trivial problems? "Use some initiative! Must I do everything? For heaven's sake, there's a sanitarium just over the hill—call the doctor and send her there!"

"What, now?" he replied, looking utterly stunned.

"Why not?" It had been a spur-of-the-moment notion, but the more she thought about it, the better she liked it. "Why not? It will show proper concern on our part—our poor little niece collapsed and we send our own carriage out into the storm to get help for her! The man isn't local, no one will have told him anything about us, all he'll be concerned about is his fee. He can't keep her alive long, no matter how cleverly he force-feeds her, but the fact that we're paying for him to try will show everyone that we're doing our best for her."

"And if he brings her around somehow?" Reggie countered stubbornly.

"How? With magic?" She laughed, a peal of laughter echoed by the thunder outside. "Oh, I think not! And just in case those meddlesome friends of Hugh's manage to get wind of what we've done, the sanitarium is the safest place she could be! No old servants to slip them inside, and even if they manage to find where she is, hidden away amongst a den of lunatics—there are guards, no doubt, meant to keep as many folks out as in." She shook her head with amazement at her own perspicacity. "Perfect. Perfect. Take care of it."

As he stared at her without comprehension, she repeated herself. "*Take care of it,* Reggie," she said sharply. "Rouse the household! Get the carriage! I want that doctor here within the hour!"

"And just what will *you* be doing, Mater?" he asked, with a particularly nasty sneer.

"I," she said with immense dignity, "will be having a truly operatic fit of the vapors. So if you don't wish to have your eardrums shattered—I suggest you be on your way."

And feeling particularly sadistic, she did not even give him enough time to leave the room before filling her lungs and producing the shrillest and most ear-piercing *shriek* she had ever coaxed out of her throat in her entire life.

She needn't have told him to summon the household after all—she was doing that quite well on her own.

Not that it was going to help Marina. Nothing was going to help her now.

20

ANDREW Pike had thought to spend his evening in his study, the room of burled walnut walls and warm, amber leather furniture that stood triple duty as his library and office as well, but found he couldn't settle to anything. Neither book nor paper nor journal could hold his interest for long, and he found himself staring alternately into the fire, and out into the gloom, as the sun set somewhere behind the thick clouds. He felt both depressed and agitated, and had ever since early afternoon. He had been a Master long enough to know that, though he had no particular prescient abilities, he was sensitive enough to the ebbs and flows of power to intuit that there was trouble in the air. And the longer he watched and waited, the more sure of that trouble he became.

He'd done what he could to cushion his patients from whatever it was, and had strengthened the shields about the place, layering walls built as solid as those of the Cotswold limestone, the red-baked brick, the cob and wattle. Now all he could do was sit and wait, and hope that the trouble would pass him and anyone else he knew by.

Moments like these were hard on the nerves of those who had no ability to see into the future. The Earth Masters were particularly lacking in that talent; their minds tended to be slow and favor the past and the present, not the future. The past in particular; Earth Masters could take up a thing and read its history as easily as conning a book, but the volume of the future might as well be in hieroglyphs for it was just that closed to them. Water Masters were the best at future-gazing when they had that particular gift, and even those poorest in the skill could still scry in a bowl of water and be certain of getting *some* clue to what lay ahead. Air Masters, known best for crystal-gazing, and Fire, who favored black mirrors, were twice as likely at their worst as an Earth Master at his best to have the ability to part the veils and glimpse what was to come. So with no more help in divining what was troubling him than any other mortal might have, all Andrew could do was wait for whatever it was to finally descend on them.

Teatime came and went with no signs other than an increasing heaviness of spirit. Eleanor felt it too, though as was her wont, she said nothing; he read it in her wary eyes, and in the tense way she moved, glancing behind her often, as if expecting to find something dreadful following. When he saw that, he increased the strength of the shields yet again, and gave Eleanor orders to add sedatives to the medications of certain patients that evening.

"Ah," she said. "For the storm—" but he knew, and she knew, that it was not the March thunderstorm she spoke of, though the flickers on the horizon as the sun sank behind its heavy gray veils and gray light deepened to blue warned of more than just a springtime's shower.

When the storm broke, it brought no relief, only increased anxiety. The storm was a reflection of the tension in the air, not a means of releasing it. This was no ordinary storm; it crouched above Oakhurst like a fat, heavy spider and refused to budge, sending out lightning and thunder and torrents of rain.

By now, Andrew's nerves were strung as tightly as they ever had been in his life, and he couldn't eat dinner. He wondered if he ought to prescribe a sedative dose for himself.

But as he sat in his office-cum-study, watching the lightning arc through the clouds, and in the flashes, the rain sheeting down, he decided that he had better not. He should keep all his wits about him. If the blow fell, and he was needed, he could not afford to have his mind befogged.

Having once shattered a fragile teacup and once snapped the stem of a wineglass when feeling nervy, he had chosen a thick mug for his tea this evening. His hands closed around it and clutched it tightly enough to make his fingers ache, and had the pottery been less than a quarter-inch thick, he was certain it, too, would have given way under his grip. As well, perhaps, that he was no Fire Master—his nerves were stretched so tightly that if he had been, the least little startlement might have sent the contents of his office up in flames.

He stretched all of his senses to their utmost, searching through the night, questing for any clue, or any sign that something was about to fall on *his* head. It was dangerous, that—looking out past the shields that he had set up around the walls of Briareley. But he couldn't just sit here anymore, waiting for the blow to fall—he had to *do* something, even if it was only to look! Every nerve in his body seemed acutely sensitive, and the muscles of his neck and shoulders were so tight and knotted they felt afire.

Suddenly, a bolt of lightning struck practically outside his study window—he jumped—and as the windows shook with the attendant peal of thunder, another sound reverberated through the halls.

The booming sound of someone frantically pounding on the door with the huge bronze knocker. Great blows echoed up and down the rooms, reverberated against high ceilings and shuddered in chimneys.

This was what he had been waiting for. Or if not—at least it was something happening at last—something he could act on instead of just waiting. The tension in him snapped, releasing him as a foxhound set on quarry.

He leapt to his feet, shoved back his chair, and headed for the door; ahead of him he saw Diccon hurrying to answer the summons, and poking from doorways and around corners were the heads of patients and attendants—curious, but with a hint of fear in their eyes.

The pounding continued; there was a frantic sound to it. Was there a medical emergency down in the village? But if there was, why come here rather than knocking up the village doctor?

Diccon hauled the huge door open, and a torrent of rain blew in, carrying with it two men wrapped in mackintoshes. The was no mistaking the second one, who raked the entrance hall with an imperious gaze and focused on Andrew.

"You! Doctor!" he barked. "You're needed at Oakhurst! Miss Roeswood has collapsed!"

Andrew folded his stethoscope and tucked it into his pocket, using iron will to control face and voice. His heart hammered in his chest; his expression must give none of this away. They must not know, must not even guess, that he had ever seen Marina more than that once on the road, or all was lost.

"This young woman is in a coma," he said flatly, looking

not at poor Marina, so fragile and pale against the dark upholstery of the couch she had been laid on, but at the impassive visages of Madam Arachne and her son. Marina might have been some stranger with a sprained ankle for all that they were reacting. Oh, certainly the Odious Reggie had come dashing through the storm to drag him here—not that he'd needed dragging—but now that he was here, Reggie merely watched with ironic interest, as if he expected Pike to fail and was pleased to find his expectations fulfilled. And as for Madam—he'd seen women evidence more concern for a toad than she was showing for her own niece. In fact— she seemed amused at his efforts to revive Marina. There was some devilment here.

Was devilment the right word? If those wild surmises of his were true, it might well be. . . .

But he could do nothing here. Especially not if his guesses were true. "She is completely unresponsive to stimuli, and I am baffled as to the cause of her state. It *might* be a stroke—or it could have some external cause. If she had been outside, I might even suspect lightning—"

There was a flash of interest at that. The woman seized on his possibly explanation so readily that even if he hadn't suspected her of treachery, he'd have known something was wrong. "She was standing right beside that window when she collapsed," Madam said, and her even and modulated tones somehow grated on his nerves in a way he found unbearable. "Could lightning have struck her through the window?"

"I don't know. Was it open?" he asked, then shook his head. "Never mind. The cause doesn't matter. This young woman needs professional treatment and care—"

This young woman needs to be out *of here!* he thought, his skin crawling at the sight of Madam's bright, but curiously flat gaze as she regarded the body of her niece. The hair on the back of his neck literally stood up, and he had to restrain himself to keep from showing his teeth in a warning snarl. *You are responsible for this, Madam. I don't know how, but I know that* you *are responsible.*

He had to control himself; he had to completely, absolutely, control himself. He daren't let a hint of what he felt show.

And he had to say things he not only didn't mean, but make suggestions he did not want followed. "—for tonight, it will be enough to put her to bed and hope for the best, but if she has not regained some signs of consciousness by tomorrow, you will need both a physician and trained nurses," he continued, knowing that if *he* showed any signs of interest in Marina, Madam would find someone else. *Devilment . . . she'll want indifferent care at the best, and neglectful at the worst. I have to convince her that this is what I represent. And to do that, I have to pretend I don't care about having her as a patient.* "A physician to check on her welfare and try methods of bringing her awake, and nurses to care for her physical needs. She will need to be tube-fed, cleaned, turned—"

"What about you?" Reggie interrupted, his eyes shrewd. "What about your people? You're not that far away, why can't you come tend her here?"

"We have a full schedule at Briareley," he replied, feigning indifference, though his heart urged him to snatch Marina up, throw her over his shoulder, and run for the carriage with her. "I cannot spare any of my nurses, nor can I afford to take the time away from my own patients to—"

"Then take her to Briareley," Madam ordered, quite as if she had the right to give him orders. "There's the only possible solution. Where best would it be to send her? You are here, Briareley has the facilities, and you have the staff and the expertise." She shrugged, as if it was all decided. "We want the best for her, of course. It should be clear to you that no one *here* knows what to do, and wouldn't it be more efficacious to get her professional help immediately?"

"It would be best—the sooner she has professional care, the better—" he began.

Madam interrupted him. "What is your usual fee for cases like this?"

She might have been talking about a coal-delivery, and if he had been what she thought he was—

He had to react as if he was.

He didn't *have* a usual fee for cases like this because he'd never had one—but he blandly (and with open skepticism, as if he expected them to balk) named a fee that would pay for a half dozen more nurses and two more strong male attendants for Briareley, a fee so exorbitant that he was sure they would at least attempt to bargain with him. But he knew that he dared not name a price so low they would think he was eager to get Marina to Briareley—much less simply volunteer to take her without being paid. He had to look as if he was exactly what Madam thought him; a quack who was only interested in what he could get for warehousing the weak-minded and insane. He was walking a delicate line here; he had to make them think he was motivated by nothing more than money, yet he didn't dare do anything that might cause them to send Marina elsewhere.

Stomach churned, jaws ached from being clenched, heart pounded as if he'd been running. Everything told him to *get her out of here*—

"Naturally," Madam said, so quickly it made him blink. "Poor Marina's own inheritance will more than suffice to cover your fees, and as her guardian, I will gladly authorize the disbursement." The Odious Reggie made a sound that started as a protest, but it faded when his mother glared at him. "I'll ring for a servant; she can be moved, of course?"

"Of course," he agreed, then did a double take, "You mean, you wish me to take her now? Tonight?"

"In the Oakhurst carriage, of course," Madam replied breezily. "I should think it would be the best thing of all for her to be in the proper hands immediately. We know nothing—we might make errors—she could even come to some harm at our hands." The woman gazed limpidly up at him. "You understand, don't you, doctor? There must be no question but what we did the best for her *immediately*. No question at all."

He shook, and strove to control his trembling, at the implications behind those words. That this creature was already calculating ahead to the moment when—she expected—Marina's poor husk would take its final breath, and Briareley would boast one less patient. If nothing else would have told him that Madam was behind this, the cold calculation in her words would have given him all the proof that he needed. This had been planned, start to finish.

"Well," he said slowly, concentrating very hard on pulling on his gloves, "I can have no objection, if you are providing the carriage. And—ah—I can expect my fee tomorrow? I bill for the month in advance, after all."

"Of course," Madam agreed, and rang for a servant.

Not one, but three appeared, and when Madam had explained what she wanted, they disappeared, only to return with heavy carriage-rugs, which they wrapped Marina in carefully. Then the largest of the three picked her up.

"My people will show you to the carriage," Madam said, needlessly.

The first two servants beckoned to him to follow, and the third carried Marina, following behind Andrew to the waiting carriage, his face as full of woe as Madam's was empty of that emotion.

The rain had stopped; they stepped out into a courtyard

lit by paraffin torches, puddles glinting yellow, reflecting the flames. A closed carriage awaited, drawn by two restive horses; one of the servants opened the carriage door, while the other pulled down the steps. Andrew got into the waiting carriage first, followed by the giant carrying Marina, who took a seat across from him, still cradling the girl against his shoulder. "Ready to go, sir."

Andrew blinked. He had expected the man to put his burden on the seat and leave. *Madam didn't order this.*

But the look in the man's eyes spoke volumes about what he would do, whether or not Madam ordered it.

Good gad. She has the servants with her. No wonder Madam was worried about appearances.

He cleared his throat as the carriage rolled forward into the damp night, the sound of the wheels unnaturally loud, the horses' hooves even louder. "When Miss Roeswood collapsed—did you see or hear anything—ah—"

"Peter, sir," the giant supplied.

"Yes, Peter—have you any idea what happened to Miss Roeswood?" He waited to hear what the man would say with some impatience. "Was she, perhaps, discussing something with Madam Arachne?"

"No, sir," the young fellow sighed. "I was polishing the silver, sir. Didn't know nothing until Madam started shrieking like a steam-whistle, sir. Then I came running, like everybody else. We all came running, sir. Madam was standing by the fire, Miss was on the hearth-rug in a heap, Master Reggie was running out the door."

Interesting. "Madam screamed?" he prompted.

"Yes, sir. Said Miss Roeswood had took a fit and fell down, sir, and that we was to send the carriage with Reggie to get you, on account of that you have to do with people's brains. Said it was likely a brainstorm, sir." The young man's voice sounded woebegone, choked, as if he was going to cry in the next moment. "I moved her to the couch, sir, thinking it couldn't do her any good to be a-lying on the hearth-rug. I hope I didn't do wrong, sir—I hope I didn't do her no harm—"

He hadn't seen any sign that anyone had hit Marina over the head—hadn't seen any sign that she might have cracked her own skull as she fell—so he was able to reassure the poor fellow that he hadn't done wrong. "This could be anything, Peter—but you did right to get her up out of the cold drafts."

"Sir—" the young man's voice cracked. "Sir, you *are* going to make her come out of this? You're going to fix her up? You aren't going to go and stick her in a bed and let her die, are you?"

Good Lord. His spirits rose. Whatever devilment Madam and her son had been up to at Oakhurst, it was clear that Marina had the complete loyalty of the underservants. With that—if there were any signs of what they'd been up to, all he had to do was ask for their help. And then there would be a hundred eyes looking for it at his behest, and fifty tongues ready to wag for him if he put out the word to them.

"I swear I am going to do my best, Peter," he said fiercely. "I swear it by all that's holy. But if there was anything going on—anything that Madam or her son were doing that might have had something to do with what's happened to Miss Roeswood—" He groped after what to ask. "I don't think this is an accident, Peter. And I can think of a very good reason why Madam would want something that *looks* like an accident to befall Miss Roeswood—"

"Say no more, sir." Peter's voice took on a fierceness of its own. "I get your meaning. If there was aught going on— well, you'll be hearing of it. Hasn't gone by *us* that Madam's to get Oakhurst if aught was to happen to Miss."

He couldn't see the young man's face in the darkness, but

he didn't have to. This young man was a stout young fellow, a real Devonian, honest and trustworthy, and loyal to a fault. And not to Madam. *Allies. Allies and spies, of the sort that Madam is likely to disregard. By Heaven—*

"Thank you, Peter," he said heavily, and then hesitated. "There might be things you wouldn't know to look for—"

"Cook's second cousin's your cook," Peter interrupted, in what appeared to be a *non sequitor.* "And your cook's helper's my Sally's sister, what's also her niece. Happen that if someone were to come by the kitchen at teatime, just a friendly visit, mind, and let drop what's to be looked for, well—the right people would find out to know what to winkle out."

Good God. Country life . . . connections and connections, deep and complicated enough to get word to me no matter what. "I may not know anything tomorrow—perhaps not for days," he warned.

"No matter. There's always ears in kitchen," the young man asserted, then seemed to feel that he had said enough, and settled back into silence for the rest of the journey, leaving Andrew to his own thoughts. Thoughts were all he dared pursue at the moment. He didn't know what had been done, and he didn't want to try anything magical until Marina was safely inside triple-circles of protection. He certainly didn't want to try anything with the girl held in a stranger's arms, a stranger who might or might not be sensitive himself.

All he could do was to monitor her condition, and pray.

Andrew rubbed at gummy eyes and started at a trumpet call.

No. Not a trumpet call. He glanced out of the window behind him, where the black night had lightened to a charcoal gray. Not a trumpet call. A rooster.

It was dawn, heralded by the crowing of the cook's roosters out in the chicken-yard.

He turned his attention back to his patient, who could too easily be a mannequin of wax. Marina lay now, dressed in a white nightgown, like Snow White in the panto—face pale, hands lying still and cold on the woolen coverlet, in a bed in a private room at the back of Briareley, a room triply shielded, armored with every protection he knew how to devise. And she lay quite without any change from when he had seen her at Oakhurst, silent and unmoving but for the slight lift and fall of her breast. She lived—but there was nothing *there,* no sense of her, no sense of anything.

No poison was in her veins, no blow to the head had sent her into this state. In fact, he found no injury at all, nothing to account for the way she was now. In desperation, he had even had one of the most sensitive of his child-patients awakened and brought to her, and the boy had told him that there was nothing in her mind—no dreams, no thoughts, nothing. "It's like she's just a big doll," the child had said, his fist jammed against his mouth, shaking, eyes widened in alarm. "It ain't even like a beast or a bird—it's just *empty*—" and he'd burst into tears.

Eleanor had taken the boy away and soothed him to sleep, and Andrew had known that he wouldn't dare allow any more of his patients to sense what Marina had become. He racked his brain for a clue to his next move, for he had tried everything that he knew how to do—ritual cleansing, warding, shielding—his medical and medical-magic options were long since exhausted. As the roosters crowed below the window, he sat with his aching head in his hands, pulling sweat-dampened hair back from his temples, and tried to think of *anything* more he could do. The fauns? Could *they* help? Would growth-magic awaken her? What if—

Someone knocked on the door, and opened it as he turned his head. It was Eleanor, whose dark-circled eyes spoke of a night as sleepless as his own. "There's someone to see you, Doctor—" she began.

"Dammit, Eleanor, I told—" he snapped, when a tall and frantic-looking man with paint in his red-brown hair and moustache pushed past her, followed by another, this one dark-haired and tragic-eyed, and a woman who could only have been his sister, eyes red with tears.

"God help us, we came as soon as we could," the man said, "We'd have telegraphed, but the fauns only found us last night—and they were half-mad with fear. So we came—"

"And we felt what happened," said the second man, as the woman uttered a heart-broken cry and went to her knees beside Marina. "On the train. Christ have mercy—how could we not have!"

"Fauns?" Andrew said, confused for a moment. "Train—" then it dawned on him. "You're Marina's guardians?"

"Damn poor guardians," the tall man said in tones of despair. "Sebastian Tarrant, my wife Margherita, her brother Thomas Buford. Lady Elizabeth's on the way; we left word at the station where to go, but half the town already knows Marina's here, and the other half will by breakfast—oh, and she'll sense us, too, no doubt."

"It's the curse," the woman said, lifting a tear-stained face. "It's the curse, right enough. Damn her! *Damn* her!" and she began to cry. Her brother gathered her to his shoulder, trying to comfort her, and by the look of it, having no success.

"Curse?" Andrew asked, bewildered by the intruders, their sudden spate of words that made no sense—the only *sense* he had was that these people were the ones he had sought for, Marina's guardians. "What curse?" There was only one thing he needed, needed as breath, to know. "What's *happened* to Marina? I've tried everything—"

"Stronger Masters than you have tried everything, and the best they could do was to warp that black magic so that it sent her to sleep instead of killing her," Sebastian Tarrant said gruffly, and patted him on the shoulder awkwardly. He glanced at the bed, and groaned. "And there's nothing we can do in the next hour that's going to make any difference, either."

Andrew shook his head, and blinked eyes that burned as he squinted at the stranger's face, trying to winkle out the sense of what he was hearing. A curse . . . a curse on Marina. But—who—how—why? The man's eyes shone brightly, as if with tears that he refused to shed. "You look done in, man," Tarrant continued. "Come show me the kitchen and let's get some strong tea and food into you. I'll explain while you eat; you aren't going to do her any good by falling over."

Sebastian Tarrant's will was too strong to be denied; Andrew found himself being carried off to Briareley's kitchen, where he was fussed over by Cook and seated at the trestle table where a half dozen loaves of bread were rising, a mug of hot black tea and a breakfast big enough for three set in front of him. He ate it, untasted, as Sebastian Tarrant narrated a story that—if he had not seen Marina—would have sounded like the veriest fairy tale. A tale of a curse on a baby, an exile to keep her safe, and all the plans undone. A tale of blackest magic, sent from a bitter woman who should have had none—

"And now I'm sorry we didn't follow her here, and damned to Madam," Tarrant said, the guilt in his face so overwhelming that Andrew didn't have the heart to take him to task over it. "But we were afraid that if we showed our faces in the village, Arachne would take her somewhere we couldn't follow, or worse. At least while she was here, we figured that Arachne hadn't worked out a way to make her curse active again, and we knew she wouldn't dare try anything—well—obvious and physical in front of people who'd known and served Hugh and Alanna. And the child didn't write, so we had to assume that Arachne was keeping too close a watch on her for us to try and contact her that way." Tarrant rubbed at his own eyes, savagely. "Dear God, how could we have been such cowards, such fools?"

"But—what is this curse?" he asked finally. "How on earth can something like that do what it did?"

"You tell me how someone without the least little bit of magic of her own could create such a thing," Tarrant countered, wearily, running his hands through his hair and flaking off a few bits of white and yellow paint. "Not a sign, not *one* sign of the Mastery of any of the Elements on Arachne *or* her son—so where is the magic coming from? And how are they able to channel it, if they aren't Masters and aren't sensitive to it? But it's there, all right, if you know what to look for, or at least *I* saw it—the curse-magic is on Marina, like a shield, only lying right under her skin, a poisonous inner skin—a blackish-green fire, and pure evil—"

Pure evil. The words hit him between the eyes and he gaped at the stranger. "Pure evil? Pure *evil?*" he repeated, as all of the pieces fell together.

Ellen—Madam and her son—the curse—the pottery in Exeter—curses, and black magic, in the traditional and legended sense of the words.

And the stories, the accounts in those old traditions of the Scottish Masters—the tales of Satanists.

And yesterday, Marina had *gone* to the pottery in Exeter, looking for whatever had attached itself, lampreylike, to Ellen with the purpose of draining her. What if she'd discovered black magic there, the Left-Hand Path, which needed no inborn abilities to walk? What if Madam realized that Marina was about to unmask that evil?

And if Madam and her son were Satanists, if they had set up the pottery as a place where they could batten on the energies of the marginally gifted as they were poisoned, physically and spiritually—*that* could be the source of the power behind the curse. That would be why no one had seen any signs of Power on or around them. They didn't have any power until they stole it, and once stolen, they had to discharge it immediately, store it elsewhere, or lose it.

And that would be why Andrew could not unravel the dreadful net that ensnared Marina. It was like no magic he or any Master he knew had ever seen before. Certainly nothing that any Master still alive had seen before.

Ah—*still alive*—

As it happened sometimes when he was exhausted, the answer came in a flash of clarity. Still alive; that was the key to this lock, the sword to sever this Gordian Knot. Because there were Masters of the past who had certainly seen, yes, and even worked to combat such evil.

And to a Master of Earth, the past was an open book.

"My God," he breathed—a prayer, if ever there was one. "Tarrant, I think I have an idea—"

"Well, I've got one, at least," Sebastian interrupted him. "Thomas and Margherita are Earth Masters themselves—not strong ones by any means, but one thing they can do is, keep Marina going. We're fresh; you're not. Do you want to get to work on this idea of yours now, or get a spot of rest first?"

He wanted to work on it now, but what he was going to try would need every bit of concentration he had. "I need to go look through my magic books," he decided aloud. "There's one in particular I need to find, what used to be called a *grammary* in Scotland and Northumberland and—"

he shook his head. "Never mind. I'll find it, make sure it's the one I need, then I'll drug myself. I'll need my wits, and you're right, if I don't get a couple of hours of rest, I won't have them about me."

"Good man." Tarrant nodded approval. "We'll make sure Marina's all right, you can leave that to us. What about the rest of your patients?"

"Eleanor can see to them—did you say your wife is an Earth Master? Would she be willing to help?" he asked, desperate for anything that might take the burden off his shoulders during this crisis.

"When Lady Elizabeth gets here, I'll tell my wife to have your nurse Eleanor show her what to do, and I'll send someone down to the village to telegraph for some more help," Tarrant promised. "There's not a lot of us out here in the country, nor powerful, but we're Devonians, even those of us who weren't born here. When need calls, we answer."

"But—the telegraph—?" he replied, puzzled.

Tarrant fixed him with a minatory glance. "Why use power we should save for helping *her* to do what a telegraph can do, and just as quickly?"

Andrew winced; it was one of his own Master's constant admonitions. *Why use magic to do what anyone can do? Save it for those things that hands cannot accomplish, ye gurt fool.*

He closed his eyes as a moment of dizzy exhaustion overcame him, then opened them. "Me for my old books, then—" he shoved away from the table.

"If you've got any clues, Doctor, you're miles ahead of the rest of us," Tarrant said, his jaw set. "And if you've the will and the strength and the knowledge—then you let the rest of us take your burdens off you so you can do what needs to be done. We'll be the squires to your knight if that suits you."

He nodded, and headed for his own room at a run, his steps echoing on the staircase as he made for the second floor. An apt comparison, that. Perhaps more so than Sebastian Tarrant dreamed.

21

AS Andrew sat on the edge of his bed and depressed the plunger on a syringe containing a very carefully minimized dose of morphine, he reflected that somewhere in Scotland, his old Master was rotating in his grave like a water-powered lathe. The old man wouldn't even take a drop of whisky for a cold; he was a strict Covenanter, and how he could reconcile that with talking to fauns and consorting with brownies was something Andrew had never quite managed to get him to explain.

Well, the old boy had a phobia about needles as well; he couldn't stomach the sight of anyone being injected, much less someone injecting him, and still less the thought of what Andrew was doing, injecting himself. Andrew pulled the needle out of his arm, and the tourniquet off, and felt the rush of immediate dizziness as the drug hit his brain. He didn't like doing this—he was nearly as against it as his old Master!—but it was the only way he was going to get any sleep.

Which I really should do now— he thought dimly, lying down.

Five hours later—long enough for the morphia to have worn off—Eleanor shook him awake. He had the luck to be one of those who came awake all at once, rather than muzzily clambering up out of sleep. "There's no change, Doctor," she said sadly as he sat up, pushing the blanket aside that someone had laid over him. He hadn't expected there to be any change—but if only—

"But Miss Roeswood's guardians have been wonderful," Eleanor continued. "Mrs. Tarrant is *so* good with the children, and Mr. Buford has charmed the lady guests—and gammoned them into thinking he's a specialist-doctor you brought in especially to see that they were all right." She brightened a little at that, for the "lady guests" were especially trying to her. And, truth to tell, to Andrew to a certain extent. There was always the worry of keeping what the real patients were up to away from them, and the fuss they tended to cause as they recovered from their exhaustion, becoming bored but not quite ready to leave. "Oh, and Lady Elizabeth Hastings is here as well. She kept the telegraph office busy for a solid hour, I think."

He nodded; that was a plus. Say what you would about the old aristocracy, but they were used to organizing things and pushing them through, used to taking charge and giving orders. That was one area, at least, that he would not have to worry about. Lady Hastings had obviously got the more mundane aspects of the situation well in hand.

And right now, he wanted to concentrate solely on the *grammary* he'd extracted from the old trunk he'd brought with him from Scotland. He'd even put it under his pillow for safekeeping before letting the drugs have their way with him. Now he drew it out, a dark, leather-bound volume of rough-cut parchment; it dated back to before the first

James—probably to the time of the Scots queen, Mary. There were no actual dates in it, but Mary had brought courtiers with her from France and had been raised and educated there—and at that time, there was something of a fad for Satanism in the French Court. Some of the Masters of the time blamed it on the Medici influence, but Andrew was inclined to think it went back further than that. There had been enough suspicious deaths and illnesses in the French Court for centuries to make him think that there had been a dark influence there from almost the time of Charlemagne.

He pulled the book out and held it; bound in a soft leather that had darkened to a mottled brown the color of stout, it was entirely handwritten, part journal and part spell-book. Sebastian had taken one look at it and pronounced it a *grimoire,* rather than a *grammary,* which at least meant that the artist recognized it for what it was. Andrew could never think of the book without thinking of the old ballad of "The Lady Gay":

There was a lady, and a lady gay, of children she had three. She sent them away to the North Country, to learn their grammary.

Most, if not all, scholars thought the song meant that the children were being sent to learn reading and writing. Little did they know the song spoke of the long tradition of wizards and witches of the North Country, who fostered the children of Masters and taught them the Elemental Magics that their parents could not . . . a tradition which Andrew himself had unwittingly replicated, though he'd gone up to Scotland rather than the North of England.

He shook himself out of his reverie. He was going to need a protector while he worked his magics, and for that, he thought, Sebastian Tarrant would be the best suited. Despite not being of the same Element as Andrew, Tarrant had more of the warrior in him than either his wife or brother-in-law. If *they* could strengthen Marina and pick up his duties—

He pulled on a clean shirt and went to find the newcomers—and predictably, two of the four were with Marina. As Eleanor had said, Margherita and Thomas were—God bless them!—tending his patients. Sebastian and Lady Elizabeth were at Marina's side, and both stood when he entered.

And the moment he laid eyes on Lady Elizabeth, he knew that she would be better suited to guard his back as he scryed into the past than Sebastian.

In fact, he had to restrain himself from bowing so deeply over her hand that he looked like a fop. He did take her extended hand, and he shook it carefully. "You must be Lady Hastings," he began. "I'm Andrew Pike—"

"We haven't time for formalities, Doctor," she said crisply, before he had done more than introduce himself. "What is it you wish us to do?"

He nodded gratitude, and hoped she saw it as he released her hand. "I'm going to use this to scry into the past, Lady Hastings," he said, holding up the book that was tucked under his other arm.

"Elizabeth," she interrupted him. "Why?"

That was when he sat down and explained exactly what he thought had been going on in Madam's household for all these years. More than once, Sebastian and Elizabeth sucked in a surprised breath. More than once, he suspected, they cursed themselves for not seeing it themselves.

But why should they? Most of those who considered themselves to be black magicians and Satanists were pathetic creatures, more interested in debauchery than discipline, in the interplay of status than power itself. They had neither the learning nor the understanding to make use of any magic that they acquired, either by accident or on purpose. And even if they'd had the knowledge, they simply

weren't interested in anything past the moment. The few
times to Sebastian's knowledge that self-styled Satanists had
warranted attention, it was the police that were needed, not
the Masters or some other occultists. In fact, to everyone except the dour lot up in Scotland, Satanic worship was more
of a joke than a threat. And perhaps, that was what had been
the protection for the few real Satanic cults in the modern
world; that no one believed in them.

*It's our protection, too, after all. When something be-
comes a fairy tale, the ordinary sort of fellow can look right
at it and not believe in it.*

"So, you're going to go look back in time to when this
book was being written and try to see what lay behind those
journal entries," Elizabeth stated, summing up his intentions
nicely. "Can you do the work here?"

"It's the best-shielded room in the place at this point," he
replied. "What I'll need from you is guarding." He frowned.
"I hope that I don't sound superstitious to you, but—" He
was reluctant even to voice his suspicions, but if he didn't
and something happened—"Look, I know that the idea of
demons is something less than fashionable among Masters
at the moment, but, well, the only way I can think of for
Madam to have done some of what she's done is to have a
servant or a slave that is sensitive to magic power. And as a
Satanist—well—I *suppose* she could have attracted some
of the nastier Elementals, but how would she have seen
them? So what does that leave but the Satanist's traditional
servant?"

Tarrant made a sour face. "I have to admit that a demon,
a Mephistopheles to Arachne's Faustus, is the most logical
answer. I don't like it. I might as well believe in vampires,
next—"

"Or brownies?" Elizabeth said suggestively, and Sebastian flushed. "I agree with you, Doctor. And that is yet an-

other good reason for us to do as little as possible magically, and make most of that passive. I had a feeling I ought to use the telegraph rather than occult means of calling the other Masters, and now I'm glad I did. I wish I knew if holy symbols really worked against demons, though." She bit her lip. "The wearing of my grandmother's crucifix is very, very tempting right now."

"I suspect that depends entirely on the depth of belief of the one using them," Tarrant replied, regaining his equilibrium. "And I will make no judgment on the state of your belief, Elizabeth. As for myself—" he hesitated. "I suspect for me, that any holy symbol would be as efficacious, or not, as any other. Doctor, if you are ready, so are we."

With the room already shielded, all he needed to do, really, was to set up the other object he had brought with him besides the book. This was an amber sphere about the size of a goose egg with no inclusions, amber being about the only material suitable for an Earth Master to use for scrying. Then he placed the book in front of it, and sat facing the sphere at the tiny table below the window, both hands atop the book, which was open to the relevant passage.

Then, after invoking his own personal shields, he "touched" the book with a delicate finger of power.

Show me— he whispered to it. *Show me your author, and what was happening when he wrote these words.*

He was hoping for a scene in the sphere, or at least a few suggestive hints that he could concentrate on to bring things further into focus. At best, he hoped for a clear image of the old Master in the midst of his single combat with the Satanic magician he had tersely described in his entry.

He did *not* expect what he got.

He was jolted—exactly like being struck by lightning— as power *slammed* into him from the pages of the book themselves, knocking him back in his chair, and breaking his contact with the volume.

"Bloody *hell!*" he yelped, shocked beyond measure. But before he—or either of the other two—could react, a column of light flung itself upwards from the open book, reaching floor-to-ceiling—a golden-yellow light, like sun on ripening corn.

"Bloody *hell!*" Sebastian echoed, as Lady Elizabeth yelped.

And in the very next moment, he found himself looking up into the eyes of a vigorous man of perhaps late middle-years, bearded, moustached, crowned with a flat cap and attired in a laced and slashed doublet, small starched ruff, sleeved gown identical to an academic gown, hose and those ridiculous balloonlike breeches that the Tudors wore. The fact that the fellow was entirely colorless and transparent had no bearing whatsoever on the sensation of *force* he radiated.

The light radiated from him, and it was as utterly *unlike* the black-green poison of the curse holding Marina as it was possible to be. Andrew wanted to drink in that light, eat it, pull it in through every pore. And as for that power, that force—

The man also radiated the palpable force of an Earth Master as far above Andrew in power as Andrew was above Thomas Buford. And more.

Details of the man's appearance branded themselves on his brain. The square jaw underneath a beard neatly trimmed, but with one untidy swirl, as if there was a scar under the hair. The bushy eyebrows that overhung a pair of keen eyes that might have been blue. The doublet, dark and sober, contrasting wildly with the striped satin of the puffy breeches and an entirely immodest codpiece ornamented in sequins and bullion. The equally sober robe he wore over both—a robe of velvet that had been badly rubbed in places, as if it was an old and favored garment that the man could not bear to part with, despite it being a bit shabby.

"God's Blood!" the man barked—audibly. And with a decided Scots brogue to his words.

Andrew started again; he hadn't expected the apparition to *speak*!

The spirit stamped his foot—no sound. "Devil damn thee black, thou cream-faced loon! Where gottest thou that goose-look? It's half mad I've been, wondering if thee'd the wit to use the book! Damme, man, thee took thy leisure, deciding the menace here!"

A quick glance at Elizabeth showed she was fascinated, staring at what could only be a spirit, as if she could hardly restrain herself from leaping up to touch it. Sebastian Tarrant, however, was as white as a sheet. But it was Tarrant who spoke.

"You—you're a ghost!" he bleated. There was no other word for the absurd sound that came out of his mouth. Formidable Fire Master Sebastian Tarrant sounded just like a frightened sheep.

The spirit favored him with a jaundiced eye. "That, and ha'pence will buy thee a wheaten loaf," he said dismissively. He stepped down off the table, which at least put him at eye level with all of them. He was—rather short. But no one would ever dismiss him as insignificant. "Aye, I linked myself, dying, to yon book, in case one day there was need and no one to teach."

"Teach about the—" he began, and the spirit made a hushing motion.

"Best not to talk about them," he cautioned. "Not aloud. And my time is short—so I'll be brief. Thee has caught it, laddie—'tis the selfsame enemy, mine and thine. *If* thee live through this, thee will have to reck out how they done this.

If; that be for later. And the on'y way thee will beat them now is to divide them. *Thou*—" he pointed at Andrew "—thou'lt confront the man. But *she*—" he pointed at Marina "—the on'y way she'll be free is to fight the mother, herself."

"But—" Andrew began

"But me no buts!" the spirit interrupted, scowling. "There be twa things thee'll need to do, an' I dinna get much time to explain them, so listen proper the first time."

Sebastian had recovered, and nodded, moving closer, as did Elizabeth. Andrew noticed then that the light surrounding the spirit was dimmer than it had been. Perhaps the power stored in the book was all that held the spirit here. If that was the case—

Later, later. Live through this, first.

The spirit continued, resting his left hand on his book. "The first thing is for all of ye—all five—t' takit hold of that cursed magic she's put on the girl an' give it a good hard *pull.* Ye shan't hurt her, but ye'll get the mother's attention. Then. . . ."

Holding their breaths lest they miss a word, the three of them leaned forward to take it all in.

Marina was in a garden. A very, very small garden. *Not* a paradise by any means; this was a tiny pocket of dead and dying growth, struggling to survive in dim and fitful light, and failing, but failing with agonizing slowness. It was walled twice, first in curving walls of brambles with thorns as long as her hand, and beyond them, a wall like a sphere or a bubble, curving gray surfaces, opaque and impermeable—but which flickered with that black-green energy that had engulfed her before she had blacked out. She was disinclined to touch either the walls of thorn or the walls of energy—assuming she could even reach the latter. She mistrusted the look of the thorns — she suspected that they might actually move to hurt her if she approached them. And she'd already had too much close acquaintance with that peculiar magical energy.

Madam was behind this; somehow she had attacked Marina through the medium of her old cradle, and sent her here. The only question in her mind was — was this "here" *real*, or a construction of her mind? And if it was real — was it solid, everyday real, was she, body and all, sitting in this blighted garden? Or was this her spirit only, confined in some limbo where Madam's evil magic had thrown her?

She was inclined to think it was the second — not because of any single piece of objective evidence, but because she didn't think that Madam was powerful enough to have created anything magical that could and would successfully hold up physically for any length of time. Why? Because if she had been able to do so, she would have done something to eliminate her niece on the journey to Oakhurst. And if Marina just vanished, there would be a great many questions asked now, questions which could be very uncomfortable for Madam.

Marina also didn't think she was dead — not yet, anyway. Elizabeth had taught her all about the magical connection of spirit and body, the thing that looked to some like a silver cord. Although she had not yet made any attempt to leave her own body, Elizabeth's descriptions had been clear enough. And now that she was calm enough to look for it, that tie of body to spirit was, so far as Marina could tell, still in existence; a dim silver cord came from her, and passed through the gray wall without apparent difficulty.

Well, there's my objective evidence, assuming I'm not hallucinating the cord. "Here" isn't "real."

So somehow Madam had separated spirit from body and imprisoned the former here.

Marina felt her heart sink. *That would suit her very well. My body is going to live for a while—for as long as she can get doctors to keep it alive. And why shouldn't she? That would neatly eliminate any suspicions that she had anything to do with what has happened to me. There probably won't be a sign of what she did. It will all be a terrible tragedy, and of course, in a few weeks or months, when—well, she'll inherit everything, with no questions asked.* She moaned; after all, there was no one here to hear her. *I suppose there's no chance it would be Andrew Pike she calls. No, it will probably be some high-fee London physician, who'll get to make all manner of experiments to see if he can "wake" me.*

Marina was able to think about this with a certain amount of calmness, in no small part because she was already exhausted from what must have been hours of sheer panic, followed by more hours of rage, followed by more of weeping in despair. There was, of course, no way of telling time here. And although she was exhausted, when she lay down in the withered grass, she was unable to sleep, and in fact, didn't feel sleepy. Another point in favor of the notion that she was only imprisoned in spirit. The evidence at this point was certainly overwhelming.

She had never been so utterly, so completely alone. She had thought that she felt alone when Madam had first taken her away from Blackbird Cottage—but at least there had been other people around, even if they were strangers.

If I am just a spirit—maybe I can call for help? The cord that bound her to her body was able to penetrate the shell around her—maybe magic could, too.

The trouble was, there was no water here; not so much as a puddle. And search though she might, she could find no wellsprings of Water energy, nor the slightest sign of the least and lowliest of Water Elementals. Small wonder the vegetation was dying or dead.

So all that remained was—thought, and whatever magic she held in her own stores. Which was not much.

And I was appallingly bad at sending my thoughts out without the help of magic. On the other hand, what choice did she have? *Perhaps I can use the cord, somehow.*

She concentrated on a single, simple message, a plea for help, trying first to reach Margherita, then Sebastian, then Elizabeth, then, for lack of anyone else, Andrew Pike. Last of all, she sent out a general plea for help, from anyone, or anything. She tried until she felt faint with the effort, tried until there were little sparks in front of her eyes and she felt she had to lie down again. But if there was any result from all of her effort, there was no sign of it.

There was no change in the walls holding her imprisoned, no sense of anyone answering her in her own mind. The only change might have been in the cord—was it a little more tenuous than before? A crushing weight of depression settled over her. She gave herself over to tears and despair again, curling up on her side in the grass and weeping—but not the torrent of sobs that had consumed her before. She hid her face in her hands and wept without sobbing, a trickle of weary tears that she couldn't seem to stop, and didn't really try. What was the use? There was nothing that she could do—nothing! There was no magical power here that she could use to try and break herself free, nothing of her own resources gave her strength enough, and she was as strong now as she was ever going to be. As her body weakened—and it would—the energy coming to her down that silver cord would also weaken. Until one day—

She would die. And then what would happen? Was it possible that she would be trapped here forever? Would she continue to exist as a sad, mad ghost here, hemmed in by thorns, driven insane by the isolation?

"Oh, my dearest—she cannot hold you then, at least—"

The sound of the strange female voice shocked her as if she'd been struck with a bolt of lightning. Marina started up, shoving herself up into a sitting position with both hands, although the unreal grass had a peculiarly insubstantial feeling against her palms.

A man and a woman—or rather, the transparent images of a man and a woman—stood at the edge of the thorns. When had they gotten there? How had they gotten there? Had they come in response to her desperate plea for help?

She had no trouble recognizing them, not when she had looked at their portraits every day of her life for as long as she could remember.

"Mother?" she faltered. "Father?"

With no way to measure time, not even by getting tired and sleepy, Marina could not have told how long it took the—others—to convince her that they were not figments of her imagination, not something sent by Madam to torment her, and were, indeed, her mother and father. Well, their spirits. They were entirely certain that the "accident" that had drowned them was Madam's doing; that made sense, considering everything that had followed. And if Madam had sent a couple of phantasms to torment her, would she have put those words in their mouths? Probably not.

Perhaps what finally convinced her was when, after a long and intensely antagonistic session of cross-questioning on her part, Alanna Roeswood—or Alanna's ghost, since that was what the spirit was—looked mournfully at her daughter and gave the impression of heaving an enormously rueful sigh.

"After nearly fifteen years of rather formal letters, I really should not have expected you to fling yourself into my

loving arms, should I?" the spirit said, wearing an expression of deep chagrin. *"It's not as if I wasn't warned."*

Marina held her peace, and her breath—well, she had lately discovered that she didn't actually breathe so she couldn't really hold her breath, but that was the general effect. Perhaps being dead gave one a broader perspective and made one more accepting of things.

Especially things that one couldn't change. Like one's daughter, who had grown up with a mind and will of her own, and who considered her birth mother to be the next thing to a stranger.

"You aren't at all as I pictured you, are you?" the spirit continued, but now there was a bit of pride mingled with the chagrin. *"Nothing like I imagined."*

Marina couldn't help but feel guilt at those sad words. Not that it was *her* fault that her parents had treasured an image of her that was nothing like the reality. "Oh, Mother—" she sighed. "I'm sorry." She couldn't bring herself to say anything more, but Alanna unexpectedly smiled.

"Don't be." Both of her parents studied her for a moment, as she throttled down a new emotion—

Lightning emotional changes seemed to be coming thick and fast, here. Perhaps it was that there was no reason, here and now, for any pretense. And no room for it. Polite pretense was only getting in the way.

This new emotion was resentment, and after another long moment of exchanged glances, it burst out.

"Why did you just—throw me away?" she cried, seventeen years of pain distilled in that single sentence. "What was wrong with me? Didn't you want me? Was I in the way?" That last was something that had only just occurred to her, as she saw the way the two spirits stood together. Never had she seen two people so nearly and literally one, and she felt horrible. Had she been an intrusion on this per-

fect one-ness? It was only too easy to picture how they would have resented her presence.

But the bewilderment on both their faces gave the lie to that notion. *"Throw you away?"* Hugh said, aghast. *"Dear child—don't you know what we were trying to prevent— what we were trying to save you from? Didn't anyone ever tell you?"*

It was short in the telling, the more so since the curse that Madam had so effectively placed on Marina as an infant was what had patently thrown her here now. She listened in appalled fascination—it would have been an amazing tale, if it had just happened to someone else.

And *why*? Why did Arachne hate her brother and his wife so much that she declared war on a harmless infant? For that matter, what on earth could Hugh Roeswood have done to anger her—besides merely existing? Hugh had only been a child when Arachne left home to marry her unsuitable suitor.

"So we sent you away, where we hoped Arachne would never find you, and left her only ourselves to aim at," Hugh finished. *"We hoped—well, we hoped all manner of things. We hoped that she wouldn't find you, and that the curse would backfire on her when it reached its term without being called up again. We hoped that you would become a good enough Master to defend yourself. We hoped someone would find a way to take the damned thing off you!"*

"But why send me away and never come even to see me?" she asked softly, plaintively. "Why never, ever come in person?"

"Haven't you ever seen nesting birds leading hunters away from their little ones?" Alanna asked wistfully. *"We couldn't lead Arachne away, but it was the same idea. We never sent you away because we didn't love you—we sent you because we loved you so much. And of all the people we*

could send you to—Margherita was the only choice. We knew that she would love you as if you were her own."

The pain in her voice recalled the tone of all those letters, hundreds of them, all of them yearning after the daughter Alanna was afraid to put into jeopardy. Marina felt, suddenly, deeply ashamed of her outburst.

"The one thing we didn't take into account was that she might become so desperate as you neared your eighteenth birthday that she would move against us," Hugh continued, with a smoldering look that told Marina that he was angry at himself. *"I became complacent, I suppose. She hadn't acted against us, so she wouldn't—that was a stupid assumption to make. And believe me, there was a will, naming Margherita and Sebastian as your legal guardians. I don't know what happened to it, but there was one."*

"Madam must have had it stolen," Marina said, thinking out loud. "She had a whole gaggle of lawyers come and fetch me; perhaps one of those extracted it." She began to feel a smoldering anger herself—not the unproductive rage, but a calculating anger, and one that, if she could get herself free, boded ill for Madam. "She's laid this out like a campaign from the beginning! Probably from the moment she discovered that—that *cesspit* at her first pottery!"

"Cesspit?" they both asked together, and that occasioned yet another explanation.

"My first guess must have been the right one," Marina said, broodingly. "That must be why she went to the pottery a few days ago—it wasn't to deal with an emergency, it was to drink in the vile power that she used on me!"

"We never could understand where she got her magic," Hugh replied, looking sick. *"And it was there all along, if only we'd thought to look for it."*

"What could you have done if you'd found it?" Marina countered swiftly. "Confront her? What use would that have been? There is nothing there to link her with it directly—and other than the curse, nothing that anyone could have said against her. She could claim she didn't mean it, if you confronted her, if you set that Circle of Masters in London on her. She could say it was all an accident. And it still wouldn't have solved my problem. All that would have happened is that she would have found some way to make you look—well—demented." She pursed her lips, as memory of a particular interview with Madam surfaced. "In fact, she tried very hard to make me think that you were unbalanced, mother. That you were seeing things—only she didn't know that I knew very well what those stories you told me in your letters were about. She thought that I was ordinary, with no magic at all, so the tales of fauns and brownies would sound absolutely mad." She shook her head. "Not that it matters," she finished, bleakly. "Not now. I could have all the magic of a fully trained Water Master, and it still wouldn't do me any good in here."

"But there may be some hope!" Alanna exclaimed. *"Your friends—that doctor and his staff—they were the ones that Arachne called! You're in Briareley as a patient on Arachne's own orders, and they've brought Sebastian and Margherita, Thomas and Elizabeth to help!"*

She stared at them. This news was such a shock that she felt physically stunned. And never mind that she didn't have a way to be physically *anything* right now. "What?" she said, stupidly.

"Wait a moment." Hugh winked out—just like a spark extinguishing—then winked back in again. *"My dear, it's better than we knew when we first came to you! They have a plan—but it's one that you have to follow, too,"* Hugh told her. *"They're going to do something to either force Arachne to break this containment, or force her inside it as well. In*

either case, you will have to be the one to win your own free-
dom from her."

He had no sooner finished this astonishing statement than
something rocked the orb and its contents—it felt as Marina
would have imagined an earthquake would feel. It sent feelings of disequilibrium all through her, quite as if her sense
of balance stopped working, then started up again. She
didn't have insides that could go to water, but that was what
it felt like.

"And that will be it, I think—" Hugh stated, as another
such impulse rocked Marina and the little worldlet. A
third—a fourth—if Marina had been in her own body, she
knew she would have been sick into one of the dying
bushes. Instead, she just felt as if she would like to be sick.

"She's coming!" Alanna gasped—and the two spirits
winked out. With no more warning than that, Marina steeled
herself. But she made herself a pledge as well. No matter
what the outcome—she was not going to remain here.
Whether she came out of here to return to her physical body
or not, she was not going to remain.

22

THE moment after Hugh and Alanna vanished, there was a fifth convulsion, worse than all the previous ones combined. It shocked her mind; shocked it out of all thought save only that of self-awareness, and only the thinnest edge of that.

For a brief moment, everything around Marina flickered and vanished into a universal gray haze, shot through with black-green lightning. She was, for that instant, nothing more than a shining spark on the end of a long, thin silver cord, floating unanchored in that haze, desperately trying to evade those lightning-lances. Something—a black comet, ringed with that foul light, shot past her before she had time to do more than recognize that it was there.

Then it was all back; the withered garden, the ring of brambles, she herself, standing uncertainly at the edge of the circle of brown-edged grass. But there was an addition to the garden. Marina was not alone.

Standing opposite Marina, with her back to the wall of thorns, stood Madam Arachne.

She was scarcely recognizable. Over Arachne's once-impassive face flitted a parade of expressions—rage, surprise, hate—and one that Marina almost didn't recognize, for it seemed so foreign to Madam's entire image.

Confusion.

Quite as if Madam did not recognize where she was, and had no idea how she had gotten here.

But the expression, if Marina actually recognized it for what it was, vanished in moments, and the usual marble-statue stillness dropped over her face like a mask.

Marina held herself silent and still, but behind the mask that *she* tried to clamp over her own features, her mind was racing and her heart in her mouth. Instinctively, she felt that there was something very important about that moment of *nothingness* that she had just passed through. And if only she could grasp it, she would have the key she needed.

And now she wanted more than just to escape—for she had realized as she watched her parents together that she wanted to return to someone. Dr. Andrew Pike, to be precise. She must have fallen in love with him without realizing it; perhaps she hadn't recognized it until she saw her parents together.

And she knew, deep in her heart, that he wasn't just sitting back and letting her old friends and guardians try to save her. He was in there fighting for her, himself, and it wasn't just because he was a physician.

I have to survive to get back to him, first, she reminded herself tensely.

"Well," Madam said dryly. "Isn't this—interesting."

Marina held her peace, but she felt wound up as tightly as a clock-spring, ready to shatter at a word.

Madam looked carefully around herself, taking her time

gazing at what little there was to see. Then, experimentally, she pointed a long finger at a stunted and inoffensive bush.

Black-green lightning lanced from the tip of that finger and incinerated the half-dead bit of shrubbery—eerily doing so without a sound, except for a hiss and a soft puff as the bush burst into flame.

Madam stared at her finger, then at the little fountain of fire, smoke, and ash, and slowly, coldly, began to smile. When she turned that smile on Marina, Marina's blood turned to ice.

"Bringing me here was a mistake, my girl," Madam said silkily. "And believe me, it will be your last."

That was when it struck Marina—what that moment of nothingness had meant. Although her spirit might be imprisoned here and unable to return to her physical self, *this place and everything in it took its shape from the minds of those who were held here.*

Madam had realized this fundamental fact first; only the faint rustle behind her and the sense that something was about to close on her warned Marina that Madam had launched her first attack. She ducked and whirled out of reach, barely in time to escape the clutching thorn branches that reached for her, the thorns, now foot-long, stabbing for her. She lashed out with fire of her own, and the thorns burst into cold flame, flame that turned them to ash—and she felt the power in her ebbing.

Belatedly, she realized that this could only be a diversion, turned again to face Madam, and flung up shields—behind her, the thorns scrabbled on the surface of a shield that here manifested as transparent armor—while inches from her nose, Madam's green lightnings splashed harmlessly off the surface.

Madam smiled—and the ground opened up beneath Marina's feet.

Andrew dismounted awkwardly from his mare's back, and walked toward the front entrance of Oakhurst. The place was quiet. *Too* quiet. It was as if everything and everyone here was asleep . . . and he knew he was walking into a trap.

He opened the door himself, or tried to—it lodged against something, and he had to shove it open. That was when he realized that it wasn't *as if* everything was asleep. For the thing that had temporarily blocked the door was the body of one of the footmen, lying so still and silent that he had to stoop and feel for a pulse before he knew for certain it was sleep that held him, and not death.

Oh, God help us. . . . Past the entrance hall, and he came across another sleeper, the shattered vase of flowers from the hothouse beside her where she had fallen. The silence was thick enough to slice.

His heart pounded in his ears. He knew—or guessed—why every member of the household had fallen. He could only suppose that Reggie had been with or near Madam when her spirit was jerked into the limbo where she had sent Marina. Somewhere in this great house, Madam lay as silent and unresponsive as Marina, for the tie of the curse worked both ways, and as long as Marina was still alive, the magic that bound them together could be used against Madam as well as against Marina. That was the first part of what the old Master had imparted to them; that using that binding, they could throw victim and predator together into a situation where neither—theoretically—had the upper hand. Their environment took its shape equally from both of them; in a fight, they both depended on the power held only within themselves.

Theoretically. But Madam was older, treacherous, and far more ruthless. . . .

He couldn't think about that now. Because Madam was only half of the equation; Reggie was the other half. Satanic rites demanded a Priest, not a Priestess, and it was in the hands of the Priest and Celebrant that most of the control resided. No matter what Madam thought, it was Reggie who was the dangerous one—doubly so, if he, unlike his mother, actually had the gift of Mastery of one of the four Elements. He hadn't shown it—but he wouldn't have to. The power stolen from all the tormented souls that he and his mother had consigned to their own peculiar hells was potentially so great that Reggie would never need to demonstrate the active form of Mastery. Only the passive, the receptive, form, would be useful enough for him to wield—which was, of course, impossible to detect. But if Reggie could see power and manipulate it, rather than working blind as his mother was, he was infinitely more dangerous than she.

And if he actually *believed?* He could have allies on his side that no mortal could hope to overcome. The one advantage to this was that such allies were tricky at best and traitorous at worst. "*I can call spirits from the vasty deep.*" "*Aye, so can I, and so can any man, but will they come when you do call them?*"

Countering this was that true believers must be few and far between, and would the Lord of Darkness be willing to squander them?

Andrew felt himself trembling, and tightened his muscles to prevent it. Yes, Reggie was the more dangerous, as this house full of sleeping servants demonstrated. Their condition proved to Andrew that Reggie was, if not a Master, a magician as well as a Satanic Priest. He had, in one ruthless move, pulled the life-energy of every servant in this house that could not resist him into his own hands, draining them just short of death. Not that he would have balked at killing them—but *that* could not be done by occult means, or at least, not without expending as much energy as he took in. So Reggie was now immensely powerful, bloated with the strength stolen from an entire household — his mother's collapse a half hour ago had given him plenty of time to array his defenses, and he would, of course, be expecting an attack.

And before he went to face his enemy, Andrew now found himself faced with a dilemma. Of all of those sleeping servants, there must be some who had fallen while doing tasks where their lives would be in danger — tending animals — near fires —

He ran for the kitchen.

Marina, transmorphing into the form of a wren in the blink of an eye, shot up through her own shields and darted into the cover of the dying bushes. All she could do was to thank heaven that she had spent so much time among wild creatures — she knew how they felt, moved, acted. She could mimic them well enough to use the unique strengths they had. And it didn't take nearly as much power to do so as it did to lash out with mage-fire or change the world around her. If she could keep attacking Madam physically, Arachne could not possibly attack Marina magically. To change into a beast or a bird or some other form cost Marina a fraction of the power it took to lash out with mage-lightning. And she was younger than Arachne; that might be an advantage too.

She left the shields in place behind her, hoping that Madam would be deceived into thinking she was still inside them.

She peered out from under the shelter of a leaf the same color and almost the same shape as she, shaking with fear and anger mingled. Green lightning lashed at the shields,

splattering across their surface, obscuring the fact that there
was nothing inside them. Madam held both her hands out
before her, lightning lashing from her fingertips, her face a
contorted mask of hatred mingled with triumph.

*Go ahead. Waste your power. You won't find any more
here.*

Marina let the shields collapse in on themselves.

Taken by surprise by the sudden collapse of those defenses, Madam lashed at the empty place for a moment, the
energies that pummeled the spot where Marina had stood so
blindingly powerful that when she cut off her attack, there
was nothing there but the smoking ground.

Madam stood staring at the place for a moment, then cautiously stepped forward to get a better look.

She was so single-mindedly intent on destroying Marina
that it had not yet dawned on her that if Marina really had
been destroyed, Madam herself should have been snapped
back into the real world again.

And in that moment of forgetfulness, it was Marina's turn
to strike.

Madam's advantage—she was swollen, bloated with
stolen power. Still. But bloated as she was—and used to
having all the power she needed—she might not think to
husband it. And here, probably for the first time, she was
able to see what her power was doing, able to use it directly
instead of indirectly. That might intoxicate her with what
she could do, and make her less able to think ahead.

Marina had to combat Madam in such a way that Madam
couldn't *use* all that stolen power directly. So it was a very,
very good thing that Elizabeth had been so very busy collecting folk ballads as the prime motive for her visit to
Blackbird Cottage—and a very good thing that Marina had
been employed in making fair copies of them.

Because one of them, "The Twa Magicians," had given

her the pattern for the kind of attack she *could* make, one that might lure Arachne into making a fatal mistake.

That curse—I can do things against it here that I couldn't do in the real world. I can see it—and I can move it. It's a connection between us, and I think I can make that work in my favor.

Swift as a thought, Marina-the-wren darted out of the cover of the leaves, and in the blink of an eye, had fastened herself in Madam's hair.

But she didn't stay that way for long.

With a writhing effort of will, she transmorphed herself again, and a huge serpent cast its coils about Madam in the same moment that the evil sorceress realized that something had attacked her.

By then, it was a bit late, for her arms were pinned and the serpent was getting the unfamiliar body to contract its coils. Belatedly, Madam began to struggle, and Marina squeezed harder.

But Madam wasn't done yet. And what Marina could do—so could she.

Suddenly, Marina found her coils closing on air, as a little black cat shot out from under the lowest loop just before she collapsed in a heap under her own weight. Then the little cat turned to a great black panther, and leapt on her, landing just behind her head, pinning her to the ground and biting for the back of her neck.

That's a ploy anyone can play— Marina became a mouse, and ran between its paws. And from behind the panther's tail, went on the offensive again; became an elk, and charged at the big cat, tossing her into the air with her massive antlers.

Ha! Into the air the great cat flew, and she came down as a wolf.

But not just any wolf—one of the enormous Irish

wolves, killed off long ago, but which had, in their time, decimated the herds of Irish elk.

Oh no—! The wolf slashed at her legs, by its build and nature designed to kill elk; Marina leaped into the air—

And became a golden eagle, dropping down onto the wolf's back, fastening three-inch-long talons into fur and flesh and slashing at the head with her wicked beak. The Mongols of the steppes and the Cossacks of Russia hunted wolves with golden eagles—

But before the beak could connect, fur and flesh melted into a roaring tower of flame, and Marina backwinged hastily into the air before the raging fire Madam had become could set her feathers alight. But evidently Madam hadn't heard "The Twa Magicians," or she would have known Marina's next transformation—

—into a torrent of water. The form *most* natural to a Water Mage.

Andrew was not a moment too soon; the cook had fallen across the front of the big bread-oven, although she had only just started the fire in it, and it hadn't heated up sufficiently to give her serious burns. One of her helpers had been cutting up meat, though, and the last falling stroke of his cleaver had severed a finger.

Blood poured out of the stump, running across the table, dripping off the edge, pooling on the floor. He could easily have bled to death if Andrew hadn't gotten there when he had.

In a moment, Andrew had the bleeding stopped, though he'd been forced to use the crudest of remedies, cauterizing the stump with a hot poker, for he hadn't time to do anything else, and blessing the spell that kept the poor fellow insensible. Another kitchen maid was lying too near the fire in the fireplace where the big soup-kettle hung—one stray ember and she'd have been aflame. He moved her out of harm's way.

That cleared the kitchen—with his heart pounding, he ran out into the yard and the stables.

There he discovered that the animals had fallen asleep as well, which solved one problem. At least no one was going to be trampled.

Here the problem was not of fire, but of cold; left in the open, the stablehands would perish of exposure in a few hours as their bodies chilled. He solved that problem by dragging two into the kitchen, which was certainly warm enough, and the third into an empty, clean stall onto a pile of straw, where he covered the man with horse-blankets.

He dashed back inside, painfully aware of the passing of time. It was too late—he hoped—for the maids to be mending and laying fires. He couldn't go searching room to room for girls about to be incinerated—

But his heart failed him. *Oh, God. I must.* He began just such a frantic search of the first floor, wondering as he did so just how long it would be before Reggie ambushed him.

Whenever it happened, it would be when Reggie was at his readiest—and he, of course, at the least ready.

Madam was running out of ideas, so she became a huge serpent, at home on land or water—which was just what Marina had hoped for.

The torrent turned immediately to hail and sleet, the enemies of the cold-blooded reptile, and the one thing they were completely vulnerable to. Marina poured her energy into this transformation—which would have to be her last, because she was exhausted, and could sense that she hadn't much left to spend. But she didn't have to kill Arachne. All

she had to do was immobilize Madam, then get her own two
hands on the woman. It was, after all, Madam's curse, and
curses knew their caster; she could *feel* the thing tangling
them together. Over the course of this battle, Marina had
been weaving the loose ends of that curse back into
Madam's powers whenever they came into physical contact.
Now Marina would just send it back, if she could have a
moment when she could concentrate all of her will—her
trained will—on doing so.

The cold had the desired effect. The serpent tried to raise
its head and failed. It tried to crawl away, and couldn't. In a
moment, it couldn't move at all. A moment more, and it lay
scarcely breathing, sheathed in ice from head to tail. The
eyes glared balefully at her, red and smoldering, but Madam
could not force the body she had chosen to do what she
willed.

Marina fell out of the transformation, landing as herself
on her knees on the ice-rimed grass beside the prone reptile.

She was spent. *I can't*—

I must. There was no other choice, but death. Go past the
end of her strength and live and return to Andrew—or die.

Weeping with the effort, she gathered the last of her
power, isolated the vile black-green energies of the curse
just as she had isolated the poison in Ellen's veins, and
shoved it into her hands and held it there. With the last of her
strength, she crawled to Madam—she didn't need to pierce
Arachne's skin for this—they were both immaterial, after
all—

She placed both hands on the serpent's head—and
shoved.

And screamed with the seething, tearing pain that followed as the thing that had rooted in her very soul was uprooted and sent back to its host.

Reggie waited for Andrew where he had clearly been for some time; in the center of a red room, with a desk like an altar in the very center of it. An appropriate simile, since on the desk lay the dead body of a woman in a superior maid's outfit, her throat slit, blood soaking into the precious Persian rug beneath.

Reggie was not alone, either. To one side stood—something. There had been a sacrifice here to call an ally, and the ally had answered in person.

It wasn't a ghost, it wasn't material—it didn't even have much of a form. To Andrew's weary eyes, it was a man-shaped figure of black-green flame, translucent, and lambent with implied menace.

Reggie pointed straight at Andrew. "Kill him!" he barked—a smile of triumph cutting across his face like the open wound of the woman's throat.

"*No.*" The figure shifted a little. "*No. First, he is Favored, and I may not touch him. Second—*" Andrew got the impression of a shrug. "*—think of this as a test of worth. Yours, and perhaps, his.*"

Reggie stared, aghast—he had not expected *this* response. "But the bargain—" he cried. "I've worshipped, given you souls, corrupted for you, killed in your name—"

"*Which was the bargain. You have received in the measure that you earned. This is outside the bargain. You will see me again only when this combat is decided.*"

And with that, the figure winked out, and was gone.

Hah, Andrew thought, with a glimmer of hope. "*But will they answer when you do call them?*"

Reggie stared at the place where it had been with his mouth agape. And Andrew took that moment to attack.

He did what another magician would have considered

madness—he rushed Reggie physically, like the rugby player he had been at university, his momentum carrying him over the desk, knocking the body of the poor dead girl off the top, and carrying carcass and Reggie both to the ground. He grabbed for both wrists and got them, pinning the other to the blood-soaked carpet.

Pain lashed him, the pain of Reggie's mage-fire raging over him, burning him physically as the fire ate into his shields. Reggie still held the sacrificial dagger he had used to sever the girl's throat; Andrew screamed in agony, but held to the wrist that held that dagger—for he knew, with a cold fear of the sort that he had never felt before, that if Reggie managed to free his hand and use that dagger, it would kill him no matter how slight the wound.

He built up his shields as the pain and fire burned them away; he bit back his screams as Reggie rolled under him and tried to throw him off. And he used tricks learned in the violence of the rugby scrum, bashing his forehead into Reggie's nose, smashing it in a welter of blood, distracting him just long enough for him to try the desperate call he hoped would be answered. He made a summons of it, calling through the channel that they had shared, hoping that she had been freed to answer it.

Because if it wasn't—he and Marina were both doomed.

"Here!"

The voice in his mind was weary, weary—but he felt Marina's spectral presence, felt her spirit, tired, battered, but alive and free of the limbo into which she had been sent! Felt her join her power with his—

And knew that it wasn't enough.

Desperately, he reached for the power of Earth—and found it closed against him, violated by the sacrifice of the servant and more blood shed over the past months, poisoned by blasphemy in a way that made it impossible for him to touch. He could use it—but only if he cleansed it. And he didn't have time.

With nose smashed aside and bleeding profusely, Reggie grinned up at him, a savage grin that made him cold all over.

And in that moment, he knew utter despair.

"No, damn it, NO!" Marina cried.

Reggie gathered his own power; Andrew felt it gathering above him—them—like a wave poised to break over them, threatening to send them both back into the limbo where Madam had cast Marina.

Then—from some unguessed depth of her spirit, Marina reached for a source of *her* power uncontaminated by the blood and black magic—reached down into the village, where a wellspring lay doubly blessed, by Elemental and Christian mage—

She should not have been able to touch it—and reaching so far and so desperately might doom her, burn her out forever—

He couldn't stop her.

She wouldn't let him.

"I love you," she said, *"And I'll be damned before I let him have you!"*

The words gave him a last burst of energy past his own strength in that last instant, and he, too, reached further and deeper than he ever had in his life—and then, two floods met—evil and good, light and dark, life and death—

Andrew was caught up in the maelstrom, and was thrown about like a cork in a hurricane. The power was beyond his control now, or Marina's, or indeed *anyone's.* It was its own creature with its own laws, supremely indifferent to the wishes of a few puny humans. In the depths of the storm he thought he sensed others—one, two, a dozen, more—who found themselves unwitting channels for a power with a will of its own. He lost sight and sense of Marina, lost sight and sense of Reggie, clung only to his own identity, desperately, praying, as the competing waves of power battered him indiscriminately, and finally drove him down into darkness.

And his last thought was that if Marina was not to survive this confrontation—*he* didn't want to, either.

The last thing he heard was a dreadful wailing, a howl of the deepest and most profound despair and defeat—and the sound of demonic laughter.

Then he lost track of everything, and knew nothing more.

He woke in a bed in his own sanitarium; he knew that ceiling—it was the one above his bed. He coughed, and suddenly there were half a dozen faces looking down at him. And among the faces around his bed was the one he wanted to see most.

"Marina!" The word came out as a croak, from a throat raw and rasping.

"Alive, thanks to you," she said, her eyes dark-circled, her voice heavy with exhaustion, her smile bright and full of an emotion he hardly dared name. "And *well*, thanks to my—our—friends. And so are you." She turned her smile on the three men, who looked equally exhausted. "Clifton bridged the power-well of the rectory to the greater power of the other Masters—and got a bit of a shock!"

"I should say," Davies admitted, rubbing the side of his head, as if it still ached. "Never have I seen such an outpouring of power—not only from the Masters we had telegraphed, not only from your Undines and the lesser Water creatures, but from the Mermaids and Tritons, the Hippocampi and other salt-water powers all the way down at the sea, *and* from the Air, the Sylphs, the Winds, the Fauns and other Earth creatures, the Salamanders and Dragons of Fire—things I can't even put a name to! They cleansed the earth for you, Andrew! And you reached for your power and it answered with more than I have ever heard of!"

"And you did exactly what that irascible old reprobate told you to do," Sebastian said, as words failed the Reverend Davies and he shook his head in wonder. "You unwound that curse and wrapped it around Reginald and tied it back to Madam, and then—" He shrugged. "Well, we don't precisely know what happened then. All we know is that when the brouhaha faded out, when Marina woke up and demanded that we go rescue you, and Thomas and I went into Oakhurst to find you, you were sitting on the front stoop looking as if you'd been in a bare-fisted bout with a champion and come out the worst. Reginald was in Madam's study, slumped over the body of the poor wench he'd killed—unconscious, exactly as the curse made Marina—and Madam was in the same condition in the next room. The servants were just starting to wake up, so Thomas whisked you away before they saw you, and I laid into the footman, trying to get him to wake up. The servants found Reggie and Madam, by the way—" He grinned sheepishly. "I did take credit for the lad with the finger he'd chopped off, though. Someone had to, and no one could prove that I wasn't the one who'd used that hot poker to save his life. They couldn't prove I was any farther into the manor than the kitchen either, which is just as well for all of us."

"Police?" he managed.

Clifton Davies nodded. "Called, been, gone. Coroner too. He says that Reggie and his darling mother poisoned each other—like they tried to poison you, my dear—" he patted Marina's hand "—and before Reggie succumbed, he killed that poor girl—Marina's maid, a lady of, hmm, negotiable virtue with a bit of a past. They say that he slaughtered her in a state of dementia. We suggested that they ought to be seen to by doctors, specialists. I'm told that they're going to be moved to some place in Plymouth, under police guard, in case they might be feigning their state."

"And meanwhile, I am living here—convalescing—until they are far away from my estate," Marina said firmly. "I do not intend to set foot there until they are *gone.*" She smiled, charmingly, a smile that made him melt. "Besides, it's perfectly proper. My guardians are here, and you're not only my physician, you're my fiancé."

He blinked. Not that he minded, but—when had *that* happened? "Now wait a bit—" he said.

"Are you saying you don't want to be my fiancé?" she asked, her serene smile wavering not at all.

Of course he wanted to! He couldn't imagine spending the rest of his life with anyone else! But she was so young—it wasn't fair to her— "No, but—dammit, Marina, you're only seventeen!"

"*Almost* eighteen," she interrupted.

"You've never been anywhere but Blackbird Cottage and Oakhurst!" he continued stubbornly. "You're wealthy, you're beautiful, you'll be pursued by *dozens* of suitors—"

"—none of whom are worthy to polish your scalpels," she said impishly.

"And I don't want you to miss that!" he cried, voice cracking, as he gave words to what he was really afraid of. "I don't want you to look at me across the room one day, and wish that you hadn't gone so fast, that you'd had your London season, that you'd had a chance to be petted and courted, seen at the opera and Ascot—had all those things that you should have—"

"Very nicely put, Doctor," Lady Elizabeth said, patting *his* hand complacently. "And she'll have all those things. A little thing like an engagement to a country doctor is not going to put off those hordes of suitors. I intend to see she gets that London season myself. And when she's had her fill of it, she'll come back here, and marry you, and between all of Madam's money and her own, I do believe you'll be able to turn Briareley into a first-class establishment."

He blinked as the three women laughed together, exchanging a glance that excluded all the mere males in the room. "Ah—" he managed, and dredged up the only thing he hadn't exactly understood. "Madam's money?"

"I'm the only heir—I'll have all her property and Reggie's too in a few months," Marina said—with just enough malicious pleasure that he felt a rush of relief to see that she was human after all. "I doubt that they'll live longer than that. I'll be cleaning up the potteries, of course—which will mean they won't be quite so profitable—but there will still be enough coming in, I believe, to make all of the improvements here that you could wish." She made a face. "And in addition to having that delightful London season, I'm afraid I'm going to have to learn how to run a business—"

Oh, my love! I won't let your season be spoiled! "You'll have help," he assured her. "Surely there must be someone we can trust to guide you through it. Or even take over for you."

"My man of business, to begin with," Lady Elizabeth said airily. "And after that—I think I can find a business-minded Earth or Water Master to become your manager. Someone who, needless to say, will be as careful of the land, the water, and the workers as he is of the pounds and pence."

"Needless to say," he repeated, and suddenly felt as if he was being swept up again in something beyond his control.

But this time, it was something very, very pleasant. And it was all in the hands of these utterly charming women, one of whom he had loved almost from the moment she had walked into Briareley to help a little factory-girl she didn't even know.

"I think I'd like to sleep now," he said meekly. "Unless—"

Then he remembered his duties, and tried to sit up, frantically. "My patients!" he exclaimed.

"Are fine. They have *my* personal physician, *and* the village doctor to attend their needs. And two Earth Masters, a Water Master, and a Fire Master." Lady Elizabeth pushed him down again. "And if that isn't enough, *my* physician is bringing in several fine nurses he can recommend who would very much like to relocate to this lovely slice of Devon."

"And *I* am hiring them, so you needn't worry where the money is coming from," Marina concluded. "Now, if you won't sleep, I *can't* sleep. So must I prescribe for the physician or will you be sensible?"

"I'll be sensible," he replied, giving in with a sigh. "So long as you are, too—"

And he whispered the last two words. "—my love."

"I will be," she replied, smiling. "My love."

One thing was very certain, he thought, as he drifted into real slumber. He was never going to get tired of those two delightful words.

Never.

EPILOGUE

MARINA'S bridal gown was by Worth, and it satisfied every possible craving that a young woman could have with regard to a frock. It should have—Worth had had more than two years to create it, and the most difficult part of the work had been making certain it stayed up to the minute in mode. Silk satin, netting embroidered with seed pearls, heavy swaths of Venice lace, *the* fashionable S-shape silhouette, a train just short of royal in length—no woman could ask for more.

The gardens at Oakhurst, cleansed and scoured of all of the blood-magic Arachne and Reggie had done there—with every vestige of Cold Iron removed and hauled off as scrap—and with a section carefully set aside as a "wild garden" where no gardener was allowed to trespass—made the perfect setting for a wedding. And it was going to be a very, very large wedding. Every room at Oakhurst was full, not only with fellow Masters, but with some of the many friends that Marina had made in her *two* successful London seasons.

Most of those were girl friends—a young lady who was safely engaged to a sober and undesirable young working man was no rival, and thus safe to become friends with. Besides, it soon proved that Andrew Pike knew an amazing number of other, quite personable young men, who, even if they weren't all precisely what a marriage-minded mama would have preferred, made very good escorts. And generally were good dancers into the bargain.

The rooms in all the inns for miles around were full. All of the stately homes and some of the not-so-stately had guests. There were even guests at Briareley, in the special, private rooms. This was a wedding long-anticipated, long in the planning, and long in the consummation.

Andrew had insisted—and had gotten his way—that they not actually get married until Marina was twenty-one. He wanted not a shadow of doubt that she was making a free choice among all the possible suitors. He had almost relented, when his head nurse Eleanor had wed Thomas Buford—finally meeting the mate she deserved over Andrew's sickbed. Thomas had moved his workshop to Briareley when Andrew burst in on the two and demanded to know just what he was going to do without the best nurse he had.

All in fun, of course, but the workshop was proving to be very useful in providing some of the poorer children with an opportunity to learn a skill. That left the Tarrants alone in Blackbird Cottage for the first time in their lives, a state which seemed to agree perfectly with them. Marina had never seen them so happy.

Margherita was Marina's matron-of-honor, and Ellen, who was now a nurse herself, her chief maid-of-honor, and Sebastian was giving the bride away. Thomas was standing up for Andrew, who, if Sebastian was to be believed, was as nervous as a cat and white as a sheet.

She didn't believe it. After all he'd been through, what

could possibly make him nervous about a little thing like a wedding?

With Ellen, Margherita, and her society friends hovering around her like a flock of twittering birds, she took a last, long look in the mirror, and was pleased with what she saw. If she was no beauty—despite what Andrew said—she thought she cut a rather *handsome* figure.

And with Lady Elizabeth in charge of the wedding itself, she'd had only to make easy decisions, and now had nothing to do but enjoy herself to the uttermost.

Drifting through the open window she heard the sounds of the string quartet beginning the melody that would end in the processional. It was time to go.

She gathered up her skirts in both hands and led the way out to the gardens, trailing brightly gowned girls like streamers behind her.

It was a real pity, she thought, that so few of her guests could see the *other* guests—fauns peeking out from every possible vantage, Sylphs hiding in the trees, a trio of Undines sporting in the fountains, and a veritable bestiary of other creatures of myth and legend hovering at the edge of the human crowd. She beamed at all of them, and if her un-magical guests thought that her smile was a bit unfocused, well, that was to be expected in someone who was only minutes from being married.

The processional began. Andrew was led to his place in front of Mr. Davies by Uncle Thomas (who was wearing what could only be described as a smirk) when suddenly, Marina lost her smile, and stared—

For there were *three* figures, not one, on the little podium where Clifton Davies stood waiting to do his duty.

For one brief moment, the two of those figures who shone with their own light smiled with delight on their daughter. Holding hands, Alanna and Hugh Roeswood made a gesture of scattering rice, and tiny sparks of Earth-magic flitted from their hands to land on the heads or the hearts of each of the guests in blessing—and two of the largest, flitting like flowers in the wind, settled softly over Andrew's heart, and Marina's.

Then they were gone. But Marina knew what they had left behind with her.

Love. Love she could accept with a whole and full heart, at last.

And she stepped forward with the first bars of the processional, and into a life she had not even imagined the day she was taken from Blackbird Cottage—and this time, it would not be alone.

MERCEDES LACKEY

The Novels of Valdemar

To Order Call: 1-800-788-6262

MERCEDES LACKEY

The Novels of Valdemar

Exile's Honor

He was once a captain in the army of Karse, a kingdom that had been at war with Valdemar for decades. But when Alberich took a stand for what he believed in—and was betrayed—he was Chosen by a Companion to be a Herald, and serve the throne of Valdemar. But can Alberich keep his honor in a war against his own people?

"A treat for Valdemar fans"
—Booklist

0-7564-0085-6

To Order Call: 1-800-788-6262

DAW 24